TURN THE STARS UPSIDE DOWN

THE LAST DAYS AND TRAGIC DEATH OF CRAZY HORSE

TERRY C. JOHNSTON

St. Martin's Paperbacks

This is a work of fiction. All of the characters, organizations, and events portrayed in this novel are either products of the author's imagination or are used fictitiously.

TURN THE STARS UPSIDE DOWN

Copyright © 2001 by Terry C. Johnston.

For information address St. Martin's Press, 175 Fifth Avenue, New York, NY 10010.

EAN: 978-0-312-98209-6

Printed in the United States of America

St. Martin's Press hardcover edition / August 2001
St. Martin's Paperbacks edition / June 2002

St. Martin's Paperbacks are published by St. Martin's Press, 175 Fifth Avenue, New York, NY 10010.

10 9 8 7 6 5 4 3

HIGH PRAISE FOR THE WORK OF
TERRY JOHNSTON

"You are there, you are really there, in Johnston's largest, most complex work." —*Kirkus Reviews* on *Lay the Mountains Low*

"Johnston is a skilled storyteller whose words ring with desperation, confusion, and utter horror of a fight to the death between mortal enemies."
— *Publishers Weekly* on *Lay the Mountains Low*

"The author's attention to detail and authenticity, coupled with his ability to spin a darned good yarn, makes it easy to see why Johnston is today's best-selling frontier novelist. He's one of a handful that truly knows the territory."
— *Chicago Tribune*

"Rich in historical lore and dramatic description, this is a first-rate addition to a solid series, a rousing tale of one man's search for independence in the unspoiled beauty of the Old West." — *Publishers Weekly* on *Buffalo Palace*

"A first-class novel by a talented author."
— *Tulsa World* on *Dream Catcher*

"With meticulous research, vivid dialogue, memorable characters, and a voice uniquely his own, Johnston has once again written the finest of historical fiction, seamlessly blending together both time and place to bring to life a world as real as our own." — *Roundup Magazine* on *Dance on the Wind*

"Compelling...Johnston offers memorable characters, a great deal of history and lore about the Indians and pioneers of the period, and a deep insight into human nature, Indian and white." — *Booklist*

"Terry C. Johnston pierces the heart and soul of the 19th century men and women he writes about so well, capturing in unforgettable and gracious stories the joys and agonies of the great westward expansion of a young America...he will make your heart sing." —RICHARD S. WHEELER, Spur Award–winning author of *Sierra*

THE PLAINSMEN SERIES BY TERRY C. JOHNSTON

Because he bravely stood and fought

beside me over these past ten years,

making possible the renaissance of my mid-life,

I dedicate this sad tale of Crazy Horse's final days

to the warrior who has many times done battle at my shoulder,

fighting victoriously so that my kids, Noah and Erinn,

will now remain with their father until it's time for them

to spread their own wings and leave my nest.

For my Montana-born Irish friend,

"Seamus" —

I dedicate this book to

JAMES ROBERT GRAVES

CAST OF CHARACTERS

Seamus Donegan
Colin Teig Donegan

Samantha Donegan

OGLALA LAKOTA
Crazy Horse / Ta'sunke Witko

Worm / *Waglu'la* (father)
Black Buffalo Woman
They Are Afraid of Her (daughter)
Hump / Buffalo Hump
Little Big Man
Flying Eagle
Walking Eagle
Jumping Shield
Chips
No Water
Lone Bear
Red Cloud
Little Wound
Red Feather
Black Fox
Big Road

Little Hawk (brother)
Black Shawl (wife)
Little Hawk (uncle)
Young Man Afraid
He Dog
Eagle Thunder
Good Weasel
Looking Horse
Kicking Bear
Woman's Dress
Little Wolf
Red Dog
American Horse
Shell Boy
No Flesh

BRULE / *SICANGU* LAKOTA

Spotted Tail
Black Crow
Good Voice

Swift Bear
White Thunder
Horned Antelope

MINNICONJOU / *MNICOWAJU* LAKOTA

Touch-the-Clouds

High Bear

MILITARY

Brigadier General George Crook—commander, Department of the Platte

Lieutenant Colonel Luther Prentice Bradley—commanding officer at Fort Robinson / commander of the District of the Black Hills

Major Julius W. Mason—Third U.S. Cavalry at Fort Laramie

Captain Daniel Webster Burke—commanding officer of Camp Sheridan

Captain James Kennington—Fourteenth U.S. Infantry

Lieutenant William Philo Clark / "White Hat"—military agent to the Oglala Lakota at Red Cloud Agency / chief of U.S. Indian Scouts (K Company, Second U.S. Cavalry)

Lieutenant John G. Bourke—aide-de-camp to General George Crook

Lieutenant Jesse M. Lee—agent to the Brule Lakota at Spotted Tail Agency

Lieutenant William Rosecrans—Fourth U.S. Cavalry

Lieutenant Henry L. Lemley—E Company, Third U.S. Cavalry

Private William Gentles—F Company, Fourteenth U.S. Infantry

Dr. Valentine T. McGillycuddy—Assistant Post Surgeon, assigned to Camp Robinson

CIVILIAN

Helen "Nellie" Laravie ("Chi-Chi") (known among the Lakota as Brown Eyes Woman / *Ista Gli Win*)

Long Joe Laravie

Frank Grouard (Grabber)

Baptiste "Big Bat" Pourier

Dr. James Irvin—civilian agent at Red Cloud agency

Benjamin K. Shopp—special Indian agent

Lucy Lee

Billy Garnett

John Provost

Louis Bordeaux / Louis *Mato*

Joe Merrival—interpreter for Jesse M. Lee

The death of Crazy Horse was in short a tragedy just as Wounded Knee was; moreover it was a "tragedy" in the Shakespearean sense as well, for a great man was slain by a lesser man.

—BRIAN POHANKA
Time/Life Books

Although Red Cloud was not as skilled a politician [as Spotted Tail], he compensated for the shortcoming with a cunning ability to manipulate both the military and his own kindred. To maintain his prominence, Red Clould would remove any obstacle which posed a threat to his political aspirations.

—RICHARD G. HARDORFF
Crazy Horse: A Source Book

As the grave of [George Armstong] Custer marked [the] high-water mark of Sioux supremacy in the trans-Missouri region, so the grave of "Crazy Horse," a plain fence of pine slabs, marked the ebb.

—LIEUTENANT JOHN G. BOURKE
On the Border with Crook

After [Crazy Horse's] surrender he was made a hero by the army officers and shown much attention by the people generally. The agency Indians, becoming envious of Crazy Horse, told all manner of stories about him, and . . . false rumors.

—CHARLES P. JORDAN
former chief clerk at Red Cloud Agency

Red Cloud had reason to be jealous. Several times during the summer, he had been pushed aside while the prestige of Crazy Horse had been bolstered . . . Spotted Tail, too, was jealous of Crazy Horse and didn't want him to go to Washington . . . [Crazy Horse] was sure in Spot's acute understanding to be the lion of the delegation and to shadow and efface Spotted Tail in the public mind and diminish his influence as a chief.

—EDWARD KADLECEK
To Kill an Eagle

It is absurd to talk of keeping faith with Indians.

—GENERAL PHILIP H. SHERIDAN

At the time, and ever since, I held that the arrest and killing of the chief was unnecessary, uncalled-for and inexcusable. It was the result of jealousy, treachery and fear, and placing too much weight or reliance on reports that Crazy Horse was again contemplating joining Sitting Bull, still in British territory, there being a manufactured propaganda to that effect . . .

A combination of treachery, jealousy and unreliable reports simply resulted in a frame-up, *and he was railroaded to his death*.

—DR. VALENTINE T. MCGILLYCUDDY
in correspondence with author E. A. Brininstool

They could not kill him in battle. They had to lie to him and kill him that way.

—BLACK ELK
Black Elk Speaks

[Crazy Horse] trusted both sides—and then they killed him.

—LUTHER STANDING BEAR
My People the Sioux

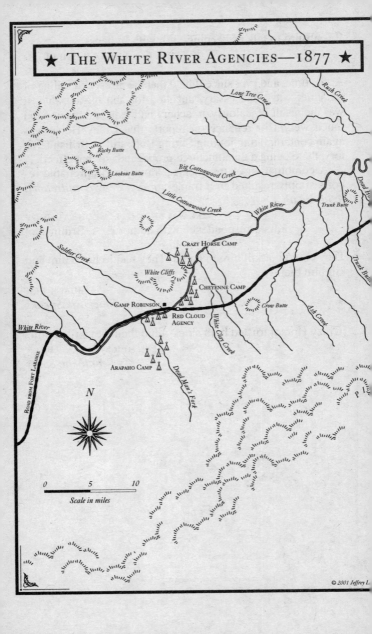

★ THE WHITE RIVER AGENCIES—1877 ★

Lone Tree Creek

Rush Creek

Dead Ho[rse]

Rocky Butte

Lookout Butte

Big Cottonwood Creek

Little Cottonwood Creek

White River

Trunk Butte

Soldier Creek

CRAZY HORSE CAMP

White Cliffs

Trunk Butte

CHEYENNE CAMP

CAMP ROBINSON

Crow Butte

Ash Creek

White River

RED CLOUD AGENCY

White Clay Creek

ARAPAHO CAMP

Dead Man's Fork

P I [NE]

N

ROAD FROM FORT LARAMIE

0   5   10

Scale in miles

© 2001 Jeffrey L.

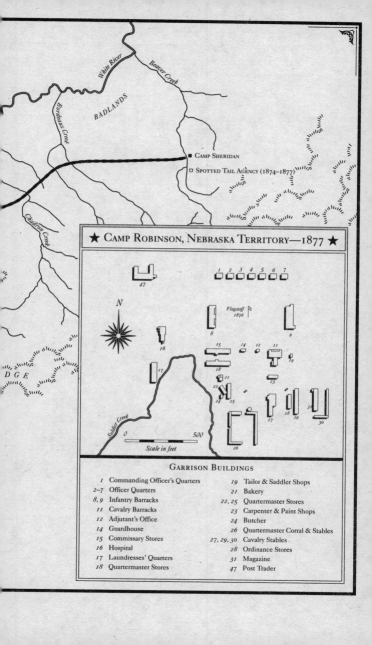

White River

Beaver Creek

Bordeaux Creek

BADLANDS

Chadron Creek

■ Camp Sheridan

□ Spotted Tail Agency (1874–1877)

★ Camp Robinson, Nebraska Territory—1877 ★

N

47

1 2 3 4 5 6 7

Flagstaff
1876

8

9

16

15   14 12   11

18   19

17

23

21

22   9

24   25

27   28   29

31

30

26

Soldier Creek

0   500

Scale in feet

Garrison Buildings

1	Commanding Officer's Quarters	19	Tailor & Saddler Shops
2–7	Officer Quarters	21	Bakery
8, 9	Infantry Barracks	22, 25	Quartermaster Stores
11	Cavalry Barracks	23	Carpenter & Paint Shops
12	Adjutant's Office	24	Butcher
14	Guardhouse	26	Quartermaster Corral & Stables
15	Commissary Stores	27, 29, 30	Cavalry Stables
16	Hospital	28	Ordinance Stores
17	Laundresses' Quarters	31	Magazine
18	Quartermaster Stores	47	Post Trader

FOREWORD

Despite all the rumor, half-truth, and fiction written about Crazy Horse, what little we do know about this mysterious man will forever be cloaked in legend.

Even as you gaze at the bloodied bayonet portrayed on the cover painting created for me by my old friend Lou Glanzman—America's most prominent illustrator—there still rages some controversy over exactly how Crazy Horse's life ended. Not only in seamy details of his "political" undoing by fellow Oglala leaders but also in the specifics of that very moment the death wound was inflicted. At that time, and even down to this day in some circles, it was believed that Crazy Horse actually stabbed himself with the knife he suddenly yanked from beneath the blanket hung over his arm in traditional fashion. To stab himself in the kidney, from behind, during a desperate struggle with his old friend Little Big Man?

As you look upon the cover artwork, ponder what sorts of covers have been on all the other books that seek to represent the death of Crazy Horse. And then remember that the *last* thing I want to write is a book about the surrender of this Oglala mystic. No, this is not a book about the *surrender* of Crazy Horse. While he did give his body over to the U.S. Army at Red Cloud's agency in May of 1877, he did not turn over his mind, his heart, his warrior spirit. In the end, this is not a story of surrender, but a tale of triumph.

This is a story about how—despite all the efforts of the army officers and the white officials, along with many of Crazy Horse's own Oglala people—this lone man succeeded in not surrendering everything that mattered most to him and, ultimately, what mattered most to the Lakota.

No, this is not a book about surrender. Instead, I have sought to tell you a story about the very personal victory of one solitary and misunderstood man.

Like other men of that dramatic era—men like George

Armstrong Custer himself, who died an early and very human death, only to rise again as mythical and immortal—so too has Crazy Horse continued to live on, less as a man and more as a symbol of steadfast opposition to white dominance. It is not this legendary Crazy Horse I seek to write about. Others have already done so. Instead, it is the Crazy Horse who has not yet appeared in film, nor between the covers of a book—a flesh-and-blood Crazy Horse who is something less than mythic hero yet somehow more than mere man.

In the afterword that follows this tragic story, I list the many sources I relied upon to write this tale of surrender, betrayal, and murder. Despite all that has been put in print about this "Strange Man of the Oglala," I found I had come to know very, very little about him from the written record. Instead, it took me walking the ground where Crazy Horse once stood, or fought, and where he ultimately died, before I felt I had come to some understanding of him ... perhaps because he was so directly, so organically, tied to the land, his land, that his country—unlike what those of us who record our thoughts and hopes in print can ever say—will remain his one true legacy for all time.

Think of it. Standing in the shadow of Bear Butte, where most sources agree Crazy Horse was born. Sitting out on the barren, wind-battered end of what is now called Scotts Bluff in southwestern Nebraska, those heights generally accepted to have been the site of this man's momentous and tragically prophetic vision quest. Walking through the calf-deep, icy snow crusted along the narrow ridgetop where Crazy Horse and the rest of his decoys lured Fetterman's freezing, frightened soldiers for what would be this young warrior's first great fight against the blue-coats. Stepping across the narrow strip of asphalt smeared atop Custer's ridge, moving from that tall, stark monument to where we used to be allowed to stand and look down the slope to the north, imagining how Crazy Horse and his warriors raced around the base of this bluff to hurl themselves against the remnants of those five companies of U.S. cavalry punching north off the ridgetop, driven back to make their last stand in what took but minutes to become this war chief's greatest victory against the blue-coats. Then you must trudge through the deep snow and January cold up a gradually rising bluff to reach the ridge where he and his last hold-outs suffered winter's cruelest bite as a blizzard closed its maw on Battle Butte. . . . Don't you sense despair seizing your heart like a hawk's talons as you realize this was where Crazy Horse fought his last fight against the U.S. Army?

Eventually I find myself standing right outside the bolted door of this low-roofed log structure where few people come to intrude upon my thoughts while I stare at the ground, feeling like I've been kicked in the belly by the realization that it was right here that a bayonet was thrust into the body of Crazy Horse, that it was right next door that he took his last breath. That it was here that the great spiritual hoop of the Lakota people was irretrievably broken for all time.

Save for the Donegan family, all the rest of the characters in my story are real, and were there, on this very ground, during those final and fateful months of Crazy Horse's life.

While a few of the scenes portrayed here may not have happened at all, or may not have happened as I have written them, you must bear in mind that I have attempted with the utmost fidelity to render this story just as true as I can make it, despite all the conflicting testimony from those who witnessed these final days.

Because Crazy Horse rarely spoke in public, even among his own people and especially in the presence of white men, little is left but the reminiscences of his friends, companions, and enemies. From them I have constructed the very psyche of the man I believe was this great Oglala chief—a man who had feet of clay, who had never desired the mantle of leadership to be laid about his shoulders, a man who wanted one woman but ended up settling for another, a father who wanted children of his own but in the end lost the only daughter we are certain he ever had. A man who weighed his obligations to his people against the hungers of his own soul.

So while not every scene in the book you are about to read may have actually occurred, I hope that by the time you close the covers on my story you will say to yourself that it had the ring of truth, perhaps saying to yourself that if we don't really know exactly what happened to undo these last days of all that Crazy Horse was . . . then perhaps this short tale is how it might well have happened.

How Crazy Horse—this quiet Strange Man of the Oglala—emerged from some two decades of warfare to turn over his people and his weapons to the hated *wasicu*, and became mired in a tangle of events that he could not escape.

Perhaps this is how it happened. . . .

TURN THE
STARS
UPSIDE DOWN

PROLOGUE

Pehingnunipi Wi
MOON OF SHEDDING PONIES, 1877

BY TELEGRAPH

———

ILLINOIS.

———

Crook on the Indians.

———

CHICAGO, May 2.—The Post has an interview with
General Crook concerning the Indian question, the
substance of which is that General Crook considers the
Indians are like white men in respect to acquisitiveness;
that if they are given a start in the way of lands, cattle and
agricultural implements, they will keep adding to their
wealth and settle down into respectable, staid citizens.

TA'SUNKE WITKO!

Oh, how he wanted to ignore that summons.

***Ta'sunke Witko! Listen! For I am calling you, Ta'sunke
Witko!***

He finally opened his eyes into the cold, chill breeze of
this springtime moon and looked around him, just to be sure
one of his friends was not playing a child's trick on him. No
one. Which was as he preferred it, for he sat alone on the
brow of this hill.

"You know me. I am the one called Ta'sunke Witko; I am
Crazy Horse," he sighed wearily, a pale streamer of his
breathsmoke whipped away on a gust of wind. "Why do you
come talk to me now, when you have not spoken to my heart
in so many moons?"

A sudden sound erupted on the wind behind him, brushing
his ears, like that of a rush of wings as a great bird settled be-

hind him, coming to rest. Closer still—he sensed the being at his back, upon the crest of the hillside where he sat staring down into the valley where the sun would soon emerge. His people were awakening below, some of the old men kicking life into last night's fires, old women starting into the brush to gather wood, the young boys leaving their blanket and canvas shelters, hunched over in the cold wind as they trudged out to the surrounding hills to bring in the first of the travois horses for their families and that day's travel.

I have always been with you, Ta'sunke Witko. Even though I had no words to speak, I have never abandoned you.

"Then why has this felt like being so alone, if you truly were with me, *Sicun*?" he asked his spirit guardian.*

You are a man, so you are not always aware I am here. Sometimes... many times, your thoughts and your heart are so busy with other matters and feelings that it may seem as if I am not here with you. But... the truth remains that I am a part of you, and you a part of me until your final breath escapes your body. Until we are freed together.

"Why have you come to me now, Spirit Guardian?"

And he closed his eyes gently, imagining the majestic appearance of that spotted war eagle that was given birth inside his breast so many summers ago. The same Winged Being that had instructed him to wear no bonnet, only two feathers** tied at the back of his long, sandy hair, their tips pointing down. The medicine pouch hanging from his neck contained the dried, shriveled brain and heart from the same golden, or spotted, eagle he had captured bare-handed in his

---

*Among the Lakota, the spirit guardian, or *sicun*, represented the power of *Wakan Tanka* embodied in a human being. This spiritual essence served to guard the person against evil spirits, often forewarned of danger, distinguished right from wrong, and controlled other humans. Raymond DeMallie states that we might call the *sicun* an individual's conscience or will.

**What he wore were the two perfectly matched feathers every eagle is born with, found bilaterally positioned in its tail.

youth, mixed with the petals and leaves of the wild aster. One of the eagle's wing bones he had used to carve a whistle that he blew each time he raced into battle.

Didn't you call me? Didn't you make the climb up this hill in the cold darkness to talk to me?

"You know that I did." Crazy Horse stared down at his hands, fingers interwoven together in his lap, his skin much lighter than that of most Lakota.*

Finally he raised his eyes to the horizon growing reddish orange below the purple bellies of the storm clouds that had soaked them all last night before lumbering off to the east with their fury. "But... how do I say the words that I have never spoken?"

You are afraid?

His pale eyes smarted with the sting of truth. "You know that I am. First it was Hump, my *kola,* taken away from me. How his death scared me so. And then Little Hawk. My own brother shot down by the *wasicu.* In the past few winters, I feel so much has been ripped from me that I cannot be brave anymore. I do not know from where my strength will come."

You must show courage, if only for a few more days, a few more miles, until this journey is finished.

"When that time comes, I do not have to be brave anymore?"

Then you will have delivered your people to an island of safety, Ta'sunke Witko. Where you will have to find a new courage in your heart.

"A new courage?" How he wanted to turn and look into the face of the spirit guardian who breathed the words at the back of his ear.

You must seek the sort of bravery that no Lakota has ever known. The other chiefs already there, they know nothing of this courage, having lived so long under the thumb of the wasicu leaders and their soldiers.

---

*Sioux is the French term the earliest of *wasicus* or white men, gave to these people of the northern plains, while *Lakota* is the word they use to refer to themselves.

"I must walk this unmarked road alone?"

You are Ta'sunke Witko! You are Crazy Horse! Isn't that what your vision first told you when you were but a boy?

"So many clawing at me, their hands and arms, reaching and pulling at me," he said, clenching his eyes and wagging his head a little with the memory of his spirit vision.* "My own people, they hold me back, pin my arms—"

Do you want your journey on this road taken from you?

He brooded on that a moment longer, then answered, "No. I have taken other journeys where no man has gone before." Crazy Horse drew in a deep breath of cold air as the lip of the sun crept over the distant brow of the earth. "Alone . . . I can walk this road too."

I will be there with you, Ta'sunke Witko. Every step you take, I will walk it with you.

"It is time for me to go," he announced, standing uneasily, finding his muscles sore from the strenuous climb up this steep ridge, cold and cramped from the long sitting in the wind. "We do not have far to go now."

Do you ever wonder upon what awaits you when you reach that place?

He stood a moment, wondering if he was shivering with the cold despite his red blanket, or if he was trembling with apprehension for what awaited him out there—a little distance and a few days from now. Finally he whispered, "I am a warrior. You have made me a man different from all other Lakota. But . . . in the end I am nothing more than a warrior."

You must remember that in the hard days to come.

"I am only what you and my people have made of me."

Crazy Horse started slowly down the hill, clutching his worn, dusty blanket around his shoulders, feeling how the gusts of wind toyed with the flaps so that the cold snaked under his breechclout.

Ta'sunke Witko! You will listen when I speak to you in the coming days?

---

*This vision was experienced on top of what is today called Scott's Bluff, in southwestern Nebraska.

Stopping, he nodded slightly, not daring to turn and look upon the guardian. "Yes, I have always listened to you, *Si-cun.*"

Turn your ears to my voice when I summon you. To-gether we will remember the days of your life. When you suffered loss ... when you turned victory in your hands.

"Yes," he whispered, turning his head slightly so that his words slipped back to the spirit guardian at his back. "To-gether ... we will remember."

Then he stepped away, down the steep slope into the val-ley, where his people were preparing for another day's jour-ney toward the white man's island on the White Earth River.

I am a part of you, and you will remain a part of me, Ta'sunke Witko. So I will stay beside you as you walk down this new road all alone. Remember that no one else has ever been called to walk this road but you.

He vowed, "My feet will not stumble."

And I promise that one day you will no longer worry about your feet, or stumbling too. For one day, Ta'sunke Witko, your spirit will take wing, and fly as high as the stars.

CHAPTER ONE

3 May 1877

BY TELEGRAPH

INDIANS.

Red Cloud's Party Coming In.

CAMP ROBINSON, NEB., May 4.—A courier brings a
letter from the Red Cloud party, which will reach this point
early on Sunday morning. Its camp to-night is only twenty
miles north of here. Forty-seven lodges have gone into
the cantonment on the Yellowstone to surrender to
General Miles.

"COULD THAT REALLY BE HIM?" ASKED LIEUTENANT
William Rosecrans of the half-breed interpreter who came to
a halt at his side.

This Fourth U.S. Cavalry officer, serving under Colonel
Ranald Mackenzie out of Camp Robinson,* anxiously
peered into the mid-distance as he threw up his hand, impatiently waving for the teamsters behind him to hurry up with
their ten wagons. Next he signaled to the half-dozen civilian
wranglers who were herding along a hundred beeves at the
end of the procession that had just come in sight of the Hat
Creek stage station.

Rosecrans had just spotted a far-off village on the move,
flowing like a great black cloud across the muddy and bar-

---

*Because of Lakota militancy in the region, this post was estab-
lished in February of 1874 when the agent Dr. James J. Saville
called for army protection at the nearby Red Cloud Agency.

ren plain, coming his way out of the north country. That crowd of people scattered across the rolling landscape, that massive herd of horses, those travois...it...it—

"Can't be no other, sir," replied young Billy Garnett, the half-blood translator Rosecrans had brought along from Mackenzie's post. "We knew we were going to run into 'em sooner or later."

Rosecrans let out a long sigh as he rocked forward in the stirrups of his uncomfortable McClellan saddle. *Who would have believed it?* he asked himself. Then he trembled slightly with the sheer anticipation. *Somewhere out there, in that small group riding in front of this village on the march, will be Crazy Horse—destroyer of Custer and his legions at the Little Bighorn, the warrior chief who fought Crook to an uneven draw at the Rosebud. The Sioux chief who time and again has confounded and befuddled Miles himself in winter battles along the Tongue River.*

"Crazy Horse," he finally allowed himself to whisper, then turned exuberantly on Garnett. "You've seen himself before, have you?"

"Not since 'sixty-five, Lieutenant," Garnett said. "I was ten years old at the time. Taken to a camp by my Lakota mother for a special ceremony. Northwest of Fort Laramie it was—where Crazy Horse himself was made a Shirt Wearer."

"You wouldn't recognize him?"

The half-breed shook his head. "I doubt it. That's twelve years of change."

Turning back again to the north, Rosecrans squinted into the mid-distance. "By damn—I don't believe I'll soon see Crazy Horse with my own eyes."

Twisting about at the sound of hooves, the young lieutenant watched the leader of some fifty Sioux scouts stop and make those hand gestures he had begun to learn from the capable Lieutenant William Philo Clark, who was serving as military agent at the Red Cloud Agency.

"H-hold on," Rosecrans said with some frustration, giving an impatient wag of his head. "I'm not as good as Clark is at this. Garnett, find out what this one wants to tell me."

After a moment of Sioux spoken between the leader of Clark's agency scouts and the half-breed interpreter, Garnett explained what American Horse was proposing.

"Yes! Yes!" the lieutenant replied enthusiastically, nodding his head to the Sioux horseman. "By all means: go welcome Crazy Horse and his headmen. Tell them I'll wait to talk with his chiefs right here!" Then he waved ahead the handsome leader, followed by his tribesmen from the agency.

They immediately kicked their little ponies into a burst of color and motion, yipping loudly, shaking their army carbines overhead, and even screaming as they bolted past the wagons in a blur. Their noisy charge came so sudden that it raised the hairs on the back of the lieutenant's neck as he watched these half-a-hundred horsemen riding hell-bent for election, off to greet their Northern brothers-in-arms. Fellow fighting men of the Sioux. The last hold-outs still south of the Canadian border, coming in to surrender their weapons, their families. These bloodthirsty demons finally brought to heel by the might of the U.S. Army. My, how that made his chest swell with pride: just to be sitting here on his prancing horse, waiting...waiting for Crazy Horse to come forward to surrender this day.

"Mr. Higgins!" Rosecrans hollered to the head wrangler as he raised himself in his stirrups. "See that your beeves don't bolt and stampede now!"

"That's easier said'n done!" the old cowman growled, then reined back to his work. "Keep 'em headed up!" he bawled at his hands. "Them redskins see these cows gettin' loose, they'll be comin' to make meat soon enough!"

"Lieutenant?" one of the teamsters cried out behind Rosecrans. "You want we should circle up the wagons?"

He watched as American Horse's galloping band of scouts spread themselves out in a broad front about the time those men in the advance of the oncoming village were crossing the Laramie–Black Hills Road. Coming ever onward.

Of a sudden the scouts' wild, blood-chilling cries faded when, some hundred yards short of their Northern brothers,

American Horse and his fifty friendlies reined up in a dusty spray and quickly dismounted, immediately sitting down on the prairie to await the vanguard that rode out in front of the approaching village. More than a dozen of those advancing Sioux slowly came up to the center of that wide line of seated scouts. In a moment American Horse and a few of his men were gesturing back toward the small escort of soldiers, teamsters, and wranglers. Rosecrans was surprised when more than a dozen of those men at the head of the village pushed on through the seated scouts, causing American Horse's men to hurriedly shuffle to either side to get out of their way. Perhaps out of some respect for those leaders. Perhaps out of fear.

By God he was going to be face-to-face with Crazy Horse in a matter of minutes, in less than half-a-mile, in only a few more heartbeats.

Over the last handful of days reports had drifted in from the north that assured Colonel Mackenzie that these last intractable Sioux were indeed on their way to Camp Robinson. Talk around the post claimed that more than a dozen years ago Crazy Horse had been friends with a few of the soldiers down at Fort Laramie. But that was back in the days before a decade of hard, bitter fighting. So a lot of the old-timers claimed that there wasn't a white man alive who had ever laid eyes on Crazy Horse. To be sure, there were some who swore they had seen the war chief at the Battle of Slim Buttes.* But heard more often were the haunted stories floating out of the Black Hills that told of all those white miners who had gone to their deaths alone. Riding down on them was the last face those men would ever see—

And here he was, watching the war chief and his attendants halt their ponies no more than twenty yards off.

"Which'un you think he is?" hissed one of the teamsters.

A second civilian observed, "Why, they ain't none of 'em painted—"

"You make about as much sense as a bung-hole in a

---

empty barr'l," a third man scolded before he spat out a brown stream of tobacco juice over the off-hand wheel of his small freight wagon. "Course they ain't gonna be painted up, you idiot! These here Injuns givin' up the ghost to the army. Ain't that right, Lieutenant?"

Rosecrans nodded, flicked a look at his half-breed interpreter, then swallowed unsurely as American Horse signaled him to come forward now that the fifty scouts had joined those village headmen and all were standing among the sage, waiting as the village slowly inched its way toward them. Riders fanned out upon their small, ribby Indian ponies, forming a wide crescent as the young lieutenant started his horse across that last expanse of open ground left between the groups—waving the interpreter, along with his sergeant and corporal, to fall in behind him. This was the moment, by God.

Back among the masses coming up behind their leaders, some of the weary, gaunt women trilled as they pushed forward to have themselves a close look at American Horse's scouts, excitedly shouting out the names of those they recognized in their shrill foreign tongue. Hundreds of eyes and cheeks turned shiny with tears of happiness at this first stage of a long-awaited reunion.

"We'll stop right here and dismount," Rosecrans instructed the three men who immediately halted just behind him. "Clark never gave me specific instructions, so I don't know for sure what the protocol is in a case such as this... but I'm sure we'll find out. Garnett, you ever done anything like this before?"

"No, can't say as I have."

"Beggin' your permission, Lieutenant," offered the old corporal in a faded blouse and tobacco-stained gray beard, "maybe we ought'n let that Sioux bugger come over to us."

"I'm damn well not going to stand on ceremony, men," Rosecrans growled sternly. "This will likely be the most auspicious introduction in my life."

Dismounting, the lieutenant waited for the other three

men to drop to the ground. Then he handed his reins to his
second in command. "Sergeant. Hold these till I return."

The soldier watched Garnett step up and hand his reins to
the old corporal; then the sergeant looked the younger lieutenant in the eye and asked, "You wasn't going over there
alone—with just this Indian-talker—was you, sir?"

Rosecrans scratched a two-day growth on his cheek. "If
they wanted our scalps, they could have taken them already."

"Yessir," replied the sergeant. "We'll have your horses
right here, Lieutenant."

The young officer tugged at the bottom of his tunic, then
brushed his gauntlets down the front of the dark blue wool,
knocking trail dust and grime from his uniform, as he started
forward. Garnett stepped out beside him, his thick-soled
moccasins padding softly on the ground dampened by yesterday's hard spring thunderstorm. The lieutenant was adjusting the bill of his kepi about the time a handful of Sioux
headmen dropped to the ground and started forward on foot.
They had taken no more than two steps when the smallest
among them turned and made a slight motion with his hand,
saying something to the rest. That done, the slim, undeco-
rated one came forward alone, likely to make the first contact with the soldier, to make that first overture.

Swallowing hard, Rosecrans blinked in consternation,
then blinked again as the figure got closer and closer, resolute and decided in his gait. The lieutenant saw how American Horse hung back with the other headmen, expectant
and waiting. Maybe he should call the scout leader forward... but Garnett should be able to tell this messenger
that the officer would wait right here in the open, on the
open ground between the two groups, for Crazy Horse himself to come forward.

By damn, if this fellow wasn't a bit more pale than the
rest of his earth-skinned fellows at the agency. Too, his
braided hair falling well past his waist wasn't black and
straight like that of the other Sioux Rosecrans had seen
around the post. No, this one's hair was almost brown—so

he was likely a half-breed like Garnett. That had to be the reason this half-blood was selected as a messenger to come out to meet him, carrying his lever-action carbine in the crook of his left arm, a dusty red blanket tied around his waist in traditional fashion, the stiff spring breeze tormenting that single feather tied at the back of his head.

Skin so light, a half-breed for sure, the lieutenant thought. *An interpreter perhaps, one whose mother had spent time around one of the long-ago fur trade posts, his father likely an old fur man who had gone to the blanket with the wild warrior bands.*

The slim figure stopped ten yards away, unceremoniously set his rifle down in the sage, then immediately crossed his arms. Rosecrans stopped, not sure what to do next.

"Take off your gun, Lieutenant," Garnett whispered uncertainly.

They both dropped their weapons, draping their gunbelts over clumps of gray-backed sage. Then the unarmed messenger motioned him and Garnett to approach.

What should my next move be? the lieutenant worried, as he and Garnett neared the pale-skinned one. Wasn't likely this messenger would understand the formality of a soldier's salute—a sign of mutual respect from one fighting man to another. So maybe he should simply put out his hand and present it to the warrior.

Rosecrans stopped mere feet away from the warrior, tore the leather gauntlet from his right hand, then slowly extended his arm, that trembling hand held out between them now that the two of them stood less than five feet apart.

For a long moment the Sioux stared down at the offered hand, long enough that the lieutenant began to consider that he should drop his arm. He started to turn to Garnett, wanting his interpreter to make some attempt to apologize for his foolishness. Such a civilized gesture had been a stupid formality wasted on this heathen warrior—

But the Indian suddenly reached out, grabbing the officer's left wrist in his right hand, and shifted it sideways so that he could grasp the white man's left glove in his bare hand. Surprised for a moment, Rosecrans eventually smiled hugely and began to shake left hands enthusiastically with this messenger.

"Yes! Yes!" the lieutenant roared with great vigor, grinning at Garnett.

The Indian said something, made a small sign with his right hand—pointing to his heart, then brushing the fingers of that hand down the extent of his left arm—ending up by signaling something to those warriors who had remained behind with their ponies.

When Rosecrans glanced at his interpreter, he found Billy Garnett frozen, staring in awe at the messenger. "Something wrong with the way I've done things?"

"Wh-what, sir?"

His enthusiasm undiminished, Rosecrans kept shaking hands with this pale-haired messenger as he instructed his interpreter, "Just tell him I want his chief to come forward now."

"Ch-chief?"

"Yes. Crazy Horse," the lieutenant replied impatiently, as his eyes raked over the others starting their way with American Horse. "I want to meet Crazy Horse."

Garnett's look of awe instantly turned into one of perplexed fascination, but suddenly brightened. He began to smile as if the white officer had just played a great joke upon him. "You want me to tell...*him*...to go get...Crazy Horse for you?"

"Yes," Rosecrans whispered with growing irritation at the delay this half-breed was causing. "I want to meet Crazy Horse, leader of the Northern Sioux."

"Crazy Horse—sure!" Garnett said, grinning widely now, his whole face animated. "Your hand...ah, Lieutenant—see...you're shaking hands with Crazy Horse himself."

It sank in slowly, while he slowly looked down at their left hands entwined together. Rosecrans rasped, "This is... is...Crazy Horse?"

"Him," the interpreter asserted, nodding toward the pale-skinned man. "This here is Crazy Horse."

For a long moment the fascinated Rosecrans studied the scar-faced, light-haired war chief of so slight a build. As American Horse brought his pony to a halt nearby, the lieutenant refused to tear his eyes from their two hands, still not quite believing.

"American Horse says," Garnett translated the scout leader's words, "Crazy Horse never shake for a long time— you're the first white man to shake his hand in more than eleven winters."

By God! I'm the first white man to shake this famous war leader's hand since he went on the warpath! That makes me the first white man ever to take his hand in ... in peace!

Sitting Bull shaded his eyes with his free hand and gently drew back on the single horsehair rein to halt his pony. The mid-afternoon sun had grown strong this far north, beginning to cast long shadows that streamed out from the sides of those two riders who galloped toward him—waving pieces of blanket, their mouths *O*ed up like the black eye-sockets in a buffalo's skull.*

Perhaps we can find enough buffalo up here, he thought as more than a double-handful of horsemen came up behind him, halting on either side of this great mystic and leader of the Hunkpapa.

The wind was strong here, whipping away the words shouted by those two riders as they raced ever closer. Young men, they were, these two brothers he had dispatched just before dawn, instructed to ride north—youngsters still full of the sap that ran strong this time of the year. And although he could not hear those shouted words ripped away from their lips by the cold spring wind that knifed its way up and down the gentle folds of this rolling prairie, Sitting Bull nonetheless already knew the message they were carrying back to him with such excitement.

Already he could hear the whispers of those who were

*This moment is said to have happened one day after Crazy Horse made first contact with Lieutenant William Rosecrans.

waiting around him. And he could barely make out the sounds of a great village on the march coming up behind them.

Turning slightly, he glanced over his shoulder at the way the procession had spread itself out as wide as the rolling hills allowed. What remained of their once-numberless pony herd was kept to the west side of their march by the herder boys. Travois were loaded with all that his people still owned. The women were scolding errant children and scampering dogs. Old men and women who could no longer walk long distances rode among the tiny ones perched atop the bundles of buffalohides, heavy loads bouncing near the ends of long lodgepoles. Some of his people—those who had spotted the two riders coming out of the distant, gray horizon—were shouting to the others now, their joyous voices struggling to be heard against the gusts of cold spring wind. Maybe they realized that they had arrived.

Slowly, with a great wave of relief washing over him, Sitting Bull drank in the chill air still soaked with a hint of the rain that had beaten against them as they had gone into camp near twilight last night. They had huddled in the lee of the low hills, throwing up what shelters they could erect and struggling to ignite a few fires where several families warmed themselves and heated some soup over the glowing embers of the dried buffalo droppings and smoldering greasewood. This Northern air felt good on a man's skin, smelled sweet. Above all else, it carried the taste of freedom to Sitting Bull's tongue as the mouths of the riders closed and they raced ever closer.

For the first moment in a long, long time, Sitting Bull felt assured that he and his people would now have peace for themselves and the children yet unborn.

As that pair of youths yanked back on their reins and their ponies came to a leg-jarring halt right before him and the other Hunkpapa headmen, Sitting Bull could see how the tears streamed from the corners of their eyes, moisture whipped by the wind and their high-speed flight across the prairie to carry him this momentous news.

"Speak," he commanded them, his eyes darting from one to the other now as he felt the anxiety creep back into his bones.

The younger one, he gulped as he glanced at his older brother.

It was he who swallowed deeply, his eyes smiling as he made his announcement. "We have been to a camp of the traders in the Cedar Hills," he explained, turning slightly and pointing behind him to the north with an outstretched arm.

Sitting Bull leaned forward, slightly, on the withers of his spotted pony, taking some of the pressure off his tailbone. "Did *they* tell you we were getting close?"

At that instant the young one's eyes grew big, his lips trembling as if he could no longer contain himself. The older boy nodded, giving permission.

"Back there." Then the young one paused and pointed past Sitting Bull and the headmen, on past the village that continued to draw closer as they spoke. "The traders said we must have crossed over sometime when the sun was near mid-sky."

"M-mid-sky?" Sitting Bull repeated, as the headmen gathered round him turned and looked over their shoulders, just as he did. He raised his face toward the sun, then quickly wheeled back on these two young couriers. "Then?"

Now the older boy proclaimed, "The trader Indians said we have already come to a new land."

Suddenly the shout went up from more than a handful of throats around the Hunkpapa leader. "The Land of the Grandmother!"

But Sitting Bull wanted to be sure before he allowed himself to believe it. He drank in another long, deep draught of that cold, moist air. "We are no longer in the land of the Americans?"

Both youths shook their heads, smiling joyously.

Around him now the older men were singing, and that soon set the women's tongues to trilling as they brought the first of the travois horses to a halt behind the advance party.

The Medicine Line! his heart exulted.

Staring behind him at that long rumple of short-grass prairie disappearing against the distant, cloud-filled horizon to the south, Sitting Bull squinted his eyes in the high spring sunlight, and wondered where the line had been that they had apparently crossed near midday. *Where had it been marked, with no range of mountains, no river's course, nothing at all to designate the boundary between what had been and what would be from now on?*

Here in this free land, he could remain a free Indian. No longer chased by the American soldiers.

They had crossed the Medicine Line and reached the Land of the Grandmother—giving the women and children sanctuary from the prowling soldiers.

His people were singing all around him now, a tumult that rocked this vacant prairie, reverberating from the very breast of the earth herself. Hundreds upon hundreds of Hunkpapa shouting their praises to the Great Mystery now that they could hunt the buffalo in peace, sleep in peace, watch their children grow in peace.

As the others, those old friends of many battles and long summers of struggle, urged their horses close around him, a blur of hands pounding him on the back, reaching out to touch his arm or brush his cheek in praise for what he had brought them through... a stunned Sitting Bull turned and looked south again.

Wondering.

Wondering and whispering a prayer for his young friend of the Oglala who had chosen a different road. Asking the Great Mystery to watch over and protect Crazy Horse.

CHAPTER TWO

6 May 1877

BY TELEGRAPH

SNOW AT DEADWOOD—INDIAN MATTERS—WASHINGTON NEWS.

Indian Affairs.

WASHINGTON, May 5.—Brigadier General Crook had a long conference to-day with the secretary of the interior and the commissioner of Indian affairs, in regard to the removal of the Sioux agencies to the Missouri river, and on the Indian question generally. Secretary Schurz and Commissioner Smith entirely concur with General Crook in his view that the Indians should be compelled to work for their grub, and the conference to-day was mainly with a view to ascertain how the labor of the Indians could be utilized in the interest of both the Indians and of the government. No definite conclusion has been reached as to the precise location of the new agencies, but it seems certain the Indians will not be removed until next autumn, as during the warm season the Indians will be disposed to straggle off on hunting expeditions, but will be easily collected on the approach of cold weather.

WATCHING THE DOZEN OR SO SIOUX HEADMEN BECKON HIM to cross the open ground between them, an animated Lieutenant

---

*Despite his being the man Crazy Horse surrendered to, Clark's greatest fame would come from the release of his comprehensive and exhaustive book, *Indian Sign Language,* published just after his death.

William Philo Clark* turned to his half-breed interpreter and asked, "That means they want me to go out to meet them?"

"A good sign, them sitting on the ground way they are," Billy Garnett whispered to the young officer, who served as the army's agent and chief of U.S. Indian scouts at Red Cloud's agency. "Shows you they're ready to talk."

Born in New York back in 1845, Clark had graduated from the U.S. Military Academy in 1868, assigned that June as a second lieutenant in the Second U.S. Cavalry. While he was affectionately known among the enlisted men as "Nobby," his fellow officers more often than not called him Philo. It was while he had served General George Crook as aide-de-camp during the Powder River Expedition, August through November of 1876, that Clark began his climb up the ladder of the frontier army. Back in January 1877, Crook had rewarded the young lieutenant, appointing him to become the new military agent at Camp Robinson when the army took over control of the Sioux agencies.

Clark yanked out his pocketwatch and glanced at its white face. Just past ten A.M.

It had been three days now since the Crazy Horse village met up with Lieutenant Rosecrans's wagons of supplies and that beef herd near Hat Creek Station on the Black Hills Road. Three days of feasting and much-needed rest before the Sioux set off again, continuing their march south.

Just minutes ago one of American Horse's agency scouts had come tearing down from the white bluffs northwest of the post, galloping among the clapboard buildings with his electrifying word that the Northern People had come in sight! About the time the far horizon had blackened with the village and its immense pony herd, Lieutenant Clark's escort breathlessly reached a stretch of flat ground a scant four miles north of Camp Robinson.

It was here, close by Soldier Creek, that Crazy Horse and his headmen rode forward onto that open ground, accompanied by Red Cloud and his agency scouts.

The young lieutenant now saw everything falling right into his hands. Through the waning days of winter it had appeared that Spotted Tail, the Brulé chief who ruled over his own agency some forty miles downriver, would get all the glory for bringing in his nephew, the famous Crazy Horse, instead of that honor going to Red Cloud, the chief in whom Lieutenant William Philo Clark had placed all his support. Red Cloud had to win, had to be the one to bring about the surrender.

Some weeks ago as spring was reaching these central plains, the aging chief had responded to Clark's promise that if Red Cloud could succeed in getting Crazy Horse and his people to surrender to his agency rather than to Spotted Tail, the lieutenant would then convince General George Crook he should restore Red Cloud to a position of power and prestige over his Oglala people ... perhaps even as chief over all the Sioux at both agencies! Highest among the chiefs. That would bring enormous prestige, not to mention immeasurable power over the day-to-day lives of his people. With the agency system, rations were distributed through the chief. The man who controlled food and blankets, kettles and beads, would have a secure grip on a position of unequaled authority.

On behalf of General George Crook, Spotted Tail had journeyed north this past winter to convince his nephew that he should not surrender to Colonel Nelson A. Miles. To come south to his agency instead. But now, William Clark and Red Cloud had whisked Crazy Horse right out from under the noses of both Spotted Tail* and General Crook.

With his mighty escort and the army's presents, Red

---

*For some time now, Spotted Tail had been receiving a salary from General George Crook—the only Lakota chief who ever received the esteem of a government salary. While it would be most interesting to know how much he was paid, and why, critics of this most famous Brulé chief have no grounds on which to claim that he was benefiting himself at the expense of his tribe, since it is on the record that he insisted that the government pay him in one-dollar bills so he could then distribute the entire amount to the poorer families on his reservation.

Cloud had gone out to persuade his long-ago friend to turn aside from the trail to Spotted Tail's camps and surrender at his own Oglala agency. Working hand-in-hand with the ambitious Clark, Red Cloud had single-handedly assured the greatest honor would go to the young lieutenant: this historic surrender of the mighty Sioux war chief Crazy Horse.*

When their eyes met across the distance now, Clark saw how smug Red Cloud appeared, having done what the soldiers had asked of him. On his dark, lined face was the look of a man who now demanded what had been promised him.

While Red Cloud and his men stood to the side, the delegation of Crazy Horse's headmen dismounted, then promptly sat down in a broad line facing the soldiers and their agency scouts.

Hearing the growing murmurs from American Horse's men behind him, Clark gazed over his shoulder again at the broad phalanx of excited agency scouts, asking Garnett, "Do these men really expect more horses from Crazy Horse?"

The half-breed shrugged. "Crazy Horse's warriors gave each one a pony or two when we run onto them a few days back...so your scouts figure to get another gift today. But one thing you can count on: them war bands won't ever give away the best of their ponies."

Fact was, as poor in possessions and as gaunt and hungry as they were, the Crazy Horse people were still rich in horseflesh, while Red Cloud's friendlies owned few ponies of their own. In the eyes of American Horse's agency scouts, the gifts of these Northern horses were a true treasure indeed.

As he moved his small party out at a brisk walk, Clark cleared his throat with the bedrock certainty that was a mark of his character. "But don't you see, Garnett? That's just what they're about to do. These Northern bands are going to turn over their weapons and their horses to *me*."

---

*With him, Crazy Horse brought a total of 899 people, of whom 217 were warriors, 312 women, 186 boys, and 184 girls, along with more than 2,000 horses and mules.

Trudging through the bunchgrass on foot, William Rosecrans clung at Clark's left elbow, while Billy Garnett hugged his right, the three of them striding across that open ground until the interpreter announced huskily, "He's the one there near the center of 'em, wearing the red blanket around his middle."

Clark moved over, and stopped right before the slim, unadorned Indian. Unsure, he quickly glanced at Rosecrans.

The lieutenant nodded in affirmation. "That's him."

Clearing his throat with authority, Clark asked, "Crazy Horse?"

Without a word, the Indian promptly rose to his feet and held out his left hand.

At Clark's left elbow, Rosecrans quietly whispered, "That's their custom."

"Garnett explained it to you?" he asked from the corner of his mouth.

"Yes," Rosecrans said in a hush as Clark accepted the offered hand in his. "He told me all manner of wrong is done by the right hand—so that's why they shake with their left. They explain that the left hand's closer to the heart too."

"Interesting," Clark murmured as he shook with the fair-skinned man, who—in the lieutenant's considerable estimation—in no way resembled the fierce war chief he had imagined Crazy Horse would turn out to be.

And that bullet scar running from the left side of the Indian's upper lip, furrowing his cheek—how it gave him a fierce look, even though he appeared to be smiling at the moment. This leader of the wild Sioux possessed a narrow face, at the middle of it a sharp, straight nose, eyes clear and light as well. As he studied the man, it appeared Crazy Horse showed little evidence of the high cheekbones that generally marked his race. In addition, the long braids that fell well past his waist weren't black and coarse at all, but a softer, brownish hue instead.

For what was a long moment, the slight Indian stared into Clark's eyes, almost as if he was taking some measure of this soldier. Then Crazy Horse said something in his native tongue, still clutching the white officer's hand.

"He's telling you he shakes with his left hand," the interpreter began, "because he wants this peace he makes with you to be a peace that will last forever."

In a matter of minutes they had made the introductions all around, Billy Garnett calling out the names of those headmen of the Crazy Horse people who had joined him in this auspicious surrender ceremony—a litany of names that for years had conspired to strike terror across the northern plains: Little Hawk,* He Dog,** Big Road, and the fierce and stocky Little Big Man. As Clark again studied the scar that puckered the left side of Crazy Horse's lip, extending on around his cheek, Garnett laid his hand around the officer's elbow, turned him slightly, and began speaking again.

"This one," the interpreter said. "You remember, I told you he's Crazy Horse's good friend. Name's He Dog."

The muscular warrior spoke, as Garnett began to translate.

"'My friend offers you his handshake in honor of our coming together to make peace. We must make it strong and lasting. The Great Mystery above wishes us to lay down our weapons, and never again make war. Looking back in the past, the land is big, so big half of it was yours, half of it was ours. We fought each other for the land. Your soldiers and our people now see the bones of many men and horses littered upon the land. The blood of many has been spilled. We have caused this, you and I.'"

As He Dog spoke, Clark had to nod in agreement.

The Sioux continued, "But on this day we will bury the

---

*This is not Crazy Horse's half brother (same father, different mother), who had been killed by some white miners when only twenty-three summers old. Instead, this is his mother's brother, who will play a minor role in the coming drama and tragedy of these final days of his nephew's life.
**He Dog is Red Cloud's nephew, a family connection that will soon exert all the more strain on his close bond with Crazy Horse.

days of our past. The blood we have spilled we will forget. We will never fight again."

He Dog stepped away for a few moments, then returned to the line of headmen, having retrieved a painted rawhide case from one of those young warriors who remained several yards to the rear with the ponies.

Garnett swallowed hard, saying quietly, "He Dog, he wants to make a gift to you."

Wary at this surprise development, an uneasy Clark watched He Dog pull back the cap of the tall, cylindrical container some ten inches in diameter, the Indian reaching in with one hand to pull forth what appeared to be a mass of beautiful eagle feathers.

The interpreter's eyes widened as he blinked in disbelief. Garnett stammered as he attempted to explain what the Sioux was saying. "This one, He Dog, he says Crazy Horse never owned a war bonnet. Never wore one in a fight. So he never had a bonnet in his life. But his good friend and . . . the one who fought beside him always, He Dog . . . he will now give you *his* war bonnet."

"This is yours, He Dog?" Clark asked breathlessly, staring down at the mass of golden eagle feathers arrayed across the Indian's hands.

The Sioux leader nodded. Beside him, Crazy Horse's face did not betray any emotion.

"I thank you," Clark replied as he took the bonnet from the hard-boned, dark-skinned warrior, running his fingers down the length of a glossy feather, all of them tipped with a white fluff and draped with several long strands of what appeared to be the coarse hair from a horse's tail. "And I thank Crazy Horse too." He looked the war chief in the eye, holding the man's gaze as he said, "If He Dog presents me this gift on behalf of his friend, I thank you both."

As Garnett interpreted those words into Sioux, He Dog took the mass of feathers from the white man's hands, shook the bonnet gently to loosen each one into its fullest glory, then spread open the skullcap and raised it, holding the bonnet beside Clark's head.

"Your hat, Lieutenant," the interpreter whispered impatiently. "Your hat!"

"Oh—yes," Clark said self-consciously, his heart leaping to his throat. Wide-eyed, he tore off the wide-brimmed hat and watched as He Dog carefully set the magnificent bonnet down on his closely cropped hair. He was sure his chest was thumping loud enough that all these chiefs were sure to hear.

He Dog said something to Crazy Horse. The war chief nodded, murmuring a few quiet words, almost shyly, as he looked away.

"What did he say?" the lieutenant asked.

Garnett gaped, his eyes twinkling as he pointed to the hat suspended in Clark's hand. "He Dog suggested they call you the White Hat, and Crazy Horse thought it was a good name for you."

"White Hat?" Clark responded.

"It's a good thing," Garnett observed. "They give you a name like this, means you're a person to 'em."

When He Dog turned to the young warriors behind them again, Clark brushed the feathers on the bonnet nestled upon his head. Without ceremony or warning, He Dog raised the tail of his war shirt and tugged it over his head, yanking one arm free at a time. Shaking it a moment so the long fringes and scalplocks hung just so as he held it out between them, He Dog uttered a few words.

Garnett interpreted, " 'Soldier chief, I give you my own shirt. My friend, Crazy Horse, he gave his over to Red Cloud a few days ago, so he doesn't have a war shirt of his own to give you. Take mine as a token for our surrender.' "

"Surrender?" Clark asked, taking the shirt into his trembling hands.

The half-breed's head bobbed. "The bonnet, and this shirt. These things are given to you in surrender."

Clark whispered from the corner of his mouth, "So when Crazy Horse gave his shirt to Red Cloud, he surrendered to him and his agency?"

Garnett nodded. "That's their custom."

Just then another young warrior approached the headmen, carrying a long, narrow case made of soft leather brightly decorated with a profusion of beadwork and quill-wrapped fringes that ran its entire length. He Dog promptly unknotted the thongs at one end and pulled out the carved stem of a pipe. To this he quickly attached a redstone bowl; then he held it out to Clark across both outstretched hands.

"Says he makes their surrender to you, White Hat," Garnett croaked, as if his throat had suddenly gone dry. "F-for Crazy Horse."

"This is He Dog's too?" the lieutenant prodded.

He Dog nodded.

Quickly pulling the shirt over his blue tunic, then replacing the bonnet on his head, Clark swallowed hard and took careful hold of the long pipe in both hands. "It will be a good thing for your people," he said, then waited while Garnett caught up with his translation. "This surrender you are making here to me. For your women, and your children. Good that the soldiers will no longer have to chase your villages. Good that you can come here to live in peace where the Grandfather in Washington makes a home for his Sioux children."

Then Clark was overwhelmed with the urge to offer a prayer of his very own. Closing his eyes, he raised the pipe and his face to the sky, saying, "Almighty God, have mercy on these people who surrender themselves to me today. Have mercy on us all. This day we are forging a peace that will last forever. All our wars and bloodshed has come to an end. We are digging a hole where we can bury all that has happened between our peoples. From this day forward, we will live in a peaceful way. I pray this in the name of God."

When the lieutenant had finished, He Dog responded, "If you are truly earnest in what you say, I want you to smoke this pipe with us now."

From a small beaded pouch the Sioux leader quickly loaded tobacco into the redstone bowl, and lit it from a smoldering ember one of the young men brought forward, held in a horn container. After Crazy Horse and his headmen had smoked, He Dog returned the pipe to the young officer. "Do as I did. Rub the smoke over your limbs to show that you mean what you prayed."

As he exhaled each mouthful of the strong tobacco, Clark captured the smoke in his hand and rubbed a little here, a little there, over his body.

"You keep the pipe," He Dog reminded when the lieutenant was done. "And this bag of tobacco too. Hold them tight. For they are a symbol of the peace we made here today."

"I am very pleased," Clark said, taking a step back so that he stood beside his interpreter once more.

"They are ready to follow you now," Garnett said quietly after He Dog spoke the words.

"Very well," Clark said, his heart buoyant. "We have pledged between the two of us that there will be no more bloodshed, and that we will cover up all the bad blood that has been between us."

Agreeing, He Dog spoke for Crazy Horse, saying through Garnett, "We will return to you all the soldier rifles we have. They belong to you. The Grandfather made them for us to fight each other. But we will fight no more."

"This is good," Clark replied. "For us to be at peace."

"And we will give you all our horses," He Dog continued. "Red Cloud told us we must give you our guns and our horses. Just as they have always done, our old people and our children can take care of our animals if you want them too."

"My soldiers will see to the horses you will turn over to me," the lieutenant explained. "Some of those horses I will give back to you, but I will keep the guns so there will never be any fighting again."

What he had worked so hard to attain over the last few months appeared to be dropping into his lap.

For so long it had appeared Spotted Tail would get the glory of bringing in the famous Crazy Horse, instead of that honor going to Red Cloud, the chief in whom Lieutenant William Philo Clark had placed all his support. Red Cloud had to win, had to be the one to bring about the surrender.

Now Clark could persuade Crook to place Red Cloud as chief over all the Sioux. Even over Spotted Tail. Highest among the chiefs. That meant immense prestige, not to mention immense power. Rations were distributed through the chiefs. The man who controlled those would be in an unequaled position of authority. On behalf of General George Crook, Spotted Tail had convinced Crazy Horse he should not go north to surrender to Colonel Nelson A. Miles. And in the last few days Clark and Red Cloud had whisked Crazy Horse out from under the noses of Spotted Tail and General Crook.

The lieutenant and the old chief both were men who understood how ambition and the hunger for power motivated the other. Clark sensed that their alliance had only begun to realize all that they might accomplish together.

"Follow me," Clark said as he beckoned toward his horse, staring down at the war shirt he wore, and that pipe across his left arm. He looked up, into the eyes of Crazy Horse. "Follow me to the agency . . . and your new life."

Ta'sunke Witko!

He immediately turned at the whisper, every bit as quickly realizing he hadn't been summoned by any tongue. Instead, he had heard his name spoken inside his head.

"I am listening," he whispered as his old friends He Dog and Little Big Man rode up on either side of him, their ponies prancing sideways as they were restrained, commanded to move more slowly than the animals would have liked, what with all the excitement heavy in the air.

Look at that old chief now—how he stands so haughty, staring at you so. Do you remember how he came to you not so long ago, almost as a beggar?

"Red Cloud?"

Yes—how he came with his gifts of the white man's agency food, a few thin soldier blankets too.

Crazy Horse sighed deeply, almost as if these were the last minutes he might use to fill his lungs, now that they had just come in sight of the agency buildings. "Before he came out to meet us on the prairie, I hadn't seen him for . . . many, many winters."

Not since he turned himself over to the white man, the way a bride gives herself to her husband on their wedding night.

For some time Crazy Horse rode on at the head of that slow procession, watching the scramble of numberless dark figures far, far ahead among the buildings, or those out among those crowded circles of smoke-blackened cones clustered both east and south of the white man's wooden lodges. Deep in his marrow, he knew Red Cloud's Bad Faces were screaming his name as they scurried to make ready this grand entrance to the old chief's agency.

"We were once the best of friends," he said to his spirit guardian.

Do you know what happened, Ta'sunke Witko?

For a moment he pondered that as the crowds gathered, swelling there in the distance—become a wildly cheering throng. Eventually he admitted there was but one answer to his *sicun's* question.

"Red Cloud . . . he gave up. Maybe he got tired—"

NO! He was seduced by the white man's shiny objects. By the white man's promise of power, prestige, and wealth. Better it was to be a big chief over a captive people, over those loafers held prisoner on this small island in the middle of a white ocean . . . than to keep his heart free.

"Yes, I see. After we drove the soldiers out of our old hunting grounds, Red Cloud was no longer a fighter, as he had been in the old days. While his feet carried him south, toward the white man and this reservation . . . mine stayed on to protect the northern country."

I want you to recall what Red Cloud asked you that night he and his agency scouts found your village already making your way south. Do you remember what question he asked you that made you angry enough that you no longer wanted to speak to your old friend?

"He sat there so smug, asking me why *I* was so selfish—

why I had brought down so much sadness and tribulation upon the heads of my people."

Do you think he meant you had brought trouble down upon all the Oglala?

"Yes. Red Cloud made it plain he and his kind blamed me for staying out so long, for fighting the white man and his soldiers so hard, for making things so tough on his agency loafers."

And now?

"Now...Red Cloud warns, we who stayed out so long, we who tried to remain free, will ultimately suffer the most," Crazy Horse whispered under his breath, so that those two close friends could not hear his darkest, saddest admission. "But you alone see what lies within my heart, *Sicun.* So you know what worries me more than everything else: to think that what I did for so long to protect my people...will in the end make this surrender even harder on them."

Crazy Horse could not begin to count them all, as their numbers swelled there along the road angling around the end of those pale bluffs dotted with tufts of a bright, spring green. The aromatic air was strong in his face, powerful in his nostrils. Perhaps the winds would blow every bit as wild and free here as they had up north on the Shifting Sands River,* in the valley of the Buffalo Tongue,** and Red Flower Creek,† or high among the bluffs above the Greasy Grass.‡

With a sudden squirt of excitement flushing through him, Crazy Horse turned and looked back over all those hundreds following him—wondering if he should feel ashamed for what he had done to bring them here. Once more he looked ahead at those who were crowding along the road, their numbers swelling in a liquid flow washing toward him as Red Cloud's people clambered to have themselves a look at

---

*The Maka Blu Wakpa, or Powder River.
**The Tatonka Ceji Wakpa, or Tongue River.
†The Onjinjintka Wakpa, or Rosebud Creek.
‡The Peji Sluta, or Little Bighorn River.

these Northern People. It was for his women and children he was coming in. Not for his fighting men, and not for him. There was no glory in surrender. No matter how much Red Cloud had tried to justify it days ago. No matter how the White Hat had talked slick and oily at their meeting on the prairie that morning. No matter...how Crazy Horse had tried to make himself believe it.

But he was man enough to do what was best for his people. Even though he would no longer be a leader here at Red Cloud's agency, Crazy Horse would see himself through this one last act of a righteous man.

"Brave hearts and fighters to the front!" had been his call so many, many times before as he led the hundreds into battle against the soldiers. "Cowards and those with knees of water to the rear! Hoka-hey! This is a good day to die!"

Brave hearts to the front, he thought again now, realizing a little of him was indeed dying at this very moment.

"Ta'sunke Witko!" the shouts washed over him in growing, towering waves of ear-numbing adulation. "Ta'sunke Witko!"

Feeling a hand on his bare arm, Crazy Horse looked down, finding that He Dog had reached out to touch him as they rode toward the cheering, chanting, trilling thousands.

"These agency people—how they call out your name!" He Dog cried loud as he could over the deafening din of voices.

Of a sudden, those headmen and warrior society leaders riding behind them began to sing, some raising their strongheart songs, others the Oglala flag song, and the rest their own powerful medicine songs as they neared the waiting throng that lined each side of the agency road like a long, throbbing gauntlet. Children darted in and out through the legs of the adults. Dogs chased back and forth, raising their shrill throats in the tumult. Women *ulu*ed their tongues in the triumph call, and the cheeks of the old men grew moist with tears as they saw him come in sight.

"He Dog is right!" Little Big Man agreed at his side. "These are your people, Crazy Horse!"

"No," he answered with a shake of his head, a little afraid of what Red Cloud and his friends were thinking now as they watched their people making such a triumphant fuss over him. "Those are not my people. No, my people," and he turned to glance behind him at the neat military rows of warriors arrayed behind the headmen, at the long scattered clutter of half-starved women and children, old ones, and their weary, gaunt travois horses, an immense, snaking procession that covered more than two miles of prairie behind him, "... those are my people. The ones who stayed out with me to wait for the ponies to grow fat on the spring grass, stayed out with me to watch their ponies grow lean beneath the wolfish winds of winter. My people stayed out and fought... until we could fight no more."

Then Crazy Horse looked hard at Little Big Man, and gestured at the immense, surging throng that pressed in around them on all sides, throwing themselves at Crazy Horse's feet, slowing their entrance to the agency grounds. "These people... they are Red Cloud's—and they are the white man's people too. These Indians may be Lakota, may even be Oglala... but they will never be mine."

CHAPTER THREE

May 6, 1877

INDIAN AFFAIRS.

We have good reason to state that the "backbone" of the Indian War is broken and that the operations of Generals Crook and Miles have resulted in an unconditional surrender of the Sioux, and they will be removed to a reservation early in the summer. The details of the surrender of

CRAZY HORSE'S BAND,

which took place May 6, at Camp Robinson, are given by the *Herald* telegram as follows: Lieut. Clark, of General Crook's staff, met the party about seven miles north of the agency and was presented to Crazy Horse by Red Cloud . . . the village resumed its march for the agency, arriving at two o'clock in the afternoon . . . The lodges were soon put up, and the work of counting the Indians and taking away their guns commenced . . . The animals surrendered number between 2,300 and 2,500 and are all in very good order . . . The lodges are not in good condition; many are badly worn and some quite useless. Crazy Horse is very taciturn, and has the reputation of never saying anything. His face is very dogged and resolute, bearing out the impression that he is a stranger to fear . . . Many of Crazy Horse's band have never been on an agency until the present movement. The guns turned in include the latest patterns of breech-loading arms of precision, but the Winchester was apparently the favorite. Of these Crazy Horse himself turned in three and Little Hawk two.

—ARMY AND NAVY JOURNAL

12 May 1877

"THIS ISN'T A SURRENDER!" GROWLED CAPTAIN JAMES KENnington, as he stared through his binoculars at the approaching procession. "It's turned into a goddamned triumphant march!"

At his elbow that Sunday stood Lieutenant William P. Clark, who had already grumbled much the same sentiment as the Camp Robinson officer corps watched how every man, woman, and child from the nearby agency were turning out for Crazy Horse's entrance to the agency, which, together with the nearby post, sat in a stunning natural amphitheater, the Red Cloud bluffs behind them. He supposed it was too much for him to have hoped that it would have been a quiet arrival of the Northern bands, but Clark figured this had to frost Red Cloud right down to his toes to witness the adulation being heaped on his one-time protégé, a war leader who had only recently seen the writing on the wall.

"I'll wager everything will turn out fine," suggested Lieutenant Henry L. Lemley of the Third Cavalry. "Now that he's here and securely under our thumbs."

Kennington sighed with relief, "At least Crook got the job done without another bone-grinding campaign, gentlemen. Last winter Congress mandated we drop the strength of our frontier army by twenty-five hundred men come the first of July. But we got Crazy Horse to surrender before the deadline."

Lieutenant William Rosecrans said, "Crook kept after him, hammering all the time. Giving Crazy Horse only two choices: fight or surrender. The last of the Sioux fighters have knuckled under to us."

"I'm not so sure as I was this morning," Clark admitted as the voices swelled around them and the screaming crowd began pushing in close around the leaders of that long two-mile column. "Crazy Horse may be surrendering the way we want him to surrender, but I've got an itch that our troubles with that one are far from over, gentlemen."

Rosecrans turned to ask, "What do you mean by that, Clark?"

He pursed his lips in reflection, then answered. "I don't think Crazy Horse sees what he is doing as a surrender. Certainly not the way we regard the surrender of those we have defeated or vanquished."

"But he's come in, for Christ's sake!" argued Lemley. "The man is now under the muzzle of our guns and the glint of our bayonets!"

"Maybe he has complied with what Crook ordered him to do," Clark said. "But . . . look there at him now and you'll see for yourself. Is that the face of a man who is capitulating to those who have vanquished him?"

"No," agreed Kennington as they all watched the Oglala headmen pass on by the adjutant's office, where they stood on the narrow porch, out of the midday sun. "That one had all the appearance of a man who has suffered no loss of leadership. Just listen to the hero's welcome Red Cloud's people are giving—"

"Damn him!" Clark growled. "These *are* Red Cloud's people. And Red Cloud is *our* leader. It's plain to see this Johnny-come-lately to the reservation is going to add a dangerous ingredient to the mix here at Red Cloud's agency."

Rosecrans turned to look at his fellow officer. "Why, Clark—it sounds as if you've already changed your mind about Crazy Horse."

"No. I *made* my mind up a long time ago," he admitted, his eyes narrowing as he glowered at the passing throng. "That Indian killed more of our soldiers than any of his kind. From Fetterman, down through Custer—and even turned back Crook at the Rosebud a year ago June. I'm going to have to get him under our thumb and be quick about it."

"He could well arouse some war fever," Kennington replied. "Get their blood running hot again."

"I think we must disarm them here and now," Clark asserted. "Without delay."

Lemley agreed. "By all means. Before Crazy Horse or any of his chiefs come up with any of their own ideas about how things are going to work."

"Exactly," and Clark nodded. "I like the way things are right now, the control I have with Red Cloud, how well he listens to the army. I don't want Crazy Horse upsetting this applecart." His eyes searched the civilian bystanders, and found the half-breed. "Billy!" he cried over the tumult.

Garnett wheeled about as if slapped on the shoulder, saw Clark waving him over, then hustled to that patch of shade where the group of officers stood watching the triumphant entry.

"You know that flat ground south of the agency?" Clark asked the translator.

"About a mile?" Garnett asked.

"That's the place," he said. "Go to Crazy Horse—before his village gets any farther and ends up camping near the other bands. Tell him you come from the White Hat, that you'll lead them to the ground where the White Hat says they can camp in peace."

The half-breed tugged down the front of his broad-brimmed hat and turned away without another word.

Rosecrans asked, "Is that where you're going to do it, Clark? The flat a mile south of the agency buildings?"

As the interpreter threaded his way through the milling, noisy throng, William Clark waited until he saw Garnett reach Crazy Horse's side. "Yes, that's where we'll take their guns and ponies away from them."

Billy Garnett was tense and edgy every moment of the nerve-wracking ordeal.

The moment the Crazy Horse village had reached the camping ground where Clark ordered them to camp, the women had begun to tear at their travois packs, lashing lodgepoles together and raising the buffalohide covers. Happy chatter, children's laughter, the barks of the camp dogs, along with the booming voices of the men as they ordered the herders here and there with all those ponies... about the time Clark showed up with his escort of agency scouts and two companies of soldiers.

Good thing he dismounted those soldiers, Billy thought, so they didn't look so damned menacing, perched there on the edge of camp. But that really wasn't what made the half-blood sweat. Trouble was that the Crazy Horse warriors out-

numbered Clark's soldiers more than two-to-one. Those
odds made Garnett pucker all the way through that afternoon's council. No telling how things would have gone if it
had come to fighting. The only thing certain is that Billy
Garnett would have been a loser either way.

His father was Brigadier General Richard B. Garnett,
who, during his ante-bellum service as commander of Fort
Laramie, had taken an Oglala wife named Look At Him.
Born near the post in the spring of 1855 at the confluence
of Saline Creek and the Laramie River, Billy wasn't quite
yet six years old when his father abandoned the U.S. Army
and went home to fight for the Confederacy. The general
became a Southern war hero, killed in Pickett's Charge at
Gettysburg. Without a father, the boy grew up among the
camps of Old Smoke and the Bad Face bands, even saw
Crazy Horse become a Shirt Wearer. But he nonetheless
kept on learning American talk, becoming good enough
that Agent James J. Saville hired him as a translator at the
Red Cloud Agency some two years back. And the moment
the Sioux War exploded, Garnett found himself recruited
by the officers at Camp Robinson, not only as an interpreter, but as a guide and a scout. Even after the last battle
had been won against Lame Deer's hold-outs on Muddy
Creek up in Montana Territory, Billy continued as a translator—working hard to do a good job for the army and the
whites. But he never expected he would be part of anything
like this day.

"Tell them they must bring their firearms and lay them on
this spot," William Clark instructed Garnett, pointing at the
ground near the toes of his boots. "All the rifles, carbines,
and pistols too. Every firearm they possess."

When the half-breed translated that order into Lakota,
Crazy Horse did not speak. Instead, he merely turned and
gave a gesture of his hand to the others. Quietly the word
was passed among the more than 200 men of fighting age
who had gathered to witness this epic event.

Some of those headmen who were seated around Crazy
Horse laid sticks on the ground, saying, "This long one is

my gun. And this little one is my pistol. I will send to my lodge for them."

The warriors began to drift off, slowly moving back into the village. Over the next half hour they came and went, a few at a time stepping through the stony-faced crowd to lay their firearms on the ground near Clark's feet. It wasn't an impressive collection at all: some out-of-date army guns, ancient muzzleloaders, a few well-worn lever-action carbines, and a handful of cap-and-ball percussion revolvers.

By the time Clark had Billy ask if that was all they were turning in, the lieutenant and his fellow officers looked over the collection with unvarnished skepticism before they had the soldiers scoop up the weapons and throw them into the bed of an empty freight wagon.

"Do they really believe we don't know better?" Clark groused suspiciously. "Only thirty breechloaders! Why—there were more than two-hundred-fifty army carbines taken from the Little Bighorn itself!"

And those thirty-five old muzzleloaders the warriors just turned in couldn't have done a bit of damage at the Rosebud, Slim Buttes, or Wolf Mountain either. Still, most of the thirty-three revolvers were serviceable weapons, to be sure. Cavalry issue: .45 caliber, single-action. Of all the dead men who had been wearing their Colt's revolvers when they followed Custer to the banks of the Little Bighorn, only thirty-three were turned in. Billy had felt his stomach do a flop again, worried that Clark would accuse Crazy Horse and his warriors of hiding weapons, demanding more from the Lakota and thereby forcing a confrontation even though this part of the surrender had been understood ... because Red Cloud had explained to the Hunkpatila war chief what was to happen and why.

Crazy Horse himself had turned in three Winchesters, and his uncle, Little Hawk, laid two at the White Hat's feet. Still the lieutenant glared at the small pile of weapons with unveiled anger in his eyes.

"I figure they cached the good weapons out there on the prairie," Clark complained to his fellow officers, his back turned to the Oglala leaders. "Many days ago and north of here, after Red Cloud told them this was going to happen—"

American Horse, Red Cloud's own son-in-law, suddenly emerged from the crowd at their side, stepping up beside Clark, then whispering in Lakota to the half-breed interpreter. In turn, Billy whispered into the lieutenant's ear. Clark nodded to the scout leader with approval; then American Horse stepped back to rejoin his agency men.

Clark studied Crazy Horse, He Dog, and the other faces in front of him a moment before he turned to Garnett.

"Billy, tell these men that my scouts have seen some of their warriors slipping off with weapons, doing their best to hide them in the brush, or beneath the dresses of their women." Clark spoke flatly, the way a man would as he tried to hold his temper when scolding a child. "Tell Crazy Horse I am going to order American Horse and his men to take those weapons away from those men who are without honor."

"W-without honor?" Billy repeated.

Clark gazed at him sternly. "Yes. You tell these men that they have surrendered to me, and that means they must turn over every firearm. No hiding a single weapon. Nothing— tell them not one rifle or pistol—must be kept back."

Sucking in a breath, the half-breed translated those harsh words, watching their harshness register on all the faces but one. Crazy Horse remained unmoved by the news that some of his warriors had attempted to hide their weapons. Without speaking a word, he turned to look at He Dog and made a simple slashing gesture with one hand.

With that it was done.

He Dog got to his feet and moved away into the crowd, speaking the sentiments Crazy Horse wanted known. These soldiers did not understand He Dog's words, but Billy sure did. Their chief was telling them that they must give up all their firearms to the agency scouts. To American Horse's men. Their chief had given his word to the White Hat. They must do nothing to weaken it.

One by one American Horse's scouts moved through the

crowd of Crazy Horse people, confronting those warriors they had spotted attempting to conceal their weapons. And one by one the rifles and pistols were handed over without a struggle, without so much as a protest now. Each new firearm was dropped upon the ground before the White Hat until there were sixteen more good breechloaders in the pile.

"One hundred–fourteen weapons in all," Clark sighed as if he were still far from satisfied, but just when Garnett feared a showdown was at hand, the lieutenant surprised him when he said, "Now they will turn over their horses. Tell them my men will lead their horses away."

"All of them?" Garnett asked after He Dog had posed the question to him. "Even their hunting ponies?"

"Yes. All of them," Clark replied firmly. "We will take every one, but give some back in a few days."

Billy had believed that would rile these warriors, these men who had been raised on the back of a pony—hunting, raiding, making war—riding all their lives . . . but the Crazy Horse people accepted this part of their surrender without complaint. It was almost eerie how none of it seemed to register on the pale, scarred face of their famous war chief.

"I want to have a talk with Crazy Horse," Clark said now that some of the herder boys had moved off with two dozen of his soldiers to start the Lakota horses toward a distant meadow.*

Billy felt the tension rise. "A talk?"

After he had settled himself before Crazy Horse and his headmen, the lieutenant explained, "I want to tell him about

---

*The army drove those Northern ponies down to Fort Laramie, where they were auctioned off for a fraction of their worth. The government held onto that money, earmarking it for the use by the Sioux in such vital matters as agriculture and education. With the way the Oglala leaders detested any talk of turning them into farmers, any mention of educating their children in the ways of the white man, just knowing that the money from the sale of their herds was to be used for that had to infuriate those chiefs beyond imagination.

how we're going to register his people. Put them on the rolls, by heads of families. Explain that we've done this very thing with Red Cloud's people, and the Northern Cheyenne who already came in and surrendered."*

Garnett swallowed, stepped over closer to the war chief, and explained that the White Hat wanted a serious talk. No preliminaries, and no need of the pipe. Just a little matter of importance to the ways of the white man. He didn't know right then which side he felt was more scared—his Lakota blood, or his white.

"Hau," replied He Dog after Crazy Horse had spoken.

Clark rubbed his hands together. "Tell them I want Crazy Horse and some of his headmen to go to Washington City with Red Cloud very soon." Clark blurted it right out, not content with preliminaries. "As soon as we have all his people registered, it would be a good thing for the chiefs to go see the Grandfather back east. It will be helpful for them to see just how mighty is our strength. How great are our numbers."

Garnett translated that as best he could into Lakota. For some moments the chiefs were quiet; then Crazy Horse murmured to the others, and He Dog spoke up.

"My chief, he says there will be a time to talk about this journey you ask him to make with the others, to see the white man's grandfather. But first, White Hat must arrange for the Crazy Horse people to have their own agency. Just as Three Stars promised if we brought our people here."

"His own agency?" Clark demanded, his eyes narrowing as if he had been caught off-guard by the question.

Billy translated, "Yes—just as the Three Stars promised them."

---

*Article Ten of the Fort Laramie Treaty of 1868 provided for the issue of rations and annuities to those Indians who complied with the treaty's terms. In order that the government's Indian Bureau could more closely estimate what was needed in the way of issue items, Article Ten further stipulated: "It shall be the duty of the agent to forward an exact census of the Indians." Every head, every mouth, was to be counted.

"Crook?"

"Yes," Garnett answered, turning back to Clark. "That's what they call the general."

Clark rubbed his chin. "Crook promised them an agency of their own?"

When he had He Dog's answer, Billy explained to the lieutenant, "When Spotted Tail came to ask Crazy Horse to come in, he carried word from Crook. Promised an agency in their own country."

Distinct displeasure grayed Clark's features. "So the general promised them this?"

"An agency in the north," Billy answered.

After a long, disgruntled sigh—the sort a man who felt himself backed into a corner he believed he had no business being in would make—Clark finally asked, "So tell me: where does Crazy Horse want his agency?"

"In the Powder River country," Billy explained after He Dog disclosed the details. "There's a nice patch of flat ground up west of the headwaters of Beaver Creek.* Crazy Horse wants his agency built right in the middle of that flat."

"He does, does he?" Clark replied sourly while Crazy Horse went to talking directly to Garnett for the first time that afternoon.

Billy watched the Oglala leader move his hands slightly, one over the other, almost in a gentle, peaceful manner—not the crude and coarse movements of sign language every frontier interpreter knew by rote. No, it was as if Crazy Horse were feeling that land in his hands, letting it seep through his fingers, perhaps even crushing some sage between his palms and bringing it to his nose the way a man might experience a piece of ground with all his senses.

Then Garnett turned to Clark with his translation: " 'The grass grows good there. Thick and tall as the belly of a horse in the bottoms. Buffalo too.' "

"Buffalo?" Clark said abruptly, as if his mind had been somewhere else rather than listening with his full attention.

---

*East of present-day Gillette, Wyoming.

"Lots of buffalo still in that country," Billy explained.

"All right," the lieutenant said brusquely, gesturing with both hands for the talk and the translation to cease. "Tell Crazy Horse we can discuss all that later. Another day. Right now, the most important thing for him to do is to go to Washington City, where he can meet the Great Grandfather. Tell him the government wants to move these two agencies east to the Missouri River. Three Stars knows the new Grandfather, President Hayes—so Three Stars wants the chiefs to go with him to Washington City so they can convince Hayes not to move the agencies to the Missouri. And when Crazy Horse gets back...that's when there can be talk about his own agency."

This talk of moving the agency came as a surprise to Garnett. Worried, Billy whispered his question: "Why are they going to make the Sioux move to the Missouri? So far from their own country?"

Leaning toward his translator, Clark explained, "Easier to transport the rations, the annuities too. Going to be a lot cheaper for the government to bring the goods upriver, rather than freighting them all the way out here across the prairie."

While Billy was whispering to the lieutenant, Crazy Horse began whispering to He Dog. Then He Dog spoke on behalf of his chief in those snappy phrases as he attempted to catch the essence of what Crazy Horse was saying.

" 'If Three Stars says we can't have the land up around Beaver Creek for my agency,' " Garnett translated, " 'then there is another place we can live—' "

Billy began to feel the tension tightening within the lieutenant beside him. Not from any palpable danger he was sensing, but more so from the way Clark and He Dog were talking to each other so quickly—without really allowing another to finish. The words were coming fast and sometimes Garnett squinted his eyes so that he could finish translating without having to turn his mind to another speaker, a different language.

"Another place?" Clark bellowed, wagging his arms in

protest. "We'll talk about that when it's time to talk about it. When Crazy Horse gets back from—"

Garnett turned to the lieutenant, finishing up He Dog's words, " 'Up at the forks of Goose Creek,* where you will find a flat of ground up against the White Mountains.' "**

Clark's face was growing splotchy with anger. "No more talk of an agency for him. Nowhere. There won't be an agency until he gets back from his trip to Washington—"

"But Three Stars promised them," Billy argued. "Said they'd have their choice if he surrendered down here to General Crook—"

"You remind Crazy Horse," the lieutenant snapped again in that clipped, even cadence of someone attempting to keep a lid on his anger, "he did not surrender to General Crook. He surrendered to *me*. That means Crazy Horse and He Dog and some of their headmen will go to Washington City, as I say, and then perhaps we'll talk about where to put his agency. For the time being, his people—every man, woman, and child—will stay right here at Red Cloud's agency for the Oglala."

After waiting until Billy had translated that to the stone-faced warriors, Clark continued, "His surrender means that Crazy Horse will take his orders from me and from Red Cloud. If I say he goes to Washington City, he goes. If Red Cloud tells Crazy Horse to camp in a certain place, then that's where Crazy Horse will camp. Do he and his chiefs understand they have surrendered to me?"

The officer and Billy waited until after he had translated in Lakota. Crazy Horse sat motionless for several moments of reflection. When he finally did whisper to He Dog, Garnett translated.

"Crazy Horse gives you his word as a warrior that he won't take up the gun against the soldiers, not no more," Billy declared. "He will listen to what Red Cloud has to say. To what Three Stars and White Hat say too. But...he

---

*Near present-day Sheridan, Wyoming.
**Bighorn Mountains.

says...each Lakota man must make up his own mind for himself."

"What?" Clark whined. "Every man makes up his mind for himself?"

With a nod, Billy said, "That's their way. Each man—"

"You tell Crazy Horse that he better do a damn good job to help his people make up their minds," Clark interrupted, his teeth gritted together as he rose and dusted off his rump once he was standing. "It's for their own good, you know, Garnett. This surrender is all for their own good."

CHAPTER FOUR

Pehingnunipi Wi
MOON OF SHEDDING PONIES, 1877

BY TELEGRAPH

CHEYENNE.

Indian and Deadwood News.

CHEYENNE, May 19.—General Crook with Major
Randall and Lieutenant Schuyler leave here in the morning
for the agencies, where the final grand council will be held,
which must be simply a formality, as the disarmament of
the Indians renders their consent to any proposition easily
obtained. A small band of Cheyennes arrived at Red Cloud
Wednesday, bringing in some two hundred horses. The
Indians are convinced that the government is acting in
good faith, and are evincing a like fidelity to the terms of
the surrender.

HE WAS A PRISONER NOW.

Even though he did not wear the iron cuffs and shackles
bound by heavy chain, Crazy Horse knew he was nonetheless a prisoner. With no weapons, nor a horse to hunt the
buffalo or track down an enemy . . . what good was he to his
people now?

How many days had it been since he brought the Northern People into Red Cloud's agency, this cluster of log
buildings that had been raised in the bottomground near the
foot of the bluffs, crouched beside the narrow and meander-
ing White Earth River. This was where the *wasicus* and
their soldiers kept the food and blankets behind tall stock-

ade walls. Stringy, greasy meat for those hungry bellies he could no longer fill with fat buffalo. Thin blankets for these spring nights so cold with the wind and rain.

No more buffalo. Now his people had only beef and pork to eat, a little flour to make their fry bread. It was not food to make a man strong . . . but—why did a man have to be strong anymore?

His old friend Red Cloud, and his uncle, Spotted Tail, too, they had grown fat eating the *wasicus'* food . . . while his own people came here lean and starving because they had been herded and harried by the army throughout the winter and down into the spring. How could some people grow fat by doing bad, and others go hungry for doing what was right? As often as he looked at the plump faces of the agency Oglala, and the famine-etched faces of his own Northern People, Crazy Horse refused to make himself over into a *wasicu* the way Red Cloud and Spotted Tail had done.

In their eyes, on their faces, it wasn't a hard thing to see— these subtle differences in Red Cloud, in his uncle too. Eight summers after Red Cloud gave up the fight . . . and it had been just as long since the white man made Spotted Tail a prisoner. The fight was gone out of them. The *wasicu* had broken them. It was clear these two old chiefs realized that Crazy Horse alone could see they were no longer the strong leaders they had once been. And Crazy Horse knew they resented him for it.

White Hat and his soldiers had taken their guns to the Soldier Town erected nearby, just west of the agency. And most of the Oglala horses had been driven south. Some said to be taken away on the white man's iron horse, perhaps sold to *wasicu* ranchers and farmers. Even the horses of the Northern People would now become something so foreign to their old way of life. Weapons gone; ponies pulling the white man's plows and wagons; and the Crazy Horse people with nothing in their bellies but the sort of food that made a man's body weak.

Had he done right?

To the east, just beyond the gently rolling ground richly

greened with spring's moist kiss, the majestic Crow Butte raised its impressive head. It was here among its heights that Crazy Horse came often in those early days of surrender, came to think mightily on what he had done. Up here he could look down upon the agency lodges, upon the Soldier Town, upon the village of his people. Theirs was a prison, with nowhere to go.

Had he ever had a choice?

Perhaps he was as helpless as the Shahiyela* had been. Only days after he brought his people to this agency, Crazy Horse had watched the army lead away the people of Morning Star** and Little Wolf, starting their long, terrible journey south to the Place of Heat and Sickness.† By reputation only, the Shahiyela had been forced to migrate to a country where the ground was as hard as iron, the water warm, and all the creeks and rivers trickled through the bottom of coulees that were nothing more than poor shadows of the streams that refreshed his beloved North Country.

The wind tormented some of his unbound hair. He pushed it out of his eyes and stared at the chalk-colored ridge rising out of the green of the earth just north of the soldier lodges. Patches of green, stunted pine dotted the slopes. But here on Crow Butte, Crazy Horse could sit among the thick stands of timber, shaded from the warm afternoon sun, and dream of what had been.

Should he have followed Sitting Bull into an uncertain future far north of their hunting grounds?

Gazing down at his lap, Crazy Horse took his *canupa*, the small pipe, from its unbeaded bag, crumpled a palmful of tobacco from the dried twist of brown leaf, and stuffed it into the hand-carved redstone bowl he had rubbed and cradled within his palms for summers beyond count.

To have followed Sitting Bull north would have con-

---

*Lakota for the Northern Cheyenne.
**More commonly known as Dull Knife to the white man. See *A Cold Day in Hell*, vol. 11, the Plainsmen Series.
†Indian Territory, present-day Oklahoma.

demned his people to a life far, far from the land of their birth, separated from the bones of their parents. But what had he achieved for his people by bringing them to this agency? How would the little ones be brought up now that they were no longer free? Would the children become loafers, just as Red Cloud's people had become coffee-coolers over the winters of their indolence? Would the children grow thirsty for the *wasicu* whiskey—grow crazy in drunkenness? Would the poor and helpless ones grow weaker still, now that they had no buffalo in their bellies, no free air to fill their lungs?

And where were the smiles? That more than anything had steadily eaten away at his resolve. No more did his friends have reason to smile. Not He Dog, Big Road, Little Hawk, even the perennially happy Little Big Man. Crazy Horse had little reason to smile himself. So he came here alone to this place to sit among the rocks at the edge of Crow Butte—just as he had walked away from the camps so many times last winter—to be with himself and the questions weighing heavy on his heart. No friend's voice, no friend's laughter reached him here. Only the soughing of the breeze through the pines that stood sentinel around his place of solitude.

Late last night two young Oglala, who had elected to stay in the north rather than ride south to surrender with the rest of Crazy Horse's people, slipped into camp, undetected by the soldiers and the White Hat's agency scouts. They carried sad news from the old country: firsthand reports of the fighting between the army and the last of the hold-outs who had rallied around the banner of Mnicowaju* chief Lame Deer. All fight had gone out of the warriors the moment Lame Deer had been slaughtered. But no, he hadn't died in honorable combat. Instead, chief Lame Deer was discussing with the Bear Coat terms of surrender for the women and children when he and his son were cut down** under a white flag of truce.

---

*Traditionally spelled *Minniconjou* by the white man.
***Ashes of Heaven,* vol. 13, the Plainsmen Series.

Embittered, and feeling as hollow as a rotted log, Crazy Horse gazed to the east for some time, watching the way the summer's wind bent the new grass far out on the prairie, and thought on those of his people who had chosen to live with Spotted Tail. His most trusted cousin, the Mnicowaju chief Touch-the-Clouds, and even his father, Worm, both had decided to live with the Sicangu,* camped so far away beyond that distant line where the earth scraped up against the summer sky. Crazy Horse felt alone, and every bit as cold as the unlit pipe he cradled in his upturned hands.

This was a good land for some. But his country lay far to the north, where he turned his eyes now. Closing them, he let his heart feel, let his heart *see* that good land far away on the Powder, where he prayed his people would be given the agency he had been promised.

It felt as if his life was thrown away now. For what did he go on living? A long time since he had been made a Shirt Wearer—one of the four who had vowed in the Wicasa Yatanpi ceremony to protect their people with their very lives. No longer did it matter that he had given back his shirt to the Big Bellies, because Crazy Horse continued to do what he knew he must for the sake of his people. Whether that was waging war or making this peace with the soldiers and the white man's loafers who had stayed back at the agencies while the fighters defended their homeland in the north. Sad men like his uncle, Spotted Tail, and his old friend and war comrade, Red Cloud.

How the face and those dark, brooding eyes of Red Cloud had registered such deep satisfaction as he watched the Crazy Horse people turn in their weapons, watched them hand over their horses. That terrible day seemed so distant now. Red Cloud had seen how Crazy Horse noticed his satisfaction. The old chief of the Bad Faces must have been sensing some great turning of fate, because he had suffered the same taking of weapons and horses by Three Fingers

---

*This is the Lakota name for this band, while the white men have always called them by their French name, Brulé.

Kinzie last autumn, just before that soldier chief pushed his men north to eventually discover the Shahiyela in a hidden valley of the Red Fork. Yes, Red Cloud knew the painful sting of that same insult. As he stood there with his closest friends, No Water and Woman's Dress, right behind the White Hat, Red Cloud's eyes had loudly proclaimed, *Now you are not so great before my Oglala, are you, Crazy Horse? Now you have no rifle, no pistol. Now you have no horses. Now your people belong to me!*

Even Three Stars had heaped scorn and insult on Red Cloud last winter, throwing him away as a chief, and making Spotted Tail the leader over both the Mnicowaju and the Oglala. How that must have made the old man's pride bleed and bleed . . . and bleed.

But whispers were that Three Stars would soon lift Red Cloud again, and make him chief of the Oglala once more . . . simply because he had been the one to bring in Crazy Horse. This was of great importance now, for a chief would be over all the others, he would command his scouts, and he would be the one given all the rations—through his hands would come the food and blankets. Now it seemed the *wasicus* were smiling on Red Cloud once again.

Hau! So Crazy Horse had come in and given himself to the White Hat, not to Spotted Tail. It was done the way the White Hat wanted, so Red Cloud would be raised, exalted, once more.

Oh, how he spent more and more hours away from camp, slipping off to be alone among the rocks, here beneath the sky, trying harder and harder to dream himself back into the Real World, seeking desperately to flee the despair of this Shadow World where everything and everyone sank deeper and deeper into the swallowing gloom. A clinging mire of hopelessness.

He drank in a deep breath and opened his eyes again, thinking how in these first days there had been much helping and sharing of this new burden for his people. The Red Cloud, and even some of the Spotted Tail people too, had offered what they had to those relations who had just come in from the north. That first day had arrived in the Crazy Horse camp with what little they could offer to fill the kettle or the skillet. But the very next morning following the surrender, the thin-faced agent had come with his wagons to distribute the first of their giving-up presents: poor soldier blankets that would never give them any warmth through a harsh winter, pants and shirts for the men and boys, long rolls of bright cloth for the women and girls to make their dresses now that the men could not hunt the deer or antelope for skins...and some small things, shiny and smooth and made by the *wasicus,* things the Northern People had never seen before...because they had never, ever, come to a reservation.

Never before had they come to eat and sleep, to live out the rest of their lives under the muzzles of the soldier guns. But now...their new life had begun on the reservation.

This prison to his heart.

As surely as if there were iron bars driven into the ground around this agency and the nearby Soldier Town, this was a prison. Although he was free to come here to this high, private place on the butte to think and look far away to the north, Crazy Horse felt as if he were held by the wide iron bands that the soldiers locked around the limbs of their captives. Many were the nights he awakened, damp with sweat, and rubbed at his ankles, massaged a wrist with his hand—just to assure himself that he did not indeed wear the wide iron bands. But he knew he was a prisoner just the same.

This was something he had done for his people. Most seemed to understand why he had brought them here. But he himself was not sure of much of anything, not anymore.

Especially when it came time that the half-breed interpreter explained that the men must register their families, give up their names, so that these things could be written down on the white man's flimsy parfleche. Then each of the Northern men were to touch the *wasicu*'s pen to signify that the names were indeed those of his own relations. Clan by clan, family by family. To give them up to the white man by giving away their names. Writing them down would rob them of their wild souls as surely as the white man's picture box could rob a man of his spirit. Like Crazy Horse, not one of the Northern men dared touch the pen. Even though they reluctantly spoke the names of their loved ones—because the interpreters explained that this was the only way they could acquire rations for their families—not one of these old men and young warriors touched the agent's pen.

Every time he walked somewhere—usually without speaking, without even noticing those around him, those he passed by—the agency Indians whispered behind their hands as he passed by, wrapped in his blanket. Trusted associates told him what Red Cloud's people gossiped about: claimed they had heard from a friend of Crazy Horse that he had not really surrendered to the soldiers, that he had come to Red Cloud's agency only to feed his people, to trade for bullets, before he would flee away to the north again.

That made him want to bray like a mule! What good was the white man's pig meat and his moldy flour in their bellies when only buffalo made a wild people strong? And what good did a handful of bullets do a man when he didn't have a weapon to use those bullets in? Yes, Red Cloud's people were full of silly talk. For years now, they had had nothing better to do than talk.

But...the reason he had come here to his private place was to decide what was best for Black Shawl. For a long time his wife had suffered with the coughing sickness that gave her great pain and made her skin hot to the touch. Women brought what roots they could find to boil for drinks, or leaves to chew on that might soothe her throat—but nothing had eased the torment. Then two days ago the half-Lakota interpreter had told him of the *wasicu* healer at the Soldier Town, the very same healer who had been among the soldiers in the fight at Slim Buttes, when American Horse* was shot through the

---

*This was the chief of the Minniconjou Lakota, not to be confused with the Oglala Lakota leader by the same name, the agency chief who will figure prominently in the undoing of and the treachery worked against Crazy Horse in this story; see *Trumpet on the Land*, vol. 10, the Plainsmen Series.

belly and a coil of his gut pushed its way out of the ragged bullet hole, bringing a night of agony before he died.

"This healer is a good man," the half-blood called Billy Garnett explained in a whisper, his eyes alert that no other should hear what he told Crazy Horse. "He has the sleeping water that took away the pain from American Horse after the fighting at Slim Buttes, so the old chief could die in peace and dignity."

But he had protested, "Black Shawl does not need this sleeping water that will help her die."

"No—but I am sure if I asked him for you," Garnett whispered, "the healer has some other medicine that will make your wife better, and take away the pain of her cough."

"I will think on this," he had promised.

So it was here at the edge of the rocks that were the very flesh of the earth, the rocks that were so much a part of his strength and power, where he came to think on this thing. Looking down at the cold pipestone in his hand, Crazy Horse decided this reservation was a new world where the old ways no longer worked. A new place, with new people and new ways. Perhaps it was best that if he could not accept and adapt himself, at least he do what he could to help those he loved most.

He hadn't been there when his young daughter, They Are Afraid of Her, was taken sick with the white man's illness and died. She was gone before he returned from a revenge raid into Psatoka* territory, her last breath taken and her death journey already begun.

Crazy Horse owed more to Black Shawl than to watch her die from the coughing sickness here in this prison. Squeezing the unlit pipebowl with fervent hope, he decided. If this *wasicu* healer possessed some powerful medicine that could ease his wife's pain and make her better, then he would ask help from a white man for the first time in his life.

A war leader, a one-time Shirt Wearer of the Oglala nation... the man who had turned back Three Stars in a day-

---

*The Crow tribe or Psa—while *Psatoka* means "Crow enemies."

long battle, then annihilated the Long Hair on the Greasy Grass, he would go to this healer and ask for whatever it would take so his wife would be spared. Although she would always remain second in his heart, Crazy Horse nonetheless owed Black Shawl more than he could ever repay her.

Even to swallowing his pride as a fighting man, as a wild and free Northern man who found himself penned up inside a small cage. Crazy Horse would do all that he could to save her life, as he would to save the lives of his people.

No matter that it might well mean he would one day have to offer up his own life in return.

BY TELEGRAPH
———

WASHINGTON.
———

Overhauling the Indian
Department Generally.
———

WASHINGTON, June 7.—Secretary Schurz, to-day, by order, created a board...to examine into the methods now in force in the finance and accounting division of the Indian bureau, especially as to an analysis of the money and property accounts of Indian agents, and whether the accounts of agents are rendered in accordance with the law and regulations; whether any expenditures are made without proper authority and whether the present system is such as to show at all times the condition of the money and property affairs at each agency...particular examination will be made as to the number and compensation of employees at each agency, and whether they are given or allowed to purchase subsistence or clothing in violation of the law...

"Eee-god, woman!" Seamus brayed with a grin so broad it nearly split his newly shaved face in half. "How long can your woman's good-byes take?"

Samantha reluctantly pulled herself a few inches away

from one of the half-dozen or so women who clustered round her at the edge of the parade ground there beside the mud-caked wall of sutler John Collins's store. She turned her head briefly, blinked her pooling eyes at him, then went back to sobbing with the lot of them—all babbling and clucking like a brood of hens who paid no earthly mind to him.

"Will you look at your mother, boy," he whispered to his eight-month-old son, the child cradled in the crook of his left arm, while he re-tucked the edge of the wool blanket around the youngster, protecting the boy from those errant gusts of early-morning breeze here in these last moments before the sun would emerge red and raw and brand-spanking-new upon the eastern prairie far, far away from these grounds of Fort Laramie.

"A man asks his wife a civil question and all she does is smile at him with those wet eyes and wet cheeks of hers, then goes right on back to what she was already about in the first place," he cooed down at the round, pink face. "Let that be a lesson to you now, Colin Teig. A little man like you might do well not getting all tangle-footed and tongue-tied with a woman...that is, when it comes the time you first start dogging after a woman's company."

His heart beat all the faster as he just stared down at the boy—seeing what he and Sam had created together. That is, the holy God above and them too. What a boost it gave his heart to just hold the boy in his big, callused, hard-knuckled hands. Just to think of what he and Samantha had made to-gether in this here cold and inhospitable wilderness once un-fit for the likes of womenfolk and children too.

And now his eyes rose to stare at the back of her head, all that spill of auburn curls she had tied back in a bit of pale lavender ribbon earlier this morning when they arose in the dark and he had shuffled off to make ready the horses—those two they would ride, and the five others, one of which would carry the small leather valises holding Samantha's and the boy's things, and the others would do to follow along if one of the riding animals went lame, or grew weary from this long journey north they were about to set out upon.

Auburn hair turning red with the coming of this new day's light. Ah, how it set her hair on fire, such light as this.

Best time of the day, he thought as he heard the shuffle of bootsoles on the gravel behind him and turned. Six of them coming. Pulling at their belts the way a man will when he has just been rousted out of his blanket. And a half-step in the lead of the other five friends strode Major Andrew W. Evans. Old comrades of the battlefield, all of these officers of the Third U.S. Cavalry.

"Donegan!" Evans cried as he approached. "Bloody good I didn't miss you."

The others were just finishing pulling their uniforms together as Evans came to a halt before the taller Irishman.

"I'd come woke you me own self, Colonel," Seamus said, using Evans's brevet rank, his gray eyes smiling down at this veteran cavalry officer who was once again serving as commander of Fort Laramie, where detachments of both the Third U.S. Cavalry and the Ninth U.S. Infantry were currently stationed.

"I bet you would at that, you old reprobate," Evans said with a grin. "You remember these fellows, don't you?"

His eyes bounced over the five of them as they smiled, nodded, and presented their hands to the civilian who had earned the untarnished respect and undying affection of all those officers and enlisted he had served with during the last fifteen months' campaign to finally put an end to the Great Sioux War on these northern plains.

"Lieutenant Colonel Mason!" he addressed the major who had stepped up to Evans's shoulder.

"Seamus," said Julius W. Mason, the first to hold out his hand. "We've had us a go at things together, haven't we?"

He swallowed the major's hand in his hard-boned horse-handler's paw, "I should say. From those days after Rosebud it was, as I recollect."

"While we followed the scattering bands going this way and that,"* Mason agreed.

---

* *Trumpet on the Land,* vol. 10, the Plainsmen Series.

"Funny, ain't it? How just last night I was laying in the dark, thinking on this ride I was about to make ... and I got to remembering how we was lucky to get Guy Henry out off the Rosebud alive, all the way back to the forks of the Tongue, without him dying on us," Seamus recalled.

With that jolt of memory, they all looked at the ground or stared at their boot-toes in remembrance of that brave officer who had been shot from the back of his horse as he sat tall and bold during a disastrous and disorderly retreat in the face of shrieking Sioux horsemen, most of them reflecting on how Seamus and an unknown Shoshone tracker had stood back to back over the critically wounded Henry, finding themselves out of bullets and forced to use their rifles like scythes and clubs against the daring enemy horsemen darting in to lay claim to the fallen man's body.

"There's nothing we can do for you?" asked Captain William S. Andrews, dragging a hand beneath his nose, and blinking his eyes.

Donegan felt the sting of tears himself as some of the other officers looked up, a mist in their eyes. Men who had once been strangers, oft-times hostile to civilian scouts. Soldiers who had eventually become the best of comrades under fire, men tested and not found wanting on the field of battle against the finest warriors on the face of the earth. No finer a friend could a man have than those who together had withstood the trials of warfare, the agony of quarter-rations, and the bitter cold or incessant rain of the northern plains.

Blinking his own eyes, Seamus glanced down at Colin, then looked up at Andrews to say, "No. We've got all we need for our journey."

Thomas B. Dewees, another officer in the Third U.S. Cavalry, said, "Your toughest feat will be to drag your Samantha away from that bunch."

He glanced over his shoulder at his wife. "Aye, Cap'n. They've been the best of friends too, don't you see? Them ladies helped my dearest bride through all them days and nights while we've been out about our business of soldiering." He sighed and turned back to look at the six faces. "The women has been good soldiers too, waiting."

"And your plans still the same?" asked Andrews.

"North by east from here to Camp Robinson," Donegan explained.

"Why not up to Fetterman?" inquired Dewees. "You change your plans to get to the Montana goldfields?"

"Closer to the Black Hills," Seamus admitted.

Mason asked, "Then you're going to make your fortune near Deadwood or Custer City rather than risk it all on a ride into Montana Territory?"

Shifting the boy in the crook of his left arm, Donegan said, "No. Plans are still to look up an old friend of mine up Montana way. But the truth is, there's more folks about the Black Hills. Towns and mining camps too. Better for mother and son I've got riding with me now to have a place here and there to lay by for a day or two as we make our way into Montana Territory."

"Going to be a long, tough journey for them, Seamus," Evans declared.

"Not near as long as the ride Sam and me made coming north from the Staked Plain in the autumn of 'seventy-five,"* he said.

"But you've got this little one now," Dewees advised.

"Time he got his first taste of riding this big land, don't you think?" Donegan asked, turning to glance once again at the gaggle of women huddled around Samantha.

She flicked her eyes at him quickly, and he could tell that it was time to go.

"Believe our time has come. Colonel Evans?" he said quietly, sentiment clogging his throat as he held out his hand to the officer.

"Sergeant Donegan, late of the Army of the Potomac," Evans replied, shook quickly, then took a step back to allow Mason, Andrews, and the rest to move forward, where they could shake the tall Irishman's hand themselves in this parting.

---

*Blood Song, vol. 8, the Plainsmen Series.

Without another word spoken between him and those comrades of battlefield and starvation march, Seamus turned and went over to Samantha. Taking the wide-eyed child from her husband, Sam nestled the boy down into the canvas duck sack she had strapped against the front of her wool coat. To the sack she had sewn a pair of wide canvas straps, cut from infantry haversacks. Then she had fashioned a short crosspiece that held the straps together with a buckle taken from a web cartridge belt. That way the straps would not have a tendency to slide off her narrow shoulders, for she had constructed the contraption large enough to fit comfortably upon Seamus's too. Either front or back, they could carry young Colin against their chests or behind their shoulders on this journey north.

"Ready, Sam?" he asked in a whisper, his throat cracking.

She only nodded, her eyes pooling as she took the reins to her horse from him.

Donegan cupped his hands before him. She laid her scuffed boot in their cradle and pushed herself and Colin onto the man's saddle, adjusting herself to the unaccustomed feel of men's canvas breeches and the long wool coat, the tails of which she flung out behind her so they draped across the horse's flanks.

"Good-bye," she barely croaked the word to her friends, each of whom had taken to bawling, hands over their mouths, dabbing at their eyes with damp handkerchiefs. She tightened up the reins and brought her horse around as Donegan turned away.

Reaching the side of his horse, he swung into the saddle, shifted, and nestled down for this long journey into the rest of their lives, now that the northern plains had been put to some semblance of peace. From around the horn he took up the lead rope to that gentle mare that carried their battered valises, four weathered pieces of leather luggage that had come west with Samantha to the Staked Plain of Texas years before, then been carried north as soon as she had become his missus.

Seamus reined around in a tight circle, and brought the

anxious horse under control. Halting, he snapped up his right arm, hand rigid against his brow. Tears tumbling down his ruddy cheeks.

Soldier to soldier, saluting fellow fighting men this one last time.

Seamus Donegan jabbed heels into his horse's ribs and it shot away. Those officers left behind not uttering a word. Heavy silence descending around them.

He knew he couldn't speak right now if he had to. So instead, he urged his horse over close beside hers, reached out, and brushed one callused finger down the tiny boy's red cheek. Then slipped his hand in her glove and squeezed tight.

Dawn suddenly broke, the reddish orb emerging over the far green lip of the earth, instantly splashing its rose light over this unsettled land as the little family rode into this first day of their new life.

CHAPTER FIVE

Pehingnunipi Wi
Moon of Shedding Ponies, 1877

DO YOU THINK SHE IS PRETTY?" BLACK SHAWL ASKED HER husband in that raspy whisper she used.

Crazy Horse realized he was staring at the young half-blood woman and turned back to gaze at his wife as Black Shawl emerged from the open door of their lodge. He studied her eyes, and realized he could not lie to his wife about this.

"Yes...she is pretty." He tried his best to put a noncommittal sound to it. He looked down at the two hands Black Shawl had clutching the blanket around her shoulders, the fingers of one hand laced around the neck of a green glass bottle. The *wasicu* was ducking his head, emerging from the lodge behind Black Shawl now. He wanted desperately to change the subject. "What did the healer give you?"

But this youngest daughter of the trader called Laravie made it impossible for him to put her out of his attention. She turned away to say something to the white man, then quickly explained in a soft voice, "It is a medicine water that will make her cough sleep."

Remembering Billy Garnett's explanation how the healer had helped American Horse die without pain, Crazy Horse grew frightened, and turned to the healer, then back to the young woman. "Will she...die?"

The trader's daughter translated. The healer spoke. The young woman explained, "She will not die, not of the coughing sickness.* This medicine he has instructed her to

---

*In his book written about these years among the Indians, Dr. Valentine T. McGillycuddy diagnosed Black Shawl as having tuberculosis.

drink four times a day—at sunrise, at midday, at sundown, and again when she is ready for bed—it will help her rest, because it will put her cough to sleep."

For a moment, he was filled with relief, not knowing what to say exactly to this *wasicu* healer. Eventually Crazy Horse held out his left hand to the white man. The healer looked down, glanced at the trader's daughter, then shook the offered hand with his left. The young woman said something in the white man's tongue and the healer smiled, pumping his arm all the more enthusiastically.

"Tell the healer I believe him to be a good man," Crazy Horse declared as they released each other's hands. "Explain to him that I took a very great chance of misunderstanding and bad hearts among my own people by asking him to come here, by seeking his help for my wife. But . . ." and he paused as his eyes came to rest on Black Shawl, "she is most precious to me. More precious than anything." Then he suddenly turned his attention back on the Laravie woman. "Ask the healer what I can do to repay him for his help?"

"You owe him nothing, he says," the half-blood woman replied. "He wants only to be your friend."

"That is not so much," the Horse said, looking into the healer's eyes with interest.

"Your friendship will mean a lot to him," the Laravie woman explained. "Says he will always be ready to help, when you or Black Shawl need him."

"Kola," he said the word again. "Tell him that is the word in Lakota, so that he will know how to say it, trader's daughter."

After the woman translated, the healer grinned warmly. Then the white man said the word in Lakota. "Kola."

"Yes," Crazy Horse said, turning away to lead Black Shawl from the shade of the lodge into the warm sunlight of this early-summer day. "Ta'shunke Witko *kola*."

Behind them, the half-blood woman was talking with the healer in the white man's tongue. He wanted to know what she was saying . . . if the trader's daughter was saying anything about him.

It was some time before Black Shawl spoke again, and not until he had helped her settle onto a buffalo robe, where she could lean back against the trunk of a cottonwood tree, the warm sun pouring down upon her.

Of a sudden, his wife declared, "She told me her white name."

He looked at her quizzically. "Who?" Then he saw how she looked at him with the deep, knowing eyes, with a look that said she knew full well that he understood exactly whom she was referring to.

"The trader's daughter," she finally said softly. "The one who looks at you with those wanting eyes." Black Shawl groaned, hanging her head a moment. Then she looked up again. "She had me repeat it until I learned to say it good."

"So she has a Lakota name?"

"No," she said. "A *wasicu* name. Nel-lie. Nellie Laravie."

Crazy Horse repeated the young woman's first name, very self-consciously, and each time he did, Black Shawl corrected him until he could say the white man's words the way they sounded coming from his wife's tongue.

"That one," she said as he watched the healer and the half-blood woman starting their way, leading their horses, "she is Long Joe's youngest."

In protest he snorted, "She is no more than a child."

"A very pretty child," Black Shawl argued. "One who looks at you with the eyes of a woman-child who wants you to notice how she looks at you...looks at you with her whole body."

Her words stunned him into silence. Finally, he turned back to his wife and admitted, "Yes, I see how she looks at me. But it is only because she knows I am leader of the Northern People. I am...only an oddity to her."

"You are a famous man," she said as they started away slowly.

She turned from looking at her husband, staring at the young woman who approached with the white healer. Then she looked at Crazy Horse again to see if he was looking at Laravie's daughter too. Crazy Horse was not. Instead, he was stoically staring off into the distance, his chin jutted proudly.

Black Shawl concluded, "Yes, you are a very famous... but also a very *human* man."

He felt his brow wrinkle with concern when he finally looked down upon his wife as she wheezed with great effort. "There will be many in this camp, especially those in Red Cloud's village, who will say I did a great wrong bringing this white healer here to help you."

She reached up and touched the back of his hand. "Thank you, husband." And a moment later, she quietly said, "Even if you lied to me about looking at the pretty trader's daughter... I love you for lying to me."

"Be quiet now, woman," he shushed her sternly as their guests drew close. "Save your throat from all these wasted, worthless words. You must rest your tongue so that the white man's medicine has time to heal you."

He could feel his wife staring up at him as they gave their good-byes to the *wasicu* healer and his beautiful translator. Embarrassed to realize how his eyes looked at the trader's daughter. But next to Black Buffalo Woman—the one he had lost to No Water—Nellie Laravie had to be the most beautiful woman he had ever seen.

As he watched their two guests mount up and ride toward the edge of camp, Crazy Horse felt his wife's eyes boring into the side of his face like two hot pokers. Nonetheless, she obeyed his demand for her silence. So he would not give her the satisfaction of seeing the look on her face, the accusation clouding her eyes.

Right now there were more important things for a man to worry about than his wife's petty jealousy. What with all the Northern People who had come to watch and wait when the *wasicu* healer and his translator had shown up in the village, asking for the lodge of Crazy Horse, he knew the tongues had to be wagging. It hadn't taken long at all for word to spread. He was sure that news of the white man's visit to his lodge had already reached Red Cloud's camp, had fallen upon the old chief's ears. Crazy Horse knew that his asking the healer to help his wife would only serve to give Red Cloud and his closest allies another hook on which to hang their growing displeasure with him.

But from the moment Black Shawl was taken sick, he had tried the sweat lodges, and having her breathe the leaves and roots laid upon smoky pyres—but none of that had cured her. So while there would be those who would say that he had turned his back on traditional healing when he asked for the *wasicu*'s help, the truth remained that Crazy Horse would do anything to cure his wife. Besides, those Oglala who were going to criticize him for this were people who disliked him already—

How surprised he was when he saw the trader's daughter turn and look back at him.

Surprised that it made him feel a little better about coming to this place and giving up his people to the agency and the army. If, as Black Shawl had claimed, this Nellie Laravie really saw something young and vital and even heroic when she looked at him, then all might not be lost by becoming less than a warrior, by turning himself over to other chiefs. Maybe she looked at him with those half-lidded woman's eyes only because he was the leader the agency loafers told so many stories about.

Then again...she might be gazing at him with the look a woman gave a man when she wanted him to possess her because she truly found him handsome and desirable— even though the scar on his left cheek gave him a stern and fierce expression. Such a thought that he still possessed a powerful personal magnetism made Crazy Horse feel a bit stronger in a very secret way, simply to have such a young and pretty woman stare at him unashamedly with such naked longing.

Now that Three Stars was coming to hold a council with the Oglala leaders at this place, all mixed up with those troubling matters Crazy Horse had to sort through regarding the soldier chief's demand that he go east to see the white man's Grandfather, or the demand he enlist as an agency

scout with the White Hat before the *wasicus* would talk
about the agency they had promised him...there was now
the question that he wasn't all that sure he would ever find
an answer for: What would his longing for that young
trader's daughter eventually do to him?

"Crazy Horse wants to know when you will give his people
the agency you promised him," Frank Grouard asked of
George Crook.

The gray-bearded general turned and dipped his head to
speak to Lieutenant Clark, their foreheads almost touching
as they whispered. Frank glanced at the Indians watching
the soldier chiefs huddled together and wondered if these
Lakota would trust anything else the soldiers said from here
on out, after the two of them had been whispering like a pair
of old women gossiping behind their hands.

Crook straightened after conferring with Clark and
asked, "Does Crazy Horse understand that I want him to go
to Washington City with Red Cloud and the others *before* we
will decide this matter of his own agency?"

The twenty-four-year-old Grouard pursed his lips and
turned back to the Hunkpatila leaders, his eyes barely passing over the face of Billy Garnett and that of Joseph Laravie,
the trader who also volunteered to translate during the visit
of so important a guest as General George Crook, come
from faraway Omaha to visit this agency and little Camp
Robinson simply because the famous Crazy Horse was here
now. It seemed everyone wanted to look upon the face of
Crazy Horse these days.

Was a time when Frank and Crazy Horse had been the
best of friends. Best of friends with He Dog too.

Frank translated the white man's words into Lakota,
shifting his eyes momentarily to the face of his former comrade, He Dog. He looked into the face of a man who had become his strongest enemy because of a woman. *Shit,*
Grouard thought. *Women were the surest way to make a fast
enemy of a good friend.*

Sitting Bull's Hunkpapa band of the Lakota had come to call him Grabber* when they accepted him into their tribe, not all that many years ago after he ran away from the world of the whites and headed to the northern plains, finding himself squarely in the land of the Lakota. They had welcomed him warmly and adopted him for what he was, even though the whites he had run across never truly believed Frank came from a faraway island in the South Pacific.** Instead, because of his dark skin, most white men on the frontier called him "nigger," declaring that he must have had black blood in him, or at least Indian blood for certain. Truth was closer to the bone than most would have imagined.

As a dirty, wretched street orphan dressed in rags when he first showed up barefoot in the Utah town of Beaver, Grouard had convinced the Addison Pratt family that his own father had been a Mormon missionary out in California, a man who had followed God's call to the South Pacific, where he had married an island woman and sired three children before returning with his new family to San Bernadino. As events had turned out, Frank had explained to the Pratts, his mother soon took her two youngest back to the islands and left Frank with his white father. Tragically, the two somehow became separated on a journey east to Utah, and Frank found himself in the kingdom of Brigham Young, the Prophet his father had so often spoken about in lofty and gilded terms.

Without hesitation, the prominent Pratts became Frank's benefactors, taking him in, educating him with the finest of books and the strictest of their spiritual teachings. Later, they tearfully bade farewell to Grouard when the young man of fifteen declared it was time for him to make a way in the world for himself. Frank found work hauling freight north into the gold diggings of Idaho and Montana territories, a fitting occupation for a youth who stood six feet tall and had

---

*Blood Song, vol. 8, the Plainsmen Series.
**Some of the most recent historical research tends to corroborate Grouard's claim that he was born in Tahiti, on the isle of Taiarapu.

200 pounds of iron-strap muscle welded on his frame in those adolescent years. He could read and write, handle animals and a gun with equal proficiency, and kept to himself— an admirable attribute on the frontier because it meant Frank Grouard kept himself out of trouble. In 1865 that was a much-sought-after combination in a mule-skinner who could haul trade goods all the way from the coast of California to the gold camps of the northern Rockies.

Yet it wasn't until January of 1870 that Frank's real adventure of a lifetime began. He had hired out to carry the mail from Fort Hawley on the upper Missouri all the way over to Fort Peck at the mouth of the Milk River. Caught in the middle of a blizzard, his horse snorted its nervous warning an instant before Frank was knocked off its back. Of the thirteen Lakota captors he found standing over him when he came to, twelve wanted to cut his throat, steal his weapons, and be done with it. But the leader of the war party smoked a pipe with Frank, and took in the dark-skinned loner.

For the next two years he traveled with that leader, who ended up adopting Grouard as his son: no less than the Hunkpapa chief named Sitting Bull. Frank had even suffered a grueling ordeal to prove his loyalty to Sitting Bull's people: remaining stoic while a shaman removed 480 tiny pieces of flesh from each of his arms, from shoulder to wrist. After the women plucked his eyebrows and face of all facial hair, then he was given a Lakota name. At Sitting Bull's direction, one of the tribe's shamans stood and pantomimed a grizzly, its arms outstretched, reaching to seize its victim.

"The Grabber" it was.

For many seasons before the arrival of Grouard, Sitting Bull had refused to trade with the white man, preferring to deal only with the Canadian Métis, those Red River half-breed traders from the north country, who brought the Hunkpapa everything from beads and bullets to guns and whiskey too. Back in the white man's world it was illegal to trade whiskey to the Indians on American soil. So when the Fort Peck trader and some army officers demanded that

Grouard lead them to the Métis camp, he felt his loyalties strained, then reluctantly agreed. When the arrests were made, three Santee Sioux in the Métis camp recognized the Grabber, and slipped away to report Grouard's complicity to Sitting Bull.

With the Hunkpapa chief furious beyond reason, it was a good time for Frank to move on. He soon found himself among Crazy Horse's Hunkpatila band of the Oglala, just about the time the war bands were harassing the Long Hair's Seventh U.S. Cavalry during their 1873 summer survey along the Elk River.* It was with Crazy Horse, along with his younger brother, Little Hawk, and his best friend, He Dog, that Frank roamed and raided, made war and stole ponies, courted young women, danced, and sang among the Hunkpatila for the better part of three years. Why, the Grabber even tried to settle down and live with one woman, the sister of his good friend He Dog. But problems with her made for bigger problems with He Dog . . . and Grouard decided it was best he disappear, after some long six years living with the Lakota.

In late 1875 he made his way into a Black Hills mining settlement, and from there down to Red Cloud's agency, where his ability to speak Lakota was a great help to then-agent Johnny Dear. Wasn't long before he came to the attention of Captain Teddy Egan of the Third Cavalry, the man who made sure Frank and what he had to offer the army were introduced to General George Crook. Those six years spent among the Hunkpapa and the Oglala, along with Frank's dark skin, gave him more in common with the Lakota than he felt in the company of white men, especially the sort of army officer like Lieutenant William Philo Clark, a soldier who always seemed to sneer at him down a long nose.

Back in the early part of that cold winter of '75–'76, Crook was searching for scouts who could lead him to where the village of Crazy Horse lay in the valley of the

*Yellowstone River.

Powder River. Not only could Frank lead Crook's sol-diers north, but he could also speak Lakota, and knew the ways of the Northern People too. The general claimed God himself must have delivered to him Frank Grouard—just the man he needed at the very moment Crook was needing him most. In the dark of night, through the maw of a winter blizzard, Grouard somehow led Crook's cavalry down on Crazy Horse's village* on March 17, just last year. Having proved himself, Frank was leading Crook's band of civilian and In-dian scouts to find the enemy wherever they might attempt to hide in the fastness of the northern plains.

Yet now that Sitting Bull had been driven far north into Canada, and the rest of the warrior bands were being rounded up and put inside corrals the white man called reservations, Frank figured he would have to find some other line of work . . . until Crook sent word he wanted Grouard to meet him at Red Cloud Agency. This time the general needed his help during the initial parley with Crazy Horse.

Here he sat: for the first time in nearly two years Grouard found himself face-to-face with the Oglala war chief, He Dog, and the other headmen who glared sullenly at the man they surely regarded as a turncoat.

Frank waited while the whispers died away and He Dog began to speak on behalf of his old friend and former Shirt Wearer.

"Crazy Horse does not know the white man. He knows only the lies of so many white men. But he wants to trust the soldier chief, the man who sits before him today. Crazy Horse wants to trust Three Stars."

---

*At the time of this story, even in mid-1877, many in the U.S. Army still did not realize, or perhaps did not want to admit, that they had not attacked Crazy Horse's village at all, but a village of Northern Cheyenne, who were on the move south to the white man's reservations, accompanied by some eleven lodges of He Dog's Oglala people, which might have accounted for Grouard's mistake identifying this Cheyenne camp as the village of his neme-sis, Crazy Horse.

"Trust?" Crook repeated Frank's word. "Of course he can trust me."

"Crazy Horse will put his trust in you," Grouard translated. "He will believe in you until your word turns false."

"Tell him that will never happen," Crook said guardedly. "Does he understand that there won't be any talk of an agency for his own people until he accompanies Red Cloud and the others to Washington City to see President Hayes?"

Frank nodded. "He understands. He Dog says Crazy Horse will go, because when he returns, you will give him the agency you promised him."

There was a sudden, stunned hush in that stuffy room filled with the smoke of pipe and too many honey-soaked cheroots. Frank felt a half-grin crease the side of his face, as he watched the way Crook and Clark and the other officers exchanged looks of surprised disbelief or even some cocky self-assuredness of the sort that claimed, *I told you so!*

Finally Crook cleared his throat and turned back to Grouard. "Frank, I want to be very sure of your translation. What did He Dog just say in regard to Crazy Horse and the journey east with Red Cloud?"

Grouard flicked his eyes for a moment at He Dog, then glanced at the impassive Crazy Horse and said, "Crazy Horse tells the soldier chief he will go with Red Cloud. And when he gets back, the soldier chief will give his people their own reservation up in the Powder River country."

Crook slapped both of his hands down on the top of his knees in exultation. "By damn! If that isn't the news I've wanted to hear with my own ears! Crazy Horse going to Washington City to see all the might and power of the nation that defeated him—"

"What about their reservation?" Grouard asked in interruption.

Perturbed, Crook turned to his translator as the other officers fell to a hush once more. "Yes. You tell Crazy Horse that when he gets back here after his trip to see President Hayes, then I will allow some of the Northern People to go on a hunt. A hunt in a late-summer moon, a journey to their old land of the Powder before they return here."

"W-why return here?" Billy Garnett interrupted the exchange now.

Crook looked even more bothered than before, his eyes narrowing above that bushy beard as he glared at the half-breed. "Grouard—tell them that I will allow them to go on a hunt if they promise to return here after forty days. Maybe that hunt will take their minds off this new agency they want somewhere up north where they'll be dangerously close to Nelson A. Miles."

"Why no talk of giving him his agency?" Frank asked.

Crook's cheeks flushed with crimson. "Because the government wants all these Sioux—Red Cloud's and Spotted Tail's Indians, all of 'em—moved to the Missouri before winter. Now you just tell them about the hunt I'm going to give his people, and don't worry about a damned thing you can't do anything about—like this business of the army moving these Sioux to a new reservation!"

Frank slowly translated the offer of that hunt in the Powder River country as the Lakota murmured among themselves, all save for Crazy Horse. He was staring—his face an impassive mask that dared not betray his emotion as his eyes flicked back and forth between Grouard and Crook.

Not knowing if he should feel a sense of elation or the impact of betrayal, the Grabber realized what promise Crook had just made to the Northern People...and what promise Crook had just taken away.

CHAPTER SIX

Wipazuka Waste Wi
MOON OF RIPENING BERRIES, 1877

BY TELEGRAPH

WASHINGTON.

Sitting Bull Will Remain North.

WASHINGTON, July 14.—Major Walsh, of the Canada
mounted police, visited Sitting Bull near the headwaters of
French creek. Sitting Bull said he desired to remain with
the Canadians during the summer; that he would do
nothing against the law; he came there because he was
tired of fighting, and if he could not make a living in
Canada he would return to the United States. Spotted
Eagle, Rain-in-the-Face, Medicine Bear, and a number of
other chiefs of the hostile Sioux, were present, together
with two hundred lodges. It is believed there must be some
four or five hundred lodges of hostile Sioux now north of
the boundary line, numbering at least 1,500 fighting men.

"YES, I REMEMBER THE SUN-GAZING DANCES OF OLD," CRAZY
Horse told his spirit guardian as its gold-kissed wings
moved restlessly inside him.

Will you offer yourself in the sacrifice dance this summer?

"No," he answered. "How can I when I have nothing to
celebrate?"

It felt as if the wings found some rest within him as he
answered the question. Perhaps his *sicun* was satisfied with
his answer. If not, at least he had put a stop to the question
that nagged at him day and night. Now that he had agreed to
go east with the other chiefs to make the soldiers happy,

Crazy Horse grew unsure he was doing the right thing by his people, for himself, for his spirit. This had begun to make him angrier than anything else—how more and more he caught himself deciding something one way and within days he felt differently about the matter. Never before had he been so indecisive. Not once in his life had he ever vacillated back and forth on a concern of his people. He had always been the sort to make up his mind, announce his decision, and move on.

But his new life here on this tiny patch of ground the army and the *wasicus* allowed his people had done something to corrupt him in a short time. He desperately wanted to be sure of things once more—to see things clearly, not blurred as if his vision were rippled on the wind-whipped surface of a pond.

Perhaps he should get away from everyone and everything as he had done before. To beg for an answer, he thought. Leave the camp and just walk into the hills on a quest for a vision. To pray and hope he was given an answer. Four days to cleanse himself and make ready to consider every matter he must consider now that this new life had begun, his people surrounded here by the white man instead of wandering free as the Hunkpatila were meant to live. As his heart was meant to roam.

He turned his eyes down the slope and watched the throngs making ready the arbor where they would erect the sacred pole and the shady arbors for the spectators, braiding the long rawhide thongs and bringing forth the grinning buffalo skulls. Clearing that dancing ground of vivid gray sage and clumps of dark green grass. Of a sudden he saw her, just beyond the sun-gazing site, as she settled in the shade of an overhanging tree on the bank of the creek. When she motioned to them, her two small children scampered off to play at the water's edge. He did not have to be any closer than this to know it was her. For the first time, he finally admitted to himself that his eyes had looked for her from the moment he had brought his people in to the agency. After all, this was where No Water lived with his good friend Red Cloud.

And her? Those close to Crazy Horse had whispered that Black Buffalo Woman lived with her two children in a small lodge behind No Water's now. Close to her husband, but not with him. She could not be happy.

Years ago No Water had chased them down, pursuing the eloping lovers so he could take his wife back from the Shirt Wearer who had wooed away the wife of a fellow Bad Face Oglala. In committing that indiscretion, Crazy Horse had made himself an enemy to one of Red Cloud's closest allies. Most Lakota men would have taken a different path than had No Water: after considering the fact that their wife had run off with another man, they would have decided they were better off without the sort of woman who did not want to be with them.

But not the quick-to-anger No Water. As soon as he had returned from his hunt and found both his wife and her former suitor missing, he knew. And had come after Crazy Horse in a blind fury.

For a moment now as he stared at her sitting in the shade, unaware of him, Crazy Horse's fingertips touched the long, jagged scar that puckered the left cheek so that it seemed he perpetually wore a scowl. Yes, he or some of his friends could have chased No Water down after the cuckolded husband had shot Crazy Horse in the face, but it was against tribal law to kill one of the group. This stealing of a wife, his making a man crazy enough to kill him—why, it irritated an already raw wound opened by the rivalry between the Bad Faces and the Hunkpatila band. As his terrible wound healed, Crazy Horse had asked his people not to take up the club, or knife, or gun against No Water and his allies. It was the only way to save the Oglala from splintering.

So No Water kept Black Buffalo Woman, and Crazy Horse got to keep his broken heart.

Looking at her from afar, he sighed. "But I found Black Shawl."

The wings of his spirit guardian were restless within. *We both know you've never been able to love her the way you've always hungered after Black Buffalo Woman.*

"It was . . . different with her."

Yes, it always is when a man finds the one woman to make him happy.

"I am happy with my wife."

No, you are content with her . . . and sometimes I wonder if you are even content with Black Shawl.

"She has been sick," he argued against the spirit. "Weak. Her fever too. And that medicine water the healer gave her to drink makes her sleep so much that she is rarely in the mood to couple—"

So more and more every day now you think about the trader's daughter. And right now you are thinking about the love for Black Buffalo Woman that once filled your heart and your loins with longing.

"I knew I would see her again one day. I knew it had to happen."

So what will you do?

"I should speak to her," Crazy Horse said quietly. "Tell her I am sorry. I never got a chance to explain that to her."

You are . . . sorry?

"Yes. For the trouble I brought her. I look at her, knowing she and her children do not live with him. I . . . I should have left her be."

Why did you ever think you could find happiness with another man's woman?

Drawing in a long, deep breath, Crazy Horse finally replied, "I was younger, stronger perhaps, and believed there was nothing to stop me. That was a time when I believed that there was nothing I did could go wrong."

Yes—those were days you felt me strong inside you.

"Aiyeee. Together I knew my days were full of strength and life."

What if you go to her now and she shows you those eyes the way she did before, hunka? What if Black Buffalo Woman shows you those hungry eyes the way the trader's daughter has turned hers on you?

"I can be strong now," he replied, trying to make it sound firmer than he felt inside. "This is good, to see my Northern

People preparing for the sun-gazing dance in the old way. I can draw strength from this dance, strength to do what I need to do. But first . . . she needs to hear that I am sorry for the way things turned out for both of us."

He waited for an answer from the winged guardian within his breast, but none came. Scratching up his courage, Crazy Horse got to his feet and started down the slope at an angle, heading not for those making the last preparations as the sacred tree that had been chosen by a virtuous woman was carried into the circle—but starting for the bank of the creek where Black Buffalo Woman sat, her hands busy rolling a piece of deerhide back and forth within them.

It made him think how she had taken his ready manhood within those same two hands and kneaded it into readiness before she climbed atop him. They had coupled and coupled again in their few days and brief hours together before No Water found them, burst into their lodge, and—as Little Big Man grabbed for his old friend's arm, hoping to forestall bloodshed, seeking to protect Crazy Horse from the infuriated husband—shot Crazy Horse in the face, the bullet from the borrowed pistol entering just below the left nostril.*

And in the seasons that followed, many were the nights that he awoke with a cold fear gnawing in his belly, his skin damp and clammy, crying out in his sleep, "L-let me go! Let go of my arm!"

The only way he had ever managed to put himself back to sleep was to think of Black Buffalo Woman, to remember how she had showered him with a passion he had never since discovered in any other woman.

He knew it would be good to make his apology. If not for her, at least for him. It was the best he could do now to make up for all the years that had been lost to others when they should have been with each other all along. Maybe that was why he wanted to trust Three Stars. Life was simply too

*This shooting took place on the upper reaches of the Powder River, sometime in the late summer of 1870, as the white man dates things.

short to go on carrying around the same old hate. The same way this sun-gazing dance, performed in the old way, would be good for his people. And even the way that hunt Three Stars promised when the first autumn winds began to dry the prairie grass would be good for his people too. This . . . this apology to her was part of making things good. If life would never be as it had been, then at least he could do his best to make life as good as it would ever be again.

Slowing his steps as he approached the trees where she sat, Crazy Horse looked at the children. The boy, older, clearly No Water's child. But the girl, younger—no more than six summers—she favored her mother, but . . . much more fair of skin. He stared, wondering about the child as she played with her miniature dolls and horses, trying to sort through the years it had been since he and Black Buffalo Woman ran away together, remembering how some had whispered that this daughter was born just long enough after the time Crazy Horse had eloped with No Water's wife. . . .

Then he turned to stare at Black Buffalo Woman. At almost the same moment she turned to gaze over her shoulder at him, as if she knew he was standing there, watching her. Instantly her eyes widened. Then her face grew dark and she looked away. Not back at her work on the hide in her hands, nor at the nearby creek rushing by her feet, but staring off somewhere else. She tugged at the blanket that lay on the ground beside her legs and dragged it onto her shoulders, over her head.

No gesture could be more emphatic than that. His heart, once strong and committed to say the words that needing saying, now broke in small, cold pieces.

She was telling him to go away. Not to look at her. Because she refused to look at him. The blanket said it all.

For a moment more he stood there, glancing one last time at Black Buffalo Woman's daughter. Her light-colored hair and pale skin. Remembering They Are Afraid of Her, the daughter who had died while he was away raiding the *Psatoka*. These two could have been sisters.

But now the one had long ago gone back to the winds on

that scaffold far to the north in a country that no longer belonged to his people. Because only the rocks and the sky live forever.

Slowly Crazy Horse turned away, his heart smaller, cold too, realizing the final words to an unfinished chapter of his life had just been written. Trying to remind himself that whenever a man turned his back on something old . . . it was best that he turn his face toward something new.

"Do you see the smoke?" he asked Samantha, pointing at the distance.

Squinting, she wagged her head.

"Look low, along the faintest part of the sky—where it meets the earth," he instructed.

"Yes," she answered cheerily. "I think I can see the smudge of it now. Where is that smoke coming from?"

"Near as I can figure from the few times I been through this country, that can only be one of two things."

"Two?"

"One might be a Injin camp. The reservation Sioux," he explained, patting the small boy on the back where the babe hung suspended against Donegan's chest.

"And the other?"

"Why, Camp Robinson itself, Samantha!" His voice rose with genuine joy.

"You mean we're almost there?"

"Damn me if we ain't, by the blessed souls of Mary and Joseph!"

She reached out to squeeze his wrist, her whole sunburned face smiling beneath the broad brim of the man's slouch hat he had bought her before embarking on this trip. They had tucked away her one good straw fedora among those new dresses, shawls, and other woman's things in the leather valises the packmare had strapped to her sides, suspended from the army packsaddle for this journey north into the land of the Montana gold diggings at Last Chance Gulch.

"Just a few more miles?" she asked with a guarded hope.

Taking that empty hand in his glove, he squeezed hard and reassuringly. "Tonight, I pray you'll sleep on a fresh-stuffed tick, Sam. And eat with your long and beautiful legs under a proper table, for sure. There's bound to be some women about—not near as many as call Laramie home... but I'm sure we'll scare up a place to stay the night, maybe two, before we move on."

She cleared her throat in that way he knew so well, a mannerism that told him to brace himself for something unexpected.

"Why must we hurry on after so short a stay at Camp Robinson?"

Seamus heard that sound in her voice, sensing the way it immediately plucked at his heart like little else ever could. He damn well knew she wasn't the trail-riding sort, even after their long ride up from the Staked Plain of the Texas panhandle. Samantha was a hardy woman, not given to complaints and such, but even a strong-boned female would find it difficult to stay in the saddle with the likes of Seamus Donegan. He had to remember that she was what she was, and the babe too.

He sighed as he looked down at their hands, fingers intertwined, then gazed into her eyes, and his began to moisten. "No reason we can't find us a place to lay by for a few days, Sam. As long a lay-over you want to have for you and Colin here. If there's no shake roof I can put over your head, I'm sure there's a post quartermaster who will let me use one of his wall tents for a spell."

"I think a wall tent would serve us quite nicely, Seamus," she said wearily, her whole face lighting up. "Every tent I saw on the grounds of Fort Laramie was far better than the small spaces most army couples are given."

"Tight quarters indeed," he replied and released her hand as Colin stirred and came awake with a cough. "The real trick will be getting my hands on a couple of new ticks what ain't been called for by them sojurs."

"We'll make do with our old ones," she said with a firm jut to her chin. "Ticks or no ticks, we'll be fine."

"You don't mind sleeping on blanket bedrolls, right on the ground?" he warned.

"I won't complain. I promise," and she held up her hand as if swearing to it.

"You're a angel, I say," he told her in a voice filled with admiration. "Don't know what I ever done to deserve a angel like you."

Giving him that rakish half-lidded gaze of a seductress, Samantha said, "Why, little Colin needed a father, didn't you know?"

Theirs had been the trip coming north by east from Fort Laramie. A week now in the journey, when the distance could have been traveled by a hard-riding man in a little more than two long and grueling days clamped atop the saddle. But instead they had traveled no more than a few miles each day, not making an ordeal of it. Lazy about getting up and stirring life back into the fire, he eventually slipped off each morning while Sam slept in, carrying the coffee pot down to a narrow stream. She only had to stir when Colin awoke, in need of his breakfast. My, but that boy took to the teat! A Donegan, that one was—surely his father's son.

In his small, grease-coated iron skillet Seamus would fry up some bacon, maybe a slab of salted pork or beef, then reheat some of the biscuits he had baked the night before in the small Dutch oven they carried along with their camp supplies. Flour and bacon and beans, pretty much the standard trail diet of a soldier. Because they were in no hurry, it was always late in the morning by the time the cooking gear was cleaned, bedding rolled up, and all of it packed away. Then the stock had to be unhobbled and brought into camp, saddled, and loaded before he finally stomped out the fire, mounted up, and moved them out. Without fail, it was never very long before little Colin began to fuss about one need or another. Either his little diapers began to smell with that horrendous telltale odor or the lad's belly had gone empty and he needed filling under some sheltering cottonwood, in a spot where Seamus could keep an eye out in all directions.

And they always stopped in a shady stand of trees a couple of hours later as the sun reached mid-sky, when Seamus might refill their canteens if he had managed to make their midday halt near a stream. Chances were Colin was already hungry again, so he'd get the two of them comfortable on a small scrap of army canvas he unfurled on a patch of green grass, close to the wide trunk of a tree. After the boy had his tummy filled most days, he was ready to nap right there against his mother's warm breast. Ah, the joy it brought the Irishman's heart to look down upon them two, mother and son, as they lay sleeping in the shade, a summer breeze nuzzling Sam's loose curls as he watched her chest rise and rise, rise and fall. And all things felt so right in the world.

Then he would turn away so he could scan the horizon in all directions, looking for smoke, or spires of dust raised by hoof or wagon wheel. Sometimes he'd smoke his pipe as they slept; other times he'd re-wind his watch and just sit with it nestled in the palm of one hand, looking at them in wonder, his heart so filled with exquisite joy that now at last they were heading to Camp Robinson, on from there to the mining towns of the Black Hills District, then striking out across the wilderness together for the gold diggings of Montana Territory.

It really had been eleven years, he often mused on this ride from Fort Laramie. Back to when he and Colonel Sam Marr first started north from Laramie with that small detail of soldiers and a Bible-thumping Reverend White, the land he was itching to reach was part of Idaho Territory. Now its sprawling expanse had a name all its own: Montana. Likely stood for mountains. The name fit, although it was these high rolling plains, the up-jutting bluffs and buttes and spectacular ridgelines, that Seamus loved all the more than hulking granite mountains. Up there in Montana Territory he would at long last have the chance to carve out the rest of his future in among the other gold seekers who scratched at the earth or shook the sluice-boxes, searching for that glint of yellow.

He'd buy her a house, he would. Have it built for the three of them. And then he'd fill it with the finest of dresses, china, and wind-up clocks too. For Colin, why, there'd not be a toy he wouldn't get for the lad . . . so his son didn't have to grow up knowing the relentlessly hard life of hand-to-mouth he and the other Donegan children had suffered back in old Eire. A Patlander come to Amerikay as a youth to look up a pair of uncles who had disappeared with little trace . . . but Seamus found them both, eventually. No, neither the Donegan nor the O'Rourke side of his blood had ever been what a man might call financially comfortable, much less well-off.

But that was about to change, he vowed each time he gazed into the limitless distance for sign of army patrol, Indian war party, or fellow sojourner.

With their midday nap over, Seamus rolled everything up once again and they pushed on until late in the afternoon when he chose a likely place to make their camp well before the sun was about to set. This gave him plenty of time to hobble the horses, putting them out to graze until he would eventually picket them in camp at nightfall. After bringing water up in the canvas bucket, he built a modest fire beneath the spreading branches of the cottonwood, so the smoke would disperse among the leaves and limbs. No sense announcing their presence.

Their canvas-sack bedrolls spread out by twilight, and little Colin asleep between them, Seamus and Samantha spent the next hours talking low of things to come, what they would see, where they were heading, and what they would do when they reached that fabled destination of Last Chance Gulch, Montana's newest strike. And when the coffee was gone, and Sam had returned from the brush for the last time before bed, he'd see that the two of them were tucked in before he took up the gunbelt once more and slipped out of the firelight. Quietly moving through the darkness, stopping often to listen intently before he moved on a few more paces, each evening he would make a wide circle of their camp, smell deeply of the night air—perhaps to pick up the scent of distant fire, animal, or even man. Only when his hour-long circuit of camp was done did he slip back toward the dying fire, as quiet as the padded feet of a church mouse, his shadowy form lit only by the crimson flicker of a few last embers.

There he took off the gunbelt once more, and laid the pair of Colt's pistols at his head, just as he kept another brace of his percussion pistols by Sam's grass-filled pillow. Most every night he ended up drifting off to sleep on his back, staring up at the brilliance of the summer sky, feeling little by little the anxiety draining from the marrow of him. Looking forward to chancing upon an old friend, perhaps running onto battlefield comrades somewhere along the way. Surely, when they struck out to the northwest from the Black Hills, he would take her directly for the mouth of Tongue River after they struck the Yellowstone, and there introduce her to Colonel Nelson A. Miles. Perhaps a lay-over of a day or so at that cantonment for the Fifth Infantry would do them all a bit of good, what with the miles they would have put behind them by that time. Then they would push on in that final stage of their journey through Montana Territory.

Every morning he awoke with the first calling of the birds in the gray of pre-dawn light, as the world around them softly stirred once more. He would quietly breathe fire back into the embers, set the coffee water to heating, then always—always—kneel over her, planting a gentle kiss on her forehead or eyelids. Without fail Sam would murmur something he never understood; then he would leave her and the boy to sleep in as long as Colin's tummy allowed them to. No rush, no need to hurry away as it had been for so many, many months with him now, no matter the season. One day put behind them at a time. One more day that stretched before them too. The slowing of his own rhythms come at long last.

Until . . . the buildings came into view beneath the powder blue of that early-summer sky, here in this most stunning natural amphitheater, the emerald bowl surrounded by the pale, majestic bluffs dotted by ponderosa. Camp Robinson. Log and slab-wood huts. Corrals and stockade fences. Along with that telltale fragrance of dung, a perfume to every horseman's nose, and by it he located the stables. Nearby stood the quartermaster's stores. Off to their right gurgled the narrow confines of Soldier Creek.

As they approached the verdant brush lining the stream Donegan spotted a lone Indian who urged his pony down the opposite bank, and into the creek. The warrior's eyes locked onto those of the tall civilian, then moved to appraise his wife, and back again, finally landing on the small boy harnessed against his father's chest. For the briefest moment, Seamus even wondered if he really was an Indian. If so, the man had to be a half-breed. Lighter-skinned than most of the Sioux he had ever laid eyes on, alive or dead. The man's hair was wrapped in braids that hung past his waist, a single feather tied into it so that it hung downward. Naked to his waist, the warrior bore no suffering scars from sundance trials on his chest or back as he looked away without emotion crossing his face, reining his pony out of the path of the oncoming white couple and their five extra horses.

For that flicker of a moment, what with the play of shadow and sunlight streaming through the treebranches, Seamus noticed something different, peculiar, something very distinctive about the man's face. But was troubled he could not put his finger on just what it was.

As much as he wanted to call out, to engage the Indian in some sign-talk with their hands, he was all the more anxious to get to Camp Robinson.

The family crossed with a clatter of hooves and a splash of water as the animals halted all on their own, pausing on the graveled bottom in the narrow confines of Soldier Creek, and drank their fill. He could let them do that now, without fear of the horses getting loggy with a long distance yet to go. Up the far bank and through the trees they moved on, his neck craning this way and that to get a look at the buildings.

"He's watching, Seamus," she announced quietly as Donegan tucked his chin and gazed down at the boy who was strapped to his chest, the child turned to the front so he could peer at his new and changing surroundings. "I really do believe he's watching."

The odors of fresh-sawn lumber reached Donegan's nose

as they pressed on past the stables, on past the carpenter's and paint shops, where his nostrils picked up the odor of soaped and dyed leather from the saddlery. Men in blue, young and old, some fresh-faced and those wrinkled with age, all passed by, giving these three curious travelers more than a cursory glance. Finally he spotted an older man, his lower face well tanned and wrinkled to the consistency of an oft-used saddle-bag, the soldier standing at ease against a building front, his infantry Springfield propped against his side.

" 'Scuse me, sojur," Seamus said, glancing at the absence of any rank on the man's sleeve, despite the short gray hairs that bristled on his cheeks and chin. "You tell me where I can find the officer of the day?"

"Right here it is," he said, jabbing over his shoulder with a thumb. "Adjutant's office this is. But...there's no one about right now, Mister."

"Where can I find the quartermaster, or even the post commander?"

The old soldier's eyes studied Samantha a moment, then came back to look at little Colin strapped to his father's chest, legs working in eagerness to get out of his harness. The man's tired eyes climbed to Donegan's face and he said, "That's where you'd find 'em, across the parade there. That row of buildings to the north—"

"By the grace of Jupiter himself!" a loud voice bawled, interrupting the old soldier's explanation.

Seamus turned in its direction, a smile instantly on his face as he peered down at the visage of an old friend hurrying across the last of those twenty yards that temporarily separated them.

The officer shoved his kepi back a bit so he could peer up at the tall horseman. "That...really is you! Gray-eyed Seamus Donegan in the flesh!"

Ripping off his sweaty right glove, the Irishman held down his hand and pumped the one held up by the officer. He watched how his old friend's eyes bounced over the child, quickly, and on to that auburn-haired rider sitting most manly astride her horse next to Seamus.

The soldier quickly ducked around the head of Donegan's claybank and came to a stop in the shadow beside Sam's knee. "This...this beautiful creature...why—you must be Samantha!"

"Yes," she responded almost shyly as she held down her gloved hand.

Sweeping off his hat, the officer kissed the back of her hand, then performed a gallant bow before he let her have that hand back. "You know you're all Seamus ever seemed to talk about on the campaign trails we shared with General Crook—when the late-night stars gleamed over our heads and the embers burned low. His talk was only of his bride Samantha. But now," the officer gushed with admiration, "oh, now it's plain to see why this homely, ham-handed Irishman is so damned fond of you—er, excuse my Irish, ma'am."

"No offense taken, sir," she replied. "After all, you will remember who I am married to!"

All three of them laughed loose and easy.

"So, Seamus," the young officer said, turning to the Irishman, "are you going to make me introduce myself in an unseemly and impolite manner to your bride?"

"Hell no, I ain't, you flea-bit, sorry excuse for a horse sojur!" he roared, gesturing grandly with one arm. "Samantha Donegan, I'm pleased to introduce to you my good, old friend: Lieutenant Johnny Bourke!"

CHAPTER SEVEN

Late June 1877

I NEVER KNOWED FRANK GROUARD TO BE SCARED OF MUCH of anything," Seamus commented to Billy Garnett at his side as their horses carried them right up to the outer fringes of the swelling throng gathered this late afternoon on the final day of the Oglala sundance.

"This here's something different than anything he's ever had to face before," said the half-breed interpreter as they reined up their horses.

Donegan rocked forward on the saddle horn, stretching the tense muscles at the small of his back. "What's so different with this that it's gonna make Frank afraid?"

"Being here," Garnett answered. "Smack in the middle of the Indians who believe you betrayed them. And you're where they can get their hands on you at long last. You get to know these Northern People, Seamus, you'll soon see how they look at things—"

"You're half-Sioux yourself."

Billy nodded. "My mother was full-blood Lakota, yes. But her people made peace with the white man a long time ago. Hung close to the fort—that's how she caught my father's eye. Just remember that the bunch Frank Grouard turned his back on is a warrior band, so they'll carry bad blood against Frank for a long, long time."

"Never saw him scared of anything near the way he was scared to come ride along with us today."

"This is where the Hunkpatila people—that's these Crazy Horse people—where they pray and make their vows to the Great Mystery," Garnett explained. "Grouard is smart enough to know he's not welcome here in this holy place."

"A holy place?" Seamus repeated as he swung out of the saddle.

"This sun-gazing is serious business for the Lakota,"

Billy sighed as they walked over to a bush that was already crowded with several Indian ponies. They tied off their horses and stepped to the edge of the crowd.

Seamus spotted young Dr. Valentine McGillycuddy and his wife, Fanny, seated across the sundance arbor, both of them perched in the shade on what appeared to be empty crates. Fanny clutched her proper parasol, watching with intense excitement from under the brim of her very proper hat, its smoke-thin veil just reaching the bottom of her chin. Donegan and the army doctor knew each other on sight, having served together during Crook's spring and summer campaign against the Sioux. So earlier in the month, not long after arriving at Camp Robinson, they had introduced their wives. Samantha and Fanny took to each other famously, and were already becoming fast friends.

As Seamus slowly gazed around the wide circle, here and there he noticed other officers he recognized, some soldiers he didn't, all of them equally intrigued by what they were witnessing.

"How many of these dances have the Sioux held?" Donegan asked.

"This is the first this summer," Garnett replied. "Lakota only hold the sun-gazing dance in the middle moon of the summer."

"Middle moon," he repeated the words. It had a nice ring to it. "So this is going to be it for sundancing?"

"Likely so," Billy said. "I figure that's why so many of the soldiers and white men turned out so they could see the wild Indians who whipped Custer's men—dancing, singing, hanging themselves from the sacrifice tree."

For a long time Seamus stared at the six dancers tugging ever harder against the wooden skewers passed under the muscles in their chest, the ends of which were tied to long rawhide ropes fastened to the top of the tall central pole. He was nothing short of amazed at how elastic human flesh could be each time the dancers leaned back, stretching their skin as they jerked a little, then continued to shuffle around the pole, right to left, following the path of the sun.

"Riding over, you told me this was their last day," he whispered as he followed Billy to the right.

Garnett nodded as they threaded their way through the edge of the crowd. Then they stopped and Billy pointed. "That's He Dog."

He stared at the dark-skinned warrior with the full face. "He's Crazy Horse's good friend?"

"And the one on his right is Big Road," Garnett said. "Got a band all of his own, but he threw in with the Crazy Horse people once the troubles started last year."

"I was there when those troubles broke out of the box."*

"On He Dog's left sits Little Big Man. He's another long-time friend of Crazy Horse," Garnett explained. "Word is that Crazy Horse put him up to riding into them talks the agency chiefs were having with the white men who came west to buy the Black Hills a few years back. Little Big Man rode his horse right onto that patch of ground between the loafer chiefs and those government men, shouting, shaking his carbine and his pistol too. Daring the soldiers to shoot him and start a war. All the time he was screaming that he wasn't only going to kill the white men come to steal the Black Hills, but he was going to shoot any of the agency chiefs who touched the pen to sell the Black Hills to the *wasicu*."

"What's that?"

"*Wasicu?* Means the white man," Billy said in a whisper. "Little Hawk, Crazy Horse's uncle, is sitting on the other side of Big Road."

Seamus saw some movement in the crowd as the throng began to part and many of the young men and older boys got to their feet and pushed out of the gathering, hurrying toward their ponies tethered nearby. His attention was immediately snagged by an Indian who rose a full head taller than all the rest, standing bare-chested, watching the dancers continue their slow circling of the sacred pole, his arms crossed before him as he surveyed the sun-gazers who kept blowing on their

*Battle of Powder River, *Blood Song,* vol. 8, the Plainsmen Series.

wingbone whistles, making a shrill, high-pitched sound that Donegan felt penetrate the base of his spine. It was a sound he had heard in battle against the Sioux, more times than he cared to count. A shrill call meant to turn a white man's heart to water, to make the enemy wet himself.

He looked around nervously while the young men and older boys flung themselves onto their horses and raced off, cleaving in two directions against the long, gentle hillside that rose behind the sundance arbor.

Seamus asked, "That tall one there—he must be the war chief Crazy Horse?"

Turning, Garnett easily picked out the big man. "Naw, that's Touch-the-Clouds."

"His name fits, big as he is."

"He's uncle to Crazy Horse, and his good friend too. They're both fighters. Touch-the-Clouds brought his Mnicowaju people into the reservation, over at Spotted Tail, just before Crazy Horse brought his folks in to surrender—"

"So where the blazes is Crazy Horse?" Donegan demanded with a little impatience. "When we was getting to know one another this morning, you said you was gonna bring me here to see the great war chief that stopped Crook cold at the Rosebud, and rode right over all of Custer's command at the Little Bighorn. I admit I never got me a good look at him at Wolf Mountain,* no matter that we was about as close to his Injins as we are to that Touch-the-Clouds fella over there. Us down in the bottom, slogging through the snow, and Crazy Horse's warriors up on a low ridge—"

"I don't see him anywhere," Garnett hissed in disappointment. "Thought sure he'd be here to watch his people dance."

"But you told me he don't dance."

Garnett nodded his head. "Said he never has."

"You know him well?"

"Just since he brought his people in to surrender," and Billy shrugged. "Not near as good as Grouard, I s'pose."

---

*Battle of the Butte, *Wolf Mountain Moon*, vol. 12, the Plainsmen Series.

"Frank got to know Crazy Horse and his kind so well that Frank had to get out by the skin of his tee—"

"I'll be damned," Billy exclaimed, his voice a good deal louder, an edge of excitement in it too.

"What's going on?" And Seamus craned his neck to see if he could discover what the half-breed was looking at.

Garnett grabbed the Irishman's forearm and said even louder now as the drumming and singing climbed in volume and intensity, "They're about to end the sun-gazing, Seamus."

"Then we've missed most everything," he said with some disappointment. "And I don't get to see Crazy Horse either."

"Most of the dancing," Garnett agreed, his voice still drenched with excitement. "But that's gone on four days already. It's not all that interesting to watch after the first couple hours or so."

"A long way we had to ride for just a few minutes of watching this dance," he said, raising his voice over the growing reverberation of the drums, the climbing crescendo of the singers' falsetto song.

"No, Irishman—we got here at just the right time," Billy declared with conviction. "It's about time for the battle to break out."

"A b-battle?" he echoed with concern, his eyes flicking this way and that.

"Not to worry, white man," Billy said with a big smile. "This isn't a real battle. Something that's always a part of the biggest sun-gazing dances. Near the end of the fourth day, they sometimes hold a . . . a make-believe battle."

"Against who?"

"The warriors divide up, take sides. Then they go at it like they did when they were just young boys: striking each other with sticks for clubs, or knocking each other off their ponies with a smack from their bows."

"Sounds like a fella could get hurt," Donegan observed as Billy tugged at his elbow and started him around the sundance arbor at the outer fringe of the crowd.

"They do get their share of bruises and cuts, that's for

sure," Garnett agreed. "There!" And he pointed at the few hundred horsemen forming themselves into two groups in the distance.

As Garnett stepped aside to talk in Sioux to a pair of older women who waited nearby, Donegan watched both sides milling around, straightening their clothing, some of the men sprinting their horses so the animals would be forced to gain their second wind.

"They're gonna make the Greasy Grass fight!" Billy squealed in excitement, his voice a notch higher as he clamped his hand on the Irishman's forearm once again.

Donegan scratched at his memory, knowing he had heard that name before. Was it Grouard, or had it been Big Bat, Baptiste Pourier, who had explained what river the Sioux called the Greasy Grass? Suddenly he remembered.

"The Little Bighorn?" he asked, leaning down slightly to gaze right into the younger man's face. "Custer's fight?"

With eyes twinkling, Garnett nodded. "Can you believe what we're about to watch? No man I ever heard tell of has ever known the story of how Custer and all his soldiers got wiped out on the Greasy Grass."

Straightening his back and peering over the milling, murmuring throng, staring at the masses of horsemen gathered on either side of a low swale of the smooth, green hillside, Donegan reflected, "So we're about to find out the story from the Injins who wiped out Custer's command, are we? The only ones to ever know for sure how all them sojurs was killed—"

"There they come now!" Garnett interrupted, gesturing with his arm in excitement. "See how them agency horsemen are lined out."

"Column of twos," Seamus said low. "Them warriors are supposed to be Custer's sojurs, ain't they?"

"That's Red Cloud's men playing the soldiers. The old woman over there told me them agency fellas wanted to play the winning side in this make-believe battle," Garnett explained. "So they chose to be Custer's men."

"Trouble is," Donegan corrected, wagging his head, "they wasn't the winners in that fight, Billy."

Garnett's eyes narrowed on the mid-distance. "The Northern People are going to show what they did to Custer a year ago this very month."

That struck him like a shot of January ice-water pouring down his spine, landing with a jolt. *By damn if this wasn't the last week of June!* A year ago, almost to the day, Crazy Horse had engineered the defeat of that flower of the frontier army, George Armstrong Custer. Civil War hero ... the man who stripped Sergeant Seamus Donegan, Army of the Shenandoah, of his stripes because he wouldn't have any part of hanging Mosby's raiders like common criminals. A soldier was given rights and dignity, even if he was a prisoner. But Custer had ordered the nooses prepared and the captives executed like common riffraff—

"Look how some of Custer's men are peeling away from the rest," Garnett pointed out.

They watched as a portion of the agency horsemen disappeared over the low saddle, gone from sight. Within minutes, another group of what was left of the agency scouts peeled aside too, taking a different course. That left the majority of the agency men continuing on their way across the side of the hill while some of the Northern horsemen suddenly swept down to attack that smaller, second unit that had split off on their own minutes before. While the mass of the agency Indians continued to sweep around behind the Northern attackers who had flung themselves against the small bunch of Red Cloud's scouts, swinging switches and lashing out with their bows in an eager attempt to unhorse their blue-coated opponents, most of the Crazy Horse people disappeared behind the low hill.

For the moment, it appeared the small band of Northern horsemen were about to be swallowed up between the two pincers of the agency fighters. But just as the large flank of Red Cloud's warriors went sweeping down on their outnumbered foes, their screams and war cries growing louder still, the mass of Northern fighters suddenly reappeared from behind the crowd, thundering out of brush along the creek bank, dashing past the sundance arbor, shouting and shaking their unstrung bows on high. The agency scouts were caught by utter surprise, wheeling and milling in confusion, with no time to prepare for the assault before the Northern men slammed into them.

Horses whinnied in fear and pain as animals collided against one another. Men shouted out in anger, bewilderment, or heart-pumping battle-fever. Dust that had been rising in small puffs from pony hooves now billowed in yellow waves, cloaking the actors in this all-too-real sham battle. Caught between two enemy forces, the agency horsemen attempted a futile retreat, just as Custer's men must have fled up that barren hillside, seeking the high ground. Before the Irishman's eyes, the Northern warriors, men who had enacted this very same maneuver to white soldiers a scant year before, herded the agency horsemen up the slope like bawling cattle, striking Red Cloud's men on the back and the head, the arm or the leg with their unstrung bows—

Suddenly a gunshot rang out. Then a second. The crowd gasped and held its collective breath as Garnett and Donegan shoved their way closer and closer to the scene among the Sioux leaders and headmen—

Then a half-dozen shots, exploding close together. Answered by another handful.

But as quickly someone was shouting above the cries of fury. A lone man walking into the open, onto that dangerous battleground, moving without hesitation on foot, both arms upraised, crying out to his fellow Sioux.

"What's he saying?" Seamus asked.

Billy was already shouting to any of the Indians who would listen, his Sioux drowned out by the angry muttering buffeting them as spectators darted one way or another, women scampering away with their tiny children in tow, men dashing off for whatever weapons they still owned.

"The agency men didn't like getting hit so hard!" Garnett explained.

"Who the hell has guns up there?" Seamus demanded, watching the slope. "Everyone back at the post told me them Crazy Horse warriors gave up all their guns."

"Not for a minute will I believe that Lieutenant Clark got all the guns they had—"

"Where's Bradley's soldiers now?" Donegan asked as he wheeled to look over his shoulder, his anxiety growing by the heartbeat.

"It was Red Cloud's men shooting. They're scouts, Donegan," Garnett declared. "So they've got their own pistols. More guns than the Crazy Horse people could ever keep hidden. When those agency Indians got angry for getting whipped, they started shooting at the Northern people."

Of a sudden the two of them were close enough to the scene that Seamus could make out the lone warrior's face, could hear what he was shouting in Sioux to both sides. Donegan asked again, "You make out what he's saying to them?"

Billy concentrated for a few moments, then began to offer a smattering of words in a running translation.

" 'Brothers you must stop! You are shooting at your own people! Put down your weapons. . . . We do not fight one another. . . . swallow down your anger. . . . Stop the fighting before someone is hurt bad. Can't you see you are shooting at your own people!' "

The more he studied that lone warrior's face, the more Donegan knew he had seen the man before. It was the horseman he had spotted as they crossed Soldier Creek, the day he brought his family to Camp Robinson. Those two long braids that fell past the man's waist, braids swaying this way and that as he addressed one group of horsemen, then the other. And that single feather tied sideways at the crown of his head. Shirtless, he wore a breechclout and buckskin leggings in this summer heat. But he carried no weapon. Not even the sign of a knife strapped at his waist. From the looks of him, the figure appeared younger than most of the headmen and chiefs, perhaps only because he wasn't a tall man by any reckoning, nor was he stocky or muscular. Despite his size, this slight, unimposing figure had interposed himself between two groups of armed men who were ready to spill one another's blood out of pride and honor, no matter that they were—as Garnett had explained—all Oglala.

"I've seen him before," Donegan confided as the groups of horsemen began to break apart and drift away in a multitude of directions.

"Where did you see him before? In battle?" Billy asked eagerly.

"No," and he shook his head. "Several days back, when we first reached the post. He was by himself."

Garnett nodded, looking at the lone man. "He usually is."

Seamus looked at Garnett strangely. "So you know that Injin firsthand?"

"That one standing alone out there?"

Yes, Donegan thought. *The solitary man who just stopped what could have been a lot of bloodshed with nothing more than the power of his will and the strength of his leadership. That man.*

"Who the hell is he?"

"Seamus," Garnett said, "you're looking at Crazy Horse."

CHAPTER EIGHT

Wicokannanji
The Middle Moon, 1877

NO WHITE MEN CAME TO THEIR SECOND SUNDANCE. THEY weren't invited.

The first had been held so the soldiers and their *wasicu* women could gape and mutter at the suffering the men endured. It took place about halfway between Red Cloud's and Spotted Tail's agencies, beside a creek the Oglala would thereafter call Sundance Creek. But this second, and much smaller, sun-gazing held at the foot of Beaver Mountain was for the Lakota alone.

Crazy Horse's uncle, Spotted Tail, had agreed to call for this private and more spiritual ceremony near his people's land, upstream from his agency, near the headwaters of Beaver Creek. The old chief had to realize how much this Beaver Mountain meant to the soul of his nephew. At the foot of the mountain's rugged slopes the Oglala and the Sicangu peoples made a clearing for the sundance arbor, carried in the sacred pole behind the long procession led by a virtuous woman, then began the first of their four days of fasting, singing, drumming, dancing ... and praying.

Since Crazy Horse had never before taken part in those sacrifices required by the sun-gazing dance—never hung himself by rawhide tethers from the central pole, nor suffered buffalo skulls hooked to the muscles of his back by wooden skewers and long tethers—five of his young followers volunteered to offer their flesh and their blood, honoring the Oglala war chief who had brought their women and children through so many seasons of war against the army. Three brothers—Kicking Bear, Black Fox, and Flying Eagle—were the first volunteering to dance in the stead of their war chief. Two of Crazy Horse's cousins—Eagle Thunder and Walking Eagle—quickly came forward, asking that they too be allowed to honor their chief by giving their bodies over to the sacrifice to the sun through the next four days.

Never was heard such a ululation from the women's throats as echoed off the slopes of Beaver Mountain that hot mid-summer morning. Now the Northern People would offer their prayers to the Great Mystery in earnest, without the eyes of the *wasicu* come to defile this narrow, sheltered valley. As the five joined the many others who presented themselves for piercing by the shamans, blood oozing down their chests, bellies, and onto the fine dust beneath their feet, the huge drums began their heartbeat rhythm. A cadence that would not cease until the sun fell from the sky that summer night, a pulse-throbbing that would be taken up the moment the great source of life once again made its appearance at dawn.

Taking only sips of water, the dancers rested out the brief cool hours of darkness here at the height of summer, rarely speaking, conserving their strength for the next day's long ordeal as they tugged and pulled on tethers and skewers captive of their flesh and muscle . . . praying.

So too did Crazy Horse pray from the circle, thinking of all the faces of friends and relatives who hadn't lived to reach this crucial point in Oglala history: this coming to the white man's prison on the White River. Offering his prayers, he asked the Great Mystery what he should do, which way was he to turn, where was he to go, and whom was he to trust. But for now, the only answer given him in the shimmering waves of heat mirage that arose around the naked brown dancers who plodded through the dust, inching around the prayer pole with tiny, weary steps, was that Crazy Horse must once more climb the heights to find what he was looking for. The same heights, to the same mountaintop, among those familiar rocks: where he had gone many times before in his search for peace.

"Build me a small sweat lodge," he asked of Little Hawk

and Little Big Man at sunrise the fourth day while the dancers took their places at the bottom of the pole.

The wrinkled, bloodied hands of the old shamans once more connected the tiny loops of braided rawhide tethers to the red-crusted ends of the sharpened, peeled willow skewers that had been shoved beneath tender, raw, and inflamed chest muscles three days before. Dust and sweat and wide tracks of blood coated the bellies and legs of all those dancers still able to stand, those few still able to hobble around the pole, blowing on their wingbone whistles and making their prayers to the infinite power above.

"How many will you ask inside?" Little Big Man asked.

The drums began their earnest thunder, and quickly the high, falsetto voices of the old men began to climb in prayer.

"Only one," Crazy Horse instructed. "Me."

"Where?" asked Little Hawk in a whisper.

His eyes touched his uncle. "Right against the foot of the mountain. There."

He watched the two of them move away without another question. They knew what to do. Cutting down the long eight-foot-tall willow, trimming off the limbs, tying the long branches together at their tops to form the low, inverted bowl, then laying over this framework the buffalo robes and blankets after they had dug a small pit in the center of the interior. Work continued throughout that afternoon, scraping out a large firepit for the rocks they selected one by one from the banks of Beaver Creek, bringing them back to the sacred mound outside the lodge, constructed with that dirt removed from the firehole. Starting from this altar, where a bleached buffalo skull faced the east with its hollow, black eyesockets, to the entrance into the sweat lodge, they brushed the loose dirt away to form a narrow path for his bare feet.

As the sun went down that evening of the fourth day of their sun-gazing, Crazy Horse stripped down to his breechclout. The crowd of hundreds fell to a hush. He stood motionless beside the altar and that empty-eyed skull while the shamans brushed him with white sage they repeatedly dipped in cool water brought from the creek, ritually preparing him for this journey from the light into darkness. When it was time, the old men stepped back and the Horse took the first step of his journey alone.

Across the warm, bare breast of the earth he walked, his naked feet following the path that quickly took him to the low, narrow entrance exposed as Big Road pulled back the flap of blanket. Dropping to his knees, Crazy Horse crawled into the semi-darkness, the only light a slim, dusky glow allowed in through that small entrance kept open while a pair of the shamans' helpers scooped the first of the heated rocks out of the nearby firepit and carried it to the doorway of the sweat lodge. There it was dropped and shoved forward with sticks until it rolled into the shallow pit. One by one, three more rocks were brought from the crimson embers of that fire, each one shoved into the heated darkness while shadows lengthened in that world outside. When the helpers had pulled back the forked limbs they used to carry those rocks and stepped away from the entrance, Big Road immediately pulled the blanket down, throwing the sweat lodge into an instant and inky black.

Crazy Horse knew there was no use in waiting for his eyes to grow accustomed to the dark. There wasn't a single slender thread of light allowed in by all the overlapping blankets and buffalohides, not even at the bottom, where the shamans had been sure to turn the covers in to prevent any of the day's dimming twilight from intruding upon his journey into the dark world.

Hunched over, he searched with his hands to the right but remembered that was the way he had crawled into the lodge, circling the pit to the sunward. So instead, Crazy Horse reached out with his left hand, and touched the large brass kettle. Feeling their way around its rolled lip, his fingers found the handle of the dipper. He swallowed, already wanting a drink of the cool water from Beaver Creek, but instead he raised the dipper, held out his left hand to feel for the heat of those four rocks, then slowly turned the dipper on its side.

That first loud hiss of water hit those rocks, each drop bursting into steam, the heavy heat of it immediately rising to penetrate his nostrils—making it hard to breathe for some moments... until his tongue, the back of his throat, and eventually his lungs grew used to the hot, stifling, sticky air.

A second, third, and finally fourth dipper he poured on the four rocks as his head began to swoon from the unremitting heat. Plunging the dipper back into the kettle, Crazy Horse took a drink, letting half of it dribble off his chin, spilling onto his sweating, heaving chest. So shockingly cold to his super-heated, tingling flesh.

Ta'sunke Witko!

"You've been here with me all along, haven't you?" he whispered.

*Since you heard the great **Wakan** explain that you must climb the mountain tomorrow at dawn.*

"Will you be with me?"

I am with you always, Crazy Horse. I have been with you from the beginning, in those dim ill-remembered days of your infancy, from the moment you took your first breath, long before you would ever come to know me. And... I will be with you at the end, when you go to join the stars.

"You know why I came here alone, without any others?"

You are always alone. No matter when you walk in a crowd of your people who sing your praises and trill of your exploits in battle. No matter how many gather around you... you are always alone.

"Wh-why?" he gasped, sensing how the heat and the rising steam pressed in upon his chest like huge hands making it hard for him to breathe.

There are only a few who can stand anywhere near such men of greatness, Ta'sunke Witko. A handful perhaps, but most will never know you as a friend.

"But I have had friends, ever since I was a child. I have friends now."

Yes, you have strong friends. But... you have even stronger enemies. Ta'sunke Witko, the truth to your life will be in learning which are the enemies to be trusted, and which friends are to be feared.

"I have never feared any man!" he hissed, feeling nauseous from the heat.

But with his empty belly he could only gag. Nothing came up.

Fear can be a good teacher. Keep your eyes on those who stand closest to the heat of your power, wanting to warm their own hands in it. A vision was given you when you were still a mere boy believing you were ready to become a man. Remember that vision and take strength from it.

"The rider coming out of the lake? I remember that."

And how Ta'sunke Witko would be killed?

He wagged his head, wondering where the memory of it was. "I–I . . ."

Your own people will cling to you, Ta'sunke Witko. They always have, because you are their strength. They will cling to you in hopes that you can save them . . . but in the end their clinging will cost you your life. You can revisit your vision on the mountaintop.

"See again . . . them holding my arms?" he asked, wiping a wet hand down his wet face, flinging the sweat onto the rocks so that they hissed. Then his fingertips brushed the long scar, as he recalled how Little Big Man grabbed his wrist when No Water shot him.

Pull away from them, break free while you still can . . . and drink in a breath of freedom on your own.

Slowly, painfully, he dragged another breath into his lungs, slowly feeling a bit stronger. Then leaned left, felt for the ladle, and splashed four more dippers onto the rocks. This time the water did not hiss near as loudly, nor did the steam fill the tiny sweat lodge near as it had. Nowhere near as oppressive now. Crazy Horse opened his eyes again, but it did no good—because there was nothing to see, not even in the clouds of steam that must be hovering right before him. He had descended deep into the belly of darkness . . . where a man had to venture before he could begin his journey back toward the light, a suffering completed in preparation for the sacrifice he would make over the next four days of his vision quest.

Pull away from them while you still can. Break free. And take a ... one final breath of freedom on your own.

With a shudder, Crazy Horse remembered that frightening part of the vision he had received in his fourteenth summer. So many hands and arms ... reaching, lunging, grasping, clawing, pulling at him by the hundreds. His people. Lakota, Oglala. Even Hunkpatila. Friends and family among them. That vision so many summers ago had assured him that no bullet would ever bring him down. Death would find him only when he was held from behind—

It suddenly shook him to his roots there in the darkness, cold sweat beading him now as if the temperature of that tiny lodge had dropped below freezing. It was as if he were feeling the approach of the death ghost itself, stinging him all the way to his marrow with a shrill warning.

They were clawing at him—the Lakota were. And the army too. He was now their prisoner, even though the soldiers had never defeated him in battle. Three Stars and White Hat too clawed at him. The agent ... and even some of his own people. The way they pestered him to go to Washington before this matter of getting an agency of their own could be settled.

But the whispers warn you that the wasicu and their army are planning to move Red Cloud's and Spotted Tail's people off their lands, all the way east to the Missouri River—no matter what you do.

"Am I so simple that I could have been deceived by Three Stars?" he demanded of his guardian spirit as his head sank between his shoulders. The steam and the heat were slowly robbing him of the last vestiges of his physical strength.

You are only one man against the many, Ta'sunke Witko. And you can only do so much—

"Stay with me," he begged in a harsh whisper, eyes heavy with fatigue.

I have always been with you. I will fly above you while

your pony carries you up the mountain tomorrow. Once you reach the rocks at the top, I will fold my wings and sit at your side while you fast and pray across the next four days.

"And then? What then? Will I finally know when I come down from the mountaintop?"

Yes. Be assured you will see farther from the top of Beaver Mountain than you have ever seen before. Ta'-sunke Witko will look down from those heights and see clearly the path where his feet are to walk.

"To join Red Cloud on this journey to the white man's country?"

When you have asked on high, the Great Mystery will tell us . . . once you have made it to the mountaintop, forsaking your body of food and water. Once you have suffered enough pain that you are finally ready to listen.

"Wakan," he whispered as his body sagged. "Is death coming soon? Tell me," he begged.

There was no answer. Not from the Great Mystery. Nor a sound from his *sicun*.

He looked up in surprise, consciously opening his eyes wider in the total darkness—breathless at the startling sight as his vision cleared: a milky cluster of countless stars brushed across the low dome of the sweat lodge just above his head. And as quickly as he began to shake with fear, the vision was gone and all was darkness again.

"W-was that the star road?" he asked respectfully.

It could have been nothing else. You've known it, seen it in the sky since your youth.

"Each star is a Lakota soul taken from this firmament," he responded, barely audible. "His earth life over so he can journey back to the Real World among the stars."

For a long time he sat hunched over, sensing the heat that rose to his face and chest gradually diminishing until the thunderous surge of blood pounding in his ears slowly subsided and he began to hear the muffled voices outside his dark world, hear the faint shuffle of feet passing this way and that. He had his directive: it was time to emerge from the belly of darkness.

Slowly dragging himself onto his knees, he rocked forward onto his hands and felt his head sag between his shoulders. Starting around the rockpit, Crazy Horse inched toward the place he remembered the opening to be. His right shoulder brushed the willow limbs until he reached the gap and lunged forward.

Of a sudden the cool night air slapped him in the face. His head and shoulders fell outside the lodge. He felt people murmuring over him, hands pulling him out and rolling him onto his knees, holding him up as a dipper of cool water was pressed against his lips.

Swallowing, he remembered the vision, and slowly looked up, the water dribbling off his chin.

It was night. Fully dark above him, where the stars glowed dimly in the blank void of the sky. He turned his head, steadied by hands, and searched. Turned some more, and still could not find it.

The star road he had glimpsed inside the sweat lodge was not to be found anywhere in the sky. He filled with utter despair... knowing that, at least for now, even the spirits of past warriors and heroes of the people had turned their faces from him.

This last difficult journey of his life he would have to make on his own.

CHAPTER NINE

Early July 1877

I THINK WHAT SHE NEEDS NOW IS SOME REST, SEAMUS," confided the army's assistant post surgeon.

Donegan studied the face of Dr. Valentine McGillycuddy with uncertain intensity. He trusted the physician, mostly because he was genuine, never having tried to be something that he wasn't. Why, McGillycuddy had regaled Donegan with many a story of how, in those days before he came west to serve with the frontier army, he had started his medical career riding with the police ambulance corps in Detroit, treating wounded sailors on the rough-and-tumble streets, dragging in the most serious to the hospital wards.

"Sh-should I be worried for her?" he asked the doctor.

"Just a little exhaustion, I'm going to assume," McGillycuddy said. Then turning the Irishman aside, and stepping away, he added in a low voice, "We don't know all that we should know about the gentler species, Seamus. Their makeup, how they're put together—we can study all of that. But . . . how women truly are different than we men," and he wagged his head, "I'm afraid we're going to be a long, long time in learning about these creatures we call our wives and mothers, sisters and friends."

Earlier that morning, Samantha had awakened with a thundering headache, and she had not gotten any better throughout the day. In fact, when she finally begged Seamus to fetch a fort physician, Sam was feeling so weak and puny she couldn't budge from her pallet of blankets and two buffalo robes Donegan had made for their bed in a wall tent he had borrowed from the quartermaster, having pitched it down by the oxbow of Soldier Creek. At least they were close to Camp Robinson's hospital.

By the time Seamus got back to the tent with McGillycuddy, little Colin was crying for the attention his mother couldn't give him and Samantha lay on her side, her legs drawn up, whimpering with the pain of the cramps knotting her lower belly.

She confided that it was far worse than the pain she had endured while delivering her first child. Seamus had seen how that declaration clouded the doctor's face with worry, McGillycuddy turning to asking the Irishman to leave the tent with the fussy child so that Samantha might be calmer, suggesting Donegan return to the hospital and ask Fanny to come back to the tent and help out. His examination of Sam was completed by the time Seamus and Mrs. McGillycuddy returned in a rustle of skirts, panting after she trotted all the way to keep up with the big-footed Irishman who dashed back with his son locked securely in his arms.

"The way she was curled up there, clutching at her belly," Donegan whispered as McGillycuddy led him a little farther from the tentflaps. From inside they could hear how Fanny cooed at the child, and talked quietly with Samantha. She was a calming influence on them both.

"It seems to have passed for the time being, whatever it was. She's had...There's nothing to indicate to me that there's something dangerously ill with her...insides, Seamus."

"You're sure?"

McGillycuddy stared up at the taller man, his gaze fixed on the older Irishman. "Listen, you thick-headed Mick. I want you to harken back to those days we shared together on the Bighorn-Yellowstone Expedition.* Back farther still to Crook's fight on the Rosebud.** I'm not about to side-talk to an old fighting comrade. And surely not about the woman he loves as dearly as you love your Samantha."

"It shows, does it?"

"Enough to know that you'd not do well if you lost her."

Breath caught in his chest before he could squeak out the words, "I-I'm not going to lose her?"

Trumpet on the Land, vol. 10, the Plainsmen Series.
**Reap the Whirlwind,* vol. 9, the Plainsmen Series.

"By heavens no!" McGillycuddy reassured him, reaching into a vest pocket. "Just give her one of these pills three times a day for the next two days, and make sure she can get to a latrine quick enough. I've got more up at the hospital when you run out of these."

"Latrine?"

"These pills will pass right through her with the power of a steam locomotive, Seamus. She'll feel weak as a kitten by the time these pills have worked their miracle on her."

He looked down at the pills in his big palm, then stuffed them down the front pocket of his canvas britches. "Starting when?"

"Soon as she is able to swallow one of them, with lots of water. Make sure she drinks plenty of it."

With a deep sigh, Seamus nodded, and laid his hand on McGillycuddy's shoulder. "When she's doing better in a week or so, we'll have a fine evening together. Have you and Fanny come down to our wee camp. I'll go hunting perhaps, make it a treat for us all—something better than army pork or skinny cow. Samantha will cook up something special for dinner."

The doctor held out his hand to shake and called softly to his wife through the tentflaps. Then McGillycuddy said, "Give her plenty of time to see how she responds before you let her take on any responsibilities—if you know what I mean. Then I'll count on us making an evening of it, old friend. How I'd like you and your Samantha to stay around the post for as long as you possibly can. Truth is, I think your wife is damned good medicine for my own!"

He grinned a little, for the first time that afternoon, shedding a little of the apprehension as Fanny came out of the tent to hand Colin over to his father's arms. "Those two have hit it off, ain't they?"

Laying his short morning coat over one forearm, McGillycuddy crooked the other for his wife to take hold of before they started away. "I'll check in with her tomorrow, mid-morning. See how you passed the night."

"Thanks, Doc," he said in a hush. "Gives me some peace

knowing an old friend of the wars is here for to take care of my special ones."

He watched the couple smile and turn away, moving off through the lengthening shadows, back toward the hospital.

"Seamus?"

He turned at the sound of her weak voice from the tent. "Yes, Sam." And started toward the flaps.

"I could use your strong hand to hold in mine," she said as he pushed through the flaps with the boy on his hip.

Her color was a little better. That ghostly pallor had had him scared. Seamus Donegan had seen that same pasty gray on enough dying men.

"Here it 'tis, my love," he whispered as he began to kneel beside her pallet, scooping her fingers inside his big paw. "You'll have mine to hold in yours . . . till all of eternity takes its last breath."

He had lain here for what seemed like an entire turn of the seasons. In reality it had been three long summer days and now into a third night, waiting. Waiting.

Crazy Horse had been gathered up by his friends from the front of that small sweat lodge, a blanket draped over his shoulders, then helped to the closest fire. There he was given small strips of boiled meat and a cup of cold creek water. Not a soul dared ask him about his time in the darkness. It was enough that he had emerged on his own, was hungry and thirsty. And, besides, he inquired if the five stones had been brought down.

"Just as you directed the young men to do before you went inside the sweat lodge," He Dog had replied.

"Where?"

"In the dance arbor." Big Road was the one who answered. "And we arranged them just as you directed."

Slowly, he started to stand, still weak, but strong enough to look hard at those on either side of him who sought to help, then backed away when they recognized his harsh glare. "I must see them, and the men who danced for me."

The five boulders were arranged in a crude V, its opening

facing to the east. A stone for each of the five dancers had been brought down from the side of Beaver Mountain by young, strong men. It was well after dark when Crazy Horse had emerged from the sweat lodge, so the fire's glow welcomed him to the site where a crowd had gathered around the five faithful warriors, each of whom was leaning against a rock, eating for the first time in days, taking small sips of creek water, his every need attended to by friends and family. It brought Crazy Horse deep satisfaction to see this closeness. The indomitable strength of the Lakota had always been, and would always remain, in family and friendships.

Crazy Horse came to sit among them, joining the five and their families at the fire that flickered off the rocks and the tired, haggard faces. These five who had offered their blood and their flesh in his honor.

"Tomorrow I go to the top of the mountain," he said quietly as the crowd fell to a hush around them.

"To pray?" Kicking Bear had asked.

Immediately Flying Hawk offered, "We will go with you."

"No," he answered sternly. "The five of you have done more than I could have asked of any man, much less all five of you. This . . . no, this I must do on my own. There are answers I alone must seek up there. To hear the whispers of the Great Mystery, my ears and my heart must be quiet."

That night he had fallen asleep on the ground and among the good friends and cousins at that fire, rolled up in the blanket beneath a dark and starless sky. And when he had awakened in the coldest part of the day, at the first graying of the horizon, Crazy Horse went in search of his pony. He had returned to the fire with the gelding and a handful of white sage. Throwing some more limbs on the embers until the flames crackled, he held the first of the sage over the fire until it started smoldering. In the graying light, he brushed the smoke over the pony's back, its strong flanks, its mighty legs, until the horse had been immersed in the sacred smoke. Then he smudged himself, completing the ritual by deeply inhaling some of the sweet, pungent incense.

That done, he had tossed the smoldering sage into the low flames, turned, and led the pony out of the five rocks where the others still slept after their exhausting trials of the last four days. Among the plum and chokecherry thickets at the base of Beaver Mountain he located the game trail he had always taken to start for the top. Crazy Horse had climbed atop the pony, and kicked it into motion.

Emerging from the trees at the top after a difficult climb, he had dismounted and turned the horse free, giving it a slap on the rump. If it should grow thirsty, it would find its way down the mountainside to the creek again, where it would once more be among friends and its own kind. He had watched it go, wondering if he would ever know that feeling, the serenity of being among his own kind.

Having brought no blanket, he lay among the rocks and what tough grasses grew on the heights of Beaver Mountain. This was a place his body knew well, a place he had come to time and again to find answers that came to him nowhere else. The cold wind knifed deep into his bones. And here he was among the rocks, stones that contained the living spirit of the earth—that spark of life they threw off when they were struck together. Yes, he would lie among the rocks for as long as it would take, for these stones were the very flesh of this earth, the same earth that each day gave his people their life.

The first night he had spent in agony, simply because he still was too much within his body, suffering the ground, every sharp pebble poking into his skin, and the cold that settled over him as the patternless stars came into view overhead.

Crazy Horse spent the entirety of that next day sitting in the sun, clutching his small pipe in his hands, praying that he would be granted an answer. Over and over he had run his thumbs over the two inverted Vs, one on each side of the red pipestone bowl, brushing his fingertips across the five raised circles he had carved on the bowl. One for each of the five small stones he had rolled together at the top of this mountain that first time he came here to pray many years ago. This was his secret place, symbolized by the two prominences of this mountain and those five rocks commemorated on his pipe.

But he did not smoke—would not until his prayer was answered. Often he thought of how White Buffalo Woman had been the one to bring the pipe and tobacco to the People, instructing them how the smoke was the rising of their prayers to *Wakan Tanka*, the Great Mystery. Crazy Horse would wait to smoke, wondering why the Creator was so long in giving him his answer.

It was here among the stones, the *inyan*, that he came to dream himself into the Real World, to somehow flee from the dark despair of the Shadow World in which all seemed madness. Time and again, Crazy Horse had lost himself in dream, striving to glimpse what really was on the other side. With dream, as in a vision, he knew he was in touch with sacred forces. The power he received in his dreams became as much a part of him as were his arms and legs. For a long time now he had believed that his dreams were even stronger than the day-to-day reality of life itself.

So it was that during the second night he began to drift in and out of dream, thinking of fights and battles and massacres. In the haze of growing thirst and hunger, he began to remember the events of so long ago in his life. As a youngster, Curly—his boyhood name—had witnessed firsthand the bravado of a young soldier chief who marched his soldiers and two cannon into a Lakota camp, demanding the thief who had stolen a white man's cow along the Holy Road. The soldier chief and all his men were cut down where they stood; then the Lakota took down their lodges and hurried away.*

The following year soldier chief Harney came looking to even the score. He found a camp of women and children and old ones on the Blue Water, and killed all who could not get away. Crazy Horse had not seen the massacre happen, but days later had come upon that camp. Never would he forget

---

*The Grattan massacre.

the sight of those bodies, young and old, or the smell of decomposing flesh. That wasn't the camp of those who had slaughtered the soldiers, but it had been a Lakota camp just the same. An important lesson was being driven home to young Curly.

Finally the Bad Face Oglala had a chance to strike back at the soldiers who had marched north beyond the Shifting Sands River. On a freezing winter day a hundred foolish soldiers followed Crazy Horse and his decoys across Lodge Trail Ridge where the trap was sprung.* Not one left standing. Not even the soldier dog slinking away through the snow until Crazy Horse shot it too. Nothing left alive.

Yet the soldiers always came back again. And when they did the army never caught the warriors. Instead, the attackers inevitably found the villages of women and children, the old and the sick, those least able to defend themselves against bullets and big-throated guns. So it was that the warriors who had surrendered with Crazy Horse had come in to Red Cloud's agency for no other reason than to save their families, to protect what they cherished most—the future of the Oglala people.

On this third night he had been slipping in and out of dream, episodes of pain knifing through him, but he no longer had the strength to move enough to end the aching in his joints, the cold in his bones. Crazy Horse remembered Lone Bear, his oldest friend from childhood. The first friend to die, cradled in Crazy Horse's arms after all the soldiers were cut down in the Battle of a Hundred in the Hand.

He began to cry on that mountaintop, not aware that he was except for the warmth of the tears gently seeping from the corners of his eyes. Remembering too his dear and trusted *kola,* his best friend Buffalo Hump, dead more than six winters. Cut down in a raid they made against the Susuni.**

There quickly followed more pain and loss. The sudden

---

*The Fetterman massacre.
**The Shoshone.

marriage of Black Buffalo Woman to his rival, No Water, losing the woman he had loved so strongly he was certain he could never love another, at least not near as much as he loved her. In a jealous fury Crazy Horse had ridden deep into the land of the Psatoka,* coming back with a pair of scalps, the only two he had taken in more than five winters. Such fighting anger was the only way he could find to fill the ache of his hollow insides.

Finally he suffered the death of his younger brother, Little Hawk—who had gone off with a war party to make a raid on the Susuni, but some *wasicu* miners had helped the enemy stand off the attack. The white men killed Little Hawk in that hot and bloody fight.

Crazy Horse had ridden deep, deep into enemy country—looking for any *wasicu* he ran across, searching for Susuni warriors. He would kill every man he came across, or he would die. Eventually he turned back east, making a wide circle through the sacred Pa Sapa,** because he had still not slaked his thirst for blood. Among the timbered shadows he had killed more than a dozen lone white men, miners searching for the yellow rocks that made the *wasicu* crazy. But none of these did he scalp. Instead, Crazy Horse left an arrow sticking in the earth beside the bodies, their faces turned to the ground.

Perhaps it had been during that time of mourning, so many tongues wagged, that he decided to give back that prized and sacred shirt the Big Bellies gave to only four to wear. Maybe with so long an absence, so long a ride, Crazy Horse had decided a man's life was too short not to reach for what he wanted most. So Crazy Horse talked Black Buffalo Woman into running away with him while her husband was off on a hunt. But No Water had come looking, taken back his wife, and nearly killed the woman-stealer.

It was while Crazy Horse healed from the bullet wound that his friend the *Wicasa Wakan,* or shaman, named Chips

---

*The Crow.
**The Black Hills, what the Lakota called the Heart of the Earth.

made a *wotawe*,* a powerful medicine bundle, for him. Inside a brain-tanned pouch Chips had placed the dried brains, heart, and claws of a spotted—or war—eagle.

"This will make you safe from any bullet," Chips had explained as he dropped the pouch cord around his younger friend's neck.

Gazing down at the powerful talisman, Crazy Horse had asked, "What about a knife? What if a man knows I am bullet-proof and tries to kill me with a knife?"

"No worry," Chips had vowed. "This eagle medicine I have made will protect you from a knife too. No blade can kill you . . . just so long as your arms are not held."

Still, the medicine bundle could never protect his heart from grief . . . a hollow, cold, devastating grief so deep and unremitting that nothing could touch it. All that he had ever held precious was torn from him. And then in the cold darkness of this vision-quest night, he shuddered as he remembered They Are Afraid of Her. His daughter born of Black Shawl. Upon his returning from a long hunting trip with He Dog and the Grabber, some friends had stopped him outside his lodge where he could hear Black Shawl sobbing. "What has happened?" he had demanded of them. Then he asked, "Where did you put her body?"

Back he rode, three days, deep into enemy country, with only the Grabber at his side. When he finally found the lonely scaffold, Crazy Horse climbed atop the bower to lie beside the still, cold body of the little child, remaining there in the wind and the rain for more than three days as he cried himself dry. Shriveling like a puckered, fallen fruit.

Some say he never was the same after losing that precious daughter. Others claimed his strangeness had started years earlier, with the loss of his *kola*, Hump. A few would admit he had become even more strange with the loss of Black Buffalo Woman to another suitor, followed so quickly

---

*Among the Lakota in general, and the Oglala in particular, Chips was renowned for imbuing objects and charms with special protective powers for those who wore them.

by the death of Little Hawk, and finally—when the man had little left to lose—his daughter was ripped from him. Cholera had claimed the girl in less than a day. How hollow was the hole inside him when he thought of cholera, and smallpox* too—together they were the double-fists that had become a curse the *wasicu* spread among the defenseless Lakota and other tribes of the prairie.

If the army could not kill off their women and children by attacking the villages at dawn, without warning, when the fighting men were away . . . then the white man would send his pestilence among the proud peoples of the plains.

From the moment he climbed down from that scaffold to rejoin the Grabber, leaving the tiny body of They Are Afraid of Her to the winds and the relentless turn of the seasons, Crazy Horse rarely spoke in public anymore. Instead, he relied upon others to speak for him in councils with other chiefs, especially in parleys with the white man. Over the years, He Dog and Little Big Man—both trusted friends— had come to recognize the many moods that Crazy Horse could express without much change in the expression on his face. Those two became his voice in the noisy crowds as he rarely spoke above a whisper. That alone was why so many found as remarkable his bellowing that put a stop to the sham battle the day of the first sun-gazing dance. Few of the Hunkpatila could remember hearing the sound of his voice, so few friends did he speak to in the last handful of winters.

Perhaps that was a mistake?

Perhaps.

"Ah! You are here, and ready to talk to me again," he said in a rasp to his spirit guardian. For the last three days and nights Crazy Horse hadn't opened his mouth to utter a sound. Not a drop of water had passed his tongue, spilled down his throat. His own voice sounded so foreign and hollow to him.

---

*The scourge of cholera came west with the emigrants traveling the Holy Road in 1849. And in 1850 a new epidemic of smallpox burned its way into Indian country.

If you always leave it to others to speak for you, then others might say something you never would have said for yourself.

He opened his eyes, sensing the breeze coming up on his cheek, in his hair—an awareness he hadn't had in more than a day. And he suddenly realized his body was in torment, lying as he was on the shards of rocks and stubby grass. In the sky above him was a sight he could not remember seeing for three nights. Stars. Hung in their familiar patterns all across the black dome of the heavens. And atop them all was the dim, milky canopy of tiny, dusty lights that tracked across the void in an arc, as if someone had scattered handful after handful of dry, glistening snowflakes.

He smiled, his dry, sunburned lips cracking painfully. It did not matter now. For some reason, he was beginning to re-feel things around him, re-sensing his world, for the first time since he had arrived at the top of Beaver Mountain. And it reminded him that he really hadn't been feeling all that much of anything for a long, long time. Not since deciding to surrender. Not really.

Sometimes hurt can remind us of who we are, Ta'sunke Witko. You were not meant for an ordinary life.

"What sort must I live?"

That is your decision from this point forward. No matter what you decide, make it your choice—not the choice of others. The white man, or the Oglala. Do not let them decide for you. There is greatness at hand—

"I never craved the adoration of others."

I said greatness, Ta'sunke Witko. The adoration you receive only comes because you have achieved greatness for your people. Let your voice be heard by the white man. Decide how best to get what you want, and speak your voice.

"Will you take this pain from my heart if I do?"

No. That pain from all the losses you have suffered has already scarred your heart. It will remain with you, no matter what joy you will come to feel.

"Black Shawl—will she ever understand about the trader's daughter?"

If that is who you want, you will help Black Shawl to understand why you need a second wife.

"And taking that long journey east with Red Cloud?"

Will they give you your own agency if you do?

"White Hat and Three Stars promise me that first I must go east. Not till I return—"

Do you trust them?

"I have to trust someone," he answered in resignation.

Do you think you will get your agency if you refuse to make the journey?

He clenched his eyes in realization. "No."

Two can play at the game Red Cloud has been playing with the white man. It is a game even your uncle, Spotted Tail, has been part of. You can learn to get what you want from the wasicu too. If all it takes for you to get what you want is to make that trip east, then you will get an agency for your people, and that buffalo hunt in the Powder River country too.

"But . . . I must do what is right for the People."

There are more ways to be a good leader than by refusing everything. What do you truly want, Ta'sunke Witko? Ask yourself what that is . . . and then go after what it is that you want most.

What he wanted was to laugh, to cry, to shout—but it would be too painful, and close to impossible as weak as he was. "Wh-what I want most is to return to my old country, live out my last days in peace, riding the back of a good horse—with proud friends and happy people in my camp. The way I remember—"

It hasn't been like that for a long time. If those old times are what you want . . . you won't have them again until I am freed from your body, until I can finally spread my wings and fly high over the land where you once rode your horse.

"But if you are freed . . . then that means—"

Yes, Ta'sunke Witko. I won't be freed until you have taken your last breath. Only then will your spirit be free once more.

For a long time he lay there, sensing the pressure of every stone against his back, buttocks, and legs, against the hard bone of his skull. Every now and then he sensed the breeze coming up, brushing across his cheeks, and realized he had been crying.

"I am ready to face what will come now," he said, after what seemed like hours had passed and the brilliant stars overhead had wheeled all the way from one horizon to the other.

Not till the sun is given birth for its new day. By then you will truly be strong enough to walk this last road that will ever be laid out before you.

CHAPTER TEN

Early July 1877

SEAMUS TOOK A LONG, LINGERING LOOK AT THE INDIAN, feeling himself being appraised. Then the dark eyes shifted to the doctor, Fanny McGillycuddy, then finally landed on the young woman who had accompanied the three of them on their ride out to the Crazy Horse camp.

"Tell him I am glad to see him," Valentine McGillycuddy instructed the half-breed trader's daughter, Helen, better known as Nellie, Laravie. "Explain that I've come to see how Black Shawl is healing."

The moment the young interpreter began to speak in Sioux to Crazy Horse, she was interrupted by the approach of four women. One of them raised her arm and waved in greeting. The other three were carrying deadfall limbs they had been collecting from the nearby hillside. Donegan swung out of the saddle a moment before McGillycuddy handed him his reins and started toward the quartet of women.

"Black Shawl!" cried the doctor in a cheerful yet somewhat concerned tone.

Helen Laravie likewise shoved her reins into the Irishman's big paw and took off at a sprint to catch up to the physician.

Looking down at his hands filled with reins, then back at the scene, Seamus turned with a shrug, looking for the war chief—and found him already starting toward his wife. Black Shawl stopped beside her lodge while her three companions continued on around to the far side, where they dropped their load of branches, dusted their hands and dresses, then inched back over to stand near the one white visitor who hadn't as yet dismounted.

"Seamus, you'll stay close?"

That soft plea from Fanny McGillycuddy brought Donegan up short. He turned and saw the concern on her face, there beneath the gauzy black veil of her pale green hat she had pinned atop her tightly wound curls. The three Sioux women dared to take another step closer, whispering to one another as a handful more Sioux bystanders closed in on the sole white woman among the visitors.

Behind Donegan, McGillycuddy was asking, "Ask her why she's on her feet, working so hard to gather wood."

"She feels better," Helen replied. "Your medicine helps her sleep."

"Not so tired anymore?" he asked Black Shawl.

Donegan watched how the Sioux women whispered to one another with amused interest. Every few moments one of them would stretch out an arm and point at Fanny's one boot, just barely sticking out from the bottom of her long dress as she sat perched atop her side-saddle.

"No, she gets sleep from the medicine you give her," Laravie explained. "Can you give her more until her cough is no more?"

"Of course," McGillycuddy answered. "I brought some right here. Tell her that. But first, I want to listen to her chest again—like I've done every visit—and have her cough for me too."

One of the more daring of the curious spectators took a step toward Fanny's horse, dropped to one knee, as if attempting to peer up at the animal's belly, at the sole of the white woman's lone visible boot. The squaw wagged her head and stood, scooting back among the growing crowd. There had to be more than three dozen women of all ages now, and at least half that many children huddled in among their knees or against their hips, everyone chattering quietly, but in a growing clamor.

"Over here," McGillycuddy instructed. "By her teepee. The two of us can sit right here in the sun while I examine her."

Glancing over his shoulder, Donegan watched how the physician was getting Black Shawl settled on the ground at the foot of her lodge, a few feet from the open doorway, while Crazy Horse and the young translator exchanged long glances. Helen stepped up beside McGillycuddy when the doctor dropped to his knees and worked at the clasp on his scuffed brown valise he positioned beside Black Shawl's bare legs.

"Seamus!"

The instant Fanny squealed in horror, Donegan wheeled back around to find one of the women lifting Fanny's dress and petticoats several inches. He stood there in horror, not knowing what to do.

"Should I kick at her?" she asked in desperation.

"Best not," he whispered harshly, inching closer to the bold Sioux woman, hoping to drive her away with intimidation. "I ... think she's just curious."

With one finger, the middle-aged woman pushed against the one boot they all could see hanging down the side of the white woman's horse. Reassured that it was indeed filled with a foot, she raised the thick layers of flowing cloth beyond the top of the boot and found Fanny's ankle enclosed in a tight cotton stocking. The moment the wrinkled woman began to daringly raise the dress and petticoats even farther, about to expose Fanny's calf, Seamus moved forward, wagging his head.

"No," he said firmly, approaching the woman.

There was no misinterpreting that word. She dropped the white woman's clothing and leaped back as all the dark eyes fixed on the tall Irishman. He stopped in his tracks and glanced at Mrs. McGillycuddy.

"I'll wager you're safe for a while, Fanny."

"S-safe?" she stammered, her voice almost a squeak of fear. "What w-was she d-doing?"

He started to smile just to think of the childlikeness of it; then when he gazed at her frightened face again, his smile immediately disappeared. "Don't you see, Fanny—to them you've just got one leg."

"One leg?" she echoed.

"There," and he pointed to the left side of her horse where she had both legs propped over their side-saddle supports.

Both legs were concealed with yards and yards of green satin, puffed up by layers of petticoats Fanny had put on for this ride out of Camp Robinson to the Crazy Horse village. With her right leg positioned higher, its boot and all completely hidden beneath the layers of cloth, it was no wonder the Sioux women believed the white woman had but one leg! And with all that curiosity from all those women and children, it was certain one of them would work up the nerve to take a daring peek for herself—if only to report to the others what did or did not lie beneath a white woman's dress.

"They can't figure out you're on a side-saddle, Fanny," he explained, containing the chuckle he felt about to overpower him. "All they see is your one boot. Far as they're concerned, you're a one-legged white gal—er, white woman."

She peered down, quickly examining the situation, then raised her eyes to face him. "If you would be so kind as to turn your head and avert your gaze for a moment, Seamus."

"What for?"

"I am going to raise my dress and petticoats just enough to show them I have two legs."

He could finally smile, because Fanny was smiling too. "Good for you!"

After he had turned, he listened to the shuffle of moccasins on the ground, the murmurs growing behind him, along with a faint rustling of the layers of starched cloth. "I'm sure as hell glad Samantha doesn't own anywhere near as many of those god-awful petticoats!"

"Out here in this country," Fanny protested firmly, "I don't have that much of a chance to get dressed up and go anywhere, Seamus Donegan. So I'll have you know, I figure your Samantha would love to dress up with just as many petticoats as I am wearing anytime she had the opportunity to fluff and prance."

"Fluff and prance, eh?" he repeated, watching how the doctor was carefully listening to Black Shawl's breathing, his ear pressed against her chest. "I'll bet you're right. She does make quite the stir when she is all trimmed out."

"You can turn around now," she announced finally.

He turned obediently.

"If you would help me down," Fanny requested, "I'd like to show these women that I can indeed stand on the two legs I have hidden under my riding suit."

Dragging the three horses over behind him, he dropped their reins and immediately held up his hands. Leaning into them she eased herself to the ground.

"There," she said, pushing herself away so that she stood alone, then delicately lifted the hem of her gown so that she could expose the toes of both boots for all to see. "When was the last time for Samantha?"

"I beg your pardon, Fanny. The last time for what?"

She glanced at him but a moment, then looked back over the women and children crowding in to have themselves a look at this astounding revelation. "The last time Samantha got the opportunity to fluff and prance?"

He cleared his throat, giving himself a moment more to reflect. "I suppose it were ... when we had Colin baptized. Back at Fort Laramie it was."

"When was that?"

"Er—a ... back, the last part of January," he answered, finally sure.

"And the time before that?"

Seamus swallowed, his hands tightening uneasily on the reins of those three horses. "Had to been our wedding day, Fanny."

"A fine husband you are," she scolded him with a grin. "Give a gal a chance to shine on her wedding day, but not again until the day she christens her firstborn? Shame on you, Seamus Donegan! You're just like every other man—"

"Fanny!" McGillycuddy called. "Could you come over please?"

As she stepped past the tall Irishman, Fanny said, "You just think about what I've said, Seamus."

He followed her over to the small group standing around the physician and Black Shawl, joining Fanny, Crazy Horse, and Helen Laravie. McGillycuddy held out his hand and helped the Sioux woman get to her feet.

"Fanny," he said very expressively, glancing at the translator, "this is the wife of Crazy Horse. Her name in English is Black Shawl." Then he had Helen explain his wife's name to Black Shawl.

"Fon-nee," Black Shawl repeated unsurely.

"And this—" the doctor began as he clutched his wife's shoulders, turning her slightly so she would face the Sioux war chief. "I am proud to introduce my new friend, Crazy Horse."

With a bow of her head and a hint at a curtsey, Mrs. McGillycuddy said, "My husband has told me so much about you, Crazy Horse." Immediately she turned to the half-breed woman, expecting Helen to translate.

Seamus watched the war chief do nothing in particular to acknowledge the white woman. He did not nod, nor offer his hand. Instead, he looked for a moment into Fanny's face, turned and glanced at Helen again, then finally looked over his shoulder, gazing directly at the Irishman.

The Sioux said something so quiet that his words were all but under his breath.

Helen Laravie looked at Donegan, and translated, "He has seen you before."

"Yes," Seamus said, returning the war chief's intent stare. "I saw him stop the shooting at the sundance a couple weeks back. And before that, I remembered seeing him the day I brought my family up from Fort Laramie, back in June."

While he was explaining, the young woman had begun to translate in her halting Lakota. As he watched, Crazy Horse wagged his head and spoke softly to the interpreter.

"He says no," Helen said. "He saw you before. In a fight . . . big battle. Army and Lakota—the Sioux against the army and the Shoshone."

Now it was Donegan's turn to wonder at that recollection. "I fought his warriors on the Tongue River. I was with Miles—the one they* call the Bear Coat—when our scouts captured a few Cheyenne women."

---

*The people of the northern plains.

After she had translated and the chief answered, Helen said, "No. Was not that fight. Summer. On Red Flower Creek."

"You mean the Rosebud?" McGillycuddy asked.

"The same," she replied, turning again to gaze up at the tall Irishman. "Crazy Horse says you were a brave man, one of the bravest among many very brave men that day. Because of that, he has remembered your face, your eyes, for a year now."

Swallowing, he recalled the noise and terror of Royall's retreat, then turned to the physician. "You and me was there, Doc. The Rosebud. Crook's fight. Crazy Horse come near to overrunning us three times."

McGillycuddy shook his head. "I only saw it from afar, Seamus—because I wasn't with Royall's men. Only heard all the stories later, how you were nearly swallowed alive."

Crazy Horse whispered to Helen, then held out his left hand.

"He wants to shake with you, his hand nearest the heart—because the right hand does all manner of bad things," she explained.

Donegan took it, about ready to speak, when Crazy Horse continued.

Helen translated, "He remembers you staying behind, at the rear of all those frightened soldiers. Each time his warriors rushed in close on their ponies, you and a few other soldiers, some of the Shoshone too, all of you turned your faces into the Lakota charge."

"Tell him yes . . . I remember."

"You were not a soldier chief?"

Donegan wagged his head, a lump in his throat, remembering the fallen. "No, not even a soldier."

After Crazy Horse quietly spoke a little more, the half-breed woman went on, "He remembers when a soldier chief was knocked off his horse at the top of the flat hill. Crazy Horse saw you stand over that soldier's dead body and fight like a mountain panther to keep his warriors from rushing in and striking coup on that fallen soldier chief. You, and one other man—a warrior—stood there. A Shoshone perhaps?"

"Yes," Seamus answered as Crazy Horse finally released his left hand.

"The chief says you are brave man to protect the body of a fallen friend who has been killed," Helen translated. "Crazy Horse had a good friend fall in battle with the Shoshone many summers ago. When he thinks about it... that memory makes him sad... because he wishes he had been able to stand over the body of his friend and fight off the enemies. But... Crazy Horse says he could never get that close to save his friend's body."

Donegan cleared his throat, finding it suddenly clogged with this talk of courage, friendship, and faithfulness, talk of fidelity in battle—standing before the mightiest enemy on the northern plains. "Tell him that the soldier chief who fell from the horse, he was not my friend."

The chief's eyes bore into the white man even more intently as Helen Laravie explained that to him.

"Captain Guy Henry?" McGillycuddy asked.

"Yes," Seamus whispered, not taking his eyes off Crazy Horse's face. "And be sure to tell him that the soldier chief was not dead."

" 'He wasn't killed?' " she echoed Crazy Horse's question.

"No, he lived."

Here McGillycuddy spoke up again, pantomiming the wound. "Like you, Crazy Horse. Shot through the face. A terrible wound, as yours must have been. But he survived no matter how hard we worked to kill him afterward."

With the faint hint of a smile for the Irishman, Crazy Horse spoke softly, then took a step backward as Helen began to translate.

"He says he honors you even more than he thought at first," she said. "Because the soldier chief was not your friend, and because you were saving his life... not just protecting his body from the enemy. That is the bravest act of a warrior: to offer his own life to protect the life of another, even when it is not his *kola,* his best friend. As he wanted to protect the body of Hump, his *kola.*"

A tight fist seized Donegan's chest. "There was lots of brave men in that fight," he said quietly. "On both sides, Crazy Horse. I am honored by your words, but I ain't no special leader. Ain't no soldier chief. Tell him I gave that up many a year ago in a war between the white men. I...I'm just a fighting man. A man who's glad he don't have to fight no more."

Crazy Horse studied the Irishman's eyes a moment more, then gripped Black Shawl's arm before he spoke again and Helen translated.

"The chief says he is glad too. He wants you to know he was just a fighting man, protecting his Lakota people. The women and the children, he fought for them. Just a fighting man who is glad like you—glad he won't have to fight no more."

CHAPTER ELEVEN

Mid-July 1877

WILL YOU SHOW ME THE KNIFE THE BIG SOLDIER CHIEF GAVE
you when you became a little chief among the soldier's
scouts?" Billy Garnett asked Crazy Horse, while Black
Shawl passed out fluffy hunks of the fry bread she had
cooked in a spitting kettle set over the fire outside the lodge.

The hot dough burned his fingers. After dropping the
bread on that stiff piece of rawhide parfleche they were using as plates, the half-breed interpreter placed his finger and
thumb inside his mouth and sucked on them, not only to
ease the pain but also to lick them clean of the savory grease
Black Shawl used to fry her bread.

"Say that American word again for me," Crazy Horse requested.

"Sergeant," Billy said in American.

Reaching behind him, Crazy Horse brought out the
leather sheath, inside it a knife with a bone handle he handed
to the young half-blood. "I like the sound of that *wasicu*
word. *Sar-jent.*"

Garnett took the sheath and pulled out the knife to inspect
this gift from Lieutenant Colonel Luther Prentice Bradley
on the occasion of the swearing in of the Northern headmen
as scouts who would serve under Lieutenant William P.
Clark. Handing the knife back to Crazy Horse, he resumed
using his mother's Lakota language: "It is the rank of a little
chief among the soldiers. Not so high a chief as the White
Hat—"

Interrupting, the Oglala leader snorted, "I would not dare
to think that I would be above White Hat!"

The other men at the fire laughed along with him.

"But neither are you an ordinary warrior like the rest of
the soldiers either," Garnett explained. He watched Crazy
Horse's eyes drop back to the low fire glowing in the pit at

the center of the lodge. And asked his question again: "It is a good thing to you—this making the vow to serve as a scout?"

"Yes," the war chief answered, looking at his new knife with admiration. "I wear this gift all the time now. It is a fine weapon." Crazy Horse laid the sheath aside and went back to tearing at his fry bread, his fingers shiny with grease. "Look here at Little Big Man, this good friend beside me. See how he wears his soldier coat to my dinner."

"This is a special occasion," Little Big Man protested proudly, his mouth still full of the stringy beef Black Shawl had prepared for their guests at this dinner. "I am *akicita!** I always wear my very best for a special occasion!"

In recent days, Crazy Horse had been officially sworn as a noncommissioned officer in the U.S. Indian Scouts. Although a quiet ceremony by army standards, it had been a momentous occasion, during which he, along with some fourteen other Northern headmen who had been enlisted as privates, promised to serve the White Hat faithfully. With his strong tradition as one of the most loyal of Crazy Horse's *akicita* leaders, Little Big Man had eagerly stepped forward to serve as a soldier scout.

Billy turned back to his host. "What about your soldier coat?" he asked, his eyes glancing about the lodge to look for it hanging from the dew-liner rope. "Where is it?"

Crazy Horse shrugged. "Oh, it is a nice color. Yes. And the buttons are very shiny too. Like an oiled gun they shine brightly. But... the cloth is too heavy for me to wear."

Big Road fingered the wool of Little Big Man's shirt and asked, "What did you do with your shirt, Crazy Horse?"

"I gave it to Black Shawl for safekeeping," he answered and continued to tear at his bread. "If she needs it to keep herself warm while she is healing from the coughing sickness, she can wear it. But... I have never liked such things."

"Even when the women and boys took all the soldier

---

*The Lakota camp police, in charge of maintaining order in camp or on the hunt.

shirts and leggings off the white bodies at the Greasy Grass!" Little Big Man roared, slapping a knee, but quickly fell silent as every eye in the lodge turned to Billy Garnett.

"I know all about that fight," Billy confided quietly, with only the slightest edge of anxiety, sensing how the others in the lodge suddenly went quiet and wooden. "The soldiers came after you. They charged your camp. Lakota and Shahiyela warriors had no choice but to fight those soldiers. There should never be any shame for killing all the soldiers you could kill that day. It was a great fight."

"Little Big Man is right!" Big Road enthused with a happy sigh that lit up his old and wrinkled face. "There were lots of soldier clothes for the women to strip off the pale, fish-belly bodies when the battle was over!"

Finally Little Hawk spoke up across the fire, looking directly at Garnett when he declared, "Our friend, Crazy Horse, has never been one to wear fancy clothing or an elaborate bonnet either."

"Only that full skin of the red-tailed hawk," Good Weasel declared.

Jumping Shield said, "It was a good fight."

"We were all proud to follow Crazy Horse into battle that day!" He Dog added.

The other headmen nodded knowingly, and they all went back to chewing at the stringy beef, tearing at their fry bread, and drinking their soldier coffee.

With an unselfconscious ease that surprised Garnett, Crazy Horse eventually broke that uneasy silence, looking directly at the half-breed translator. "You must start teaching me to eat in the white man's way."

Billy noticed how Crazy Horse held up three of his fingers on one hand and made a poking motion toward the slab of beef on his rawhide platter. "They call it a *fork*," and Garnett pronounced the last word in English.

"Fork," Crazy Horse repeated the sound without too much trouble and smiled like someone proud of himself for it. "Yes. I will need to know how to use this fork before I go east to visit."

Garnett said, "After you protested that you wouldn't go for so long, White Hat was very happy when you finally told him you would journey with Red Cloud and the others, to see the *wasicu* grandfather."

When Crazy Horse was silent for a long time, Looking Horse observed, "Red Cloud and Spotted Tail want our chief to go with them when they make their protests to this *wasicu* grandfather. So that the strong word of Crazy Horse will be listened to, and the government will not make the agencies move to the Muddy Water River."*

But Crazy Horse did not elect to take up this subject of tribal politics. Instead he set his bread down and stared at Garnett. "I have another question of you."

"About eating?"

"No," the war chief replied. "How does a man...How will I...relieve myself if I am in the wooden house that rolls on the iron road?"

"In the wooden house, the soldiers will show you a small room where you can go to be by yourself," Billy explained with an impish grin, thinking how foreign a concept this must be to a people who did not even understand the white man's use of privies and latrines. "There you will be in private, where you can remove your breechclout, and will sit down to relieve yourself."

Crazy Horse thought about that, an uncertain shock crossing his face. "What I leave behind...it stays in that small room?"

"N-no!" Billy said with a chuckle. "It drops through a hole below you, and falls on the ground of the iron road."

"Ah, this is good," the chief responded with a wry grin. "I imagined how that small room would smell even worse than those little lodges the white man uses to relieve himself, instead of going out to the bushes."

The Lakota headmen all nodded, knowingly, slyly glancing at one another as they grinned with that joke on the backward *wasicus*.

---

*Mnisose, the white man's Missouri River.

After taking a few more bites, Garnett broke the silence. "Is it true what I am told: that you never danced at a sun-gazing ceremony?"

Little Big Man leaped in, "Crazy Horse has never taken part in any dance our Northern People have ever held before coming here to the agency."

Looking Horse nodded. "He's never danced."

"I leave the sun-gazing to others," Crazy Horse explained, holding up his tin for Black Shawl to re-fill with hot coffee the moment she entered the lodge with a steaming, blackened pot. "And I am not an energetic young man anymore."

"Especially when the only reason we are dancing is to put on a show for the white people," Little Hawk grumbled.

"For the longest time, all the *wasicus* had to do was to talk about the wild Indians of the north—in those summers you were fighting for the Powder River country," Garnett explained. "Now these whites finally have a chance to see those same untamed Indians: dancing, drumming, singing— acting every bit as wild as the frightening nightmares they had of you!"

They all began to roar with hearty laughter; then Crazy Horse commented, "They do like coming out to our camp to watch the young men and women dance, don't they?"

"And they think Indians always wear blankets!" He Dog sputtered around a piece of meat in his mouth. "So they want us to wear our blankets . . . even when it is now the mid-summer moon!"

Billy leaned forward slightly, in that manner of a man about to confide a secret confidence, and said to the Hunkpatila headmen, "I have overhead many of these white men and women talking about how excited they become just to watch the dancing and the drumming, knowing they are looking at people who, only a few moons ago, were making war on their army and killing their soldiers. It makes their hearts beat so much faster to think they are watching your warrior bands do what you have always done in freedom—"

That made Billy cut himself off abruptly, seeing how that

last word affected the rest of them. A sad and bitter silence fell over this lodge with its canvas cover rolled up so the summer breezes could drift through as they sat around the empty firepit and took their supper in the age-old manner of Lakota men. Garnett's belly did a flop, not knowing if he should apologize or wait for someone to strike up the conversation anew. He realized he was the youngest man there, and only half-Oglala at that. The rest were full-blood, men who had lived their entire lives on the open prairie.

In that strained, painful silence, he began, "I shouldn't have said something so thoughtless—"

"It is no matter," Crazy Horse interrupted him with barely a whisper, and a slight gesture of his hand. "We know where freedom is . . . and it lies in the north."

"Not here, no," Billy said, thankful and wagging his head, staring at the empty firepit, his heart made heavy to know he had brought up something so painful.

"Here we eat the white man's spotted buffalo," He Dog grumbled, gazing down at his rawhide platter.

"But his flour is good," Crazy Horse replied, surprising many of them with the lightness in his voice. He looked around the firepit at the faces. "It does no man's heart any good to dwell on what was. On what we once had. This young half-blood's heart weighs heavy now because he feels he ruined the dinner I invited you all to attend while I asked him about important matters in the *wasicu* world."

"But I am afraid I have ruined your dinner for you," Garnett apologized.

"No," the Horse said. "I have made up my mind no man can make my life miserable but me and me alone. No, young man," he said, putting out his arm to lay a hand on Garnett's shoulder, "we can remember the freedom we once had and become bitter. Or we can remember that freedom and choose not to be angry. Freedom was only what we once had, like something that we lost back upon our way to this place . . . something we now cannot find. I do myself and my people no good if I mourn its loss now."

How undeniably sad that made Billy feel, wondering why

his Oglala blood did not boil when he thought about what had been taken from these people, when he considered how the white man had surrounded and corralled his mother's people, driving these free-roaming bands onto this tiny reservation by killing off enough of the buffalo and causing the children to starve. It stabbed him deep inside to sense how his white blood mingled with his Lakota spirit. He had grown up in both worlds, learning both languages, absorbing all that he could of both cultures—worlds apart that they were.

"Don't take any of these old men so seriously," Little Big Man said with a hint of a grin. "It is only that in our bones we have such a distrust for interpreters."

"It's dangerous, not knowing what the translator is saying about our words to the *wasicu* and his soldiers," Big Road agreed.

"What do you think about Grabber?" He Dog asked the young half-blood.

He saw how all their eyes were trained on him as he considered his feelings about Frank Grouard. "He has never given me a reason to distrust him."

"Just wait," He Dog snorted, tearing off a chunk of fry bread between his teeth.

"The soldier chief, Three Stars, believes in him," Billy asserted, scratching for some reason for him to support Crook's favorite interpreter.

"Maybe that is so," Crazy Horse said. "As for me, we trusted him once . . . but will never trust him again. Not as far as I could spit."

"If the Grabber comes along as a translator, will that change your mind about going to Washington with Red Cloud?" Garnett asked.

"No. I will still go, because Three Stars and White Hat say I have to do that to get my own agency," Crazy Horse declared. Then he looked around the firepit at the others. "Those of you here tonight realize that there are fewer and fewer of those I can trust among our own Oglala people."

"The talk is strong behind your back," Little Hawk declared.

"It makes me laugh," Big Road said, "how every time the white men come to visit the agency, they don't come to see Red Cloud and the old chiefs anymore."

"No!" snorted Little Big Man. "They come to see Crazy Horse!"

He Dog nodded, saying, "Red Cloud has always been a jealous sort—given to rumors and intrigue, this old man. But what I fear most is that Red Cloud and those who whisper in his ears will one day believe their own poisonous words."

"Wh-what words are those?" Billy asked.

The dark-skinned Shirt Wearer turned to Garnett and explained, "This preposterous story that claims the white man and his soldiers will make Crazy Horse the head chief over all the Oglala, even head chief over Spotted Tail's Sicangu as well!"

Billy admitted, "I never heard any whispers of this—"

"Such talk isn't true!" Crazy Horse protested. "More than once I've told the White Hat and the soldier chief I don't want to be chief over anyone! Not over my uncle's people. Not even to be a chief over Red Cloud's people.... I am tired and do not want to carry that responsibility at all. No matter what I say to the soldiers, this bad talk has been given birth, and taken on a life of its own, so not even the truth will ever kill it now."

Little Big Man said, "A man needs only look at Crazy Horse, to come to this village to see us—then he will understand that Crazy Horse is not wanting to be chief over Red Cloud and his people."

"This is Red Cloud's agency," agreed Little Hawk. "Let him be chief here."

"We want our own agency in the North Country," Crazy Horse said quietly. "Let Red Cloud have to deal with White Hat and the *wasicu* agent here."

After a long silence in the lodge, Garnett gazed at Crazy Horse. "Before you go east with Red Cloud, I want to teach you everything you want to know about the white man's ways, to prepare you for your visit to the *wasicus'* grandfather."

"Perhaps in the time left before I go on this journey, you can teach me some more about that land far to the east, where you say the white man is like the blades of grass."

Billy wagged his head, a shiver of regret shooting through him. "I don't know much about that land to the east. I have never been there."

"But you can teach me about the white man, yes?"

"I will teach you everything I know before you leave."

Sipping at his coffee, Crazy Horse said, "I am thinking this will be a quiet summer, here on Red Cloud's tiny island in the middle of a sea of white men. Later we will leave for our hunt White Hat has promised us."

"Has the White Hat told you when you are going to hunt in the Powder River country?" Garnett asked.

"Soon," Crazy Horse responded. "Soon...is all White Hat will say and right away he wants to speak of the trip east, or changes to talk of another subject."

"So what do you want to do for the rest of this summer until the Northern People go on your buffalo hunt?" Billy asked.

"Me?" the war chief asked. "In these long days of summer, I don't want to do anything but to eat, sleep too, and couple with Black Shawl—once she has healed and is stronger from her coughing sickness."

"So what about our new agency?" He Dog reminded.

"Yes," Crazy Horse said. "That's why, more than anything, I want all my people to go on the buffalo hunt the white man has promised us. Men and women, children too. Not only so we can make meat for the coming winter...but so I can show Three Stars and his soldier chiefs the country where they have promised to put my agency."

CHAPTER TWELVE

Wicokannanji
THE MIDDLE MOON, 1877

"NOW THAT CRAZY HORSE HAS AGREED TO GO EAST WITH
you," No Water grumbled to Red Cloud, "White Hat and
the new agent—all those stupid *wasicus*—can't seem to do
enough for him!"

Red Cloud brooded. That was indeed a thorny problem.

More and more every day he had taken to worrying about Crazy Horse, his popularity with Red Cloud's Oglala people, his growing influence on the white men who at one time had feared and distrusted the Northern war chief.

Brushing some stray hairs out of the corner of his mouth, Woman's Dress* licked his lips and hissed, "No one should have ever trusted Crazy Horse."

Red Cloud turned his head and peered at this man who would be a woman, a friend who had been tapped with a very special medicine. As a child he had been called Pretty One, because of the fine features of his face. In their youth, Pretty One had played with Crazy Horse and his younger brother, Little Hawk. Soon enough the boy had taken a different path from the rest: instead of playing the rough-and-tumble games of youth, he stayed behind in camp with the girls, concentrating on learning what it was that he must know to become most like a woman. And soon he was wearing the ear- and fingerrings, the bright vermilion paint, even the decorative dresses of an Oglala woman. At one point there was an argument among hotheaded youngsters, strong words were spoken, and Crazy Horse ended up smashing a clenched fist into Pretty One's nose. Much later in life Red Cloud's Bad Faces and the Hunkpatila parted ways—when Red Cloud realized the great might of the white man and

---

*He was one of the more well-known of the Lakota *winkte* (literally meaning "a man who wants to be a woman"), those men who dressed like a woman and preferred a woman's role, beading and cooking, to making war or stealing horses. In their youth, they usually played girls' games. In adulthood, it was not unusual for a *winkte* to become a warrior's consort, although there is some ambivalence in Lakota culture concerning the propriety of a man having sex with a *winkte*. Theirs was a powerful medicine, so strong that they were often asked to give secret nicknames to newborn children, the sort of ribald and often obscene names that were rarely uttered in public. Some of those more earthy names were censored, or changed, when the Northern People were enrolled following their surrender at Red Cloud Agency.

brought his band to the agency, while the Crazy Horse people continued to fight for the North Country. Fiercely loyal to Red Cloud, Woman's Dress came to this place on the White River with his chief.

"You only say that because he broke your nose as a child," Red Cloud said, goading his friend into an unpleasant remembrance. "It's natural that you've never liked him."

Red Dog, never far from Red Cloud's shadow, asked the chief, "Did you?"

"Did I what?" Red Cloud asked and brought the dipper of cool water to his lips.

"Ever like Crazy Horse?"

He drank, long and deep, refreshed on this hot summer afternoon. "Yes. I liked him, very much." Wistfully he gazed into the distance, and finally said, "Things might have been different."

"How?" No Water demanded, clearly upset.

Red Cloud looked at this man who had refused to let his woman go with Crazy Horse, even when she had run away from No Water, openly showing all the Oglala that she no longer wished to be No Water's wife—fleeing with her husband's worst enemy. Because No Water could not give her up, a war was almost started. A war that Crazy Horse made sure did not explode in their faces.

"He could have used his powers to help me," Red Cloud admitted. "To help all the Oglala, instead of surrounding himself with the obstinate ones."

"The stubborn men like himself," No Water spat with a sneer.

That had been a most precarious time for the Oglala, when No Water went after his wife and nearly splintered the tribe for all time with his selfish act. But after he had healed, Crazy Horse hadn't sought revenge for his terrible wounding. Instead, he went off by himself, eventually gathering around him more and more of those who were of like mind, rather than openly, publicly breaking with Red Cloud. For that Red Cloud knew he would always be grateful. But for that same act of kindness Red Cloud would always be resentful too. By not forcing a show of power at that moment in their people's history, Crazy Horse had forever denied Red Cloud the supreme seat of Oglala power. In his saving the tribe for Red Cloud, Crazy Horse had assured that he would one day rise to a prominence that would threaten his former chief and mentor.

For his not destroying the Oglala with a vendetta Red Cloud would always be grateful and love Crazy Horse. For what he came to do by retreating into the Powder River country and surrounding himself with like-minded lovers of freedom who refused to believe in the might of the white man...Red Cloud would always begrudge and hate Crazy Horse.

And for now, that hate was heating to a boil.

He himself had been far to the east, talking with the white man's grandfather and all his little uncles too, seeing with his own eyes the might and far-reaching ingenuity of the *wasicus*. For the longest time now, Red Cloud had believed that all Crazy Horse had to do was go east and he would be made a believer too. Such was a conviction that had allowed Red Cloud to be used by White Hat simply to bring in Crazy Horse. Last year, in Canapekasna Wi, the Moon When Leaves Turn Brown, Three Stars had become terrified that Red Cloud's Oglala would escape from their reservation and break for the north to join the wild Northern People. The soldier chief had ordered his soldiers to surround Red Cloud's camps, to strip the Oglala of all their horses and confiscate their guns. Then Three Stars even raised Spotted Tail over Red Cloud, making him chief of both agencies.*

Biding his time in shame and humiliation, Red Cloud had waited through a long winter for Three Stars to reinstate him as chief at his own agency. He had never made any trouble. He had not run away and gone to war like the others. He had not wiped out all those soldiers the way Crazy Horse had. So time and again through the long, agonizing seasons of that war in the North Country, Red Cloud had wondered why it

---

A Cold Day In Hell, vol. 11, the Plainsmen Series.

was taking Three Stars and the *wasicu* leaders so long to lift him up before his own people again, to make him a powerful chief once more—the man who had the say of when and where and how the rations were distributed to the Oglala. For a people who did not roam nor hunt, that was an immense power for one man to wield.

As he had waited out the winter, word drifted in that the Bear Coat was attempting to lure the Hunkpatila north to the mouth of the Tongue River. About the same time, Three Stars sent out Spotted Tail and a mighty escort to bring in his sister's son, Crazy Horse. Not to be outdone, the upstart little soldier chief they called White Hat had convinced Red Cloud that the one and only way he could ever get the attention of Three Stars and the *wasicu* rulers was himself to be the man who brought in Crazy Horse for White Hat.

Little did it matter to Red Cloud at the time that White Hat would wreath himself in unimaginable glory for having brought Crazy Horse to surrender at his agency near Camp Robinson. It simply made sense that this was what he had to do to get himself reinstated. Red Cloud had gone north to see that old friend he hadn't talked with in many a summer—only to discover that Crazy Horse was already bringing his people in...but had decided on Spotted Tail's reservation. Red Cloud convinced him that the Hunkpatila belonged with the rest of the Oglala. They were family, of the same blood.

But when Crazy Horse had come in to surrender, it was not as a prisoner, and Red Cloud was hardly treated as a hero for his success! Instead, he had been shunted aside while all the attention and light was turned on the Strange Man from the North.

Under these circumstances, there was little for Red Cloud's friends to do but wait and keep their ears open. He kept his spies out among the people in all the camps, even among Spotted Tail's Sicangu people over on Beaver Creek too. Some would watch and listen around the army's Soldier Camp, hoping to hear whispers of talk as to when Three Stars would again raise Red Cloud.

But instead the soldier chiefs and *wasicu* leaders wanted so badly for Crazy Horse to go east with Red Cloud and the other headmen that the white men courted and played up to the Northern war chief, anything to win him over to their campaign to take him east to see the white man's grandfather. And lately, rumors had it that when Crazy Horse returned to the White River because he had been so powerful and fought against the army for so long he would be made chief over all the Oglala! Some said he would even be raised over his uncle's people at the Spotted Tail Agency too!

Flies buzzed annoyingly around their faces in the heat. Red Cloud gently wagged the horsetail swatter he gripped in his left hand as he brooded.

He had done everything White Hat asked of him in the spring. But now he and the new agent were both going to betray Red Cloud and install Crazy Horse above him! Chief over all these people, with all that power stripped from Red Cloud's hands.

"Can we lure White Hat away from the others some day," Red Dog suggested, "get him alone? . . . For he is easy to convince when you flatter him."

"Yes," Woman's Dress said, his face lighting up with conspiratorial glee, "we could kill him and blame it on Crazy Horse—"

"No," Red Cloud interrupted gruffly. "The *wasicu* are not like the Lakota. We can't kill one man and be done with it. Even if we get rid of White Hat, the white man will send another to take his place . . . and besides, there are more men than just White Hat who are talking now of making Crazy Horse chief over us all. The murder of one man won't do."

"Then how?" asked Woman's Dress, smoothing the front of his long calico skirt he wore over blue wool leggings trimmed with silver buttons attached along the fringe at the outside seam. "Perhaps we should kill Crazy Horse."

"No, that will not do," Red Cloud said, shaking his head. "There would be too many questions, too many problems raised for us if *we* killed Crazy Horse. Murder will not do."

Standing Bear spoke up for the first time, "Something

must be done about Crazy Horse soon, because the White Hat and Three Stars are ready to give his people a long hunt into the buffalo country—"

"And if the Hunkpatila go north on their horses, with their guns and women and children too," Red Dog snarled, "then we know Crazy Horse will never bring them back here again."

"Perhaps that is where our path lies," Red Cloud said softly, sensing the flutter of hope.

"Where?" asked Woman's Dress. "To go north too?"

"No," Red Cloud answered. "To convince the soldier chiefs that if they allow their shiny chief Crazy Horse and his warriors to go north with ponies and firearms and all their families...the Hunkpatila plan to go back on the warpath."

"Killing many, many *wasicus!*" Standing Bear cheered.

Red Dog agreed, "Both soldiers and white women too!"

"We might have time, before we go east," Red Cloud suggested, "to start convincing White Hat and the others that Crazy Horse is really evil, that he has only fooled them into thinking he has surrendered."

Woman's Dress clapped his hands ecstatically, finger-rings clattering together. "Oooo! I think we can plant that little story in just the right ears!"

Red Cloud felt immensely proud of himself. "Yes, my friends, I think we can succeed at our plan. We can convince the soldier chiefs that Crazy Horse only came in to bide his time, fatten his horses on the early-summer grasses, to acquire ammunition not for the hunt but to renew the war... and then he will be gone one morning, right from under the noses of these sleeping dogs at Camp Robinson!"

Billy Garnett watched Crazy Horse carefully, intently studying every small move of the war chief's facial muscles as the Oglala leaders sat beneath the awning in the afternoon* heat, listening to the new agent who had just come to the

---

*27 July 1877.

reservation, Dr. James Irwin,* and the agent's special guests.

There were times when Billy knew Crazy Horse couldn't be listening, not staring off into the shimmering afternoon sunlight the way he was, his mind clearly drifting far, far away from these talks with Indian Inspector Benjamin K. Shopp, come from a long distance to make plans for the chiefs' forthcoming visit to Washington City. Then Billy would translate a piece of dialogue for one of the white civilians who had been accompanied here by an army escort, and something would seem to prick Crazy Horse's attention—immediately bringing him back to these talks. For a few moments Crazy Horse would appear to listen intently to Billy's translation, his eyes often boring into the white faces as he listened to Garnett's Lakota.

And for an instant, all Billy could think of was that day when an unarmed Crazy Horse stepped between the two angry groups at the sundance grounds.

"Brothers, you must stop!" he had shouted at those Oglala prepared to shed Oglala blood. "Can't you see you are shooting at your own people!"

Many talked of how brave Crazy Horse was in battle, whether it was luring the soldiers into the trap at the Battle of a Hundred in the Hand or at the all-day fight against General Crook's column. But to Billy, Crazy Horse had never been braver than the day he stepped into the center of those hundreds upon hundreds. In the midst of all that confusion and madness, shouting and anger, any one of those infuriated Oglala could have fired his gun and killed the Northern chief without any man knowing exactly who had committed the murder. Yes, courage in battle against a known enemy was one thing . . . but to expose your breast to your own people, not knowing who really were your friends and who were those whispering against you and seeking your downfall, that was courage of an even stronger sort—

"Garnett?"

---

*Irwin, a civilian, had become agent on July 1, ending direct military control of Red Cloud Agency.

He blinked and turned his head slightly, finding a perturbed Lieutenant Clark calling his name a second time.
"Yes, sir."

"We need you to translate what I just said to the chiefs,"
the officer instructed.

Clearing his throat, Billy apologetically asked Clark to
repeat his statement.

"As soon as we have laid down firm plans for our journey
to Washington City," Clark said, "General Crook has given
his full permission for the Northern People to begin preparations for making a fall hunt."

Then it was no longer a rumor, something that could only
be hinted at . . . then withdrawn because it was not a fact.
White man's promises. Only smoke on the wind.

When he told the chiefs their hunt was going to happen,
there were murmurs among the headmen. Happiness and
celebration among the Hunkpatila. Concern and thinly
veiled anger among the Red Cloud people.

"And once you return from making meat for the winter,"
Clark continued his declaration, reading from a piece of
folded paper he had taken from inside his uniform, "the trip
east will commence, at a time when the weather has turned
colder."

Their hunt would come in the Moon When Leaves Turn
Brown, Garnett told the whispering leaders there in the
buzzing summer heat of that late morning. And the journey
east would take place in the Moon When Leaves Fall. By the
middle of October, Crazy Horse would be taken east, wooed
by the power and majesty of the government and cities, rail-
roads and long graded pikes that connected one center of
commerce with another. But if there was any reason to sus-
pect that Crazy Horse had not been converted—exactly as
Red Cloud had become a dependable leader—then the war
chief might never return from his visit. Instead, with him far
away from the protection of his friends and his people, the
army could slap iron shackles around his wrists and ankles,
throwing him into a boxcar bound for the Dry Tortugas, that
death prison Billy had heard so many whispers about.

Clark leaned over to put his head close to Garnett's ear. "Why don't Red Cloud and his friends seem happy about this news? After all, they've gotten what they wanted. Crazy Horse has agreed to go east with them."

Garnett shrugged. "No telling what it will take to make any of 'em happy," he confessed, not willing to venture his opinion, his fear.

"Then let's tell them about the feast," Clark suggested as he leaned back.

"Yes, by all means," Irwin agreed, turning to the Indian Inspector.

Shopp rubbed his hands together, saying, "Mr. Garnett, I want you to tell these men that I am very pleased with how much work we have done today, making our plans for the trip to see President Hayes. So pleased that I have been authorized to conduct a feast."

Billy translated that, and the murmuring immediately ceased. Shopp and Garnett had every Oglala's attention.

Continuing, the Indian Inspector said, "I can provide three cattle for a great feast, together with some coffee and sugar too. We want the Oglala to dance and sing and eat their fill—for this feast is a chance to celebrate our new friendship, after so much misunderstanding and war."

"When?" Billy turned to the white men after Woman's Dress asked the question.

"As soon as you decide you want to hold it," Shopp replied. "The cattle can be here in a matter of a few days."

This time No Water asked a question: "Who will host the feast?"

"H-host?" Shopp echoed the word, bewildered.

Clark was quick to explain the tradition to the civilian official, that even a feast given by the white man such as this had to have an Oglala host. Someone who would be honored by being selected.

That's when Young Man Afraid got to his feet, taking a step closer to the white men as they sat on their canvas stools. "It would be a good thing to have the feast held to honor Crazy Horse."

Garnett translated, watching the eyes of the white men, and the Oglala too, narrow on the war chief as Young Man Afraid pressed on.

"It has been a long time since he came to this agency, a long time without a feast to welcome him. We should hold the feast at Crazy Horse's lodge."

The white men muttered among themselves a moment, their voices barely above a whisper, as Clark helped Irwin and Shopp understand the nuances of Sioux custom. "If we allow the feast to be held at Crazy Horse's lodge," the lieutenant explained, "that would make him the symbolic giver of the meal. A very great honor."

"Yes," Shopp said, nodding agreeably.

Garnett quickly translated the announcement into Lakota, "'Crazy Horse will be given this very great honor to host this feast on the white man's cattle—'"

At that moment the rustle in the crowd silenced Garnett's translation, and drew the attention of the white men. Like them all, Garnett watched as Red Cloud and three others rose to their feet in the midst of the gathering, turned, and shoved their way out of the group. Purposefully, the trio followed their chief past a crowd of curious onlookers to take up the reins to their horses. Behind Red Cloud, the trio—No Water, Woman's Dress, and Red Dog—mounted and rode away as the first whispers from the Crazy Horse people broke the stunned silence.

Young Man Afraid was asking his question again, a little louder now, so Billy concentrated on translating. "'Then it is decided?'" he asked the civilian officials. "'Crazy Horse is to be honored by this feast?'"

"Yes," Agent Irwin answered, his faced pinched with a little irritation at being put on the spot by Young Man Afraid as the whispering grew around them. "Crazy Horse will be the host."

CHAPTER THIRTEEN

July 27, 1877

WHEN FRANK GROUARD STEPPED INTO THE DIM LAMPLIGHT of the cramped office, he had been invigorated by the mile-and-a-half ride through the black, starry night, summoned to Red Cloud Agency from Camp Robinson, the post where he was a sometimes translator for the army.

"What's the rub?" he growled at the four civilians huddled around the desk in the yellow corona of light put out by a small lamp.

Grouard glanced at the lamp, thinking they could have turned up more of the wick...so they must have purposefully wanted to keep the light dim.

"We need you to translate for us."

"Who are you?" he asked the speaker.

"James Irwin—"

"So you're the new agent," Grouard interrupted. "I thought Garnett was your agency interpreter. Why'd you go and drag me out of my bedsack?"

"Agent Irwin already told you, Grouard," a second, fleshy-faced man said with no small amount of irritation. His ample cheeks were clearly flushed with something other than the mid-summer night air.

"I take it you can't find Billy?"

"He might be off visiting one of the camps," Irwin declared, pressing his hands together.

With a snort, Grouard responded, "You're afraid he's gettin' a little cozy with them Oglalas, are you?"

In the dim lamplight, Irwin stretched out his arm, indicating a darkened corner of the small office. Waving his hand, he gestured two men forward—but they came only as far as the edge of the light. Frank stared at them suspiciously, clearly Indians. The smell of them, moccasins too, and both had blankets pulled over their heads and shoulders, concealing not only their faces but anything particular about their hair, or feathers, or their shirts too. This pair certainly did not want to be identified... and coming here in the middle of the god-damned night, when few, if any, people were up and about the agency. When a man should be wrapped in his blankets, dreaming deliciously about warm legs and willing—

"These two have come knocking on my door," Irwin continued to explain. "Since none of us can speak Sioux, and we don't find Garnett in his bed next door, I sent a runner for you over at Robinson."

Turning to the pair without another word to Irwin, Grouard asked in Lakota, "Why are you here?"

"We came to speak to the agent."

Try as he might, Frank could not put a finger on that voice, especially since the speaker used a whisper to further disguise his identity. He pointed to the disheveled Irwin. "This one is the agent."

"We know."

Scratching at the side of his cheek, Frank asked, "What is it you want to tell him?"

He listened to their terse and angry words, then turned to the white men. "These two come from chief Red Cloud himself."

"Is there trouble?" Irwin squeaked.

"Maybe will be," Grouard replied, "if you hold some feast for Crazy Horse. That's what they're angry about."

Shopp leaned an arm on the small desk. "Angry about the feast?"

"They say you shamed Red Cloud today," Grouard explained.

Irwin nodded. "So that's why he got up and walked away in the middle of our making plans with Young Man Afraid."

"Young Man Afraid? He's the one who gonna do his best to make all sides come together," Frank said. "He's a good talker, that one. A fair man—fair as they come."

"So what is Red Cloud's argument against the feast?" Shopp inquired.

Volving a sore shoulder, Grouard answered, "Seems the

feast is a good idea—but they want you should make Red Cloud the host, 'stead of Crazy Horse."

Irwin drew in a long breath, while he stared at the shadowy, blanketed forms. "They tell you why they have a problem with Crazy Horse?"

"He hasn't been at the agency for long," Frank told the white men after the pair explained their protestations. "This feast is a great honor you give away. I know that my own self. So I gotta agree with 'em: Crazy Horse doesn't deserve such an honor."

For several moments Irwin and the others fell silent; then the agent said, "I just remembered someone telling me that you spent time with the Crazy Horse band a few years back, didn't you, Grouard?"

He shrugged. "I never tried to hide it."

His face growing more animated, Irwin took a step closer to Frank, saying, "Then you must know enough about Sioux practices to give me some solid advice on this matter. You're saying it isn't a good idea to go against Red Cloud and his friendlies about this feast—"

"I said I agree with these two Injuns here," Grouard interrupted.

"A-agree . . . about Crazy Horse not hosting the f-feast?" Irwin stammered.

Frank nodded. "Yeah. But mostly, I agree with what they was asking me to tell you about Crazy Horse."

"There's something more?" Shopp asked.

"It's true what they told me to say to you: that Crazy Horse isn't a friendly. He ain't an agency Injun at all. By no means."

"Explain yourself," Irwin ordered.

"He might've come in to surrender, but Crazy Horse ain't given up—not by a long shot, gentlemen."

Irwin sighed sourly, staring at his cluttered desk. "I had come to wonder if he truly was reconstructed or not. From his sullen and morose behavior, everything points to the fact that he hasn't really given up his backward, marauding ways."

"This is sad," Shopp groaned. "Very, very sad. After all the plans we've made to take him east with the others."

"We can still do that," Irwin suggested, hope registering in his voice. "No reason why we can't. He'll be under our complete control, away from his warriors and his people. He'll be ours to convert to the fold . . . or ship off to prison as General Sheridan recommended we do."

"You ain't ever gonna make a agency Injun outta Crazy Horse," Grouard reminded them. "Not the way you done it to Red Cloud."

"Grabber," one of the two visitors whispered his Lakota name for emphasis, then began to tell him more.

Frank thought of old friends like He Dog, Little Big Man, and all the other closest allies of Crazy Horse as he listened to the visitors' snarling epithets against the Northern People. Then he turned back to the civilians and informed the white men, "If Clark goes ahead with Crook's plan to give them Crazy Horse people a hunt sometime in September . . . these two here are right."

"Right about what?" Irwin demanded.

"Crazy Horse and the rest of his warriors won't ever be coming back to your agency."

"Won't come back from the hunt?" Shopp squealed in dismay. "But . . . they've given their word to us they would return when the—"

"What's the word of a bunch of bastards been killing, scalping, and stealing all their lives? You gonna trust their promise?" Grouard demanded. "When it's the easiest thing to them warriors to lie to you . . . then turn right around and raise your hair in the next breath."

"You're telling me Crazy Horse will lie to us?" asked an ashen-faced Shopp.

Frank explained, "You fellas ain't been out here long, so you don't know the truth of the tale. Clark can tell you, others too. Just ask 'em. But for now I want you to remember how the other chiefs throwed Crazy Horse away. Took his shirt from him, all his power as a leader, because he had disobeyed 'em. One thing for sure, the chiefs don't have no more faith in him now than they did when they stripped him of his shirt. If his own people can't trust him . . . how do you figger you can?"

After a long moment, Shopp eventually leaned toward the stunned Irwin. "James, maybe they're right."

Nodding slightly, the agent said, "With all this less-than-flattering talk about him, maybe we should be very, very cautious—even wary—of this Crazy Horse."

"I think it best that we cancel the feast," Shopp suggested, "until we can sort things out and see where his loyalties really lie."

"By all means," Irwin agreed, looking up from the floor now, a deep furrow between his eyes as they came to bear on Grouard. "Tell these two they can carry my word back to Red Cloud. Assure the chief there won't be any feast, not for now. And certainly not with Crazy Horse as the honored party."

After he had translated that good news to the two blanketed visitors and the Lakota had slipped out the door and back around the corner of the agent's office, disappearing into the night, Grouard thought it was time to reassure the white men about their misgivings and distrust of Crazy Horse.

"You're doin' the right thing," Frank stated emphatically. "Anything goin' on with Crazy Horse and them warriors who stick real close to him—why, it's bound to stink to the heavens soon enough."

Red Cloud waited among the tall pines on the long, gentle slope at the base of Crow Butte, watching from the mid-morning shadows as a pair of horsemen approached. He turned to smile knowingly at the two old friends who had joined him here after they had reached their decision over breakfast. He found Red Dog and No Water were smiling too.

Two nights ago they had begun closing the first of the two pincers around Crazy Horse, when he sent a pair of his friends to carry word of his dismay to the new agent and the *wasicu* from the east. That first prong of their two-part plan had been set into motion quite handily: convincing the white man that Crazy Horse had not changed at all when he surrendered at the agency, easily convincing the *wasicus* that if allowed to go hunting in the Powder River country the war chief and his people would never return to the White Earth River...and might well ignite a new war against the white man.

Now they were preparing to start closing the second of the two pincers on Crazy Horse in their shadowy plan to assure that Red Cloud—and Red Cloud only—would hold the real power here on his agency. All three had reason to smile as they watched the two riders enter the shady stand of trees just below them. It was sure to be another hot day. Better to wait here in the cool shadows...where no one would have any idea that Woman's Dress was bringing Long Joe Laravie to meet with Red Cloud.

Letting his chest swell with his own sense of indignation, Red Cloud knew that he was the one and only chief of his people. Not Spotted Tail of the Sicangu, raised above Red Cloud by Three Stars. And surely not Crazy Horse! When Woman's Dress was sent to the French trader that morning, Laravie would have jumped at a chance to have a private audience with Red Cloud, even though he wouldn't have the least idea what they were to discuss. Only that Red Cloud could not be seen publicly talking to the trader...at least if he and his friends wanted to make sure it never appeared that Red Cloud had anything to do with their maneuvers to undo Crazy Horse from even the bottommost rungs of power on this reservation.

He watched how Laravie's suspicious eyes tapped the other two men, then came to rest on him as the pair of horsemen came to a halt, then quickly dismounted and tied off their ponies in the pines near the other three.

"You speak good Lakota?" Red Cloud asked the trader.

His head bobbed, and so did his prominent Adam's apple. "Good enough my wife understands me," he answered with that low creek frog of a voice.

"Come, sit," he instructed, turning sideways and indicating the buffalo robe stretched out in the shade. "We will have us a little smoke . . . then talk of important matters."

Perhaps it was because Long Joe was a white man, but he appeared impatient during the filling and ceremonial smoking of Red Cloud's pipe while the five of them sat at the outer edge of that buffalo robe.

"You have three daughters," Red Cloud declared when the pipe went out and the tobacco in the bowl had turned to ash.

"You want a new wife, eh?" Laravie replied, grinning toothily as if immensely proud of himself for catching onto Red Cloud's intent. "That would make me your father-in-law."

"No, not for me," the chief answered, watching how quickly the man's smile disappeared.

"So . . . why do you ask about my daughters?"

"There is one, I think she is your second—"

"Helen," Laravie interrupted, his eyes narrowing with a father's concern.

"Heh-lawn," Red Cloud mimicked the sounds Long Joe had made to declare the young woman's name.

Nodding once, the Frenchman said, "But around the trading post and agency, she's known to the *wasicus* as Nellie."

"Nell-eee?"

"Yes, Nellie. You asked me here to talk about her?"

Red Cloud pushed a loose strand of hair from his eye. "Has any man come to speak for her?"

Laravie quickly glanced at the other three Bad Face leaders; then his eyes came back to Red Cloud. "No. No one has come to ask for her in marriage. One of these two want a wife?" he asked, indicating Red Dog and No Water, but not pointing out the *winkte*, who clearly had the special woman-man medicine. "I know each of them already have their own wives—"

"Not for them," it was Red Cloud's turn to interrupt. "But it is true that the husband we have picked out for your second daughter already does have a first wife."

"Who is this man?"

Red Cloud took a long breath, his face a study in composure. "He is not a wealthy man. So he will not have much to give you for your daughter."

"Oh? Then tell me why should I be interested in marrying my daughter to a poor man?"

"Because *we* can make it worth your while," Red Cloud said with a knowing grin.

"I'm a trader! That means I have my own wealth already," Long Joe argued. "There isn't much that you could offer me that I don't already possess!"

"We can offer you horses."

"Yes, horses," Joe responded, less cocky now. "Horses . . . are a good thing."

"But . . . at first, the new husband for your second daughter would only be able to give his new wife's father two ponies."

"T-two?" Laravie squeaked an octave higher. Then his face grew red as he began to bluster, "Any daughter of mine is worth far more than two ponies!"

Red Cloud let the Frenchman spew a few more moments. By all rights he should remind the trader who he was dealing with. After all, he was the only Lakota who had ever won a war against the *wasicus* and their army! He was the only chief—all the way from the land of the brown ones in the south clear up to the land of the Grandmother in the far north—who had made the soldiers retreat and abandon their attempt to take the hunting grounds between the Powder and the Bighorn rivers away from the Lakota! Now here this small-time trader was trying to tell Red Cloud the number of horses he wanted for his daughter in this arranged marriage?

"Perhaps you should talk to one of the other fathers, a half-breed maybe, someone who hangs around the agency," Laravie bluffed. "Like Pourier or Garnier . . . either one. You can marry one of their daughters to this *poor* man who cannot afford a decent dowry—"

"His name is Crazy Horse," Red Cloud said quietly.

Laravie almost choked on that revelation. "C-crazy Horse? The Northern chief?"

He only nodded, enjoying how that both perplexed and pleased the white man at the same time.

It was a moment before the trader spoke again, asking, "You want me to give my daughter...t-to Crazy Horse?"

With a grin, Red Cloud said, "Haven't you seen how they look at one another when he comes to the agency?"

"Y-yes, I have seen—"

"And haven't you heard talk of the way Crazy Horse looks at her when she comes with the white healer to visit Black Shawl, Crazy Horse's first wife?"

Licking his lips with the pink tip of his tongue, the wide-eyed Frenchman asked, "So he is a great chief...but all he can afford for Helen is two ponies?"

"That is what we can arrange for him to give you for the time being," No Water answered for his chief. "But when we are assured that Crazy Horse changes his mind about going east to see the *wasicu* grandfather...there will be much more in this for you, Long Joe Laravie."

The trader squinted an eye mercenarily, asking, "How much?"

Red Cloud leaned toward the white man a little, saying, "The White Hat wants me to tell you that I can promise you something good."

"What does he say you can promise me?"

"If things come out right, the White Hat wants you to know you will be well paid."

"H-how much?"

Wearing a big smile now, Red Cloud answered, "No telling how many horses a man might eventually get for marrying his daughter off to the famous fighter named Crazy Horse...once Crazy Horse is convinced it is not safe for him to go to east this coming autumn."

"So, if I understand you right," Laravie rubbed his palms down the thighs of his canvas britches there at the edge of the buffalo robe in these shadows of the fragrant pines, "*if* I allow my daughter to become Crazy Horse's second wife...

and *if* I get her to talk Crazy Horse into changing his mind about going east with you, then there will be much more wealth in it for me?"

Red Cloud turned and nodded to his friends, self-satisfied that he had played the white man perfectly. "See? I told you Long Joe Laravie was a smart trader!"

The white man demanded, "How many horses?"

Again he leaned toward the Frenchman meaningfully, and said, "How many is your daughter worth?"

With a half-grin, the trader appeared to grow cagey. "How many horses do you think the second wife of this Northern chief will be worth to you? Especially . . . when she will use all her charms to get Crazy Horse to change his mind and refuse to go east with White Hat and Three Stars?"

Wagging his head slightly, Red Cloud got a dour look on his face. "Ah, but the agent and the soldiers have taken so many of our horses already, don't you understand?"

"W-wait a minute here," Joe stammered. "Are you taking back your offer already?"

"No, we just don't own so many horses as we used to," Woman's Dress argued, brushing dust off of one leg of those blue wool leggings decorated with their shiny silver buttons.

"How m-many will you give me when Crazy Horse refuses to go east with you and White Hat?"

Red Cloud regarded that question a moment; then he answered by asking, "What is Nell-eee worth to her father?"

"My prettiest daughter?" he retorted, leaning back as if insulted. Then quickly Laravie rocked forward, his elbows on his knees, and studied Red Cloud's face intently. "Three-times-ten and not one horse less—"

"This woman is not marrying Red Cloud!" No Water fumed. "Crazy Horse is no high chief of the Oglala!"

"Ten horses," Woman's Dress proposed. "Not one horse more!"

The trader regarded that for a long moment. "Make it two-times-ten, and we have ourselves a deal."

Red Cloud held out both of his hands. "Ten horses, Long Joe. Ten, plus the two from Crazy Horse."

"All . . . all right. Ten plus the two . . . in trade for my pretty Nellie."

Red Cloud raised his right hand, fingers spread apart and held a few short inches from the trader's face. "Two from Crazy Horse when she goes to live in his lodge. Five more my friend, Red Dog, will bring to tie at the back of your store that same day."

Laravie turned his eyes to look at Red Dog, asking, "So what about the other five horses you will owe me?"

"Those five . . ." said Red Cloud, pausing. "No Water and Woman's Dress will bring you the five best horses from my own herd when Crazy Horse has informed the White Hat that he refuses to go anywhere his new wife does not want him to go."

CHAPTER FOURTEEN

Wasutun Wi
MOON WHEN ALL THINGS RIPEN, 1877

HAVE SEEN HOW YOUR EYES SPEAK TO HERS, MY FRIEND," HE
Dog said to Crazy Horse that warm summer night after the
stars had come out in a fiery bloom.

"Why do you talk of another woman here at my home?"
Crazy Horse whispered low, his eyes flicking from the face
of his old friend to the faces of the others who had gathered
with him beneath the rustle of the cottonwood leaves.

All of them were friends; most had charged into battle
with him. All were Oglala except the White Hat, the little
chief of the soldiers, who had joined their circle for what he
explained was an important discussion.

Crazy looked again at He Dog. "My wife is Black Shawl.
What if she should hear you speaking of another woman in
this manner?"

"This is meant to honor you," Young Man Afraid explained while the half-blood interpreter went on whispering
at White Hat's shoulder, busy translating without interruption. The famed Lakota diplomat gave a long disapproving
look at the soldier chief sitting among them, then continued,
"Since the agent decided against you hosting the feast, we
have been considering how we could honor you for the
courage you showed to bring in the Northern People to the
reservation."

"More and more I hear whispers of bad talk against me,"
Crazy Horse said.

He Dog said, "Just silly talk. From people who should
not matter to us."

"If Red Cloud's friends do not want me around, perhaps I
should go live with my uncle at his agency," Crazy Horse
declared stubbornly. "When I live there I won't have to lis-

ten to the chattering of so many magpies who have nothing else to do but to spread their bad stories about me."

"You can't go to Spotted Tail's agency," Billy Garnett said nervously, translating what the White Hat had instructed him to say.

Crazy Horse turned to the white man and his interpreter. "Why can't I go where my father lives?"

"This is your new home."

The war chief blinked a few times, considering his answer. "My home is wherever I have relatives. Spotted Tail is my uncle. I think I would find more peace living somewhere close to Beaver Mountain."

"White Hat says I should remind Crazy Horse that he has relatives right here among his own Oglala people," Garnett said unsurely.

"My friend," He Dog explained to the chief, "the White Hat did not come here to listen to you talk about leaving to go live with your uncle at his agency. He and our friend, Young Man Afraid, came to smoke with us and talk about how we can honor you."

"The *wasicus* want to plan another feast for me, then take it away again?"

For a moment, He Dog and Young Man Afraid exchanged weary glances. He Dog said, "No. They came to talk of plans to honor you with another wife."

Crazy Horse took in a deep breath as his eyes looked around. He Dog was sure he was looking for some sign, perhaps a sound, something to tell him of Black Shawl's proximity to this informal gathering and a smoke among old friends.

"Another wife," Crazy Horse repeated finally, his voice more subdued than it had been. "This is why you asked me about the trader's daughter."

"A great leader such as you should be honored," Young Man Afraid explained as Garnett went back to translating at White Hat's ear. "The little chief of the soldiers, and your friends, we have talked about this before we came to you with our question."

"Whose idea is this?" Crazy Horse asked, turning back to He Dog. "Is it yours?"

"No," he admitted. "The White Hat thought you would be honored with a young, pretty wife."

Looking at White Hat a moment, Crazy Horse finally asked the little chief, "Why another wife?"

The White Hat waited while Billy Garnett translated, then spoke to the interpreter. His answer was, "A feast will fill your belly for only one night. I thought a new wife would last a long, long time. And make your life happier here at the agency."

"Young Man Afraid and I," said He Dog, "we know how Black Shawl has been ill for a long time with her lung sickness—"

"She is getting a little stronger every day," Crazy Horse interrupted him, rubbing the redstone bowl of his small pipe between his palms.

"We thought another, younger wife would not only make you happier," He Dog professed, "she would be a great help to Black Shawl in your lodge."

They watched Crazy Horse stare at the small personal pipe held between his hands, studying the weighty proposition they had just laid in his lap. Even the half-blood translator was silent now, everyone waiting.

"She speaks the *wasicu* tongue very good," Crazy Horse commented without looking up from his hands.

"Yes," He Dog said softly. "And she is very pretty."

Young Man Afraid joined the refrain, "Very, very pretty."

Now Crazy Horse looked up, a smile in his eyes. "She is very pretty, yes."

He Dog reiterated, "Think of how good it will be if Black Shawl does not have to work so hard."

With a sigh, Crazy Horse asked, "What does the young woman know of this?"

"The trader has agreed," Young Man Afraid declared. "Long Joe Laravie says he is honored to have his daughter marry you."

"But . . . what does he expect from me in payment for

her?" Crazy Horse asked. "He is married to a Shahiyela woman, so he will expect some gifts from me."

He Dog said, "Laravie does not expect that much—"

"Surely Laravie knows I am a poor man," Crazy Horse averred. "I have my clothing and my pipe." He held it up briefly, making certain White Hat understood the half-blood's translation. "But I no longer have many horses, and I no longer have my weapons. A warrior always had his weapons."

White Hat made some quick gestures to Young Man Afraid, holding up two fingers on one hand, then moved those two fingers across the palm of the other hand.

"Just two horses," Young Man Afraid stated. "That's all Long Joe says he will take for his second daughter."

Surprise came over the war chief's face. "He is a rich man, is he not? Isn't he wealthy by the standards of the *wasicu*?"

"Yes," He Dog replied. "But he told the White Hat that he does not have need of anything. He has all the blankets and beads and finery any man like him could ever want, so Laravie told the White Hat that he needed nothing more from you than the two horses."

"You have two horses to spare, my friend," Young Man Afraid said. "And if you do not have any that you will let go, I have two horses to give in your stead. I would be honored if you would allow me to present them to the trader on your behalf."

"Or you can have two of my horses too," Little Big Man spoke up for the first time, his full face animated with excitement. "If this new wife will make my long-time friend happy here in his new life...then I will give away all the horses that I call my own!"

"You are a metalbreast now," Crazy Horse said. "Wearing the soldier coat and the *wasicu* badge. *Akicita* like you will always have the best horses, won't you?"

"I wish only to honor my good friend," Little Big Man protested. "We rode many trails together, raiding for horses and scalps—Psatoka, Susuni, fighting *wasicu* too. I am happy as an *akicita* here, walking a new road, Crazy Horse. So I want to do all I can to make your heart happy too."

"Do you like her, nephew?" asked Little Hawk, leaning toward the war chief.

Crazy Horse's eyes touched the young interpreter. "Billy, I ask you not to give White Hat my Lakota words I am about to say, because I want to talk to these men as my friends and relations. Will you hold your tongue until I am done, when I say that you can make *wasicu* words for him?"

Garnett swallowed and nodded once there beside the White Hat.

"Good," he said, laying a hand on He Dog's knee a moment before he continued. "The *wasicu* are a strange people, aren't they? Their black robes and holy men tell us our people are evil because a Lakota man can have more than one wife... but here sits the White Hat, speaking for all the *wasicu* chiefs above him, offering me a second wife because I think he believes it will make me happy."

"Won't it make you happy, old friend?" asked Jumping Shield in a grave voice.

"She is very pretty," Crazy Horse admitted. "And very young too."

"Black Shawl needs help," Looking Horse observed. "And Worm has given his approval too."

Crazy Horse looked at his uncle, Little Hawk. "Yes, my father must have agreed, or Little Hawk would not be here to smoke and talk, trying his best to convince me to take this young woman into my lodge."

By this time White Hat was whispering nervously to Billy Garnett, in all likelihood demanding to know why the half-blood wasn't interpreting while the Lakotas talked one to another.

"Tell him," Crazy Horse spoke up, his voice louder than it had been for some time, "that you were only making sure of the words we have spoken before you translated. Say that I trust my friends coming to me about this question. If he had come to me alone, I would have suspected the *wasicu* wanted something of me. But since my good friends are

here, and my uncle too, then I trust there is nothing underhanded in you asking me to take the trader's daughter as my
second wife."

Garnett translated the White Hat's words, " 'When he
came to me, the trader wanted only to ask some way to
honor Crazy Horse. That is why he offered his prettiest
daughter to you, why I came to your friends to ask them how
you would accept this gift of the woman.' "

Looking at the war chief, He Dog reminded him of
Lakota etiquette: "My friend, you cannot insult a man who
wishes to give you a gift."

Then Young Man Afraid stated, "Black Shawl will be
glad for the help in her lodge."

"When will this happen?" Crazy Horse finally asked.

"Tomorrow," He Dog answered. "Unless you want to
wait."

Crazy Horse looked at the White Hat for a moment, and
eventually answered with his eyes locked on the white
man's. "No. There is no reason for me to wait." He sighed.
"Thank you, my friends, for this honor you have given me. I
accept the trader's daughter as my second wife."

"It is done," He Dog said with a smile.

And as soon as the half-blood translated Crazy Horse's
agreement to take Helen Laravie as his wife, the White Hat
slapped both hands down on his thighs and roared in glee,
"It is done!"

He could barely catch his breath as the young woman rocked
slower and slower atop him, his manhood impaled within
the trader's daughter.

No, she is no longer Long Joe Laravie's daughter, Crazy
Horse thought to himself, sensing the sweat leaking from
every place on his skin where flesh was pressed against
flesh. *Now she is my wife.*

For now he called her Nellie, which she explained was
not the name given her as a newborn. That was Helen. So
that first night she had come to stay in their lodge, Crazy
Horse had explained that among the Lakota, children began

life with one name, later they were given another. Not only full-blood men but women too. So it was not unusual, he had told Nellie in the presence of Black Shawl, for her to have been born with one name, and to have another now that she had become an adult.

Adult. Nellie was no more than seventeen winters old. Half his age. Her body still taut and new, never having known the pleasures of bonding with a man until she had come to find him by the river this third night of their marriage.

Pressing her hips against him there in the twilight, half-hidden by the tall willow and rustling branches of the overhanging trees, Nellie had laid her face into the hollow of his neck and told him how she had waited two nights already for him to make her his wife in fact, and not just in promise.

"I cannot come to your blanket in Black Shawl's lodge," he had replied, feeling how stirred his manhood became as she molded herself into him, slowly moving as if by some ancient force.

"That's why I came to find you here," Nellie had told him, reaching down to pull up the bottom of his loose cotton trader's shirt, running her eager hands over his cool flesh.

"The horses." He had tried to explain that he needed to tie the ponies in the nearby trees, those three animals he had taken down to the riverbank for water before returning them to stake them near the lodge.

"They won't wander far," she had whispered against his mouth. "And if they do, everyone knows the horses of Crazy Horse anyway."

By that time one of her hands had played itself down his belly and slithered its way inside the front of his breech-clout. Nellie released a muffled squeal.

"So this is what becomes of a man's member when he is aroused enough to mount his woman!"

As soon as she wrapped her fingers around his throbbing manhood, Crazy Horse's hands grew hungry—one of them encapsulating a small, hard breast, the other quickly yanking up the bottom of her trader's cloth dress, feeling her bare hip, brushing across the top of her bare thigh, and then finding her heated moistness ready for his touch.

They had both groaned as he caressed her there, legs quivering, while Nellie's hand squeezed and squeezed until he thought he would be mad. No longer did the three horses matter.

Not as he cupped both of her buttocks in his hands, lifted her slightly, and tipped her onto the grass below them. Quickly she had ripped aside his breechclout, her fingers finding him again, and sought to guide him where he was already aiming his heated eagerness. They spent themselves all too quickly, then lay together, still as the stars, while the night darkened and the insects began to sing from the branches around them.

She had pulled his shirt from his arms sometime later, lightly massaging his chest as he explained why he bore no scars from the sun-gazing dance like many other Lakota men.

"You are man enough that you don't need to prove yourself to anyone," she had cooed to him as her slim fingers once more sought him out.

But when he had attempted to roll her aside so he could mount her again, Nellie instead pushed him back and threw a leg over his hip. Grabbing his manhood, the young woman had settled it within her with a groan, then began rocking slowly atop him as Crazy Horse's hands found both of her breasts. He kneaded them fiercely as she pulled up the bottom of her dress, yanking it off her arms and over her head to straddle him completely naked, but for the ankle-high moccasins strapped around her feet.

That time it had lasted exquisitely long.

"Does Black Shawl make you feel the way I make you feel?"

For a moment he studied her face. "Sad things have happened in our lives. When we were married, she was not as young as you—"

"So I am better than Black Shawl with you?" she prodded, both of her hands outspread on his bare chest, sliding across his damp skin.

"We have not been together for some time," he explained, gazing up at her. "She has been so sick."

"That is the only reason you were so hungry for me?" Nellie begged. "Or . . . was it only me that made you so ready to mount me?"

"You," he admitted. "I can remember how your eyes told me long ago that it would be just like this."

"It will always be like this between us too," she whispered, reaching down to take his hands off her sweaty hips, placing them on her breasts, pressing hard and closing her eyes as her head rocked back slightly.

"Yes," he vowed. "You can remain my second wife for as long as we both shall live."

That's when she opened her eyes and brought her face down closer to his. "Husband, I want you to live a long, long time."

"Yes," he said, knowing his flesh was sated and limp, but feeling inside the stirrings of a renewal of desire for this woman who—if he were not careful—might just consume all of his flesh.

Her long, lustrous hair hung down so that the fragrant ends almost brushed his face when she said, "To live a long, long time with me, Crazy Horse . . . you must stay safe."

He smiled up at her in the starlight. "I am safe. There is no more fighting. And if we ever break free for the old hunting ground, I will take you with us. No white man's bullet will ever kill me."

"I know. My father told me of your vision," she said, inching his hands down from her small breasts to place them on the flat of her adolescent belly. "But that does not mean a white man cannot make a prisoner of you."

"A p-prisoner?"

"Yes, when you go east with Red Cloud and the others," she whined in a small, childlike voice.

He chuckled softly. "No *wasicu* will ever make a prisoner of me. This agency is already as much a prison as they will ever find that will hold me. And perhaps not even this—"

"You cannot go," she said with fiery urgency.

"Go?"

"To see the white man's grandfather," she whimpered. "If you go away from here, I know they will put the iron ropes on you and never let you return to me!"

She fell against him, nestling her long black hair against his cheek as she sobbed atop him, her whole body quaking. "Don't let them take you from me!"

"It is only a journey to make the *wasicus* and White Hat happy," he argued. "Three Stars will give us our own agency when I return. Then you can live with me in the country of the Powder R—"

Surprising him, she sat upright in an instant. "No—they will never give you your agency."

Feeling horror and disbelief, he demanded, "Why would you ever make up such a story?"

"I know the truth," she confided. "I hear the white men talking. You know I understand their language. When they don't know I am listening, I hear a little bit of a story here, a little bit more over there."

Studying her face for some sign that she had betrayed herself in this joke, Crazy Horse asked, "W-what are you saying?"

Tears came to her eyes as she leaned over his face, hot drops spilling on his cheeks like summer rain. "There are plans to keep you from ever coming back again!"

"But the promises—"

"How many promises must they break before you believe that the *wasicus* plan to keep you a prisoner far from here?" she pleaded. "Far from me and the country you will never see again?"

"This is hard for me to believe."

"Don't you see, husband?" she said, taking his face between her small hands. "The white man and his soldiers are too scared to move the agencies while the terrible Crazy Horse is still around. So they plan to start you on your way east . . . then put you in a prison where you can't raise a hand to help your people!"

For a long time he stared at her face, not wanting to believe that everything he recently had come to believe was true had in reality been constructed of lies from the beginning. What they had promised to persuade him to bring his people in... what they had sworn to in convincing him to take the journey east with Red Cloud. Surely she must know. Nellie spoke the white man's tongue. She was the healer's translator now. The young woman moved in circles where she would hear the *wasicus* and the soldiers talk.

She was his now, so she was showing him her allegiance and loyalty. No longer only a half-blood trader's daughter... Nellie was the wife of a Hunkpatila war chief. Second wife to the renowned Crazy Horse.

He felt her begin to grind her buttocks atop his thighs again in that dance that had driven him to madness.

"I feel how your manhood grows beneath me again," Nellie whispered as she rocked forward onto her knees, found him with her fingers, and massaged him into instant readiness.

Then settled atop him again as his breath caught high in his throat.

"Promise me, husband," she whispered as she bent over him, her hair in his eyes, her mouth almost brushing his. "Promise me you will tell them you have changed your mind."

"Changed?" he murmured, his eyes closed below hers.

"Tell the *wasicu* agent that you won't go east with Red Cloud."

"No," he repeated in a hoarse whisper. "I won't go."

"You must tell the White Hat too," she said as her hips began to rock with more fervent heat, "tell him you are not going to see the white man's grandfather until they have given you your agency first."

"Just as... I told them... when I came here," he said between gritted teeth, seizing the tops of her arms as he drove himself upward, thrusting into her fiercely again and again in time with her rhythm.

"But don't ever tell them it is because you want to stay here with me," she whimpered as she bent over him, her face low, long, fragrant hair spread across his face, as she took his ear between her teeth. "So we can be together like this every night."

Crazy Horse opened his eyes when he felt he was beginning to lose himself, staring right into the heavens through that opening in the trees overhead, saw the sky spinning as the stars became a blur.

CHAPTER FIFTEEN

Wasutun Wi
MOON WHEN ALL THINGS RIPEN, 1877

BY TELEGRAPH

———

ILLINOIS.

———

Remains of General Custer at Chicago—
Other News Items.

———

CHICAGO, July 31.—The remains of General Custer
arrived here to-day from Fort Lincoln, and were forwarded
at 5:15 P.M. by the Michigan Southern railroad, to West
Point, where they will be interred in the receiving vault
until the funeral in October. The remains of Colonel
Cooke, Lieutenant Reilly, and Dr. DeWolf arrived on the
same train...

MAYBE HE WAS WRONG ABOUT THESE IMPORTANT THINGS.
Crazy Horse sat beside the White Earth River and
brooded on how life had changed for him ever since he had
decided he would come in to the agency.

For so long he had resisted every threat or entreaty from
the soldiers, fighting on and on till it seemed there was little
left to fight for. Their old hunting grounds were being surrounded, invaded, stripped away year by year. And even the
buffalo were all but gone. Perhaps the great black beasts
would come back one day, stronger than ever, blanketing the
prairies so the Hunkpatila could once again grow strong.

But for now...he had changed his mind about keeping
up the fight, and for now he had brought his people here to
this prison on the White Earth River.

Once he had come here, the *wasicus* made his ears hurt,

they talked so long and loud of how they wanted him to go east with Red Cloud's delegation, there to see all the marvelous things the white man had made of his world. For the longest time he had resisted every plea, deciding that this was where he had come, and this is where he should stay. After all, he had no desire to see that world east of the Muddy Water River. Perhaps it was true that the *wasicu* had made something of that country. Still, Crazy Horse knew in his marrow that this was the country that the Great Mystery had made for the Lakota. Why would a man ever decide to live where other men made their world something artificial, when he could live in a country where the Creator Himself had carved out the hills and valleys, rivers and streams, the animals and the sky too, all of it for His children?

So Crazy Horse had refused the invitations, asking only that he be given what had been promised when he agreed he would bring in his people to Red Cloud's agency ... refused until the spirits on the mountaintop convinced him that he could do well for his people if he used this power the *wasicus* and the soldiers were convinced he possessed. That was amusing, he thought, to consider how his old enemies gave him so much more prestige and influence than he had ever possessed as a poor man of the Lakota. Crazy Horse a leader of great power? No, only a simple man with no title and no responsibilities, a warrior at best.

So was it that he had made a mistake about the young woman? Could he have been wrong to let the others convince him to take her into his lodge? Her flesh was soft and smooth, and she brought him to the heights of such pleasure he had not experienced since his few days spent in the arms of Black Buffalo Woman ...

So how could he have refused the honor of her being offered to him by his friends? That would have been an insult. One did not turn down a gift from friends. Yet ... until she had come into his lodge, and laid in his arms, Crazy Horse was decided he could do best for his people by going east—doing what the *wasicus* asked of him so that those *wasicus* would be forced to do what they had promised him.

Could it be that he really was in danger to go east? That was the question he had asked himself over and over in the last handful of days since she had convinced him that she knew what his white enemies had planned for him. They dared not take him here at the agency, where too many would rise up and free him, fleeing from this prison and making for the old country. Perhaps it did make much more sense that the white man would lure him back east, lulling him into believing he was safe, just so they could close the jaws of their trap around him. To kill him outright would be far better than... for them to put iron shackles on him and keep him locked up inside four walls, beneath a roof, cramped between other prisoners. That would be unbearable—the death of his spirit!

Although friends told him about the place, Crazy Horse had no interest in seeing the *wasicu* prison lodge at the Soldier Town. While Little Big Man had been inside, and described how dark it was, how the foulest stench assaulted the nostrils... the idea of such a place simply repulsed Crazy Horse, knowing how it would grip his belly with torment to look upon men whose freedom had been stripped away. Better to die than to find himself stripped of his freedoms.

So he had listened to the description of that place given by Little Big Man and Billy Garnett... then put those terrible thoughts out of his mind... realizing he had been thinking about little else but the young woman, how she knew of the plotting of the *wasicus* around the agency, brooding on the white man's evil plan to imprison him. And if he fought, they would kill him.

Perhaps all he needed to feel better was to look forward to going off to do some hunting on his own. That way he could clear his head, think about the two women, and consider where each one would have a place in his life. And when he returned from those days away from the camp, he would feel much better for having been alone among the rocks, alone beneath the stars. Oh, how he tried more and more to make his mind dream himself back into the Real World, to tear himself from this Shadow World where everything reeked of despair—

Turning at the sound of the hoofbeats, he saw Young Man Afraid approaching with Good Weasel and He Dog on horseback. They were coming from the direction of the Soldier Town.

"Crazy Horse!" He Dog sang out. "We have found you!"

He got to his feet there in the shady overhang of the trees as the grasshoppers buzzed out in the bright splash of sunlight. "Found me? But I haven't been lost!"

"Grave news," Young Man Afraid announced, his mouth turned down.

From the hard look on their faces, he knew it must be serious. "Come rest, and we'll talk."

Tying off their ponies, the three came to the cool grass and sat with him, four old friends.

He asked, "This is because I changed my mind and will not be going east with Red Cloud?"

"No," Good Weasel replied. "The White Hat is very upset that you won't go, but this news is not about that."

He Dog said, "Young Man Afraid has been at the Soldier Town for the last two days."

"The half-blood translator who is friendly to us," Young Man Afraid explained, "he has been telling me what news has been coming over the white man's talking wires."

That was a relief. Nothing in regard to the white man could be so serious to him anymore. "What news of the *wasicus* would be of importance to me?" Crazy Horse snorted, pulling up some blades of grass between his fingers.

"Reports of a new war," Good Weasel declared.

"Who?" he demanded uneasily. "I thought that Sitting Bull had crossed the Medicine Line with his people long ago."

"The soldiers are not fighting the Hunkpapa," He Dog advised.

"Who then?" he asked. "Are there others still in the North Country who we don't know about? Our brothers and cousins who have not surrendered and fight on?"

Good Weasel shook his head.

But it was Young Man Afraid, the well-known Lakota diplomat, who answered, "The Nez Perce."

For a moment Crazy Horse could not remember who those people were. Then he finally answered, "Oh. They live far, far away to the west. Beyond the mountains. I have never fought any of them, although some Lakota have done battle against them when the Nez Perce came east to visit the Psatoka and hunt buffalo—"

"They are coming east again," He Dog confirmed. "That seems to be all the white men and soldier chiefs are talking about at the Soldier Town."

"So the Nez Perce will have a hunt of their own," Crazy Horse said. "We will go north and hunt too. There are enough buffalo—"

"I want you to understand that the soldiers are *chasing* the Nez Perce," Good Weasel interrupted. "Talk is that the army has been doing a lot of fighting while the Nez Perce fled their homelands for the buffalo country. The soldiers here are already talking about marching north to fight the Nez Perce when those Indians reach the land of the Psatoka."

Crazy Horse considered that for a long time, picking one green blade of grass from the ground at a time, tossing it aside before he picked another one. So on and so on, until he said, "If these people do come east to Psatoka hunting ground, and these soldiers go to stop them, then there will a lot of fighting near our old buffalo country."

"Where we want to go for our hunt," He Dog asserted.

"Soldiers and Psatoka and Nez Perce all mixed up in that country," Young Man Afraid said, wagging his head. "Three of our enemies already up there where we are going to do a little hunting before winter."

"This is soldier talk we must listen to very carefully," Crazy Horse declared. "Be sure that the young half-blood knows that we are thankful for all the news he can give us about the *wasicus* chasing our old enemies."

"What about Nellie?" He Dog asked. "She knows the white man's tongue like it was her own. Why don't you ask her if she would listen to any talk about the Nez Perce running toward the land of the Psatoka, how the army is trying to surround them?"

"Soldiers are coming from lots of places," Young Man Afraid said. "But so far they can't stop the Nez Perce. One fight after another, and the soldiers still haven't stopped them from coming this way."

"Soon enough," Crazy Horse said gravely. "One day soon the army will have enough soldiers in that country to surround our old enemies. The same way we won our first fights against the soldiers...until the white man wore us down."

Good Weasel agreed, "The same will happen to the Nez Perce."

"But Three Stars and the soldier chiefs might take away the promise for our hunt," He Dog said. "If the Nez Perce are coming into that country up north, the *wasicus* will not let us go up there to hunt buffalo."

"We must learn everything there is to know about these people fighting and fleeing the soldiers so far away," Crazy Horse said, hope ringing in his voice. "You must remember: if there is a chance that all the soldiers will be going to fight those enemies...perhaps we'll be free to make our own run to the North Country."

"Grouard, I want you to tell the chiefs why I called them to my office," instructed William Philo Clark.

The young lieutenant was nearly busting his buttons that morning in early August, unable to contain himself until he could watch the expressions on the Oglalas' faces when he told them the news just telegraphed him from General Crook's office in Omaha.

"This better be some good news," grumbled James Irwin, Indian agent.

"We're all due some good news," Clark agreed. "Maybe this will be what it takes to convince Crazy Horse again that he should agree to visit Washington City with Red Cloud's delegation."

"We best remind him that if he doesn't go," Irwin said, "he won't stand a ghost of a chance of getting an agency of his own...anywhere."

"Let's take first things first," Clark said soothingly. "If we give a little on something, perhaps he will change his mind again and be convinced that it's in his best interests to accompany the delegation when it departs for the east in October."

Irwin, a pinched and acerbic man to Clark, merely gave him a wave of his hand, gesturing for the lieutenant to proceed. If it hadn't been that General Crook needed to have Irwin sign off every move of this sort on the reservation, Clark would have called these chiefs to meet him over at Camp Robinson instead of gathering here, beneath an awning erected beside the agent's cramped office.

Looking over those who had answered his call to assemble, Clark was undeterred that Red Cloud had refused to show. The old chief was growing more and more indignant that Crazy Horse was being given all the more prestige.

"He's not even a chief!" Red Cloud had protested time and again.

"And for now you still aren't chief of the Oglala," Clark had always reminded him.

"You promised me that I would be raised to chief again if I brought you Crazy Horse," the Oglala needled the lieutenant.

"General Crook won't recognize you as leader until we've taken Crazy Horse to see the president," explained the lieutenant. "Once that is done, we expect Crazy Horse to return and be very cooperative with our efforts to pacify the Northern bands. He'll be given a little agency of his own—nothing of any consequence—and you will once more be our leader here."

Again Clark had emphasized that Red Cloud was the soldier's chief, the white man's chief. Like Spotted Tail was over the Brulé on his reservation. Both leaders were allowed to stay in power only so long as they performed as the white man dictated. Their rights to chieftainship did not come from the people they ruled, but from the distinction that they were the chiefs who the army officers believed would best follow the wishes of the white man. So Clark never lost an opportunity to remind Red Cloud that the only reason he was allowed to have any say over anything at the agency after Crook removed him from power almost ten months ago was that Red Cloud always did what Crook and Clark wanted of him. He was an obedient Oglala; that's why he would one day be returned to a position of prestige among the tribe.

As for Crazy Horse? Well, that was a pony of a different color. Right from the start, the war chief hadn't done much that Clark or Crook asked of him. Why, he hadn't even shown up for that first face-to-face meeting with the general back in May! On top of that, when it came time for rations to be doled out to his people, the highly suspicious Crazy Horse refused to make his mark in the agent's ledger. And what with him demanding his reservation before he went east, it appeared that all of their plans would go awry ... until Crazy Horse had suddenly reversed himself and agreed to go. Everything had been falling into place. Crook was ecstatic, and Clark was basking in the glow of success and the heady acclaim of his fellow officers, when word came that Crazy Horse had recanted. He had changed his mind again and would not go east until he was first given his agency in the Powder River country.

So the telegraph wires had hummed, not only with the faraway news of the pursuit of wild, breakaway bands of Nez Perce, but they buzzed with discussion between Crook and Clark as to how they could convince Crazy Horse it was in his best interests to be agreeable. The official go-ahead was given to grant the Northern hostiles something they had been wanting ever since they limped in during a rainy, soggy spring.

"General Crook," and Clark paused while Grouard translated for the Hunkpatila and those delegates Red Cloud had sent to the council on his behalf, "informed me yesterday that he has granted his official permission for the Oglala to take leave of their agency on a hunt ... for them to be gone from the reservation for a period of forty days."

Clark paused again, studying the copper faces as Grouard

translated the news into Sioux. Among the Hunkpatila, there wasn't one face that didn't register exceeding joy at the announcement. But ... in looking at the Red Cloud emissaries standing on the edges of the assembly, the lieutenant was not surprised that clouds seemed to darken the countenances of those who saw this as a dramatic and signal victory just handed the upstart Crazy Horse and his unreconstructed hostiles.

The lieutenant thought, *Perhaps Red Cloud would now think twice about dallying with the power of the White Hat!*

When Crook was here, Red Cloud gave the general all the deference his rank and power deserved. But the general wasn't at the agency all that much anymore. That meant that William Philo Clark was the power to be reckoned with when it came to making decisions that would affect the Oglala in general, and Red Cloud in particular. The chief had better give the lieutenant his due and toe the line ... because right now Clark was showing the Red Cloud camp that the White Hat held power over their lives, whether they were Hunkpatila or Bad Face Oglala. One of the most powerful weapons the chiefs had handed the lieutenant was their own petty jealousies and toxic envy for one another. When Crazy Horse surrendered, it created all the deeper a friction between the leaders—and Clark did everything he could to aggravate that friction. Once more he was proving the old maxim of divide and conquer.

"The trader will be allowed to sell you and your warriors ammunition for a limited time," Clark continued his electrifying announcement when Grouard had finished and turned back to him, "between now and the last day before you leave for the hunt."

The one he knew as He Dog got to his feet beside Crazy Horse, asking his question that Grouard translated.

"When will we start north on our hunt?"

"I haven't picked a specific date yet," Clark admitted. "But I will schedule it to begin early in September. In less than a full month."

Grouard translated that, and the smiles grew bigger

among the Crazy Horse people. Now they had something tangible to hang their hopes to. No Water, Woman's Dress, Red Dog, Little Wound, and the rest of Red Cloud's cronies grew more stony-faced than before while Clark discussed the specifics.

"We will have enough horses along to carry the meat and bring back the hides?"

Clark answered, "Yes. We will take as many horses along as it requires for you to hunt in the old way in that country."

Frank Grouard translated another question, "Our children and women will come along too?"

But the lieutenant didn't have an answer for that. There had never been any discussion with Crook on that matter of taking the whole village along.

Leaning forward, the half-breed translator whispered, "That's the way they hunt, Lieutenant. Bring their whole damned families."

"Now you've stepped in it," Irwin grumbled sourly. "You and Crook have stupidly put all our feet in it too!"

Scratching at his chin, Clark explained to Grouard, "Tell the chiefs that the general has not decided on that yet. But I will ask him if he will grant permission for the women to go along."

Soon enough the one called Little Hawk stood and petitioned, "We do not hunt without the women along. Our men hunt and make the kills. But the women are the ones who butcher the buffalo. They skin off the hides. They pack the meat and fold the hides onto the spare horses to carry back to our camp. We must bring in meat for our bellies this winter, and the robes to keep our people warm."

Looking Horse stood to make his point, "If the women come along with us on the hunt, who will stay behind with the children? There will be no one to watch over the little ones. Everyone must go. They all have a job to do when we chase down the buffalo."

Now the murmurs were growing, louder, as the Oglala leaders discussed it among themselves, as Red Cloud's Bad Face delegates grumbled contemptuously.

Finally Clark waved his arms, gesturing for silence. "Quiet! I must have quiet! This isn't something I can decide by myself. General Crook must tell me who has permission to go with you. As soon as I hear from him, I will call another council and tell you his decision."

He smiled, feeling a sense of accomplishment, and with that he dismissed them. After all, the chiefs seemed satisfied with his response to their concerns about their families. The Sioux leaders got to their feet, talking with one another, and moved off toward their ring horses being held by a crowd of younger men. Soon he was left alone with his translator and Irwin.

Furiously slapping both hands down on the thighs of his wool suit pants, the agent got to his feet beside his ladder-back chair. "I want you to understand that I am sending General Crook a strongly worded protest this very afternoon, Lieutenant."

"Protest?"

"The very thought of what you've proposed!" Irwin whined. "Granting these warriors permission to purchase ammunition from the trader. I'm sure Johnny Dear will be very happy about that!"

"Perhaps he will—"

"But I don't think Crook has even considered the possibility of danger," Irwin said as four of the Red Cloud delegates motioned Grouard over to their corner of the canvas awning. "Danger in selling ammunition to a captive people. Who the hell knows if those bullets are for hunting, or for murder."

"M-murder?" Clark echoed.

"Let them go on a buffalo hunt," Irwin argued. "Just like the old days . . . why, the next thing you know, they'll take up their savage practices once more. Just like the old days."

"You write your wire to the general," Clark agreed. "And I'll send it to him for you."

"You best see that you do," Irwin said. "I'll make sure others in Washington City know about this foolhardy plan of Crook's too."

"All the way to the top of the War Department?"

Irwin glared at Clark a moment. "By all means, Lieutenant. Just as high as I need to go to get the general's order rescinded."

Watching the agent stomp away around the corner of the log agency office, the lieutenant turned to start for his horse when Grouard and the five Oglala hurried over and stopped in a semi-circle around him.

"These men, they want to talk to you," Grouard explained, his eyes furtive, bouncing in one direction, searching in another.

"What do they want to talk over?"

"Want you to know I agree with 'em too," Grouard said. "Like I told you before. This hunt Crook is planning for 'em ain't a good idea. It will cause more bad than good."

"The ammunition that Agent Irwin is worried about?"

Wagging his head, Grouard said, "No. Red Cloud and his headmen think you and the general are making a very big mistake."

"With the hunt?"

"Yes. You allow Crazy Horse and his warriors to go on this hunt to their old war grounds," Grouard declared, "they won't come back at the end of your forty days."

For a moment Clark looked over the eyes of those four friends of Red Cloud. Then he fixed his gaze on Grouard once more. "What makes these leaders right and General Crook wrong?"

The interpreter snorted humorlessly. "Crook don't know any better that he's come up with a bad idea because he's a white man. But these chiefs... well, they damn well know what them Crazy Horse people are bound to pull once they're off the reservation—because they're Lakota themselves!"

CHAPTER SIXTEEN

RED CLOUD'S CAMP DOGS HAVE BEEN AMONG THE *WASICUS* for too long!" Crazy Horse snarled. "They have been loafers for so many winters it seems they have forgotten that when a Lakota makes a promise, he holds true to that vow . . . on his very life!"

The friends around him murmured their agreement that warm summer evening after his brother-in-law, Red Feather, came to tell Crazy Horse that among the bad whispers being spread about the Hunkpatila chief, now there was louder talk from the Bad Face leaders, bellowing like wounded buffalo calves, that it was very wrong for Three Stars and White Hat to approve the forthcoming hunt to the North Country. No longer content to whisper behind their hands, Red Cloud's allies were now spreading talk far and wide that the only reason the Crazy Horse people wanted to go north for a buffalo hunt with ponies, weapons, and their families along was so they could break out, take up the war road again . . . because the Northern People never had any intention of returning to the reservation when the scheduled allotment of four-times-ten days was done.

"Unlike Red Cloud and those at his elbows," growled Crazy Horse, thinking of his old nemesis, No Water, and Red Cloud's nephew, Woman's Dress, "we are men who keep our vows. The Hunkpatila will return from our hunt because we are men of honor!"

Little Hawk appeared dubious of their chances. "Nephew, we must convince the White Hat that Red Cloud's warnings are the whispers of a toothless old woman."

"Can't White Hat see the truth?" he asked angrily, thinking to himself, *Why can't the* wasicu *see the truth, see when he is being lied to and manipulated?*

"No, he can't see the truth," Little Hawk said with bitterness, "because Red Cloud has the white man's ears, and we do not."

For a long moment, Crazy Horse gazed in admiration at his father's brother. He thought of how Worm and his two Sicangu wives were living on Beaver Creek, having chosen to camp with Spotted Tail's people rather than staying with Crazy Horse on the Red Cloud Agency. Again and again it had made Crazy Horse angry, how the Oglala were not allowed to go visit friends and relatives at the other agency. Without the white man's permission, they were forbidden to travel down the White Earth River to visit Spotted Tail's agency. So it was that whenever Crazy Horse had some advice to ask of his father—realizing that there were far too many eyes watching him on both reservations—Little Hawk volunteered to ride in darkness to Beaver Creek, seeking out Worm's lodge in complete secret. Time and again Little Hawk had been successful in hiding from those who would alert the Sicangu chiefs—next then the chiefs would tell the agent, and finally the agent would tell the soldiers that one of the Northern People had been spotted where he was not supposed to be.

On his last trip to Spotted Tail's agency, Worm had admitted to Little Hawk how heartbroken he was that even the Sicangu chief was starting to talk against his own nephew, Crazy Horse. Not only were a growing number of Spotted Tail's people saying that Crazy Horse was a troublemaker...but in the last few days Spotted Tail himself had taken up Red Cloud's refrain that the Northern People would bring down on the heads of all Lakota the retribution of the army when they broke out and did not return from their hunt. Spotted Tail had even added his voice to that of Red Cloud in giving a warning to their agents: Three Stars must not allow the planned hunt!

How it had saddened Crazy Horse when Little Hawk told

him how Spotted Tail was talking so hard against his nephew: saying the soldier chiefs must take back their offer and tell the Northern People that everyone must stay in their place, on their reservation, and make a new life for themselves. No one could ever go back to the way they used to live.

On that last visit to see Worm, Little Hawk had waited out the following day, safe from prying eyes inside Worm's lodge, hidden behind the tightly closed lodgedoor, slipping away only when it was completely dark and Worm found the path to escape was clear. Little Hawk had dashed into the shadows, hurrying up Beaver Creek on foot until he reached the trees where he had tied his pony the night before. Riding all night to get back to Red Cloud's agency, Little Hawk brought a report to his nephew on everything he had learned from Worm.

The poisonous words being spoken about Crazy Horse on this very agency were spreading like glowing embers scattered by the wind on summer-dry grass. Miles away, more and more of Spotted Tail's Sicangu had begun to echo those Bad Face warnings hissed into the ears of the *wasicus* and soldiers.

"Crazy Horse will never be an agency Indian."

"He will forever stay a wild Northern warrior."

"Crazy Horse cannot be trusted."

"The Northern leader will always lie to a white man to get everything he can for himself."

"Ta'sunke Witko is going to bring terrible trouble down upon the heads of us all!"

"What will it take for me to get the attention of the white man's ears?" Crazy Horse asked his friends.

"Perhaps you must play at the white man's game the way Red Cloud has done?" He Dog suggested.

"Only Crazy Horse can answer that," Little Hawk responded with a wag of his head. "He must be true to the voice of his spirit."

"I speak the truth," Crazy Horse said. "While others tell lies about me, and make the *wasicu* believe them."

"It is easy for the white man to believe the bad words Red Cloud's friends tell them about you," Looking Horse said, "because they do not want to believe you could be a truthful man. The soldiers fought you for so long, they see you only as their enemy."

Crazy Horse nodded, saying, "And while I fought the soldiers, Red Cloud, No Water, and the rest stayed right here, loafing in the shade of the Soldier Town—friends and cronies to the *wasicus.*"

Kicking Bear said, "White Hat and the agent believe that Red Cloud's people should know you best, so they must surely speak of things that really are."

"Perhaps the time will come when we can show White Hat that our vow is our honor," Crazy Horse said grimly. "There was a time when I let myself think that we might stay on in the north country, to spend our winters on the Powder River, and live as free men. But maybe the best we can do for our people now is to go on this hunt with our families . . . and when our time is over, we will come back here. Just so we can show the *wasicus* that our word is who we are."

The face of Black Fox grew long and sad. "I don't know if we will have a chance to prove that to White Hat."

Crazy Horse's eyes touched his old friend. "The soldiers have decided to listen to those old women like Red Cloud and Spotted Tail who whimper against me?"

"Perhaps," Looking Horse said. "Or the hunt might be canceled because new reports have the Nez Perce escaping this way . . . at least until the soldiers lost track of them. If the army goes to fight a war in our hunting grounds, Three Stars and White Hat won't let us leave this reservation."

Crazy Horse asked, "Your heart tells you the white man is going to take back this hunt?"

But it was Black Fox who answered grimly, "Yes. The soldiers will refuse to let us go when it is time."

That made his heart go as cold as a stone. Eventually Crazy Horse said, "This means there will be no parfleches stuffed with dried buffalo to see us through the winter, no smoke-cured bladders of *wasna.** One more promise broken."

---

*Meat mixed together with fat and powdered bone meal.

"Is there anything any white man tells us that he will stand by!" Kicking Bear roared.

"I came here instead of going to my uncle's reservation with Touch-the-Clouds because Red Cloud brought me White Hat's promise for my own agency," Crazy Horse reminded them. "Now I must first go see the white man's grandfather before Three Stars will talk about our own agency in our own country. They dangle their empty words in front of my face. Telling me we can go on our hunt, then ripping that promise from us when it does not suit them. What can I believe when all around me the white man and my fellow Lakota are lying to me . . . lying *about* me?"

The night fell hushed, tree frogs softly cheeping by the river.

For some time Crazy Horse stared down at his hands, empty now when once they had carried on the fight for his people. Now they were idle, with nothing to do. "What is a man to do when he no longer has a clear enemy to fight? Now I am set upon by my own people, by all the old friends who once stood around me—like snapping wolves leaping in from all sides to slash at my hamstring?"

He Dog warned, "Watch who is at your back. Remember your vision. After all, death will take you from behind."

"Yes, old friend," agreed the impassioned Little Big Man. "All you can do is watch who is at your back."

These days He Dog did not know which Crazy Horse he would run into, which Crazy Horse he would end up talking to. Sometimes he would sit and smoke, recalling the old days they had spent as Shirt Wearers with his long-time warrior friend. And then there were the days when Crazy Horse's eyes seemed vacant, oft-times hollow, as if He Dog had never truly known the man behind them. So it was that He Dog watched with disappointment each time his old friend rode off alone for Crow Butte. There he might stay for the afternoon, or not return until the following day. Taking only his little pipe and a blanket, leaving Black Shawl and the trader's daughter behind so he could be by himself among the rocks.

The more Crazy Horse heard of the whispers people were making behind their hands, the more despondent He Dog's friend became. Red Cloud's cowardly whisperers had won too, because the Northern People had learned two days ago that their hunt had been taken away from them.

"No surprise," He Dog had told a despondent Crazy Horse. "We knew Red Cloud and his friends would steal the hunt from us."*

Angry, He Dog and Little Big Man had gone with Little Hawk to see the agency trader called Dear. As if he had been waiting there of a purpose, the half-blood Billy Garnett helped translate the exasperated white man's words.

"He wants to sell you weapons and bullets," Garnett spoke in Lakota, then pointed to a paper the trader held in his hands. "But this tells him he will get into trouble with the soldiers. There won't be a hunt, so now he can't sell you any guns or bullets."

Little Big Man had snatched the paper away from the white man, roaring at Garnett, "Tell this *wasicu* I am an Indian policeman! I am not his enemy! I am a metalbreast and he cannot treat us this way!" But as long as Little Big Man stared at the paper, he still could not read the marks made upon it. Finally the *akicita* begrudgingly turned the paper back over to the trader.

"No hunt. No trip to visit the east," He Dog later reported to Crazy Horse. "And surely no reservation of our own. Winter will be hard living here, camped with all these people."

"Already there isn't enough to eat," Crazy Horse murmured gravely. "How will the *wasicus* feed our old and the very small when the snows come?"

The day after they were told the hunt had been taken away from them, Billy Garnett came with two other interpreters to tell the Hunkpatila that they had to move their camp right beside Red Cloud's.

---

*You will recall that He Dog is Red Cloud's nephew.

"Move our village?" He Dog asked, "Why, when we are comfortable right here opposite the mouth of White Clay Creek?"

Garnett shrugged, his face a little sheepish with apology to his mother's people. "The white men want you to be closer to the agency. And they have made plans to hold another council with all the chiefs."

"So Three Stars is making another visit to us?" Little Big Man asked, his tone provocative. "Is that why we are going to hold another council?"

"The *wasicus* come to take something else from us?" demanded Little Hawk.

"After you move your lodges next to those of Red Cloud's people," Garnett explained, "there will be a big council to talk about what the white man will do for the Oglala people."

"They can let us have our hunt," He Dog grumbled as he stared at the interpreter's back when the half-blood had turned and started away.

"They can give me my own agency," Crazy Horse said. "I will not go sit in a council with the bad-faced one who sends his messengers to talk against me to the agent, convincing the white man not to hold the feast in my honor. No, I will not go. Nor will I move my camp where they tell me I have to go."

As the stars twinkled over them that night, the headmen sat and discussed the White Hat's sudden demand that the Hunkpatila move their lodges beside Red Cloud's camp. Crazy Horse quietly declared his opposition, then fell more subdued than ever, and for the longest time too, listening to the speeches of the others.

"What you do is up to you," he said to them with undisguised disgust. "I am not moving so I can live closer to the bad-faced one who sent his messengers to talk against me to the agent. Why should I sit in a council to honor the man who lied about me so the agent would decide against a feast in my honor?"

"All the headmen are coming," advised Young Man Afraid, peacemaker among the three Oglala bands.

"Why should I do anything good for the whites who have lied to me?" Crazy Horse countered. "Why should I go live beside the Oglala who continue to lie about me?"

"The white man wants us to be more like Red Cloud's lazy lapdogs," Little Hawk said.

He Dog thought and thought on this as the discussion dragged on. And for the first time in his life, he found himself dismayed that he was considering putting his feet on a path different from the one Crazy Horse was taking. Perhaps, he thought, since they had surrendered, giving up their weapons and their horses, talking was indeed better than fighting. If their women and children were surrounded by soldiers and agency Lakota, maybe it was better to talk, negotiate, hammer out the best bargain they could with the *wasicus*.

"When the White Hat sends the interpreter to tell me I have my own agency in the North Country," Crazy Horse explained steadfastly, "*then* I will move my camp. But until the white man gives me what he has promised . . . I see no reason for me to take my people anywhere just to please the *wasicus*."

"Even to take them across the river to camp closer to Red Cloud's village?" He Dog dared ask his old friend.

"Those of you who want to raise your lodges next to Red Cloud's people," Crazy Horse said, his eyes steady on He Dog, "are free to move across the river. And those who think there has been enough of this empty talk and these worthless promises . . . can stay here with me."

Wagging his head, He Dog said, "This is not the time to make a stand, my old friend. We have no weapons, no way to defend our women and little ones when the soldiers come to punish us for not doing as they say and moving close to Red Cloud."

For a moment, Crazy Horse seemed to study him. "Y-you are saying you will go?"

"Yes," He Dog replied sadly. "And everyone who doesn't

want your wives and children cut down by soldier guns should move across with me."

"You seem most troubled by your decision, my friend," Crazy Horse said.

"Something bad is coming," He Dog warned, sensing the presence of something he could not put his finger on. He was a fighting man, not a mystic or a seer. Just a simple man who admitted, "I don't know what will happen. But in recent days there are too many signs that point to trouble already coming this way."

Crazy Horse asked, "Is this because of the news that the Nez Perce are bringing a war to our old hunting ground?"

"No," and He Dog wagged his head. "Not that."

"Perhaps you are worried because rumors say that Sitting Bull will strike across the Medicine Line and cause troubles for us down here?"

"No, what I feel does not have to do with someone else...nothing to do with some*where* else," He Dog attempted to explain the unexplainable. "Trouble is...very, very close."

"Trouble will come this winter because the agent doesn't have enough flour for us," Crazy Horse said. "Trouble will come because we are not allowed to hunt the buffalo for our winter meat. Yes, He Dog...trouble will come because the starvation that is coming will drive a wedge between old friends."

He Dog understood immediately. For the first time in their many winters of friendship, Crazy Horse was telling him that he could not think for himself. Drawing himself up with a long sigh, He Dog decided he must speak to all that they had been as friends for many, many summers.

"If we cannot be friends because I choose to move where the white man tells me to go," He Dog said quietly, but with firm resolve, "then so be it. We will no longer be friends—"

"I am no white man!" Crazy Horse interrupted, taken aback as if his old friend had just insulted him. "No man loses my friendship simply because he decides he wants to live in a different place. There is plenty of room for all of us. Camp wherever you wish to raise your lodge."

"Even if I choose to cross the river?" He Dog asked.

"Yes. I won't be like the white man drawing a line in the dirt, saying to you, 'Those on this side of the line are my friends. Those on that side are my enemies.' No, He Dog— only the white man can cause us to disagree like this," he said very sadly as the listeners around that council circle fell silent. "Only the white man has ever caused the Lakota to go against Lakota. To pit the Oglala against...his fellow Oglala."

In that council, the headmen were hushed, considering his words, but before anyone else could speak, Crazy Horse said something that shocked many at that gathering: "I am not a leader anymore. Better that Little Hawk lead you. I don't want to have others depend upon me anymore. Those days are past, long ago now. For the rest of my time, I want to live quietly. So the rest of you can choose to live where you want. As for me, perhaps I could find another place to finish my days. Maybe out there...somewhere in the hills among the rocks and the trees."

He Dog understood. Crazy Horse was saying he no longer thought he should live among people. Maybe it really was better for him to live among his sacred rocks, *inyan.* Up close to the sky. *Only the rocks and the sky last forever,* he thought. And the days when he and his old friend Crazy Horse were free men were behind them now. On the face of Crazy Horse, in the way Crazy Horse held himself, there was such a profound gloom. It tore at He Dog's heart so.

As he watched Crazy Horse get up slowly and leave without any word of parting, He Dog felt an immense melancholy wash through him with cold waves of yearning for the old days of the hunt and the chase, the fight and the fierce camaraderie.

What use was there for men like them anymore?

CHAPTER SEVENTEEN

Late August 1877

BY TELEGRAPH

KANSAS.

An Imposing Military Funeral at Fort Leavenworth.

LEAVENWORTH, KS., August 3.—Yesterday evening the Chicago, Rock Island and Pacific brought the remains of Captains Yates and Custer, Lieuts. McIntosh, Smith, Calhoun and Worth. The bodies were placed in the Post chapel, and a guard of honor was stationed and remained during the night. This morning a large number of people visited the chapel and viewed the caskets containing the remains of the honored dead...The fact that the lamented dead had lived at this garrison and were well known and honored by our people created an intense feeling of sympathy among the entire community. Five of the bravest soldiers in the army have thus been tenderly placed in their final resting place in the beautiful Leavenworth cemetery with all the honors due to men of noble and daring deeds, and their memory will be cherished by every patriot in the land.

SEAMUS QUIETLY SLID HIS LEGS OFF THE LOW PALLET OF blankets and buffalo robes, reached over to snag his boots, then slowly stood up. For a moment he gazed down at the two of them, sleeping on their tick stuffed thickly with tall, fragrant grass he had gathered up close to the white bluffs. Sighing with contentment, Donegan silently parted the canvas flaps and stepped out of the tent.

A few yards away he settled on an upturned chunk of cottonwood log and stuffed the cuffs of his britches into the tall stovepipe tops of his prairie boots. He stood, briefly looking over their little camp beside Soldier Creek, then straightened his hat, and started off for Benjamin S. Paddock's saloon, located north of the laundress's quarters and the post hospital, where his friend might well be ready for a drink.

"No, I can't join you right now," Valentine McGillycuddy said with a real measure of disappointment. "We've had us a batch of new ones come on sick call this afternoon."

"You come over for a drink later?"

The doctor nodded. "Think I can slip away sometime, Seamus. Can't say when it'll be though."

"No matter," Donegan said. "If it ain't today, I'll buy you a drink tomorrow."

McGillycuddy asked, "How's Samantha?"

"A little stronger every day," he said with relief. "Another couple of weeks and she thinks she'll be strong enough to ride to Deadwood."

Quickly glancing over his shoulder through the open doorway, McGillycuddy turned back to the Irishman and inquired, "She really going to let you put your hands to digging gold?"

"Fastest way I can see to getting a roof over this family's heads."

"Just remember they haven't driven all the wild Sioux onto the reservation, Seamus."

"Better them Injins . . . than tryin' to drive the wild and thirsty Irish onto some dry and parched reservation, Doc!"

McGillycuddy winked, grinning as he moved away, stepping back through the open doorway, entering the ward where two hospital stewards were bathing soldiers' faces down both sides of two long rows of tented beds.

Benjamin Paddock's saloon was cool and shady that afternoon, and damn near empty too. Through the open doorway drifted voices of some officers' wives discussing the colors of cloth and dress patterns with the trader from the store attached to the log saloon. Paddock had served as post sutler since January, a franchise for which he paid three cents per soldier per month. In turn he could take as much wood as he needed from the ricks of post timber brought in by the enlisted men. It was to the common soldier that he mostly dealt in whiskey, while he carried canned oysters and the latest fashions for the officers' wives.

Donegan's eyes adjusted to the shadows as he scanned the room, eventually finding only one thirsty soldier elbowed over his empty glass at a small, wobbly table. When Seamus stepped up to the unmanned plank bar to wait, the soldier spoke.

"Paddock told me he'd be comin' right back," he said without looking at the Irishman. "I told him to take his time with them ladies, for it didn't matter none to me."

He eyed the much-older man, figuring that he could easily have been a veteran before the War Between the States. But, for some reason, the soldier had climbed no higher in rank than a private. Donegan asked, "This late in the month, I'll wager you already run outta your whiskey money."

Finally raising his head to look Seamus in the eye, the soldier said, "Ain't that. Seems I run outta whiskey."

"We'll have him here shortly," Donegan promised.

"Don't make no difference to me. Sutler can't serve me nary a splash for 'nother three hours."

Taking a step closer to the soldier's table, Seamus leaned an elbow on the bar and asked, "What's with them three hours?"

"The general's new rule for us soldiers," he explained, looking back down into the last film of whiskey at the bottom of his cloudy glass. "Been less'n a week since the rule started, as I recollect now. General and his fine officers was havin' too much a problem with us enlisted boys, so it seems."

"You in the Fourteenth?"

The private nodded. "Footsoldier I am. F Company."

"So the post commander got the right to say how much his men can drink?"

"And when we can drink too," the soldier explained. "Only two drinks a day, an' there must be three hours atween 'em."

Seamus wagged his head. "Don't seem right, not letting a

sojur get good an' drunk when there's nothing else out here
for him to do."

"That's a problem, least according to Bradley."

"Br-Bradley?" Seamus repeated, that name touching a
raw nerve.

"General. Post commander, that one," the soldier declared.

"You know his first name?"

"Don't think I ever heard it. He ain't commander of the
Fourteenth. Makes no goddamned anyway....I'm just a
footsoldier."

"Got any idea where this Bradley come from?" Donegan
inquired. "Where he served ten years ago?"

With a shake of his head, the old soldier ceremonially
raised his cloudy glass and slowly licked at the last dribble
of his precious whiskey with his tongue. Closing his eyes, he
appeared to enjoy it immensely. When he opened them
again, he set his glass upon the rocky table and stood,
sweeping up his dusty kepi and plopping it down askew on
top of his disheveled graying hair.

"No. Don't know nothing but walking and shooting. I
does some sentry duty. Don't ever know nothing 'bout the
officers."

"But you got a name, sojur," Seamus said, holding out his
hand.

For a brief moment the man stared down at the civilian's
big hand, then took it and began to shake. "William Gentles.
Private: F Company, Fourteenth Infantry. Born County Ty-
rone. That's in Ireland, I'll have you know."

He smiled hugely as they let go their grips. "By the by,
I'm a lad born in County Kilkenny."

"You don't say!" He leaned close and whispered, "You
ever serve you a hitch in this goddamned army?"

"Army of the Potomac," Seamus said proudly. "Sheridan's Army of the Shenandoah too."

"You wasn't footsoldier, eh?"

"Horse. Took almost two years—then I made my
sergeant's stripes."

"Officers curse at me a lot," Gentles admitted. "Maybe why I'm still a private an' never got no higher in grade. Listen, friend—my fellows call me Willy."

The tall Irishman said, "So Willy it's gonna be. I'm Seamus Donegan."

"I seen you around," he stated, tugging his kepi down on his unruly hair, then sighed, "Time for me to find my bunk. Standing guard again come dark."

"Sentry duty is about the worst duty a man can have."

"Bradley has us stand four two-hour reliefs," Gentles explained. "Most times I get my eight hours off to have a drink and crawl into my bunk for a nap before I stand another eight hours at one of the other sentry posts."

"Two eight-hour walks in a twenty-four-hour day?"

"Yup. It beats digging latrines." His face went sad, a bit lonely too. "Beats getting hit with a lead ball. I took a wound at Pilot Knob in 'sixty-two. That's in Missouri. Damn if them Rebs didn't give us hell."

"When you come to Amerikay?"

Gentles's eyes grew wistful as he said, "I was all of twenty-six, strong as a country ox. Back to 'fifty-five that was. After I couldn't find much work, I signed up—come west to serve in the Mormon War under Albert Sidney Johnston. Now there was a general could grind Bradley under his heel any day o' the week."

"Thought all of the Fourteenth was tranferred outta here."

The old soldier's face went sheepish as he began to explain, "I got in trouble with the whiskey, I did. Landed my arse in the guardhouse for twenty days of hard time.* When

---

*On 13 August 1877, Private William Gentles was court-martialled for "unauthorized absence from his company." He was sentenced to twenty days at hard labor, in addition to his forfeiture of one month's pay ($12.00). Although he was not released to return to his duties as sentry until 3 September, I have taken license here to have him meeting our fictional hero, Seamus Donegan, here at Benjamin Paddock's saloon at Camp Robinson the last few days of August.

I got out, my company was gone, pulled out, shipped back to Utah. So Bradley keeps me round to stand sentry duty—a lot of it at that guardhouse where I rotted for twenty days and twenty nights of stinkin' hell."

"So you been a sojur more'n twenty years now?"

The old man shrugged as he ran the back of his hand under his reddened nose. "It ain't much, but it's all I can do. The army, soldierin' . . . it's what I am."

Behind the old soldier at the open doorway Seamus spotted Frank Grouard trudging up on foot.

"Maybe next time I can buy you a drink, Willy."

The soldier smiled and held out his hand to shake again. "I could tell you was a soldier once."

"Horse."

"Don't make no matter to me," Gentles replied with a grin. "Just had a notion you was a soldier once."

He watched the two of them pass just outside the door. Gentles gave no greeting to the dark-skinned half-blood interpreter, and Grouard made no effort to address the soldier as he stopped just inside the doorjamb and looked about, letting his eyes become adjusted.

"Well, I'll be damned, if it ain't the Irishman I find squattin' here in this whiskey hole!"

"C'mon over here, Frank—and help me hold this bar down till the trader gets here."

"I'm coming right now, fellas," Benjamin Paddock said as he hurried in from the store. "If it ain't canned oysters for a captain's wife, its a bolt of red material for a major's wife. What can I do for you fellas?"

Seamus turned toward the sutler. "This new rule the post commander put on this place—it mean us civilians too?"

Paddock shook his head. "Naw. General Bradley issued those orders for his soldiers. Maybe gonna cut down some of the wild drinking they do soon as they get their pay. Causing trouble, raising hell, getting thrown in the guardhouse for it. Some of 'em having to stand extra guard duty or dig new latrines."

That made Seamus shudder. He'd dug enough slip-trenches before in his time. Hands blistered and back aching, standing over a long hole scratched out of the ground, the stench so strong it made a man's eyes water, slowly filling in the latrine one shovelful of dirt at a time.

"What's it gonna be?"

He looked at Grouard and said, "My friend and I would like three fingers of your finest whiskey."

"Finest?" Frank responded in surprise.

"I got hard money," and Donegan patted the back pocket of his britches.

"Good whiskey it is," Paddock said, bending down to work at a padlock he kept on a cupboard behind the bar.

For a moment longer Seamus stared at the sutler's back; then he asked, "This Bradley, your post commander. You know his first name?"

"Luther," the trader answered. "Why?"

The realization sent a shiver through him. "We met long time ago."

"You serve under him in the war?" Grouard asked.

"No. We was both up in Montana Territory together. Ten years ago."

Rising with a bottle in his hand, Paddock asked, "Where was that?"

"On the Bighorn. Post called C. F. Smith."*

"That's where you served under him?" Frank observed.

Wagging his head, Seamus said, "I was a civilian there. Haycutter. Bradley wasn't my boss. That was a fella named Al Colvin. He'd been a Johnny Reb in the war."

"Damn them southerners anyway," Paddock growled, pulling the cork out of the bottle.

"Colvin was a good man, the sort I'd want to stand at my back anytime," he argued. "As for Bradley—"

"Grouard!"

They both turned in surprise to find Lieutenant William P. Clark lunging through the open doorway, squinting as he left the bright sunlight behind.

---

*Red Cloud's Revenge, vol. 2, the Plainsmen Series.

"Looks like I won't get to buy you that drink after all, Frank," Seamus said as Grouard took a moment to peer longingly at his empty glass.

"Pour us," Grouard ordered the trader, turning his back on the lieutenant.

"General Bradley needs you, Grouard," Clark instructed as he stepped over to the bar, giving the Irishman a long appraisal.

"To translate during afternoon tea?"

Seamus heard the bottle clink against the rim of Grouard's glass.

"No, dammit," Clark growled. "I got He Dog to come in to talk. He's broke off from Crazy Horse, so I'm gonna try to figure what's really up with Crazy Horse these days."

"He Dog?" Seamus asked as Paddock poured him some whiskey.

Frank explained, "He was the one I told you about winter before last. The reason I run off from the Oglala. Been best friends with Crazy Horse."

"Not anymore. You coming, Grouard?" Clark demanded, standing there with his balled fists on his hips.

"Man can't finish his whiskey?"

"Not when General Bradley's got business with He Dog about these rumors Crazy Horse is about to break out," Clark said snappishly.

"Mind if I come along?" Seamus suddenly asked.

Grouard turned to Clark, then said, "Don't make me no mind. He can come, can't he, Lieutenant?"

After appraising the tall civilian down and up, Clark said, "Just so you come now, Grouard."

With that both of the civilians tossed back their whiskey and slammed their heavy-bottomed glasses on the plank counter, as Donegan scratched into his pocket for the coin.

"I couldn't do that with the saddle varnish you serve us usual," Grouard complained. "But that was some fine whiskey, Ben Paddock." He turned to Seamus as he put on his wide-brimmed hat. "Thanks for a taste of what officers like Lieutenant Clark here get to swallow all the time."

Through the trees and across the grass they followed the officer in a fast walk across the short distance that brought them to the post commander's office. As they stepped onto the porch and through the open door, Donegan recognized Bradley immediately. Ten years older, and a bit paunchier too, but it was the same man who had nearly cost the lives of his quartermaster's employees back in August of 1867. The officer glared at Grouard, but gave only a cursory glance at the tall Irishman, who slipped back to a corner where he could stand out of the way during this parley. There was only one Indian in the office. Dark-skinned, much more so than the one called Crazy Horse, Seamus decided. He could even smell the grease on the warrior's braids, so close were they in this room.

As Grouard and Clark went to stand between Bradley and He Dog, Seamus noticed the warrior giving him a sidelong look of appraisal.

This had been Crazy Horse's best friend. Chances were he had been in the same huge war party that pinned them down for a long summer day at the Crazy Woman Crossing back in '66. And a few months later, up on that snowy jut of land when the Sioux and Cheyenne massacred Fetterman and eighty brave men. Surely when Crazy Horse got his warriors to fight like disciplined cavalry against Major Royall's retreating troops at the Rosebud. There was no doubt this He Dog had watched the fall of Custer's five companies at the Little Bighorn, maybe even led part of the attack on Crook's cavalry at Slim Buttes later that summer. And the last time the two of them might have been close enough for Seamus to hit with a bullet could have been at Battle Butte, when Miles's Fifth Infantry drove off Crazy Horse's warriors into the teeth of a howling blizzard.

So this was the mighty He Dog.

It was plain to see just how uncomfortable the warrior and Grouard were at that moment, brought so close together after all the shadows of their tangled history were resurrected.

"Make sure he understands that I appreciate him coming

to see me," Bradley was saying. "Can't be easy slipping away from Crazy Horse's camp these days."

Grouard waited for a reply, then said, "Says he don't live in Crazy Horse's camp now. When you called for a council, Crazy Horse didn't want to talk. Didn't want to move like they was ordered to. But He Dog brought his people across the river to camp near Red Cloud—like the White Hat asked him to."

"So He Dog and Crazy Horse aren't friends anymore?" Clark asked.

"They're still friends," Grouard grumbled. "Shirt Wearers, he wanted me to remind you. But Crazy Horse decided to stay at his old camp, and He Dog decided he would give some talk a chance to work."

"Talk?" Clark asked.

"He Dog figures talk is better than fighting."

Bradley nodded, staring at the warrior's eyes. "Does he know I was the soldier chief who gave Crazy Horse a fine knife in a sheath?"

"He knows of the knife. Crazy Horse wears it all the time now," Grouard translated.

"Tell him I'll give him one too," Bradley offered coyly. "If he's helpful to us."

He Dog nodded when Grouard explained that to him in Sioux.

"So ask him my question," Bradley instructed. "Since Crazy Horse did not obey the orders to move his camp closer to Red Cloud's village, is it true what Red Cloud, Spotted Tail, and many other chiefs fear—that Crazy Horse is planning to make a break off this reservation?"

They all waited while the words were translated into Sioux, then watched how He Dog's eyes slowly moved to touch Bradley, then Clark, and finally he turned his head sideways to look at the civilian standing back in the corner of the office. Finally the warrior spoke.

"He Dog says Crazy Horse will hold to his word," Grouard said. "He came to the agency to make peace. So he will keep the peace. He won't break his word and run away."

"Then why is Crazy Horse refusing to do what I ordered

him?" Bradley demanded, his jaw muscles working.

The warrior spoke, and his words were translated, "'Crazy Horse has a strong medicine. The most powerful medicine I ever knew among our people. Maybe . . . I think Crazy Horse's medicine is telling him something. Warning him. Telling him to beware of coming across the river and living with Red Cloud's Oglalas.'"

"What could be his suspicions?" Clark asked.

And instead of verbalizing an answer, He Dog only shrugged. Then he spoke almost in a whisper to Grouard.

The interpreter said, "He wants to go now. If your talk is done, he wants to go."

"He won't tell us his suspicions?" Clark demanded.

Grouard tried again, but He Dog just stared at a spot on the wall behind the officers and said nothing.

"I don't think he's going to tell you anything more, Mr. Clark," Bradley observed.

"Damn him," the lieutenant said. "I bloody well want to know what's making Crazy Horse's *medicine* so suspicious now!"

He Dog spoke again, clearly irritated; then Grouard translated. "He wants to go, General."

"Yes," Bradley said. "Tell him he can go."

Seamus watched the warrior wheel about and leave the office. Outside he heard He Dog lead his pony away from the front of the log structure on the gravel.

"He didn't like being here with me," Grouard explained. "That's why he wanted to go, why he wasn't going to tell you any more. Maybe you better get yourselves another translator next time you wanna talk with that one."

"You and he know each other?" Clark asked.

Grouard stepped over to the open doorway, staring out at the bright sunlight, watching the warrior walk his pony before He Dog leaped onto its back and started it east toward the White River, away from the grounds of Camp Robinson. "We go back some, yeah."

Seamus came to stand beside the interpreter, watching the Indian ride away.

"Who are you?" Bradley demanded.

When Donegan and Grouard turned, the officer was just settling into his chair behind a desk, its top cleared but for two neat stacks of paper pushed to one side.

Donegan saw the colonel's eyes on him. "Me?"

"Yes, you," Bradley said. "I take it you're a friend of my translator here."

"Him and me, we go back a ways too," Frank explained as he and the Irishman stepped back to the middle of the room.

While Clark settled on the edge of the commander's desk, Bradley's eyes burned into Donegan's until he asked, "Do I know you?"

"I doubt you'd remember me." Seamus steeled himself, feeling the flush of a ten-year-old anger.

"Then, we have met," the officer said, laying one white hand atop the desk and spreading out the fingers.

"Yes."

"And where was that?"

"Fort C. F. Smith, Montana Territory."

For a moment that brought surprise to Bradley's face. Then he asked, "You served under me at Fort Smith, did you?"

"I'm glad I never had to serve under you anywhere, General Bradley," he said low and even, using the officer's brevet, or ceremonial rank, a distinction awarded by the army for some act of meritorious service or bravery, perhaps courage under fire. But Seamus knew the army hadn't awarded this brevet for courage in the face of the enemy.

The officer's second hand suddenly shot to the top of the desk to lie beside the first as Clark pushed himself away from the desk and stood the instant Donegan's slur had been uttered.

"I . . . I beg your pardon, civilian," Bradley said with a stammer, his jaw jutting haughtily. "Did I understand that you were at Fort Smith, but are glad you never served under me?"

"I was a quartermaster's employee for the better part of a

year," Donegan explained. "Worked around the fort: digging picket posts, raising walls, seeing to stock, and when spring came, I went to work with Al Colvin's bunch...out in the hayfield."

Bradley's eyes narrowed. "Now I remember you. Your name eludes me, but I remember you and Colvin—that whole unruly civilian bunch." The officer turned to explain to Clark. "We had some rebellious workers cutting hay several miles from our post during the summer of 1867."

Clark tore his eyes off the Irishman to ask, "You were post commander at Fort Smith on the Bozeman Trail, sir?"

With a nod, the officer continued, "Early in August, as I remember, the Indians gathered for a mass attack on Fort Phil Kearny, and another mass gathered to attack us."

"But the Injins hit our hayfield corral first," Donegan explained, turning to Clark, having seen the expression of keen and unequivocal interest cross Grouard's face. "Even when we managed to send a rider racing them four miles back to the fort after more'n three hours of fighting, he found the fort gates locked!"

"I had perfect reason to believe that my post might come under attack," Bradley said coolly to Clark.

"Because Cap'n Hartz come down from the side of the mountain—where he could see the Injins riding round and round our corral," Seamus growled, glancing at Grouard. "But after he told you what he'd seen, you locked the gate and didn't send out any relief to us! Not even a patrol to come find out what become of us!"

"I had a supply of ammunition to protect," Bradley protested, turning to Clark. "If those Sioux had gotten that ammunition—"

"Turns out," Donegan interrupted, turning to Clark himself, "that it took us civilians to hold off them hundreds of Injins...till Bradley screwed up enough courage to act like a real soldier—"

"I resent that remark!" the colonel roared, bolting to his feet so fast that his chair went spinning, clattering into the log wall behind him.

"Maybe we'd better go," Grouard recommended as he took a couple steps toward the door.

Clark glared at the tall civilian, saying, "Do you know that General Bradley could have you thrown in the guard-house for your slur against his character?"

"I damn well know the army's covered up his cowardice," Donegan said, then saw the red rise to the cheeks of the in-furiated colonel. "So there ain't no way to prove it to you. Just his word against mine."

"The word of a . . . a mule-skinner?" Bradley snarled.

"'Cept if you ever run onto Captain Hartz, or maybe Major Burt," Seamus said to Clark. "I fought with Burt at the Rosebud."

"You're dismissed!" Clark said suddenly as Bradley started around the side of his desk, hunched over in fury. The lieutenant coyly stepped in front of his commanding officer. "I suggest you make yourself scarce on this military post, or you might find yourself thrown off."

"No, wait," Bradley ordered, his eyes become serpentine, his voice calm and cold. "I remember Donegan now. After Carrington was demoted and removed from command at Fort Phil Kearny, you were shipped up to Fort C. F. Smith. We learned you spent quite a bit of your time in the guard-house down there at Fort Kearny. I remember it now: drunk and disorderly, insubordination to officers, unruly and unbe-coming conduct—"

"Only with puffed-up braggarts like them who went against Colonel Carrington," Donegan said. "I worked hard for you, General Bradley. I gave you more'n a day's work for a day's wage while I served at Fort Smith. But you . . . how can a man like you sleep at night?"

Bradley whirled on his heel and leaped behind his desk, jerking open a drawer.

"I'm not armed, General," Seamus warned, holding his arms out from his side.

"But if you do not leave this very minute," Bradley vowed as he pulled out a long, slim cheroot from that drawer, rolling it between his white fingers, "you may well be spending the remainder of the summer behind the bars in *my* guardhouse."

"C'mon, Frank," Seamus said as he turned, laying a hand on the back of Grouard's shoulders. "Let's go finish that drink we was having when this soldier business came up."

CHAPTER EIGHTEEN

Wasutun Wi
MOON WHEN ALL THINGS RIPEN, 1877

BY TELEGRAPH

News from the Indian War.

WASHINGTON.

General Sherman's Report: Pittsburgh Wants a Garrison.

WASHINGTON, August 4.—General Sherman, in a letter
to the secretary of war, says: "With the new post at the fork
of Big and Little Horn rivers and that at the mouth of the
Tongue river, occupied by enterprising garrisons, the Sioux
Indians can never regain that country, and they can be
forced to remain at their agency or take refuge in the
British possessions. The country west of the new post has
good country and will rapidly fill up with emigrants, who
will, in the next ten years, build up a country as strong and
as capable of self defense as Colorado..."

"WHAT ARE THOSE TWO FAT *WASICUS* CALLING ME?" CRAZY
Horse asked his second wife, as he gazed at the two big-
bellied white men waving to him from behind a half-dozen
young warriors who stood barring the visitors' way.

There weren't so many of the Hunkpatila who had remained with him in this village anymore. So many had followed He Dog, moving their lodges across the river to camp
near Red Cloud's people, just as the White Hat had ordered
them to. *Like He Dog*, he thought, *they must fear that trouble
is coming soon...and they don't want to be near me when
trouble shows up.*

"These men are calling you a name used for important soldier chiefs," Nellie Laravie explained.

"What is that word? Say it in the tongue of the white man."

"General," she said and he began to silently try out the term. "They're calling you General Crazy Horse. One of them just called you Mister," and she said that last word in the white man's language as well.

"Are both of those words good talk?"

She flashed him her dark, liquid eyes while Black Shawl came up to stand near them in the morning shade beside the lodge. "Yes," Nellie said. "You are the only leader they want to have sit for them and take your . . . your—"

"These are more of the men who bring the shadow boxes?" he demanded, flushing with irritation.

"Yes," she answered, refusing to look at Black Shawl's face. "You see those two horses they brought with them? They have their shadow boxes tied on the horses. These white men are ready to capture your image."

"No!" he growled. "The white man takes everything from me. He has taken my country. And he's taken my freedom—"

"It is just a picture of you," Nellie cooed. "So you can see how others see you."

He fingered the long scar on the left side of his face and said, "I can peek into a woman's looking glass to see my face. I do not need these *wasicus* to make a picture of me. No. They have taken almost everything from me. Their sickness took my daughter. . . . Then their bullets took my brother too."

"Let me go explain it to them," Nellie suggested, taking hold of her husband's hand. "Someone should tell them why you don't want this."

"Because I don't want them to take my spirit away and hold it in their little shadow boxes," he hissed, muscles growing tense along his shoulders. "Isn't it enough that they hold my body prisoner here on this tiny patch of ground, that these fat-bellied white men shouldn't try to capture my spirit too?"

"I will go tell them," she said softly, taking a step away.

"Yes. Go tell these *wasicus* never to come back with their shadow boxes again."

He watched her move away, her hips swaying beneath the cloth trader's dress, its colorful fabric shifting from side to side over her rounded buttocks. He liked watching the half-blood woman walking, for it stirred something inside him, causing him to remember how the skin of those buttocks felt in his hands whenever they coupled.

Turning his back on the white men, Crazy Horse said to Black Shawl, "I thought these shadow catchers had stopped coming."

"It has been a long time since they have troubled you, yes."

"At first, after we came to this place, it seemed they came to beg and plead with me almost every day," Crazy Horse muttered, glancing over his shoulder at the young woman, watching her talk with the two white men. "But she will know what to say to them. She knows their tongue as well as we know ours."

"She is half-wife, husband," Black Shawl reminded, an edge of jealousy in her voice. "So too is her heart."

He watched Black Shawl whirl around and flee to the shadows of their lodge that late morning. Then he raised a hand to shade his eyes and watched Nellie as she waved farewell to the pair of white men and they turned their horses away. She wasn't long in returning to him, both of her hands clenched in front of her like fighting fists.

"I have something for you, husband!" she squealed in delight, her eyes searching for Black Shawl. "Where did she go?"

"Inside," he said, not caring that Black Shawl was angry with him or jealous of the trader's daughter. "What did they give you? Something to bribe me into letting them capture my spirit in their little boxes?"

Nellie stepped close, so close she brushed her hip and thigh against him. He felt the surge of desire that always came with being next to her.

"Here," she whispered, holding up her left hand and

opening the fingers slowly, like they were being peeled back. In her palm lay a shiny red folding knife.

"They gave you this for me?"

"It is red," she declared, "for the Indian that you are."

He glanced at the other hand. "And that one. Is it a gift for you?"

"No," and Nellie brought up her left hand, opening the fingers slowly again. Inside lay a blue folding knife.

"Blue," he said with dismay. "But these fat *wasicus* aren't blue!"

"No, but the clothing of their soldiers is. And part of their war flag too."

"Yes," he said quietly. "The white stars are sewn on the blue."

She sighed and laid her head against his upper arm. "The colors are why they wanted you to have these two knives together."

"I cannot take them," he said, stepping back. "They give them so I will be seduced into making a picture for their shadow boxes."

"No," she said, slipping the knives into his hands. "They just want you to know how much they admire you. They think you are a great, great chief. Like I think of you."

"I am not a chief," he grumbled. "I am not even an important man. Not anymore."

"But they think so—and I do too," Nellie said. "I am going to ride over to the agency now."

"To see some friends?"

"Perhaps. I would like to visit my family too."

"You saw them yesterday, didn't you?" he asked.

She bent to untie the pony's long rein from a tent stake. "Those two *wasicus*—they promised if I came to the agency right now, they would take my picture with their shadow boxes."

"T-take your—"

"It is all right, husband," she assured as she hurried by him in a rush, wheeled, and flung herself atop her pony. "You don't have to worry about me!"

"Yes," he groaned in panic, "I do have to worry that they will capture your soul in their black boxes!"

She turned around on the bare back of her pony and called out to him as the horse carried her away for the agency. "You must never worry about something like that... because"—and she giggled in that young woman way of hers—"I have no soul for them to capture!"

He heard the tinkle of her laughter fade as she turned around and slammed her heels into the ribs of her horse. For some moments after she had disappeared through the trees along the river, he stared down at the two knives in his hands; then he went inside to show them to Black Shawl.

He watched her face as she inspected the shiny knives, turning them over in her hands. Her own color was so much better lately, and she was finally putting on some weight again, despite the fact that they had nothing more to eat than the white man's poor flour and his stringy beef. She had grown so thin and pale before the soldier healer had saved her life for Crazy Horse. Now there was more meat on her bones, and she had become more eager to please him whenever the trader's daughter rode off to the fort as she often did and they were alone.

Two wives was not such a bad thing, he brooded, looking at her with desire now, wanting her to pull off her dress so that he might couple with her. The white man looked very stern at the Lakota who had more than one wife... yet they had approved him taking the trader's daughter into his lodge. So be it. She was an amusement that had quickly become an addiction. And in some small way, the half-breed had reached inside him and touched that hidden part no one had touched since he gave his heart to Black Buffalo Woman. When he admitted it to himself, Crazy Horse knew that his heart could never be the captive of one woman. Instead, he fondly remembered lying with his manhood inside No Water's wife... and how good it felt when Nellie grabbed him and hurried him inside her moistness. Even Black Shawl continued to satisfy him.

He looked at his first wife, thinking on those shadow

catchers—how much in a hurry Nellie was about everything. To have him climb atop her, or to hurry back to the agency to have her picture captured by them. Perhaps it was her white blood that made her in such a hurry.

Why was it that the *wasicus* would not let him be? Why was it so important to the white man that the Lakota became like them? What was it about the *wasicu* that made him work so hard to make everyone else over in his own image?

Was that why rumors had it the soldiers were going to offer Crazy Horse a chieftainship over all the Lakota if he would only lead both agencies to those new homes the white men were making for them on the Mnisose? Did they really think they could bribe him with material things, even the promise of the sort of power that was all-important to the *wasicus*?

Did these white people think that Crazy Horse was so simple? Or was it that the *wasicus* were just stupid themselves?

He was beginning to doubt that the Lakota and the whites would ever understand one another.

"General Crook wants your help," Clark was droning on, finally getting around to the purpose of this council being held in the largest room they had along officers' row, the drawing room in Colonel Bradley's house.

Seamus Donegan sat against the wall, right behind the few soldiers who huddled up front with Clark and the two interpreters. Frank Grouard had invited him along this afternoon, claiming that the Irishman would get a chance to see most of the war chiefs the army had been fighting on the northern plains gathered in one place. The second interpreter brought in today was Louie Bordeaux, a half-blood trader's son, who was known among his mother's people as Louis Mato, or Bear. Bordeaux had received a good formal education in Hamburg, Iowa, before returning to Brulé country. The delegation he had accompanied upriver from Spotted Tail Agency was led by Crazy Horse's own uncle, Touch-the-Clouds.

"How tall is that one?" Seamus had whispered in awe at

the back of Grouard's ear when the huge chief ducked his head to enter the room earlier.

"Clark told me he goes over seven foot," Grouard had said softly.

Donegan now watched Clark pace back in the opposite direction, his body tense, appearing a bit impatient too, as Grouard painstakingly translated Crook's request for help from Sioux scouts.

"The Nez Perce have broken away from their reservation far to the west," Clark finally continued. "The army does not really know where they are going, or what they will do. But the army intends to catch them, and force them back to their homes. It seems they are heading for the Yellowstone River country. This is the reason why General Crook can't allow you to go north on your hunt."

Clark took a long breath after Grouard finished that part of translation; then he pressed on, "The general wants to enlist scouts from both agencies to go with him when he goes after the Nez Perce."

Grouard finished and the room fell silent, save for the breathing of all, and an errant cough from time to time. The Sioux were fidgeting, glancing at one another in bewilderment. Donegan had no idea why they appeared so furtive, almost suspicious of what had just been told them. Even Crazy Horse, and the two on either side of him. Seamus recognized He Dog at Crazy Horse's right, but he could not remember ever having seen the older man who sat next to Crazy Horse's left side.

Finally that older man spoke up, and Grouard translated, "Little Hawk wants to ask: Crook says for them to go north with him . . . to scout against the Nez Perce?"

"Yes," Clark answered emphatically.

Then Little Hawk asked, and his words were interpreted, " 'The soldiers want us to . . . to fight?' "

Again Clark answered enthusiastically, "Yes. You go north to scout for Three Stars. You will be with us to fight the Nez Perce."

Interesting, how both groups of Sioux talked that over

among themselves. At one side of the room sat Red Cloud himself, the older chief who had orchestrated the many attacks on the Bozeman Road forts. And at the other side of the room sat Crazy Horse, Touch-the-Sky, and their loyal supporters. Voices low and their hands gesturing emphatically, both sets of Sioux appeared to be tearing apart Crook's proposition into very fine pieces indeed. How different this was from anything Seamus could have ever imagined: watching the war chiefs and headmen argue and debate among themselves in hushed tones, as if any of the white men with them in that stifling room could not grasp that tense atmosphere of give-and-take, despite the language barrier.

Finally the quiet discussions faded and the older man sitting beside Crazy Horse spoke to Grouard.

Frank translated, "Little Hawk speaks the words the others have decided."

"Go ahead," Clark prompted, rubbing his hands down the tops of his thighs in anticipation.

" 'The white man and the soldier chiefs wanted the Northern People to come in,' " Grouard said. " 'They came in and untied the tails of their ponies in peace. The White Hat came to their camp and wanted to take away their horses and guns—so they gave those to the soldiers too. Very soon you wanted Crazy Horse to go see the Grandfather with Red Cloud, and he said yes to that. Then Three Stars gave the Oglala a buffalo hunt, but that's been taken away. Now the White Hat wants them to go to war.' "

Grouard took in a sigh, pausing in his translation, his eyes moving from Clark's face, to those of the warriors gathered around Crazy Horse, He Dog, and Little Hawk to his left. Frank continued Little Hawk's speech, " 'When we came here to the White Earth agency, we untied our horses' tails. We came for the peace you said we would have for our women and families. Tell Three Stars that we have done everything he has asked of us, but we do not want any more war. Instead, we only want to go north to hunt buffalo and make meat for the winter."

Seamus immediately saw how that refusal struck Clark.

The lieutenant's eyes narrowed, and that grin of anticipation quickly disappeared as his face turned to stone. Even though one of the headmen who sat beside Red Cloud was rising to take his turn at speaking, Clark rudely cut him off.

"Grouard, you tell them that's impossible!" he growled. "Tell these chiefs that the army can't allow them up there!"

From one face to another, Seamus watched how the mere tone of those words immediately slapped the Sioux. Even though they had no way of understanding a single word Clark was hissing at them, there could be no mistaking the meaning behind what the lieutenant was saying.

"There's fighting going on up there! It's preposterous to think we'd give them permission to go hunt now! General Crook needs them to go scout—just the men! No hunting with their families along," Clark continued to grumble, Grouard hurriedly attempting to capture this phrase or that.

"The whites, the settlers and townspeople—if they see the Crazy Horse people wandering around up there," Clark was saying, his voice even louder and more strained, as he leaped to his feet and gestured emphatically with his arms and shoulders, waving them over the seated Indians, who watched him with horrified eyes, "what are those whites going to think? They're going to think the Oglala have broken off their reservation and gone to war! Then where is that going to leave everyone? They'll cry for the soldiers and we'll be in a real goddamned Indian war; that's where we'll be!"

From the looks on some of the copper-skinned faces, Seamus could read something of what they were suffering. With the loud yelling and the harangue Clark was giving them, it was as if they understood they were being scolded, parent to child. Donegan felt embarrassed for the young lieutenant, even ashamed for the way he had lost control of himself in this delicate situation.

"There can be no hunt!" Clark repeated, his face gone livid with anger. "You must do what Three Stars commands of you. Go scout for him, and go to Washington. You must do what he tells you!"

Grouard struggled to keep up, staring at Clark's face as he turned the words into Sioux for the Indians.

"If you don't go to scout for him," Clark's volume dropped a little while his words became tense and threatening, "there will be no buffalo hunt. And ... there will never be an agency for Crazy Horse."

His voice quickly fell away and he stood there above the delegates, dramatically enfolding his arms across his chest as Grouard finished his translation.

None of the delegates spoke, not so much as a whisper, as they sat in silence and mulled over the tongue-lashing they had just been given by the young officer. It was some time before anyone said anything, so it stunned Seamus when it was Crazy Horse himself who stood and began to speak.

Grouard translated for Clark, " 'Little Hawk told you my words. We came here for peace. We are tired and want no more war.' "

Quickly looking around the room, Donegan saw how most of the Sioux watched this slim man with a mix of awe and reverence, how the power of his presence and the strength of his being had command of that room, even held Clark's rapt attention. Only Red Cloud, and that handful of those men seated closest around him, looked at Crazy Horse with something approaching scorn, or jealousy, even outright hatred itself.

" 'You, the White Hat, and old Three Stars too,' " Grouard went on with his running translation, even as Crazy Horse was speaking, " 'and the new white agent—you have all told us lies. Not just one lie, but one after another, like knots on a rope.' "

Clark started to respond to that, but he suddenly shut his mouth like a man who thought better of it.

" 'You have made promises, but they were as empty as the cold wind,' " Grouard translated. " 'Still ... we want to do what you ask of us, because we came here to make a peace with you. If Three Stars wants us to go north to fight the Nez Perce ...' " and Frank paused, concentrating on what Crazy Horse was saying, " 'then we will go north and fight until a white man isn't left.' "

That slammed Donegan in the belly with the force of a man's boottoe. Fight until a white man wasn't left?

Was Crazy Horse so angry about the broken promises and the lies that he was saying he and his warriors were going to use the trouble along the Yellowstone to break out and go back on the warpath?

"N-not a white man left?" Clark shouted in fury.

The fire in the lieutenant's words clearly shocked Crazy Horse and the other delegates, as if they had no idea that this bold, direct challenge to Clark would make the white man so angry. It was almost... almost as if the two men weren't understanding the other. As if they did not really know what the other was saying... as if Frank Grouard had made a terrible mistake in his translation.

For the first time Donegan noticed that the interpreter appeared momentarily flustered. Then the older warrior stood beside Crazy Horse, gesturing, and Frank translated.

"They can't understand why you're yelling at them. Little Hawk's saying Crazy Horse just told you he'd do what you want—"

"What I want?" Clark had turned shrill again, loud. "I want them to scout for Crook and this son of a bitch, high and mighty Crazy Horse, says he's going to ride north to kill every white man he can find? That's what I want?"

Suddenly Donegan looked at the second interpreter, the trader's son named Bordeaux, and recognized a look on his face that said all was not as Grouard had represented it—

One of Red Cloud's men suddenly leaped to his feet, pounding his chest with a fist and pointing at Crazy Horse, his face gone red, spittle foaming at the corners of his mouth.

"His name is Three Bears." Grouard's voice grew loud over the noise of so much pandemonium. "He says if Crazy Horse wants to kill anyone... then Crazy Horse should start by killing him!"

"He didn't say anything about killing white men!" Bordeaux roared, lunging up from his seat behind Grouard and Clark, leaping in front of Frank to wave an accusing finger. "You're a goddamned liar!"

Grouard slapped it out of the way as Clark jumped between them.

The trader's son from Spotted Tail's agency growled something at Grouard in the Sioux tongue.

"You shut your damned mouth, Bordeaux!" Frank hissed. "If you know what's good for you—"

"Tell Clark that you twisted the words around!" Bordeaux said, shaking with the first flush of anger. "Tell him!"

Clark demanded, "Twisted the words?"

"You *bastard!*" Grouard growled, coming off his stool.

Seamus was there, his big hand clamped on the translator's shoulder as Frank's arms shot toward Bordeaux.

"You lying *bastard!*" Grouard shouted. "I'll teach you to lie about me!"

"*You* lie, Grouard!" Bordeaux screamed back. "Just like the Oglala say about you—the Grabber lies!"

Frank snarled something back at Bordeaux in Sioux; then in English he roared, "You're just like all these red bastards! You're always making trouble for me!"

Wheeling on Clark, Grouard jabbed the lieutenant in the chest with a finger and said, "Every word was the goddamned truth. No matter what this bastard Bordeaux thinks, I told you just what Crazy Horse thinks."

Then as Donegan and the rest of them in that room watched in stunned horror, Frank Grouard turned to look directly at Crazy Horse with a strange light in his eyes for but a moment, before he shoved past the delegates and hurled himself out the door. The room was shocked into silence as Grouard slammed the door closed behind him, its terrible thud slowly dying.

Finally Clark whirled on his heel, hunkering over Bordeaux accusingly as the trader's son settled back on his stool. "What do you mean, Grouard was lying?"

The interpreter said nothing, did not even meet the lieutenant's gaze.

"You're not going to talk to me?" Clark's voice went shrill again. "Have it your way, damn you. You're from Spotted Tail anyway, so I can't really trust you. So just sit there with your mouth closed if you want."

Straightening, Clark waved his arm at a soldier as the Sioux in the room began to murmur among themselves again. "You, Private—go to the agency on the double. Bring me back the interpreter called Garnett. Billy Garnett."

And when the infantryman had hurried from the room, Clark turned back to Bordeaux. "You see? I don't need your translating anyway. I'll get someone I can trust."

Donegan's eyes quickly moved over the gathered chiefs and headmen, but always returned to Crazy Horse, and those closest to him, as they whispered, their eyes glancing about suspiciously. Perhaps malevolently. Seamus looked to where the window was—how far away was that door Grouard had fled through—wondering how a man could make an escape from all these Sioux if trouble broke out. Surely some of them had pistols secreted under a blanket draped over an arm. If not that, then knives or a tomahawk hidden perhaps. The way those two sides of the room were talking and whispering, one faction or the other had to be plotting against Clark and the few soldiers stationed in that tense room.

Thinking of Samantha and little Colin, how they would be playing in the shade of the cottonwoods back at their camp, thinking only of them as he kept his eyes moving, the tense moments slowly became minutes ...

And suddenly Billy Garnett was in the doorway.

It was as if Seamus hadn't taken a breath since Grouard escaped.

Clark was shouting orders at the young half-breed who wedged his way through the crowd, even as some of the Sioux leaders hollered their words at Billy too. Voices rose again; men grew tense.

Back and forth the Indians shouted angrily while Clark

gave Garnett his version of what Crazy Horse had said when he was ordered to take his men north to hunt for the Nez Perce.

"The Nez Perce," Billy repeated, after hearing from Little Hawk and He Dog. "That's what Crazy Horse says he told you. They'd go north to fight the Nez Perce like you asked 'em to."

Clark shook his head, staring at the Sioux chief. "No. He told me he would go fight until not one *white man* was left."

With a snort, Garnett chuckled, "Is that what Grouard told you?"

"Yes, goddammit!" Clark was growing angry again.

"Then Grouard got it wrong," Garnett said firmly. "Crazy Horse says he told you he does not want to go to war, but if Crook wants...he will take his young men and go to the north country, and there they will fight until not a Nez Perce is left standing."

"N-nez Perce?" Clark repeated with a squeak.

"Grouard got it all twisted around," Billy said, then suddenly turned to Bordeaux. "Why didn't you tell him what Crazy Horse said? You could've told him that Grouard made a bad mistake with his words?"

Bordeaux never met Garnett's eyes, his face sullen. Instead, he only shrugged off the question.

"Why would Grouard ever want to make that kind of mistake?" Clark demanded of Garnett, Bordeaux, of anyone who could answer. "Why would Grouard do that?"

Donegan turned to look at Crazy Horse, finding the man unmoved for all the turmoil that still swirled around him. The war chief found Seamus gazing at him, and for a moment the two of them shared that same sort of unspoken recognition they had shared on that afternoon he accompanied the McGillycuddys to the Sioux camp.

It was almost as if the eyes of Crazy Horse were telling Donegan, *Now you see that for too long...you have believed in the wrong man.*

CHAPTER NINETEEN

August 30, 1877

BY TELEGRAPH

———

Indian News—Very Serious
Trouble in Texas.

———

THE INDIANS.

———

Sitting Bull Heard From.

———

WASHINGTON, August 8.—A letter from the United
States consul at Winnipeg says: Near Sitting Bull's
encampment a war party of twenty-seven Sioux robbed the
traders of powder and one bag of bullets. Besides Sitting
Bull's band there is an equal number of Sioux refugees
from the Minnesota massacres of '62 and '63, over whom
Sitting Bull seems to exercise much influence.

BILLY GARNETT TURNED TOWARD CRAZY HORSE AND TRANS-
lated the question Lieutenant Clark had just asked, " 'If the
Grabber said the wrong thing to the White Hat, what is the
truth Crazy Horse wants spoken to the little chief?' "

The chiefs looked back and forth between Garnett and
Clark, the expression on their faces saying: *We already told
you the answer to that question.*

"Can't you see the mistake you made?" Billy whispered
to the lieutenant from the corner of his mouth.

"What the devil are you talking about?" Clark demanded.
"Grouard is the one who lied."

"I mean the mistake you made bringing Grouard together
with that interpreter from Spotted Tail." Garnett kept his
voice barely audible. "The two of them got a lot of trouble

between 'em. Grouard hasn't ever gotten along with traders' sons—Richaud or Bordeaux, any of 'em."

Turning on Bordeaux, the lieutenant demanded, "Why didn't you speak up when Grouard made the mistake?"

But the trader's son didn't utter a word, still refusing to even look at the officer.

So Garnett explained, "That's the Indian way. Around the white man anyway. In an argument, when a man loses his head, others just go quiet, won't say a thing."

"Is that why Crazy Horse and the rest of them won't speak now?" Clark turned away from the interpreter, having become even more agitated as the Lakota delegates refused to speak, refused to answer his question.

His heart must be beating like a drum, Billy thought, looking at the officer's crimson face when the lieutenant grew exasperated with impatience and asked the chief again.

"You're not going to speak to me now that the truth will be made of your words?"

Then Crazy Horse surprised Billy when he began to speak, slowly moving his eyes to the lieutenant. "Now I believe that you will hear the white words that speak the truth of what I tell you."

Clark repeated, "Will you go north with Three Stars and track down the Nez Perce?"

Nodding slightly, Crazy Horse looked at Billy and said, "Tell him yes. Yes, we will go north with Three Stars. We will take our women along and have a little hunt. Tell him we need the women along to help with the buffalo."

But when Garnett translated that, Clark's face grew red again and in frustration he swiped his open hand down the length of his face before he said, "No! You can't go hunting up there until we chase the Nez Perce away! It's foolish for you to think of scouting and making war with your women along! Women don't belong when men go to do fighting!"

Billy watched how that made some of the elders and headmen put their hands up to their mouths, not in amazement, but to hide their amusement at the rash foolishness of the White Hat's words. These warriors knew better than the short-tempered army officer.

In the hush of that room, Crazy Horse eventually spoke again, softly: "Remind the White Hat that the Oglala have done some good fighting with our women along. We ride fast enough to get away too when we are done fighting . . . but always we have done good fighting with our families along."

As Garnett translated the chief's words, Clark's eyes narrowed. Billy figured he understood that Crazy Horse was making him the butt of an Oglala joke on the army and its inability to win a decisive victory over the Lakota.

The lieutenant's breathing got louder for a few moments, until he finally bellowed, "No! I don't give a damn what they say about taking their women along. If they go north, they are going to scout and fight—not for some goddamned buffalo hunt!"

Billy realized the tone of Clark's voice was already expressing everything to the Oglala. They didn't need Garnett to turn the White Hat's words into Lakota to understand the bad talk coming from this little chief. These warriors did not deserve to be talked to so rudely. This was not right, Billy thought as he continued to translate for the angry Clark and some of the Hunkpatila headmen began to murmur among themselves. He was glad Grouard was the army's translator and not him, because he did not like the way the army treated his mother's people—

"Where the hell are they going?" Clark demanded as Crazy Horse and those right around him got to their feet and began to push back through their own delegation, starting for the door.

"Come, my friends," Crazy Horse said to those Hunkpatila around him, adjusting the red blanket over his left arm. "I can see these are people who don't know very much about fighting."

"Won't you stay and talk until everything is decided?" Garnett asked in desperation.

Crazy Horse stopped. He turned slowly, his eyes sad yet filled with a toughened resolve. "No," he said in that hushed room as Clark fumed behind Garnett. "The White Hat and Three Stars are trying too hard to put blood on our hands again and blacken our faces in war when we have untied our horses' tails and promised peace."

Billy pleaded, "It's better to stay and talk—"

"No," Crazy Horse said, wagging his head sadly. "Tell the White Hat I am leaving this place now. Tell him that there has been too much talking here already."

"What the hell were you trying to do?" Donegan demanded, grabbing a double-handful of Frank Grouard's shirtfront.

The half-breed interpreter immediately shoved both of his wrists upward, freeing the Irishman's grip on him, and lunged backward a step. Menacingly, he said, "Don't ever you touch me like that again."

"You owe me an answer."

"I owe you nothing!" he growled, turning away.

"Damn you son of a bitch," Seamus snapped, seizing Grouard's arm and whirling the interpreter around.

Grouard immediately froze in a half-crouch, his hand almost touching the butt of the revolver sticking from his belt like the huge hoof of a goat.

"You gonna shoot me? That it, Frank?"

"You put your hand on me again, I might just cut it off."

He stared at Grouard's eyes, could see that the man meant it. In those same eyes he had read everything from fear to stoic courage over all the miles they had crossed and the battles they had fought together. But now, there seemed to be something new there too. An enemy glaring back at Donegan. The interpreter slowly straightened and dropped his gun hand, turning his back on the Irishman, then starting away again.

"At the very least you owe me an answer, Frank," Seamus pleaded. "All we been through together, you owe me that."

His words seemed to hit Grouard squarely between the shoulder blades, stopping the man in his tracks. For a long moment he didn't turn around.

But when he finally did, Frank said, "It don't make no difference now. Soldiers like Crook and Clark, they're gonna believe what they wanna believe. And the Lakota won't ever change what they believe either."

"I don't give a damn about them," Seamus said, taking a step closer to the man who was once his trusted brother-in-arms. But Grouard tensed up, took a step back, so Donegan stopped where he stood. "Awright, I ain't coming any closer. Just tell me why, 'cause I gotta know for my own self."

"Don't make a hill of shit to any of 'em," Frank said.

"Tell me why you told Clark that Crazy Horse said something he didn't say," Seamus pleaded, "especially when the army already thinks Crazy Horse and his people are gonna break out and go killing white folks between here and the Powder River country."

With a shrug, Grouard said, "It's what the bastard was thinkin'."

"What he was thinking? What in blazes does that mean?"

Frank glared at him, saying, "I only told Clark what Crazy Horse was thinking of doing, what the red bastard wants to do if he sees a chance. So I said it for him! Right out, I said what he's been thinking he would do anyway!"

"How do you know?"

His mouth curled up, his eyes half-closed in a feral warning. "Oh, I know, Seamus. I know damn well what those bastards like Crazy Horse and He Dog are thinking. I lived with 'em long enough."

"They could've killed you, any day they wanted," Donegan said, wagging his head in disbelief. "But they took you in after you run away from Sitting Bull's camp. Kept you safe, made you one of theirs. Even let you marry one of their women—"

"That's all in the past now!" Grouard snapped. "You're a stupid bastard yourself if you think I owe Crazy Horse or any of 'em a damned thing!"

"Don't you owe 'em your hide?"

Grouard bleated with some humorless laughter. "I owe the Hunkpatila nothing—nothing but all the grief I can give 'em for the grief they give me at the end of my stay with them red bastards!"

Shaking his head, Seamus said, "They made you one of their own. Let you marry one of their sisters, one of their daughters. And this is the way you repay these men who put their trust in you?"

Now it was Grouard's turn to take a long step toward the Irishman. He was shaking with fury as he said, "Who the hell do you think we were fighting when we took Crook north to jump that village on the Powder River a year and a half ago? What bastards was we fighting all day at the Big Bend of the Rosebud? Huh? Those same red sonsabitches! So what do I owe them, Seamus? You tell me that."

"Fighting an enemy, making him less than a man and nothing more than an enemy—that's what we all do when we're at war, Frank," Seamus explained. "You done it, and I done it, lots of times. Nothing wrong with fighting and killing when you're at war. Back when we first run onto each other working for Crook, it wasn't no problem for me to understand why you become a scout to track down the Injuns. You was back to being white again, Frank. But this I don't understand—"

"Spit it out, Irishman."

Seamus took a long sigh, then said, "I could see you fighting them Sioux—Crazy Horse, He Dog, and the rest. Stand-up and eye-to-eye . . . like a man does in war. But this, Frank . . . this was underhanded. This lying to Clark to make it out like some words come out of Crazy Horse's mouth that didn't—"

"He won't ever be a agency Injun like Red Cloud or Spotted Tail."

"Maybe he won't," Donegan admitted. "But he appears to be a man brave enough to stand up without a weapon, right in front of his old enemies—like you and Crook and all the army—and speak what's in his heart, no matter the consequences!"

Grouard's hands were tensing into balled fists. "You saying I ain't a man now?"

He saw the man ready to lunge at him, or pull that pistol out of his belt, and realized he hadn't buckled on his pistols since bringing his family to what he thought was the serenity of sleepy Camp Robinson. A man like Grouard who was ready to fight an old friend, or even to pull a gun on an old comrade, he damn sure wasn't worth all this trouble.

"I s'pose I got my answer," Seamus said with great melancholy.

"I asked you if you figgered I wasn't a man no more!" Grouard growled menacingly. "That's what it sounded like you said."

"You was a man I admired for a long time, Frank," he admitted with deep regret. "The way you found that village on the Powder in the middle of the night and a blizzard to boot. The way you never give up and stuck your neck out to do your job, no matter how Reshaw worked to convince Crook you was gonna betray him and his soldiers. But now, I find out you got enough hatred chewing away at your insides that you could out-and-out lie about an old friend like Crazy Horse—"

"He ain't my friend no more!"

"You could lie about him, because it don't make you ashamed to do that to a man who was once your honored enemy."

"Ain't nothing to honor in that red bastard," Grouard said, flexing his fingers.

"That's why I guess we don't see eye-to-eye no more, Frank," he said quietly. "That's why we won't be friends no more."

"Fine by me."

"Sad is what it is, Frank. Sad because you was my friend all them times we was saving our hair and our hide. Sadder still because of what you done to play this cruel trick on that Injin, a man who I figure will tell the truth...even when it won't get him nowhere."

Grouard shook his head. "I don't get what you're saying."

"I know, Frank. I don't think you ever will."

"Go to hell, Donegan!" he growled as he whirled on his

heel and started away. "Go straight to hell right here."

For some moments he watched the interpreter's back as Grouard disappeared among the post's buildings.

"I sure hope that ain't where I'm going," Seamus admitted with a shiver. "Place'll damn well be crowded with lying bastards I once thought was my friends."

Omaha, Aug. 31, 1877.

Gen. Crook.
Comdg. Department,
On West-bound train, Fremont, Neb.

Dispatch from Colonel Bradley just received. Crazy Horse and Touch-the-Clouds tell Lieut. Clark this morning that they are going out with their bands; this means all of the hostiles of last year. Probably more troops must be brought here, if this movement is to be stopped. I think General Crook's presence might have a good effect?

R. Williams
Adjt. General

Grand Island, Neb.,
September 1, 1877.

General Bradley,
Camp Robinson, Neb.

Your dispatch received. I cannot come to Robinson. If Spotted Tail can, with his own people and the help of the troops now at Camp Sheridan, round up Touch the Clouds, you have sufficient force to do the same with Crazy Horse ... If there is any danger of the Indians becoming alarmed by the arrival of troops from Laramie, you should so arrange matters that they shall arrive dur-

ing the night and make the round up early the next morning. Use the greatest precaution in this matter. It would
be better not to say anything to the Indians about it until
the night previous when you can consult the head chiefs
and let them select their own men for the work. Delay is
very dangerous in this business.

George Crook,
Brigadier General.

Chicago, September 1, 1877.

General Crook,
on West-bound train,
Sidney, Neb.

I think your presence more necessary at Red Cloud
Agency than at Camp Brown and wish you to get off at
Sidney and go there. Colonel Bradley thinks Crazy Horse
and others will make trouble if the Sioux scouts leave. I
will ask Bradley to detain them until you reach Red
Cloud…

P. H. Sheridan,
Lieut. General.

CHAPTER TWENTY

Wasutun Wi
MOON WHEN ALL THINGS RIPEN, 1877

BY TELEGRAPH
———

The War in Europe—
Resumption of Hostilities.
———

President Hayes to Adopt a
New Indian Policy.
———

THE INDIANS.
———

General Sitting Bull Gives Rise to a
New Indian Policy.
———

OTTAWA, August 15.—A commission has been appointed
by the United States government to make a treaty with
Sitting Bull for a return to the reservation with his tribe.
While in Washington lately, Hon. Mr. Mills fully explained
to President Hayes the Canadian system of dealing with
Indians. The president expressed his intentions of adopting
a similar line of policy and give the management of the
outposts to experienced army officers, and do away
altogether with agents. The Canadian Indians of the
northwest are fiercely jealous of the advent of hostile Sioux,
and it is feared they may at any time make war upon them.
It is expected that the new policy towards the Indians, about
to be adopted by President Hayes, will bring about the
withdrawal of American Indians from Canadian territory.

TA'SUNKE WITKO!
He did not open his eyes to know that it was still dark.

Just the smell, the very feel of the air told him that it was the coolest time of the night outside this lodge, in these moments just before dawn would break beyond Crow Butte. All was quiet around him, so quiet because so few of the lodges remained around his. Only Red Feather and Little Hawk had their lodges raised nearby in a family group.

"I thought perhaps you had gone," he said to his spirit helper.

Because I have not spoken to you for so long? You thought I had deserted you?

"No, that would have been foolish of me. So, why come speak to me now?"

You haven't needed me for some time.

"That's where you have been wrong, Spirit Guardian. I have needed you every day."

Not the way your heart has been, Ta'sunke Witko. You have let others rule you, whether it was the way you allowed your anger for, and distrust of, Red Cloud to decide things for you... or you allowed your lust for the trader's daughter to make you believe things were strong inside your heart when your heart was not strong at all.

For a moment he listened to the breathing of the two women in his lodge. From across the fire came the sleeping sounds of the young woman who had such passion in her mouth and body and those dark, flashing eyes. Then he moved his hand and felt Black Shawl beside him. First wife who was struggling to fight off the white man's coughing sickness, even while he failed to fight off the seduction of the young woman who wanted only to take Black Shawl's place as first in his heart.

"Yes, I've been a fool about a few things," Crazy Horse whispered.

What have you decided about going north with Three Stars on his search for the Nez Perce?

"I gave the White Hat my answer yesterday," he said. "But then nothing the *wasicus* want from me ever turns out the way they promise."

You won't talk to the little chief anymore?

"It serves no purpose. Here in the final days of the Moon When All Things Ripen...all things terrible have indeed come to bear their bitter fruit."

Crazy Horse felt Black Shawl stir a bit beside him. Patting her arm beneath the blanket, he listened while the woman's breathing became regular and deep once more.

You are thinking more and more of that north country.

"Yes, how I would like to be there now. Away from this place where men's hearts grow small. Up there in my country, the land is big, and men's hearts grow bigger for it. Down here..." and his whisper faded.

How can you take your people with you, thinking you won't have to watch them suffer when the soldiers come after the villages of women, children, and the old ones?

"Just like they did during the winter when we had so little to eat, when the snows were so deep, and the babes cried out in their dying. No," he whispered, his eyes stinging, "I cannot do that to the mothers and the children ever again."

Do what, Ta'sunke Witko?

"Ask them to sacrifice themselves, as a warrior willingly sacrifices himself—even unto sacrificing those most precious to him."

Just the way you believe you sacrificed They Are Afraid of Her to the white man's disease she contracted because you had a little contact with the wasicus and loafers at the forts?

"My daughter was sacrificed because of me—"

She died because of the white man, not because of anything you did. And Black Shawl did not grow sick because of you either. Still... your heart tells you all things will be better when you are far, far from this place, doesn't it?

"Yes," he answered fervently. "To be where the white man would not molest my people...but I can't take them along, won't take them because I don't want to chance so many of them dying to the cold and the hunger, to the constant running and the soldier bullets when the wasicus eventually find and attack our village."

But you will go and take the two women with you?

He thought on that; then he sensed what he had to answer, although his spirit guardian would already know.

"I don't think I will ask the trader's daughter to go," he answered. "I will send her to visit her family for a night, so she won't be around when we go away in darkness."

Half her blood is white, so you realize that if you asked her to go north with you, she might decide she would tell her family. And her **wasicu** *father would likely tell the soldiers, so they would come to make a prisoner of you before you could escape. In the end, the army would send you away to the Hot Place.*

"Where they sent Little Wolf and Morning Star, and their Shahiyela," he answered, remembering how they were led away from the agency by a soldier escort, ordered on foot to a new home in Indian Territory far to the south, where the waters were hot and the earth so dry it grew parched and cracked. "No, I will take only Black Shawl with me. Perhaps Little Hawk will bring his family too. Red Feather will want to come because of his sister, I am sure—"

"Crazy Horse!"

He opened his eyes, jerking at the raspy, whispered call coming right through the lodgeskins. "Who is there?"

"You are awake, Crazy Horse? I heard you talking—"

"Is that you, Little Big Man?"

"Yes. I come early because I have news to tell!"

"Wait, and I will come out there to talk with you."

He gently pulled away from her, slipping from under the blanket, and dragged on his trader-cloth shirt. Quickly he stepped over and stood for a moment looking down on the trader's daughter, staring at her one bare leg protruding from under her blankets. How childlike she looked in sleep. Crazy Horse sighed with disappointment and ducked out of the doorway, letting the flap slide back in place.

"Ever since yesterday," Little Big Man said the moment Crazy Horse emerged outside in the rosy light of sunrise, "the white man's talking wire has been crowded with the name of Crazy Horse!"

"Why?"

"Perhaps because you told the White Hat you would not talk anymore," Little Big Man surmised.

"So I am important to them only because I refuse to talk."

"Every time you won't come to a council, or every time you refuse to do what Three Stars or the *wasicus* say you must, you make trouble for yourself—can't you see?"

"This is what you came to say? That I am making trouble for myself?"

Little Big Man nodded grimly. "The soldiers believe the old woman talk from Red Cloud and Spotted Tail now. You made them believe you really are going to break out with our people and run for the North Country."

For a moment he thought of asking his old friend to come along. One of the few friends he had ever trusted. Even though Little Big Man had grabbed his arm when No Water had jumped inside that lodge and fired his pistol at Crazy Horse, he had meant well by it. Little Big Man was one of the few he felt he could trust with his life.

"That is what the little chiefs are saying?"

"The talking wire is buzzing with words to and from Three Stars," he said. "I hear this from the half-blood who does not want to see our people hurt."

He knew Little Big Man was speaking of Billy Garnett. "These soldiers have nothing better to talk about?" He started away from the lodge, afraid these whispers might frighten Black Shawl if she should awaken. "What old women are these soldier chiefs—"

"There is word from the Pa Sapa too," Little Big Man interrupted as they moved away to the nearby trees bordering the riverbank. "The earth-scratchers there, they are offering a big bounty for Indian scalps, Lakota or Shahiyela."

"Aiyeee," he whispered low. "Money for Indian hair? All those earth-scratchers left in the Pa Sapa who are afraid of dying, eh? They cower in their settlement towns, their hearts turned to water because we have killed too many of them when they are out scratching alone."

"*You* have killed too many, Crazy Horse," Little Big Man said. "Over this summer, with all the rumors of Crazy Horse breaking away from the reservation, those *wasicus* are very scared of your people coming to the Pa Sapa to kill all the whites you can find and drive the rest out."

"Lately, I have started to think that Three Stars does not want the Hunkpatila to go north with him to fight the Nez Perce."

"Why?"

Crazy Horse said, "I am thinking Three Stars really wants us to scout for our old comrade, Sitting Bull."

"That can't be!" Little Big Man whispered in disbelief. "Why would Three Stars have us go after Sitting Bull when the Hunkpapa have already escaped across the Medicine Line?"

"Because everyone knows that Three Stars always pits one tribe against itself. The way he used Lakota to hunt Lakota. Shahiyela to hunt down Shahiyela. This is why Three Stars is trying to trick me into hunting down my old friend, Sitting Bull."

"I recall hearing the reports that Sitting Bull's men have been coming back across the Medicine Line to raid for horses," Little Big Man said thoughtfully. "Some of the soldiers think Sitting Bull will come south again to join up with the Nez Perce and drive the white man out of that country for all time."

"That is why Three Stars believes he should go after Sitting Bull," Crazy Horse declared. "To keep him from joining up his warriors with the Nez Perce."

For a long time Little Big Man was deep in thought; then he said, "Now it's easy to understand why you don't want to scout for the soldier chief."

Crazy Horse considered it a moment, then told the *akicita*, "Still, I have been thinking of going north, my friend."

Little Big Man looked at him quizzically. "So, you've changed your mind again? Now you are going to scout for Three Stars?"

"No! They are such fools, not letting us have a little when we ask for a hunt, asking only for our women to come along on the scouting."

The muscular man's eyes narrowed. "Even though you won't go with Three Stars...you said you were wanting to go north?"

Quickly looking around for the ears of any who might be going into the bushes to relieve themselves early of the morning, he whispered, "I won't take all the people. I do not want to bring trouble down on the heads of everyone."

Little Big Man wagged his head, clearly confused.

"A few of us can slip away, my friend," Crazy Horse explained. "Just me and you and some of the other old friends—"

"I can't go—"

"Each man can bring his wife and—" Then Crazy Horse stopped abruptly. "You said...you can't go?"

"No, I can't."

"They won't come looking for so few of us."

Little Big Man wagged his head again. And pulled at the tails of his blue soldier shirt. "They probably wouldn't come looking for me, or Red Feather, or even Little Hawk...but one thing is for certain: they will come looking for *you.*"

"Am I that important for them to keep me penned up here like an unbroken horse in a pole corral?"

"Yes, Crazy Horse. And"—it was clearly hard for Little Big Man to say this—"the agent and soldier chiefs would make me come after you too."

"Even you?"

Staring at the ground, Little Big Man confessed, "Yes. You know I have a new life now. How I have taken up wearing the metalbreast for the agent. They will tell me I have to go after you because you are supposed to stay here...and I will have to come after you and bring all the people back to this reservation."

He felt relieved by that, saying to his old friend, "But I am not going to take the People with me when I go! I have given my word to the White Hat and to the agent too. I promised not to lead the Northern People away from here. But that does not mean that a few of us can't drift away one night soon. One lodge at a time. The *wasicus* won't miss one lodge each night. We would all go north to the White Mountains, where we can meet again on Goose Creek in the Moon When Leaves Fall."

"A few others might not be missed at all," Little Big Man admitted. "But . . . the little chief and the agent would miss *you*. I would have to come and bring you back."

"You . . . would?"

"I am sorry, my friend," he said, and his eyes spoke their apology. "But I would come after you because it is my new responsibility, and I am a man of honor. And . . . because I would want to be sure none of Red Cloud's friends shot you down."

"Ah, my friend—even when we are taking different trails in life, you would protect my life with your own."

Little Big Man smiled. "Yes, old friend. Even though I am a metalbreast, even though I would obey my orders, I would do everything I could to keep others from killing you."

"But . . . will you tell the *wasicus* that I might slip away?"

"Don't," Little Big Man warned sadly. "Please don't make me have to come after you."

"What if I decide only to go visit my uncle's people on Beaver Creek?" Crazy Horse asked. "You would come after me if I went to visit my father on Spotted Tail's reservation?"

"If you are supposed to stay here, then I would have to bring you back here."

Crazy Horse smiled. "What if I resisted, and struggled with you to get away?"

With a laugh, Little Big Man grinned. "You would not get away from me, old friend! Look at you, so small! And me, I am much stronger than you!"

He grinned too. "Yes, it would be a fierce struggle between us—"

"Crazy Horse! Little Big Man!"

They turned to find Red Feather approaching with his young son, hand in hand.

"My brother!" Crazy Horse said to Black Shawl's

younger brother. "Go call the rest of the men together. I have something important I must tell them first thing this morning."

Red Feather glanced at Little Big Man, his eyes regarding the soldier coat, and the shiny badge pinned to it; then he looked at his leader. "You have decided something, Crazy Horse?"

"Yes," he said with enthusiasm. "I want to tell our men that they are to stay home."

"We are not to obey Three Stars?"

"No," Crazy Horse said. "I want to tell our men that we are not going to hunt for the Nez Perce."

After Red Feather swept the young boy into his arms and started away, Crazy Horse slapped a hand down on his friend's shoulder, pressing against the wool of that soldier shirt. "Little Big Man, my faithful friend—so you would use all your strength to protect me from Red Cloud and his betrayers?"

The stocky warrior nodded, pressing the flat of his palm against Crazy Horse's heart. "This I swear to you. I will do everything in my power to keep others from hurting you... even if that means I must prevent you from doing something foolish that could bring you harm."

CHAPTER TWENTY-ONE

2 September 1877

BY TELEGRAPH

Another Indian Fight in the
Black Hills.

———

DEADWOOD.

———

Another Desperate Fight Between Miners and Indians

———

DEADWOOD, August 25.—The party of two hundred
persons who left here about two weeks ago for the Little
Missouri river, returned to-day, and state that last Tuesday
evening the party discovered Indians close to them. They
selected high ground, dug rifle pits, and had been digging
about thirty minutes when nearly five hundred Indians
appeared on the bluff opposite, about four hundred yards
off, and commenced firing at them. The fight lasted nearly
four hours. Thos. A. Carr, quartz recorder of the Deadwood
mining district, was shot through the head and killed.
Twenty-seven horses belonging to the miners were also
shot. After dark the Indians withdrew and the miners
escaped, being obliged to walk one hundred and fifty miles
to reach the city.

"WHO IS THAT COMING?" GENERAL GEORGE CROOK ASKED OF
those around him as he leaned out from the front of the army
ambulance he was riding in the moment his driver began to
slow down their two-horse hitch.

Just ahead of the ambulance rode Lieutenant William
Clark and his pair of interpreters, all three of them having

stopped the moment a lone Indian on horseback broke from the trees farther up the trail, racing toward their party.

Clark turned in the saddle. "The one called Woman's Dress."

"Whose Indian is he?" the brigadier general demanded as he clambered down from the seat, onto the front wheel of the ambulance, and stood in the middle of the narrow trail.

The lieutenant replied, "He's one of Red Cloud's closest and most loyal."

"Ah, I can see now," Crook said. "He's wearing a soldier's blouse."

"Yes, General," Clark said. "One of my scouts."

Crook glanced at the second, and older, of the two interpreters, Baptiste Pourier, more well known as "Big Bat." This half-blood son of a French trader, who had served Crook throughout the Sioux campaigns, only nodded in recognition as he and young Billy Garnett came out of the saddle. The general turned, watching the solitary rider approach. "Why would he be out here all by himself, and not at the council grounds?"

That bothered Billy too. Why this *winkte*, the Lakota man-woman with a very sacred personal medicine, a man who often dressed and acted like a female, would show up out here on the trail that was taking the soldier chiefs and their escort to a scheduled council with the chiefs and headmen of the various agency bands.

Three days ago when Crazy Horse walked out of that council with Lieutenant Clark, bluntly telling the officer that he would be leaving the reservation, both the agency and nearby Camp Robinson began to buzz with dangerous talk. With his patience worn down to the most slender of threads, Clark wired Crook about the worsening situation. Early the following day, 1 September, Crook had telegraphed orders to have Crazy Horse arrested, and to disarm all of the disaffected Northern Sioux. But because Clark and Bradley, on the scene, didn't believe they had enough men to make the arrest and seizures with any certainty of success, they convinced Crook to rescind his orders.

The telegraph continued to hum with all the trouble the

white men saw coming. Not only Clark and post commander Bradley, but General Sheridan himself back in Chicago. He ordered Crook—who had just arrived at Fort Laramie, on his way to Camp Brown on the Shoshone Reservation to put together his final preparations for starting the march after the Nez Perce—back to Camp Robinson to solve this nettlesome matter of Crazy Horse's refusal to allow any of his men to serve as scouts on the forthcoming campaign, and his threat to flee the reservation.

Crook had rolled in that very mid-afternoon, grumpy, tired, and sore from the long ambulance ride up from Fort Laramie. He was clearly in no real mood to entertain any guff from the Lakota leaders who had surrendered months ago. Not long after his arrival, the general sent riders to the various camps to instruct the chiefs and headmen that he would meet them in council some two miles southeast of the fort, in a well-known grove of cottonwoods on the banks of White Clay Creek.

Next, he called a meeting with Bradley, Clark, and Lieutenant Jesse M. Lee, military agent up at Spotted Tail Agency, who had hurried down to Camp Robinson on this most urgent business. Before all these officers, Crook had young Billy Garnett explain how Grouard must have simply made a mistake in his translation of Crazy Horse's words. In turn, Billy told the general that Crazy Horse was upset because the promise of the hunt had been broken and his own agency had been taken from him too. Still, Crazy Horse had given his word and would not take his people north to make trouble. And Agent Lee agreed. The two of them believed that Grouard had not only made a mistake, but had defamed Crazy Horse and his people by purposefully mis-translating the chief's words and intent.

But Clark was quick to protest, saying that for some time he had had the feeling Crazy Horse was a born liar and had only been biding his time before he could get his hands on guns and ammunition before breaking out.

"A leopard never changes its spots, General," the lieutenant declared.

Billy saw how Crook had one voice of reason in one ear,

a voice of distrust and suspicion in the other. To settle the matter, Crook said he would listen to everything the chiefs had to tell him in council; then he would decide what was the truth about Crazy Horse. In that way, everything would be straightened out so he could get moving after the Nez Perce, reported to be heading north for the Yellowstone country.

Now in the heat and stifling dust of that late-summer afternoon, Crook quickly glanced back at his escort of soldiers halted around the ambulance, all of them awaiting the approach of that lone Indian loping up on horseback, his flowing cloth garments captured by the occasional breeze, sunlight glittering off the engraved silver buttons that were sewn down the outer seam of his dark blue leggings.

"I come to talk with Three Stars," Woman's Dress announced breathlessly as he brought his pony to a halt right in front of the two interpreters.

"He has a council to go to now," Pourier snapped impatiently.

Woman's Dress looked directly at Crook now. "Tell Three Stars that what I come to tell him is a matter of his life."

"What bad story are you carrying now?" Garnett demanded suspiciously.

The *winkte*'s eyes glowered at the half-blood with undisguised contempt. "Maybe you stand too close to Three Stars' enemies to know the truth when it stares you in the eye."

"Just tell us what you have to say," Pourier declared, shooing a big deerfly away from his face. "We'll tell Three Stars what your talk is, then be on our way to the council."

Turning his haughty gaze to Pourier, Woman's Dress hissed, "Three Stars can't go to the council. You tell him that. Crazy Horse is planning a trap for Three Stars!"

"A t-trap?" Billy sputtered, half wanting to laugh. "You have hated Crazy Horse ever since you were children—back to the days when you were called Pretty Fellow!"

"How would you know, little boy!" the *winkte* growled haughtily. "You weren't even born yet!"

Billy continued, "I know about you, how you've wanted to get even with him ever since he accidentally broke your nose in child's play!"

"This is not child's play!" Woman's Dress snapped, refusing to look directly at the younger man now. Instead, he went back to addressing Baptiste Pourier. "It will happen when Three Stars arrives at the council grounds. Crazy Horse will be there with at least six-times-ten of his faithful warriors. He will make a handshake with the soldier chief, so that Crazy Horse can hold onto Three Stars's hand tightly while he brings out a pistol from under his blanket. When he shoots Three Stars, the rest of his warriors will fall upon the other soldiers and quickly do away with them."

Billy studied the Lakota man closely, despairing that there really might be the slightest kernel of truth to this rumor. Over the last few weeks, Crazy Horse had become more and more distant, harder and harder to speak to and deal with. It seemed as if he were lending credence to all the bad whispers and furtive talk about him preparing to escape the reservation. Crazy Horse had been doing nothing to counter-act the bad talk made about him by the White Hat and Red Cloud's friends. Then he had put the top on it by walking out on that council with Clark, declaring he was leaving.

And now as he watched how Pourier's translation of Woman's Dress's warning was striking General Crook and Lieutenant Clark, Billy could see that Crazy Horse had done himself no good in refusing to bring his camp closer to the agency, in not showing up at some of the councils Clark or Crook had called, in trying to remain a wild Indian on a pacified reservation. The time when Billy could have helped Crazy Horse had passed. Too many wheels had already been put in motion.

"You know this for yourself?" Garnett demanded of the *winkte*. "Heard it with your own ears?"

With disdain, Woman's Dress glared daggers at the younger man and said, "Lone Bear's brother, Little Wolf, has been staying in the Crazy Horse camp to court a girl who lives near Crazy Horse's lodge. He was listening outside the chief's lodge when he overheard the plot being made with Crazy Horse's friends. So Little Wolf hurried to tell Lone Bear—and Lone Bear has just told me of this plan to murder Three Stars."*

"Little Wolf?" Pourier asked. "The same warrior who fought so hard against the soldiers at the Greasy Grass?"

"Yes!" Woman's Dress answered. "Since the Greasy Grass fight he has become a good-hearted man and does not want to see Three Stars killed!"

"Lone Bear and Little Wolf, they're Bad Faces," Billy grumbled, remembering that it was said of Lone Bear that he had cut out the tongue of a Custer trooper, and still kept that battle trophy in a medicine pouch. "All of you are Red Cloud's friends."

"No matter what *you* believe, little talker," Woman's Dress accused as his eyes narrowed to slits, "I speak the truth."

"You Bad Faces are like camp women," Garnett growled with disdain. "All of you wanting to be chiefs over other men. To cling onto some little shred of power...so you use tricks and schemes when you can—"

"Perhaps the soldier chief needs to know that this little talker cannot be trusted at his side, eh?" Woman's Dress asked Pourier.

---

*According to the record left by Lieutenant William P. Clark, he did indeed enlist the help of one of his Indian scouts, asked to commence a liaison with a Hunkpatila girl who resided in the lodge right next to that of Crazy Horse, simply so he could monitor the chief's intentions and the comings and goings of the chief's allies. Clark himself never did reveal the name of this Indian scout, but in his interview with Judge Eli Ricker, He Dog stated that both Lone Bear and Woman's Dress were spying on Crazy Horse's lodge for Clark.

"I am not afraid of you or what you may say about me," Billy said. "I am known to speak nothing but the truth. While you are a petty man trying to play big with the soldiers."

Turning back to Pourier, Woman's Dress said, "Remember that your wife is my cousin. I will trust only you to speak for me to Three Stars. This little talker is a bad man."

After watching all the back-and-forth between his translators and Woman's Dress, Crook took a deep sigh and arched his trail-weary back, gazing at Garnett. "Well, Billy—what do you make of this one's story?"

For a long moment he considered speaking what lay in his heart—his doubt that Crazy Horse could ever think of committing such a cowardly act as cold-blooded murder—but then he remembered how strange Crazy Horse had behaved in recent weeks, Garnett wondered if Crazy Horse could somehow feel justified, driven to this rash act of madness.

Finally he told Crook, "This is too big a thing upon me to answer. And a bad time with lots of words and feelings and actions all mixed up. I cannot answer in my own heart if this Woman's Dress speaks the truth of what will be."

His face still a blank slate, Crook next turned to Pourier and asked, "What about you, Bat? Is this a man to be trusted? Someone I can believe?"

After a brief moment, Pourier said, "I never knowed him to speak crooked, General."

Crook ground one of his bootheels into the dirt, brooding, then suddenly turned to the sergeant of his escort and Lieutenant Clark. "I don't want to make a mistake, for it would, to the Indians, be the basest treachery to make a mistake in this critical matter. So I've decided we'll go on to the council."

"General!" Clark squealed in dismay. "Don't you realize what lies waiting for you out there?"

Irritated, he whirled on the lieutenant. "I never set off to go anywhere but what I didn't get there."

Clark sputtered, "B-but this man has brought us news of a secret conspiracy to kill you!"

Scoffing at that, Crook said, "In every battle I've ever fought, believe me, there have been men who have wanted nothing more than to kill me."

"But this is something different, General," Clark protested. "What's been planned is going to be a murder committed by a man who will kill you under the pretense of shaking your hand at the beginning of a peace talk!"

"Outright murder?"

Clark nodded. "Crazy Horse's reformation does not run very deep at all."

His eyes narrowing, Crook turned to Clark, saying, "Such a cowardly act would pretty much do it for Crazy Horse, wouldn't it?"

"He's been on a collision course with you for a long time, General," Clark agreed. "I can't help but think of General Canby's murder, how Canby trusted that Modoc, Captain Jack, when he sat down to negotiate a peace—and the bastard chief shot Canby in cold blood!"*

"Truth be known, in the back of my mind I've been concerned about just this sort of thing since the man met my troops on the Rosebud last summer," Crook admitted. "I wouldn't doubt that Crazy Horse has considered murdering the man who drove him off from that fight, scattered his warriors after we caught him napping at Powder River, and we drove him off again at Slim Buttes. Yes, I am certain in my bones that he could indeed hatch such a plot to murder the man who has dogged his every step for most of a year."**

---

*April 11, 1873: Reverend Eleazar Thomas and General Edward R. Canby were murdered by Modoc leaders during a peace council in the Lava Beds. See *Devil's Backbone*, vol. 5, the Plainsmen Series.
**According to the thesis of James H. Gilbert, author of "The Death of Crazy Horse," which appeared in the scholarly *Journal of the West* (January 1993), "General Crook had previously been targeted for death under similar council meeting circumstances prior to the surrender of Crazy Horse, only to be saved from murder by an Indian informant." None of Gilbert's assertions am I able to substantiate in Crook biographical materials.

"Because you are his nemesis," Clark stated. "You are his conqueror, General. Even if he died in the act, I am certain Crazy Horse is just insane enough to kill you in the middle of a peace council, with your soldiers and subordinates around."

Crook turned to gaze at Woman's Dress, while he spoke to Pourier: "Bat, ask him to confirm that Crazy Horse is planning to run, to flee with his people, once he has killed me."

Woman's Dress nodded when Pourier asked the question. "Yes. He is going to steal all his people away from the agency and go north to kill whites."

With the gray of concern coloring his features, Clark said, "General, we've got to get you back to the post now. There's no telling if Crazy Horse has his agents watching for our approach at this very minute. They might even attempt to commit their assassination right here on the road to the council. We've got to get you out of here!"

Billy watched Crook, seeing how things boiled inside the man like the roiling surface of a coffee pot. Behind the two officers that escort of soldiers muttered among themselves, turning this way and that, watching the trees, searching the hillsides for any sign of attackers.

Suddenly the general spoke and broke the brief, uneasy silence: "We're turning back for the agency. Bat, you and Garnett ride on ahead to the council grounds and select those chiefs you know are entirely loyal to the agent. Get them off to the side and order them to meet with me at the post in two or three hours. Just the ones of a loyal brand— Clark himself will tell you who they are. Don't—and I repeat don't—let Crazy Horse or any of the Northern leaders know of this secret meeting."

Garnett wanted to tell Crook then and there that Big Bat and Woman's Dress were related, how Pourier was married to the Lakota's cousin. And Billy wanted to tell the soldier chief that no man should ever trust anything that had come down to him from three tongues, one to the next to the next. Especially from Red Cloud's lodge dogs.

But Pourier slapped him on the shoulder and things were already in motion around him.

"Let's go, Billy," Big Bat said as he turned back to his horse.

Garnett leaped into the saddle, his heart in his throat. Wondering if by their poisonous words Woman's Dress, Lone Bear, and Little Wolf hadn't already accomplished the death of Crazy Horse for their leader, Red Cloud.

CHAPTER TWENTY-TWO

2 September 1877

BY TELEGRAPH
—

Death of Brigham Young.
—

Indian News—Sitting Bull
On His Way Home.
—

Chief Joseph in Search of
General Howard.
—

UTAH.
—

Death of Brigham Young.
—

SALT LAKE CITY, August 29.—Brigham Young died at 4
o'clock this afternoon.
—

WASHINGTON.
—

Sitting Bull Heard From—Returns to United States.
—

WASHINGTON, August 29.—The government is
informed by telegram, from General Miles, of the
crossing of Milk river by Sitting Bull in the
neighborhood of the Little Rocky Mountains, and about
50 miles east of Fort Belknap. Sitting Bull's presence
again in the United States, with a large force, will cause
additional activity at the war department in dealing with
the Indian problem.

THE CHIEFS AND HEADMEN* BEGAN TO MURMUR THE MO-
ment William Clark brought Woman's Dress into the drawing room of what was Colonel Luther Bradley's personal
quarters, although Bradley hadn't been invited to this secret
meeting. Clark and Woman's Dress came to stand near General Crook and Frank Grouard, Billy Garnett, and Baptiste
Pourier, the three who had just explained to the Sioux that
they would now learn why the white men had never made it
to the peace parley.

"Garnett, have this man tell the chiefs what he told us after stopping us on our way to the council site this afternoon,"
Crook instructed the young half-breed.

Always one to dress and strut in a showy manner,
Woman's Dress was not a shy speaker in the least. As he
warmed to his subject, the man began to gesture dramatically as he described how Little Wolf had sneaked up behind
Crazy Horse's lodge to listen to him laying his plot to kill
Crook, Clark, and the other soldiers before they bolted from
the reservation. As the Indian went through his recitation,
Clark kept an eye on Crook, measuring how the general was
weighing things, especially this matter of the story coming
through three mouths, through three Sioux who held no
goodwill for Crazy Horse.

But this was hardly a difficult case for William P. Clark to
decide. Easy to figure out that once Crazy Horse discovered he
would not have anything like the freedom he once enjoyed on
the wild prairies, the war chief had become less than cooperative. At first it was only with minor things, like his refusal to
sign the agent's ledger for the rations and goods his people
were drawing each bi-weekly ration day. Then it was a most
vexing problem: his refusal to go to Washington with the other
chiefs to visit President Rutherford B. Hayes. And beneath it
all was the rumbling current of those rumors and the talk from

*Those placed at this meeting were Red Cloud, Red Dog, Young
Man Afraid, Little Wound, Slow Bull, American Horse, and Yellow
Bear, along with interpreters Frank Grouard, Baptiste Pouier, and
William Garnett.

the spies Red Cloud put out, their ears and eyes open to every-thing. Not that Red Cloud wasn't a carping, grasping, insecure man, a leader who had surrounded himself with a loyal cadre of venal lieutenants, some of whom held more jealousy, dis-trust, and animosity—read that: more outright hate—than even Red Cloud himself had for Crazy Horse.

But at least Red Cloud and Spotted Tail were the white man's chiefs. And Red Cloud, well . . . make no mistake, he was William P. Clark's Indian. They were both going to help put each other on the map. Clark had convinced Red Cloud that by working together they could reinstate Red Cloud to his former position of prestige and power over all of the Oglala. By so doing, Clark would be vaulted into a position of prominence not only at Camp Robinson, or in the eyes of Department Commander George Crook . . . but Clark was fully aware that Lieutenant General Philip H. Sheridan and Commander of the Army William T. Sherman were both watching the unfolding of events with much interest. The success that Clark had been crafting for himself and Red Cloud was about to bear fruit.

How he had played Crazy Horse like a fine-tuned violin! By first grabbing the honor and the limelight for accepting the war chief's surrender back in May, and now for backing the man into a political corner so that he would refuse all overtures from Crook to do what the government was re-quiring of him. The man was nothing more than a savage warrior, one who thought in no other terms but fighting all the efforts of the white man to acculturate him into the new life he must lead here for the rest of the nineteenth century. With emotions so primitive, it had been almost child's play for Clark to guide and manipulate both Red Cloud and Crazy Horse into playing their opposing roles, one antago-nistically against the other—with Lieutenant Clark becom-ing all the more important for it!

Not that Crook was easy to deal with on this. That old soldier had seen it all, done it all, and a man didn't rise to his stature without having learned a thing or two about the poli-tics of the army's command structure. When Woman's Dress finished re-telling his story to the quiet room of loyal chiefs, Crook questioned Woman's Dress again about the details of Crazy Horse's plot. Clark figured that cross-examination probably made the general feel as if he were really getting to the bottom of the scheme.

For a moment the lieutenant turned to look at the face of No Water, sitting there between Red Dog and their chief, Red Cloud. No Water turned and gazed at Clark for but a moment, his eyes steady, just the hint of a smile in them. Then the warrior looked away, a gaze of serious and rapt attention returning to his face as he stared at Woman's Dress.

I wonder if he has the slightest idea that I know he orchestrated this whole charade, Clark thought to himself. *Does No Water realize that I know who created this whole jumble of lies?*

"Bat, you or Grouard ask the chiefs now what they think of this man's testimony," Crook instructed. "Do we have something to worry about? And if we have something to worry about...do these chiefs realize they have a problem in their midst?"

As soon as Baptiste Pourier put the question to the Sioux, some of them began to mumble to one another, their eyes furtive and darting. But...every one of these men had something to say. Finally, it was Red Cloud's faithful mouthpiece who stood to speak.

When Red Dog had finished, Pourier translated. "'We have a trouble-maker among us. Crazy Horse will never be one of us. He will always be wild and...'I can't think of how to translate that word—"

"Take your time," Crook said.

"'Crazy Horse will never learn to be a reservation man,'" Pourier continued. "That's as close as I can make it."

"Good," Clark said, feeling assured. "What else did Red Dog say?"

A look came over the faces of all three interpreters at that point, and they glanced at one another knowingly. Grouard looked away. Garnett nodded to Pourier.

So it was Bat who made the startling announcement.

"The chiefs say to tell you they will kill Crazy Horse if Three Stars wants them to."

For a moment the room was hushed, even to every breath being held. Clark could not believe his ears! He had brought the chiefs here, hoping at the best they would fall into line behind a plan to arrest Crazy Horse and get him out of the way, shipped off to a prison cell where he could rot far, far away from Clark's reservation.

But these men must truly fear Crazy Horse. If they only hated him, were only jealous of him, then these chiefs and headmen would just want to have the despised one taken away from the reservation so that he could never again rally around him all those who were dissatisfied, disaffected, yearning for a breath of the old days and the old ways. But...Red Cloud, American Horse, Little Wound, No Flesh, High Wolf, Little Bear, and Red Dog...they were damn well afraid of Crazy Horse!

And that was an emotion Clark could understand. The only way you rid yourself of the source of your fear was to get rid of it once and for all.

"K-kill him?" Crook blustered, clearly taken by surprise with the offer from the chiefs. His eyes briefly touched the stunned Garnett, then Clark. Beneath his beard, the old warrior had blanched. "No. N-no, that would be murder. We can't condone murder."

The room was quiet, the chiefs looking at one another, studying Crook's face too. Then the general realized that nothing was happening.

"Bat—tell them that, goddammit!" Crook bellowed.

"I think it was a mistake to make scouts out of the Northern Indians in the first place," Pourier complained. "No one had any business giving them guns—"

"There was nothing wrong with my decision to make them scouts!" Clark bawled like a wounded man.

"Just tell them I can't approve of murder," Crook said firmly, jabbing a finger at Big Bat. "No. Tell them I can't approve of them murdering Crazy Horse."

As soon as the general's words were spoken, the chiefs

went back to murmuring among themselves. Clark was reminded how much they seemed like a pack of wolves worrying over the bones of a carcass at that moment. The question had been decided! No longer was there going to be any worry over how Crazy Horse would react to this or react to that. No more would he have to be concerned with the sullen, unresponsive, melancholy, brooding savage who thought far too highly of himself. Crazy Horse was going to be out of Clark's hair, one way or the other, from this hour on!

" 'Winters ago,' " Pourier started to translate Young Man Afraid's words when the chief stood to talk, " 'the white man put Spotted Tail in a prison because he did not do what the white men wanted him to. Spotted Tail came back to his people a changed man. His heart was softened toward the white man. Perhaps we can we do this to Crazy Horse?' "

Clark almost felt sorry for Young Man Afraid, knowing how close he used to be to Crazy Horse, in their old army-fighting days together. But with his surrender, Young Man Afraid had vowed to make a new life for himself and his people, and had been doing everything he could to make things better for his band...whereas Crazy Horse took no interest in the affairs of the reservation. Young Man Afraid was looking beyond tomorrow, while his old friend Crazy Horse was still thinking only of the past. Clark felt his heart tug for Young Man Afraid—knowing how hard it must have been for him to suggest what the others were already agreeing to, nodding their heads as the chief spoke to Crook.

"So say all of you?" Crook inquired. "Bat, ask each one of them if they are in line with taking Crazy Horse into custody."

One by one by one, the chiefs and headmen solemnly nodded their assent to making the arrest.

Crook rubbed the flats of his sweaty palms down the front of his unbuttoned blue vest with a long sigh, as if wiping his hands clean of any blame in the coming confrontation.

And Clark realized there would be a confrontation. Bloody and messy, and probably deadly too. Crazy Horse would not let himself be taken alive. The lieutenant quickly looked over the chiefs in the room, studying their eyes and faces, men he had begun to know. How many of these men realized, Clark wondered, that Crazy Horse was already a dead man because they knew he would not allow himself to be taken alive?

"One thing is imperative, Mr. Clark," Crook said. "These Indians must be in on the arrest. It cannot be made out to be the U.S. Army or U.S. soldiers arresting this notorious chief. Think of the way the press would play that up! No, when the soldiers go to make this arrest, they will be acting in concert with, and supporting, these chiefs and their warriors."

The general saw Clark nod in agreement; then he turned to Pourier. "Bat, tell the chiefs they will make the arrest. Say how important it is that it will be a show of these headmen taking control of a troublesome situation. How vital it is that this is a Sioux solution to a Sioux problem. The army is only going along to help if...if major trouble breaks out and there's a break off the reservation."

Clark was euphoric. He never would have hoped for so stunning a solution! The chiefs murmured for a moment, their heads nodding; then Red Dog and American Horse voiced their strong support for the joint operation to arrest Crazy Horse in his camp.

"I will leave the details of the operation to Lieutenant Clark here," Crook said after the chiefs had offered their hand-picked warriors for the arresting posse. He turned and removed his rumpled coat from the back of a chair, draping it over his arm as he began to re-button his vest. "Captain Kennington, if you would be kind enough to arrange an escort for me back to the Sidney station so that I can catch a train to carry me on west. I have men and supplies already arriving at Camp Brown for this campaign to capture the wild Nez Perce who Generals Howard and Gibbon haven't been able to stop."

"But you will, General Crook!" Clark cheered, buoyed by this opportunity to make Crazy Horse a prisoner. "If anyone can catch the Nez Perce, it will be George Crook, sir!"

"Hera, hera!" James Kennington agreed. "I'll go see to getting your escort formed up, General."

The colonel left the room as the chiefs continued to talk among themselves. Crook turned, speaking low and meaningfully to Clark, whispering so his words would be heard by no others.

"Make this clean, Philo," he said, using Clark's middle name, how a mentor would address his protégé. "Do all in your power to pull this off without making a mess. You don't botch it, there's a feather in your cap and another rung in the ladder for you."

"You have my word, General."

Crook placed his hand paternally on the young lieutenant's shoulder. "Whatever it takes—iron shackles or bald-faced lies—I want Crazy Horse out of here as quickly as possible and on his way to Omaha. I'll leave word for Bradley and my staff to have the prisoner transferred from Omaha on to Florida."

"F-florida?"

Crook looked at Clark strangely. "Yes. The Dry Tortugas. Where in the hell did you think we would send a man of Crazy Horse's history?"

"The Dry Tortugas," he repeated. "Of course, General. It's the only place where the bastard won't ever be a thorn in our sides again."

He Dog could tell from the way Billy Garnett stammered his words that he was very upset, probably even scared. The half-blood interpreter had rushed off to find some of Crazy Horse's old friends, he said, finally locating He Dog and Red Feather at the agent's office more than a mile and a half from the Soldier Town.

While Red Feather hurried away to tell Crazy Horse of the sinister plan that had been set into motion, He Dog and Agent Irwin hurried back to Camp Robinson, seeking out Crook, even soldier chief Bradley.

"The commanding officer of this post wasn't even invited to this little planning session with the chiefs?" Bradley roared as Garnett translated for He Dog.

The four of them stood inside the soldier chief's small office. Bradley went to the door, and shouted for a sentry to bring him Clark.

"How did you expect to get away with this, Lieutenant?" he roared once William Clark had hastened into the room.

"We're not getting away with anything," Clark argued. "This was the plan constructed by General Crook himself."

Bradley's eyes narrowed. "So where is the general now?"

Clark glanced at the door. "He's on his way to the railhead at Sidney, sir. From there to Camp Brown to continue his preparation for—"

"Who the hell did he leave in charge of this operation to arrest Crazy Horse?"

Stiffening, Clark responded, "Me, sir. I was at the business of notifying the company commanders to ready their troops because we would be leaving the post tonight, accompanying the chiefs—"

"*You* . . . you were readying *my* troops?"

Clark swallowed. "Yes, sir. Under orders of General Crook."

"And just how long did you figure I would be kept in the dark about you using my troops to arrest Crazy Horse?"

"As soon as I had everything in motion, I was going to report to you."

"Dammit, Clark!" Bradley roared. "I am your commanding officer. Not General Crook. And this is *my* post. The last time I looked you weren't in command here, and neither is Crook. Do I make myself clear?"

He shook his head slightly. "N-no, sir. Not clear."

"If there is going to be an operation to arrest Crazy Horse that will involve my troops, it will be under my orders. The very nerve of it!" and he slammed a fist down on his desk, with language and anger even He Dog could understand without Billy Garnett's translation. "Going after a man like Crazy Horse in the dark! That's the act of cowards!"

Clark bristled. "W-we're not cowards, General—"

"Any man who will sneak up on another under the cover of darkness and take him at night is a coward in my book! We're going to execute this in broad daylight—do I make myself clear, Mr. Clark?"

"You've made your point, sir," Clark backed down.

"This operation of yours should be carried out by the light of day. The life of Crazy Horse is just as dear to him as my life is to me," Bradley declared. His eyes fell to the floor and he stared at his boots. "It's as plain to me as the rising sun that it was a mistake in the first place to give him a pistol and a gun."

The lieutenant said, "When he surrendered last May, I don't think any of us knew it would turn out like this."

"Now it's up to you to clean up the confusion you've caused," Bradley said.

"Confusion?"

The colonel turned to Garnett. "Go to the chiefs. Be sure they understand that no one is going to arrest Crazy Horse tonight. Tell them they aren't supposed to come with their warriors until we send them word that we are ready." Bradley turned to glare at Clark, saying, "That's when the soldiers will go with them to make the arrest, when we have enough troops. I will go now to wire Laramie and see that they send me up some cavalry companies."

"How many do you propose, sir?" Clark requested.

"At least four."

"I'll make the request in your name, General," Clark said. "With your compliments."

"You may carry my orders to have those troops sent up here, Lieutenant. But you don't have my compliments, by any stretch."

"General Bradley," Clark said apologetically, "these are General Crook's orders."

"This is my post, Lieutenant—and you're letting yourself step awfully close to insubordination."

"Yessir."

"Now what in blue blazes did you and Crook figure you

were going to do with Crazy Horse if you managed to capture him alive?"

"You and I are to see he gets put on a train and sent to Omaha. From there to the Dry Tortugas."

"Maybe it will be better for him to be out of here, away from his people for a while," Bradley said. "Things might settle down."

When Billy quietly explained that to He Dog, the old warrior sensed the breath seeping out of his body and he gritted his teeth in shame and anger.

"So you and Crook are taking Crazy Horse out of my hands?" Bradley asked. "Is that the plan?"

"Yes, sir. To get the man as far away from here as possible, so he can't cause any more trouble for you."

Bradley turned and stared out the one smudged window in his cramped office. When he finally spoke again, the colonel only said, "Lieutenant Clark, you have your orders. Get those troops up here from Laramie—on the double."

CHAPTER TWENTY-THREE

BY TELEGRAPH

Horrible Details of the Sacking of Saghra.

The Turks Jubilant Over Their Successes.

WASHINGTON.

The Sitting Bull Commission.

WASHINGTON, September 1.—Gen. A. G. Lawrence, of
Newport, R.I., has accepted the position on the Sitting Bull
commission representing the interior department and will
act in conjunction with General Terry in conferring with
the Sioux chief, provided he still remains in the British
possessions.

"WE ARE ALONE?" ASKED RED FEATHER.

Crazy Horse looked strangely at his brother-in-law,
winded and excited as he was that early evening when he
came running up to the nearly deserted camp. "Only your
own sister is here. Why?"

The younger man's eyes were watchful, darting here and
there. "Where is the trader's daughter?"

"She is staying the night at the agency," Crazy Horse explained, sensing his brother-in-law's unease. "Visiting her
family. So we are alone."

"Truly?" Red Feather asked.

"We can talk, brother. Rest a moment, because you need
to catch your breath."

"There is so little time," Red Feather huffed in excitement, his eyes wild and wide. "You never came to the council grounds."

"We watched from the hillside for Three Stars, but he never showed," he answered. "Why should I go somewhere I am not wanted, go to talk to someone who doesn't show?"

"Woman's Dress turned him around. He told Three Stars you have plans to kill the soldier chief."

If such a betrayal hadn't been so serious, Crazy Horse would have felt like laughing. He heard a tiny gasp, and turned to see Black Shawl's eyes fill with terror above her hand that kept the sound of utter fear rushing out of her throat.

"Did Three Stars believe Woman's Dress?"

"It seems so," Red Feather admitted. "He sent on his two interpreters to the council grounds, where they talked only to the agency chiefs."

Crazy Horse took his eyes off his wife, saying to his brother-in-law, "How can they think that I would plot to kill Three Stars? I have given my word and we have already untied our ponies' tails! Have these old chiefs so muddied Lakota honor that the *wasicus* can believe such a foolish lie as this?"

"I see the White Hat's hand in this," Crazy Horse grumbled. "When I first came in, he acted as if he had just become my new best friend. But when he found out I was not going to be his lapdog like all the rest of Red Cloud's and Spotted Tail's men, the White Hat turned his face against me."

"Three Stars told the chiefs they were to gather at the Soldier Town, but not in a big group."

"Yes, he would want them to come in twos and threes, so it would not look suspicious to any of our friends." Crazy Horse felt a tensing of that warrior spirit that lay deep beneath his breastbone, like the flexing of a muscle he had not used in a long, long time. "They went to the Soldier Town?"

Red Feather nodded and gulped. "All of the chiefs who

have whispered behind their hands went into a secret council with Three Stars, the White Hat, and another little chief too."

"Behind their log walls?"

"Yes," he answered his brother-in-law. "I did my best to find a place in the shadows to hide and listen, but the soldiers came and drove me away."

"So how is it you know these things they said about me?"

"I hid and watched until their council was over," Red Feather disclosed. "I saw the half-blood translator come out. I followed him until I could talk to him in secret. He told me of the plans to come for you."

"They are coming for me?" he asked, his chest tightening.

"The agency loafers—they were asked to pick their own men. A lot of them are coming here together," Red Feather admitted. "Along with some soldiers...to take the Crazy Horse village."

"Aiyeee! All this for one lone man?" Crazy Horse said, shaking his head. "I can see their cowards' faces—these brave men who come in a crowd for me."

Nodding, Red Feather said, "The White Hat offered a sorrel horse and a lot of the *wasicu* money for the man who killed you."

"So this little chief really doesn't want to make me a prisoner, does he?" he asked, knowing he had finally discovered the truth about the White Hat after so many moons of lies and bad talk behind his back.

"No Water stood up and made a vow that he would be the one to kill you himself."

"Ah, my old friend, No Water," he growled. "He could not kill me as a man, so he comes after me with many others, like a pack of hunting dogs running down the fox."

"Even Young Man Afraid..."

He saw how sad that made Red Feather to tell him that. And Crazy Horse swallowed hard with the stab of that news. Young Man Afraid, a childhood friend. So long, so long.

"How about Little Big Man?" he asked with anxiety. "My old *akicita* friend who has become an agency metalbreast?"

":The half-blood did not mention his name," Red Feather admitted. "I don't think he is the kind to come after you in a pack like the other yapping dogs."

With a sigh of relief, Crazy Horse reached out and touched Black Shawl on the arm. "By the time they get here, we will be gone a long time."

"Three Stars has given orders for extra bullets and guns to be handed out to the friendlies."

"When?"

"The half-blood told me they will come for you tomorrow morning."

"That does not leave us much time to go," he said with bitterness. "There is so much to do to get so many packed up and started away from this place—"

"My brother," Red Feather interrupted, putting his hand on the chief's arm, "you must no longer think of everyone else. Now is the time to think only of yourself...because most of the others who have depended upon you for so long—now you won't be able to depend upon them."

He studied Red Feather's eyes for some time. "I am alone?"

Squeezing his brother-in-law's forearm, Red Feather said, "Not completely. Your truest friends will always be at your back."

"When I first came to this place, I wanted nothing more than peace and quiet, to be left alone," Crazy Horse explained with deep regret. "Instead, I was talked to and talked to by the white man—morning, day, and night. So many voices talked to me until my mind was a whirl of confusion and I could not sleep. I haven't slept in so many nights."

Turning, Crazy Horse reached behind him and took from the leather loops that rifle the White Hat had presented him the day when the Northern People became scouts for the army. He ran his hands down the barrel, caressing the smooth wood of the stock. Then handed the weapon to his brother-in-law.

"Go now, brother. Tell the others everything, exactly as you have told me. If they are going to stand beside me, they must be ready to ride at any moment. That is, *if*... they are going to stand beside me."

Red Feather could barely choke out the words as he stopped at the doorway: "We will never desert you... even unto the death."

Sept. 3, 1877
Hqs., Dept. Missouri

General Crook
West-bound Train
Union Pacific Railroad

I do not like the attitude of affairs at Red Cloud Agency, and very much doubt the propriety of your going to Camp Brown. The surrender or capture of "Joseph" in that direction is but a small matter compared with what might happen to the frontier from a disturbance at Red Cloud.

Philip H. Sheridan,
Lieut. General

The White Hat's scheme to capture Crazy Horse did not go off as he had hoped the morning of the third because Lieutenant Clark was still waiting for those cavalry troops to arrive from Fort Laramie.

All that day and on into the night of September third, when three additional troops of Third U.S. Cavalry rode in, Billy brooded darkly on that—why it was going to take so many Lakota and so many hundreds of soldiers to take one man into custody. If the soldier chiefs were worried about all the Northern People putting up a costly fight to protect their leader, as Lieutenant Clark argued to justify the overwhelming force he was gathering, then to Billy's way of thinking all those spies the White Hat had in the Crazy Horse camp weren't doing a very good job at all.

While it was true that the Hunkpatila chief had surrendered with more than 200 warriors back in May, by now, in the first flush of September, those still fiercely loyal to Crazy Horse had to number less than half-a-hundred. Why, even his old friend He Dog had moved his own clan's lodges away from the camp weeks ago, out of concern for the safety of the women and children in that highly charged atmosphere of rising tensions.

As the moon rose that warm Monday evening, Lieutenant Jesse M. Lee, agent over at Camp Sheridan, learned by accident that in secret Clark had sent for chief Spotted Tail to come to Camp Robinson as quietly as possible. Barely able to contain his anger at this maneuver pulled behind his back, Lee demanded to see Colonel Luther Bradley so that he could ask the district commander to order Spotted Tail back immediately, where the chief might better control his own people when they learned that Crazy Horse had been arrested at the Red Cloud Agency. Receiving Bradley's permission to depart Camp Robinson during this tense time, Spotted Tail and Agent Lee, along with his translator, Louis Bordeaux, prepared to depart at three o'clock on the fourth, right after moonset, their small escort well armed for what they believed might well be a perilous journey.

From the back of his horse in the dark that had swallowed the land, Lee looked down at Clark and the White Hat's two interpreters, quiet in giving his advice: "Mr. Clark, don't let Crazy Horse get away. He might make a break for it and run our way, to Spotted Tail's agency."

"There's not a ghost of a chance of that, Mr. Lee," Clark scoffed almost sarcastically. "Crazy Horse can't make a move—he can't sneeze or take a piss—without my knowing it. And I can damn well seize him any time I want him. I'll send you news of our success in writing by a dependable courier when we have him in hand."

With the coming of a rosy dawn on September fourth, Billy stood with a cup of coffee steaming in the cool air, watching the hundreds and hundreds of army horses moving back and forth across the parade, while almost 400 Lakota warriors waited in the background, and two Gatling guns were noisily rolled out by their nervous gun crews, hitched to the trained teams that would pull them down White River toward the Crazy Horse camp some six miles distant. Those agency warriors who had no guns were allowed to draw weapons and ammunition for the day's dangerous duty.

Across the last day and a half now Billy had hoped that this plan of Crook's and Clark's would be pulled off without bloodshed. If overwhelming force was used, perhaps Crazy Horse's supporters would decide not to put up a fight. Perhaps Crazy Horse himself would see there was nothing he could do but surrender. With such an array of might as this, Billy reasoned, the man could actually be captured without an outbreak of trouble. Then Crazy Horse could be shipped off to spend some time in prison . . . just as his uncle, Spotted Tail, had been. When he came back—like his uncle had eventually returned to his Sicangu people—Ta'sunke Witko would be a changed man too. Things would be better on the reservation. Better than if events continued in the direction they were headed right then . . . because to Billy it seemed a dead certain thing that someone would kill Crazy Horse by accident, if not on purpose.

"It's almost nine!" Clark bellowed impatiently that Tuesday morning as he clomped out of the adjutant's office. "We're ready to go, Colonel Mason," using the major's brevet rank.

"Very good, Mr. Clark," Major Julius W. Mason replied. He in turn mounted up and rode over to his cavalry, placing at the head of the column those three companies he had brought in from Fort Laramie only hours ago—D, E, and G of the Third U.S. Cavalry.

The horse soldiers turned neatly in form and moved out, starting down the east bank of the White River with Garnett along, the artillery rattling behind them. At the same time, Clark mounted up and led his agency scouts: the Oglala who swore allegiance to Red Cloud, American Horse, and Little Wound, along with a few Arapaho, and even a handful of friendly Cheyenne who had somehow managed to remain at the Red Cloud Agency when their chiefs and people were shipped off to Indian Territory. Among the Lakota moving down the west bank were men like No Flesh, Young Man Afraid, No Water, along with three Hunkpatila from Crazy Horse's camp—Big Road, Jumping Shield, and Little Big Man—Oglala whose loyalty to the whites might be severely tested this very day. Because of this, Clark had Frank Grouard instruct the other, more steadfast warriors to stay together and be wary of those less than trustworthy should events come to a fight.

"Better to know who is at your side and at your back," Clark had warned Grouard, "than to be sorry after the shooting starts."

The column hadn't put Camp Robinson far behind them when the first of the couriers sped away from Clark, carrying news to the village some six miles away that they were coming and did not want to stir up a fight by frightening the Crazy Horse people unawares. At five miles both soldiers and warriors in the long march were quiet, every man thinking on what was to come on this historic day. Four miles and the bright autumn sun warmed them. Then at three miles the first couriers came galloping back with a rumor that Crazy Horse must have fled, for they could not find him.

Downriver, through the shimmering distance, Billy fixed his gaze on a large, black object more than a quarter of a mile away. As he shaded his eyes in the morning light, Garnett thought he spotted a smaller piece of the object move to the side and disappear into the timber bordering the White River.

"I'm going ahead to see something!" he abruptly shouted to Lieutenant Clark as he jabbed heels into his horse's ribs.

It wasn't until he was a couple hundred yards away that he finally made out the shape of that large object. Reining up beside the carcass of a dead pony, he was gazing down at the many fresh bullet wounds in its chest and head when a figure slipped out of the brush.

"Hau! Half-blood white-talker!" the Hunkpatila cried as the startled Garnett leveled his carbine on him.

Billy caught his breath. "Looking Horse! You surprised me. I came to see what this was in the road—"

"Red Cloud's friends killed my pony!" the Hunkpatila man cried as he started toward Garnett's horse with a limp, favoring a leg.

"They shot it?" he asked, finally close enough to notice how badly Looking Horse's face was beaten.

"And they pounded me up too," he groaned, wiping some more blood from under his oozing nose.

Garnett saw how dusty and torn were the man's shirt and leggings, bruises already starting to purple his cheeks and jaw. "They hit you with their hands?"

"Hands, yes—then guns and clubs," Looking Horse said through swollen lips. "Because I am a Crazy Horse man."

"Who of Red Cloud's friends?" he demanded through gritted teeth, angry to think of any man being outnumbered and made to suffer such a terrible beating.

"Woman's Dress!" he whimpered. "He did most of this to me. The bad one who shot my horse."

"There had to be others."

Looking Horse nodded, squinting with a swollen eye in the morning light. "Three others. I don't know their names—because they were Red Cloud men, loafers. Never knew them before."

"How did this happen?"

"They were coming to the Crazy Horse camp when they bumped into me. Woman's Dress signaled with his arm in a friendly sign, and when I rode up to them, thinking everything was good, he suddenly shot my horse. As it fell down, the other three jumped off their ponies and beat me bad."

"Didn't you have any weapons with you?"

For a moment Looking Horse glanced on up the road to where the soldiers were approaching; then he explained through puffy lips, "I hid my rifle and pistol from the soldiers when we surrendered...but I lost them today when Woman's Dress stole them from me."

"Didn't have a chance to shoot any of the men who attacked you?"

With a shake of his head, Looking Horse grumbled, "It is

not right for Oglala to fight Oglala. I could never kill one of my own people ... the way Red Cloud and his kind will do."

"What are you going to do now?"

Looking Horse quickly glanced up the road again, concern filling his eyes. "I will hide in these bushes again. That's what I was going to do when I saw a rider coming, but soon I noticed it was you. I will hide again and let all the soldiers go by."

"There are a lot of agency men coming too," Billy warned.

"Red Cloud's?"

"American Horse's men too."

"Thank you, white-talker," Looking Horse said with real gratitude as he turned and hurried away at a crouch for the thick undergrowth on the bank.

He watched Crazy Horse's friend disappear into the brush, then wheeled his horse around and started back for the head of the column. By the time he arrived back among Clark and his most trusted scouts, Little Big Man had grown visibly upset. The moment Garnett rode up, the metalbreast started chattering, asking Billy to tell the White Hat that he wanted permission to race ahead to the Crazy Horse camp.

"Why does he want to do that?" Clark demanded.

"He's getting really worried now that his old friend will do something that might get him killed. Maybe he can say or do something to convince Crazy Horse that it would be for the best to allow the arrest to take place ... instead of fighting it and getting a lot of men killed."

Nodding, the lieutenant gave his permission, and Little Big Man bolted off.

"It is a good thing," Billy said. "Maybe we can do this without anyone getting hurt."

It wasn't long before Little Big Man loped back to Clark, in the company of some of the other couriers who had already gone to the camp. The White Hat called Billy over to translate.

"Crazy Horse has gone," Garnett translated for the lieutenant. "He took his full-blood wife."

"Black Shawl, yes," Clark said impatiently as the columns on either side of the river continued to move along at a steady pace.

"But he has taken some friends with him," Billy continued his translation.

"Ah-ha!" Clark said with certainty. "I knew he would gather all those hot-bloods around him! So they've prepared to make a stand of it, eh?"

"No," Garnett explained, "only two chose to go with the chief."

"On-only two?" the officer echoed.

"Lieutenant!"

At that cry from Mason across the river near the mouth of White Clay Creek, Clark and the others peered at the nearby hillside where the major and some of his men were pointing. On the brow of a rounded knoll some six hundred yards from the cavalry column, more than seventy warriors had assembled. Clark and his 400 Indians immediately turned into the river and began their noisy crossing. As they splashed onto the east bank and loped in two directions along the halted cavalry, one lone horseman spurred his pony off the top of that hill, making for the soldiers.

"Who is that?" Clark demanded.

"They don't know," Garnett announced after listening to the Oglala around them. "Only that he's from the Crazy Horse camp."

"Tell the scouts to stand aside," ordered the lieutenant. "It's likely the others have told him to surrender because of his young age."

As the hundreds watched in silence, the youth galloped through the ranks of scouts and brought his pony up when among some of Young Man Afraid's Oglala. They began to talk quietly among themselves.

Clark turned to Garnett, saying, "That proves just what I feared, Billy. Crazy Horse does have his agents among our Indians at this very moment. We better watch our backs if this comes to a fight."

"But Crazy Horse has gone," Billy argued.

Wagging his head, Clark said, "I'll wait to see for myself."

"This is not good," Billy warned, pointing at the ceremonially dressed warrior starting down the long slope, riding away from the rest of the Hunkpatila on the brow of the hill.

"Anyone know who that is?"

"I don't," Garnett said, shaking his head, noticing that the advancing horseman was dressed in his finest war regalia, including a showy double-trailer war bonnet that spilled off the rear flanks of his prancing pinto. Concerned that someone was going to get shot, he asked for advice from Little Big Man.

"Name is Black Fox," responded Little Big Man. "He's a Crazy Horse man, and dressed for war."

Of a sudden Black Fox kicked his horse into a spirited gallop, riding straight for the soldiers until he was almost fifty yards away, and suddenly veered to the left, racing along the line of march, shouting out his challenge to Lakota and soldier alike as he shook a Springfield cavalry carbine in one hand and a Colt revolver in the other—both weapons taken from the Greasy Grass battlefield.

"What the hell is he saying?" Clark demanded.

"'I have been looking all my life to die,'" Billy translated, listening carefully as Black Fox approached, yelling at the top of his lungs. "'I see only the clouds and the ground. I am all scarred up.'"

"What does that mean?" asked the lieutenant. "All scarred up?"

"He has seen many battles," Garnett said, watching the middle-aged Black Fox take a skinning knife from the scabbard at his waist and put it between his teeth as he rode even closer to the Indian scouts. "He's survived many fights before—was in the Custer battle. This is a very brave man—riding right toward the bullets that can kill him. A very brave thing to do—"

"We must stop this bad show!" American Horse cried as he pulled his horse up with Clark's and Garnett's.

"Go do what you can," the lieutenant pleaded. "If we don't have to, I don't want anyone killed."

Nodding, American Horse immediately advanced his horse several paces as he pulled his own pipe from a beaded pouch slung over his shoulder. With this held in one hand, he stretched out his arm and began to shout to the onrushing warrior.

"Think of the women and children behind you!" American Horse yelled above the noise of those around them. "Come straight for the pipe, Black Fox! The pipe is yours to take!"

Gradually the warrior began to slow his horse, then reached up and took the knife from between his teeth. In moments he had halted his pony right before American Horse and the agency scouts. "Hau!" he cried to the leaders of the agency scouts.

"The pipe is yours," American Horse repeated. "Let's smoke."

It did not take long for Clark and a half-dozen of his leading scouts to dismount and seat themselves on the ground in a small circle with Black Fox. While they loaded and lit the pipe, beginning its path around the ring, Mason's cavalry waited in formation and the Hunkpatila cautiously rode down from the top of the hill, parading back and forth across the gentle slope in a drill, watchful and staying very close to their leader.

"Crazy Horse is gone," Black Fox said when he had smoked and passed the pipe to his left. "He has listened to far too much bad talk about him. I told my friend that we had come in to the reservation for peace, to stay here in peace . . . but he listened to all this bad talk about him. Now he has gone and the people belong to me. I came out riding to die this morning—but you saved me, American Horse."

"Gone?" Clark demanded as Garnett was giving a running translation. "Where's he gone? Is he fleeing north?"

"No, I don't know where he will go now," Black Fox said, then turned and hollered to his warriors, "All over. Go back to camp now."

With Clark, Billy watched in surprise as the Hunkpatila horsemen immediately turned their ponies around, started up the hill, and eventually disappeared from sight.

"We were coming to take Crazy Horse and his weapons," American Horse explained to Black Fox. "But since he is gone, it is up to you to bring the people closer to the agency."

"Yes. This will be good to do," Black Fox agreed. "You saved my life. It is a good notion to bring the people in closer now that Crazy Horse is gone—"

"Look!"

Everyone seemed to be yelling at once, soldiers and warriors both. Most of them pointed at the four figures visible in the distance, just emerging from behind a faraway knoll and racing to the northeast...in the direction of Spotted Tail's agency.

"The scouts think that must be Crazy Horse!" Garnett yelled above the hubbub.

Clark was digging in his saddlebag for his field glasses as he demanded, "Who's that with him?"

"Little Big Man already told us that a few minutes ago," Billy said sadly. "Only his wife and two trusted friends are fleeing with him...vowing to stay with Crazy Horse to the death."

CHAPTER TWENTY-FOUR

Canapegi Wi
MOON WHEN LEAVES TURN BROWN, 1877

THEY ARE COMING!" SHOUTED THE YOUTH AS HE CAME TEARing into the nearly deserted camp. Shell Boy had some strands of his long, black hair plastered to the sweat on his face. "And they have two wagon guns with them too!"

Crazy Horse drew in a long sigh as he looked at his wife. "We can't take anything."

"I don't need much, husband," Black Shawl said, turning toward her horse, to which she had already tied two small parfleches of her most precious personal belongings. "We . . . never have had much, besides each other."

On all sides of them the last of the most faithful were finishing their frantic labors of tearing down the lodges, loading the covers onto travois, packing up children and belongings. Some of the women had begun to stream out of camp, their men starting back toward the agency and Soldier Town to do what they could to delay the attack. But most had already gone before dawn, when riders told Crazy Horse that few were already making a break for the north. Instead, his people were fleeing the danger and hurrying for the safety they believed they could find in Red Cloud's camp.

His heart had grown more and more hollow as he looked all around him, seeing how they were deserting him in this moment. Rather than escaping north into the badlands together, rather than fighting together as they always had . . . the Hunkpatila were scattering, abandoning their leader.

But—he thought—that was all right now. He did not want to force any of them to choose between escape and staying behind, between life and death.

So when the terrible news came, Crazy Horse made sure the word was spread through this camp. Last night he had chosen to go alone, taking only Black Shawl with him. Everyone was free to go where they wanted now, he announced. He was no longer their leader. Still, Red Feather would not let the two of them go without him. Kicking Bear—half brother to Black Fox—and the youngster called Shell Boy either. The three vowed to stay with Crazy Horse to the end.

"We are coming and you cannot stop us," his young brother-in-law declared. "You might just need us at your back when trouble comes."

And they all knew that it was just a matter of time—a day, maybe two at the most—before trouble caught up to them.

"No," Crazy Horse said. "I want you to go with Black Fox, who is leading the others. Stand with them as the men have always done. Put yourselves between the soldiers and our families."

"Is that the best way I can protect my sister?" Red Feather asked.

"Yes, because you can give us time to get started on our escape."

So they watched Black Fox lead out the eight-times-ten of those warriors most committed to their chief, then turned away from the last of the women struggling with uncooperative animals, or left to choose between what to take and what to leave behind, because very few horses still belonged to the Oglala. Crazy Horse leaped atop the bare back of his gelding and started them away from that camp.

Only the four on a run now: a wanted man, his ailing wife, and two young warriors who rode behind, ready to defend their chief to the death.

Instead of racing north onto the open prairie, he had chosen to make the long ride for his uncle's agency. Spotted Tail could give him some measure of safety while the evil of all those lies against him were put straight once more. Liars like

Grouard—who could trust the Grabber anymore as it was? Or trust No Water? Every Oglala knew that No Water had won back the body of Black Buffalo Woman, but ever since that day when No Water shot Crazy Horse in the face she had been nothing but an empty shell.

How could the *wasicus* trust those who lied again and again until it became so natural? How could the soldiers want to arrest, imprison, even murder Crazy Horse, when he had never spoken anything less than the truth all his life?

As Black Shawl and the rest of the women in camp had hurried about making preparations to scatter on the winds or flee to Spotted Tail's agency, Red Feather and Black Fox kept an eye on the Soldier Town, and on Red Cloud's camp too. They were to signal with mirrors the moment either of them saw the soldiers and their dog pack of friendlies on their way. That morning they came.

After riding a short distance, Crazy Horse turned and looked back at the deserted camp. His hollow, aching heart felt every bit as empty.

William Clark's belly boiled with the acid of bitterest disappointment. Just watching Crazy Horse fleeing in the distance made every nerve in his body scream out in agony.

The lieutenant bawled his orders to the half-breed interpreter. "No Water! Take your best men on the strongest horses and go after Crazy Horse!"

The sorting out began immediately, with each of the twenty-five men who were going on this chase making his choice of a horse of his liking from those who would remain behind. No Water had already grabbed the reins of two extra horses to take along on the chase.

Yanking his horse around in a half-circle, Clark found another of Red Cloud's most trusted leaders. If any two men could be counted upon to capture that outlaw, it would be No Water and, "No Flesh! Pick thirty of your finest fighters and put them on your best horses. You are going to bring Crazy Horse back to me!"

" 'What will the White Hat give me for bringing back the trouble-maker?' " Garnett translated No Water's words.

Clark raised himself in his stirrups and bellowed, "I will give two hundred dollars and my fastest horse to the man who brings me back the scalp of Crazy Horse!"

Billy Garnett barely had the words out of his mouth when No Water yipped wolfishly, reining about on his pony and kicking the animal savagely with his heels. The two spare horses lunged away behind him the moment No Water snapped on their lead ropes. It was clear to Clark that this longtime enemy of Crazy Horse would spare no effort to stay in the lead and snatch the bounty offered for the capture of the fleeing criminal.

With a sigh of satisfaction, Clark looked over at Major Mason. "Colonel, I believe we're ready to march on to the camp and see what we can make of things now."

"Is that our quarry?" Mason asked, pointing off in the direction the agency scouts were taking in their race, yipping and howling like wolves on the chase. "Have you sent them after Crazy Horse?"

"Don't you worry about Crazy Horse, sir," Clark said. "We don't have a thing to worry about now."

No Water could almost taste the fury burn at the back of his throat. At long last he was given sanction to chase down and kill this lifelong enemy of his. Ever since childhood, he and Crazy Horse had been dancing toward this day, preparing for the moment when No Water would not only kill, but rip off the scalp of the man who had caused him so much shame and ridicule.

Far, far in the distance he noticed one of the four turn to look over his shoulder. They could see that No Water was gaining a little on them. He must be yelling at the others. Perhaps that rider was Crazy Horse himself.

I hope he recognizes me, No Water thought to himself. *Then he'll know death is riding on his tail!*

The horse beneath him began to falter, even though he

kicked and kicked it again, forcing it to gallop up the steep hill. At the top it stumbled and nearly went down with him. Flecks of whitish foam were plastered around its jaws, sweat crusted in the horse's mane, in patches beneath his bare legs. The animal fought, jerking its head every time No Water kicked it hard in the ribs, forcing it to race on down the slope for his quarry. As it continued to toss its head, the warrior dropped the reins and leaped to the ground.

Some of his men were succeeding in coming up the slope behind him. He had to keep himself in the lead, and slow up the progress of the others.

"Shoot this horse!" he shouted to the first warriors to arrive.

"Why shoot it?" one of them hollered up the slope at No Water.

"I have run it into the ground!" he screamed before he turned away from the animal just then collapsing to its knees. "Do as I order you and give this horse a merciful death!"

In a couple of bounds he was on top of a fresh horse, wheeling it away, down the hill from the crest where that first exhausted animal rolled onto its side, and weakly thrashed its legs.

"A merciful death for that stupid beast," No Water cursed under his breath as the wind came strong into his face, pushing this new horse to a furious speed. "When I catch up to him, there will be no such merciful death for Crazy Horse!"

He doesn't stand a chance against me! No Water thought as he unstintingly whipped his pony with a rawhide quirt. *Crazy Horse has but one horse, only one he will have to carefully pace ... while I have two left me!*

The good doctor had done everything he could think of in attempting to make the army give his friend, Crazy Horse, evenhanded treatment.

Days ago, the moment he learned from Louis Bordeaux

that Grouard had made the mistake in translation and hadn't attempted to correct the mistake, Valentine McGillycuddy went to see George Crook himself. But the general said he trusted Grouard, had for a long time, so the matter would stand, especially after he had learned of Crazy Horse's plot to kill him a couple of days ago. From what the doctor could see, that lie about a murder plot had sealed the chief's arrest... and there would be no turning back now.

When Crook sped away from Camp Robinson, heading west to begin his campaign against the Nez Perce, McGillycuddy hastened to see Luther Bradley, asking permission to visit the Crazy Horse camp.

"I hope to get at the truth of this matter, General," the doctor explained. "If I can talk to Crazy Horse, I can find out what he really said, what he really meant."

"All fine and good, Doctor," Bradley had replied. "But I can't give you permission. It would be far too dangerous at this point. Too much already set afoot, you see."

"They know me, Crazy Horse and his warriors," McGillycuddy pleaded. "Besides, if I take Fanny along, they'll know I have come for a medical visit—"

"Take your wife?" Bradley spewed. "My god, man! Are you daft? Why would you sacrifice your wife to those savages who are worked up to no good? No—I won't allow you to go and that's that!"

So here he was tagging along as surgeon to those eight troops of cavalry and some four hundred friendlies, riding down the White River for the Crazy Horse village about six miles from the post. It seemed the only way the doctor was going to get a chance to see for himself just how this arrest would play out. Then word came back to the army's side of the stream that Little Big Man was saying Crazy Horse was fleeing, and that he had left some eighty warriors behind to delay the soldiers... and a sudden flurry of activity among the scouts was explained as more than fifty hand-picked warriors were set off after their prey. Crazy Horse had been seen escaping in the distance.

"He's likely got his sick wife with him, Colonel," McGillycuddy explained to Mason, using the major's brevet rank.

"Why not leave her behind if she's so ill?"

The doctor said, "This is proof he's not making a run for his old country. He's going to Spotted Tail's agency."

"Perhaps. But I happen to think it's proof that he's fleeing the reservations entirely," Mason advised. "He'd leave her behind if he were merely in fear of his life. The fact that she's with him clearly shows that he's escaping, and taking with him all that he holds dear."

Clark loped up and halted his horse, explaining that it was time for the cavalry to continue on to the Crazy Horse camp, accompanied by the balance of his agency scouts.

There wasn't a lot left to the village Valentine had come to know so well. Not even one smoking fire. It was clear the women hadn't taken the time to cook any breakfast that morning. Perhaps news that the forces were assembling at the post had reached the camp and the warriors set their women to tearing down the lodges and packing the travois. No more than a half-dozen lodges were still standing, another handful nothing but lodgepole skeletons, stripped bare of their canvas or buffalohide covers, left standing because of the approach of soldiers.

Sending out Clark's scouts to see what they could determine as the direction of the escapees, Mason posted guards to watch from the surrounding heights while he and his officers decided what to do next.

"It appears the bastard is running for Spotted Tail," Clark reported as he rode back up to the major.

Mason asked, "Is that where the rest of his people are fleeing too?"

Shaking his head, Clark said, "No, for the most part they're scattering, and a lot are racing south for Red Cloud's camp."

"Where it's safer for them."

"Damn right, Colonel," Clark said. "So I'm taking my leave of you and following those scouts I already put on his trail. With any luck at all, we'll have him by nightfall."

"Lieutenant Clark?" McGillycuddy said.

He turned to the surgeon. "Yes, Doctor."

"I will ask you as a personal favor to me," and Valentine considered how best to put it, "that you take special pains to be sure some of your scouts won't act too enthusiastic about their duty."

"Oh," and the lieutenant smiled, "I've already seen to that, Doctor. I've offered a reward and my best horse to the man who...arrests Crazy Horse." He immediately turned away and snapped a salute to the major.

Mason returned Clark's salute and said, "Let's pray you don't have to pursue this outlaw all the way into Burke's jurisdiction."

"Not a chance, Colonel!" the lieutenant cheered as he reined away. "I'll have him back at Robinson by sunrise!"

From time to time Crazy Horse turned on the back of his pony and looked over his shoulder at the pursuers. At places where the terrain allowed, he could see behind them far enough to make out some of the horsemen. But most often, Crazy Horse could only see the wisps of dust all those hooves spun into the hot late-summer air as they raced down the White River for his uncle's agency.

Still, there was that one rider who seemed obsessed in his pursuit, staying far out in the lead, ahead of the others whenever Crazy Horse looked back. At first the horseman had two ponies strung out behind him. Then there was only one spare animal, convincing Crazy Horse that one horse had already been ridden into the ground. That rider could only be one of two men who pursued him with such dogged determination, with old, nagging scores to settle. It might be Woman's Dress...but then he realized it had to be No Water. There wasn't another man he could name who would be pressing the chase with this much zealous energy.

Right at the first of their flight, the three of them had put Black Shawl out in front, shielding her as Lakota men are taught to do for the women and children, for the old and the sick ones, whenever a village had to flee attacking soldiers.

They rode behind her up and down every hill, and sometimes one of them had to whip her horse to make it run faster.

And run they did, across every flat and down every hill. But when they came to a slope they had to climb, Crazy Horse had them rein up and slow to a walk, attacking the slope at an angle if possible, giving their horses a chance to save their strength. Once the top was reached, he and the others would yell to the animals, urging the utmost from the horses as they raced headlong to the bottom and across the flat until they reached the next hill. Then they would again slow to a walk, conserving every ounce of energy from these Indian ponies... while he was certain that No Water was beating his animals to death, not only with his rawhide quirt, but with his obsession to race up and down every hill without slowing, without paying heed to conserving his horse's strength.

The sun was about to set. In the mid-distance he could see the first smudges of firesmoke rising from the hundreds of lodges tucked in the valley of Beaver Creek. They must skirt far to the south around the Soldier Town protecting the agency of Spotted Tail's Sicangu people. Not that anyone could have alerted the soldiers here of his flight from Red Cloud's agency. Just that under the *wasicus*' laws a Lakota was not allowed to move from one place to the other without prior approval, even when he had friends, not to mention relatives, on his uncle's agency. He thought of his father, wondering how things would be now for Worm. Hoping his uncle would take him in and let him live on Beaver Creek... a magical valley that held so many special memories for him.

Up ahead he saw the first of familiar faces, Mnicowaju warriors emerging from the camp of Touch-the-Cloud, his dear, old friend and uncle on his mother's side. This band of Northern People would understand his need. For many summers they had fought to defend the old hunting grounds with him, so these men would see that his wife was protected. They would be his shield... placing themselves between him and those mad dogs whom Red Cloud, American Horse, and the White Hat had loosed on his back-trail.

Everything would be different now that he had made it to the camp on Beaver Creek. His heart lifted—oh, how he wanted to sing out a brave-heart song in joy!

Everything would be all right now!

CHAPTER TWENTY-FIVE

4 September 1877

Camp Robinson, Neb., Sept. 4, 1877.

General Crook,
Fort Laramie.

The cavalry and Indians started out at 9:30 this morning.
Crazy Horse's village broke up last night and when the
Command got out to the ground, there were but few
lodges to be seen and these making for the Bluffs; some
of them came in and others were captured. We have
about half the village—forty-odd lodges—and the
Agency Indians are after the balance and are sure to cap-
ture some of them. Crazy Horse left the village this morn-
ing with his sick squaw for Spotted Tail, and we have
twenty picked Indians after him who promise to bring
him in. All the friendly Indians behaved extremely well,
Little Big Man among them. Will telegraph you to-mor-
row at Cheyenne.

Bradley,
Lieut-Colonel

"DAMN HIM TO HELL!" WILLIAM CLARK GROWLED IN EXAS-
peration when he caught sight of No Water in the distance,
coming to the realization that no one was going to catch
Crazy Horse before the war chief reached Spotted Tail's
agency. "Damn his soul to hell!"

About the only thing the lieutenant had to show for all the
hours and all those miles put behind them was the fact that
most of the Crazy Horse people had already chosen to join

one of Red Cloud's camps, being herded in that direction by large parties of his agency scouts. Minutes after he had dispatched No Water and No Flesh with their chosen posses to pursue Crazy Horse, Lieutenant Clark had asked Red Cloud and Red Dog, American Horse, and Big Road to divide their warriors into search parties that were to scour the country surrounding what had been the Crazy Horse camp on Little Cottonwood Creek. They were to bring in all members of the Northern bands.

"Those who will not comply willingly," Clark told them through interpreter Billy Garnett, "then police them. Do what you have to—but just make sure they don't escape downriver for the other agency."

After more than 300 warriors were on their way in four different directions, Garnett assured the lieutenant that the scout leaders understood that word *police*.

"*Akicita*," the translator said for Clark. "Just like the Lakota have always done when it comes to keeping men in the camps, when they are close to a buffalo herd, or making sure people behave on the march—for the good of the band. *Akicita*...they understand what you mean by bringing them in."

Only a few families, lodges, or individual warriors had managed to escape the valley of Little Cottonwood before the noose closed around them. Very few slipped through and reached Spotted Tail Agency on the heels of Crazy Horse. But the mere fact that a few of them had made fools of Red Cloud's friendlies did nothing but make those agency scouts seethe with anger. Bands of the scouts came pouring out of the hills to join Mason's eight companies in covering those last two miles of their approach to the agency, itching for a fight—even though it would mean a fight within their Sioux family. So it struck Clark as odd when Mason ordered his battalion to turn aside and make for Camp Sheridan and Red Cloud's Oglala continued for the nearby village.

Of a sudden they heard piercing war cries and angry

shouts. Mason called for a halt as they prepared for possible attack. As it turned out, the soldiers were in no danger— only Red Cloud's scouts. When the agency friendlies showed up near Touch-the-Cloud's village, those northerners who were supporters of Crazy Horse boiled out of the camp, brandishing what weapons they still owned. A few carbines to be sure, but hardly a match for all the firearms the army had issued to its scouts. Mostly the Northern warriors carried long lances, rock-or nail-studded clubs, waving tomahawks in the air as their ponies hurtled them on a collision course for the Oglala.

And just before it appeared he would witness the bloody outbreak of a civil war among the Sioux, Red Cloud called off his men. *And a wise thing he did,* Clark thought to himself. Although the scouts had more guns, the fact that those warriors racing out to confront the friendlies had been the very men who destroyed Custer's men when the Seventh U.S. Cavalry had possessed more guns was a sobering reality for any man who might consider attacking a camp of those Northern bands under the war hero named Touch-the-Clouds. Making grand and showy gestures with a mighty lance, one of the Minniconjou joyfully herded none other than No Water and his played-out horse toward the stockade walls at the agency.

But at that moment, Spotted Tail's Brulé warriors began to show up, intending to drive back Touch-the-Cloud's Minniconjou, by quickly riding around the outskirts of the Minniconjou camp to join up with their allies among Red Cloud's scouts, making a formidable force. In Touch-the-Cloud's village women were screaming orders, shouting to gather their children, hurriedly tearing down their lodges, preparing to make a break for freedom and safety while their men formed a barrier and sought to protect their families from Red Cloud's war party. Both sides fiercely drew up their lines, shook their weapons, dared the other to strike first, shouting insults and shrieking their war cries at one another—but neither side had suffered a casualty. So far.

"You're the expert here, Lieutenant," Mason bawled as he brought his horse to a halt beside Clark's. "What do you think? Is Crazy Horse hiding himself in that camp?"

"I don't think those Northern hostiles would have put up this fierce a show if they didn't have any reason for turning back Red Cloud's posse," Clark grumbled.

Mason cleared his throat and asked, "What's your take on the situation then? Should we force our hand and go in after him?"

"No," Clark said after some consideration. "I suggest that we take our troops on to Camp Sheridan. Captain Burke commands only two companies to withstand any attack on his post. I want to talk to him and Agent Lee to see if we can come up with a way to convince Crazy Horse to come in for a talk, try to convince this outlaw to give up peaceably and without a struggle that will clearly leave a lot of soldiers and our friendlies dead—not to mention how the Northern bands will bolt and scatter across the prairie."

"Another goddamned Sioux war to put down," Mason growled.

"Mind you, all I want is one Indian," Clark reminded firmly. "I want him in irons, taken back to Robinson, and on his way to Omaha and the Dry Tortugas as General Crook ordered."

"That's what Sheridan wants done with him?" Mason asked, referring to their division commander.

Clark regarded the older war veteran a moment, then carefully stated, "Yes, sir. I am acting under Lieutenant General Sheridan's instructions to General Crook. That's where I derive my authority."

"Very well, Lieutenant," Mason sighed. "I'm turning my men aside to Camp Sheridan, which means you'll have your shot at convincing Crazy Horse to surrender to you on his own."

"My brother!" Touch-the-Clouds called out as he hurried forward on foot toward the four riders who had just raced into his village.

Four people could have caused no greater stir among these people who had fought to the bitter end with Crazy Horse at Red Flower Creek, then at the Greasy Grass, at Slim Buttes, and finally in the last skirmish against the Bear Coat on Buffalo Tongue River while a blizzard descended upon the battlefield. This was like returning to the fold of friends and family, seeing familiar faces, hearing their calls of greeting as they crowded around Crazy Horse, his wife, and the two brave friends who had accompanied them here to safety.

"My horses, they are very tired," Crazy Horse confessed.

"See that they are watered!" Touch-the-Clouds ordered, and it was done. Four young boys leaped through the throng to take the lathered ponies off to the creek. "My heart is frightened for you, brother," he said as he laid a hand on Crazy Horse's shoulder. "You have come from far away, against the laws of the *wasicus* and the soldiers—on four weary horses. Are you being chased?"

"No Water will be the first to show up," he told his mother's brother. "If he does not kill the last of the three horses he rode after me."

"Why would No Water be chasing you here?"

For a moment Crazy Horse stared back to the southwest, gazing up the White Earth River in the direction of Camp Robinson. "Because the soldiers and Red Cloud's chiefs have made a pact to take me prisoner."

Around them more than a hundred women shrieked in terror. Men shouted that this must finally mean war against Red Cloud's loafers. Touch-the-Clouds, all seven feet of him, held up his arms and bellowed for quiet. Finally he asked the fair-skinned one before him, "What will they do with you if they take you prisoner?"

He shook his head. "There have been too many lies told about me already."

"The Grabber?"

"Yes, you know about that lie," Crazy Horse said. "But another, more serious lie comes from the lips of Red Cloud's most faithful: Woman's Dress, and his brothers."

"What have they said against you?"

"That I was plotting with my friends to murder Three Stars when we met in a council," he answered, feeling Black Shawl's weight lean against him. "Brother, can your people find a place where my wife can lay her head and rest? It has been a very hard ride."

Touch-the-Clouds put his arm around Black Shawl's shoulders, helping support her as he said, "And she has been so weakened by the white man's coughing sickness too." He waved two women over.

Crazy Horse briefly clutched his wife's hand before she started away with the Mnicowaju women, swallowed by the crowd of murmuring people who were listening to the story.

"We will not let them take you by force," Touch-the-Clouds promised. "We must see that you have a chance to tell Three Stars and the White Hat that the words of Woman's Dress are nothing more than lies intended to destroy an honorable man."

"Thank you—"

Shrill shouts burst from the lower edge of the camp. Everyone turned, and the women began to shriek at once. In the distance they all could see the dust being raised by the many hooves. Beneath the clouds of spinning dust turned golden in the slanting afternoon light came more soldiers than they had confronted at the Greasy Grass. And with them rode half as many Lakota horsemen, blood of their blood, but riding on the side of the loafer chief Red Cloud and the *wasicus!*

"Strike the camp!" Touch-the-Clouds gave the fateful order. "Tear down the lodges and prepare to flee!"

All around them now the headmen were issuing orders to their society members as the women wheeled away, searching desperately for their children here in the heat of a late-summer afternoon when the little ones would be scampering about on the prairie, or down by the creek, perhaps playing in the nearby hills of the Beaver Valley. Frightened women combing the camp for their little ones, then turning back to tear lodgecovers off the poles as the hundreds of soldiers and agency scouts came loping toward them.

"Protect your families!" Touch-the-Clouds led the cheer. "Put your bodies between the enemy and the innocents!"

Crazy Horse's head burned in utter dismay. He had caused this, bringing this terror down on these people who had already lived through so much, stayed loyal so long, been faithful to him day after day of fighting and running. There were a few of his Hunkpatila here, men who had made the race from his camp, following on his heels . . . but the majority were Touch-the-Cloud's people, who were clearly prepared to defend this one lone Hunkpatila against a mighty array of Bad Face warriors come to snatch him away.

"Tell me!" Crazy Horse yelled above the tumult. "Among those who are coming to take me prisoner, does anyone see my old friend, He Dog?"

When the question was shouted to the approaching Red Cloud forces, the answer came back. One of the Northern men turned and relayed the message, "No, He Dog did not come with the *wasicus'* scouts. But they tell me that Little Big Man, Young Man Afraid, and Big Road did come along on the chase."

"O-old friends," Crazy Horse said. "Even old friends have turned their backs on me, betrayed me this day."

It caused him such heartache. Despite their falling out in recent days, He Dog had stayed behind rather than join this mob clamoring to get their hands on Crazy Horse. Perhaps he had refused to come because of all that they had shared in the old days. Now it was clear that three old friends had shown up—like the worst brand of betrayal—making his heart shrink and grow so cold.

"Come with me now, nephew," Touch-the-Clouds said, leaning down closer to Crazy Horse's ear. It was hard to hear in the midst of the yelling and screaming, the taunts and the threats as those two lines of warriors drew up to challenge one another.

"Where?"

"To the lodge of the agent."

"A *wasicu*?" he asked in horror, stopping in his tracks.

Touch-the-Clouds looked kindly upon his relative. "He is a fair-minded man, Crazy Horse. You must go to him so you can reveal the sinister evil behind these lies being said about you."

"Crazy Horse is here?" Jesse M. Lee asked his interpreter to repeat, startled at the news in light of Clark's plans to arrest the Oglala leader back at Red Cloud's agency.

Interpreter Louis Bordeaux said, "Yes, Crazy Horse has come to the camp of Touch-the-Clouds."

"And he's alive? Not wounded?"

Quickly, Bordeaux questioned the young courier from the Minniconjou camp. "Yes, Crazy Horse is alive. Not hurt, no."

This young lieutenant in the Ninth U.S. Infantry, who had been serving as Indian agent for Spotted Tail's reservation since early May, turned to look at Captain Daniel Webster Burke, post commander at the nearby Camp Sheridan. "How in Hades has this happened, sir?"

In the complete darkness just after moonset, in the wee hours of that Tuesday morning, Lee and Brulé chief Spotted Tail had put Camp Robinson behind them with an armed escort of more than twenty Indian soldiers, not reaching the chief's camp until ten o'clock. They immediately went to the village, calling together the chiefs and headmen so Lee could explain to them that over the next few days their people might well hear rumors of trouble at Red Cloud's agency upriver. He wanted them to remain calm, since the army was going to sort out with Crazy Horse and his closest friends a story that Crazy Horse was planning to assassinate General Crook. With the leaders' promises not to become aroused by rumors and unfounded tales, the weary lieutenant mounted up and made the short three-mile ride on in to his quarters at the agency itself.

Feeling as if he were sitting on a powder keg, and wondering when—and who—would light the match, he immediately went to bed at midday. It seemed no time had passed at all before loud voices outside their quarters awakened him. Looking from the window, Lee spotted Louis Bordeaux and another interpreter, Joe Merrival, at the center of a small gathering just outside his office, the two translators talking to an excited young man who was tightly ripping the reins attached to a horse white with foam. As he buttoned up his shirt and stepped out the door, it was plain to see that the young Sioux rider had come from some distance, punishing his animal in the bargain.

"What's he got to tell me, Joe?" Lee asked.

The dusky-skinned half-breed turned to find the agent stepping down from the plank porch. "Says he come from Red Cloud's agency. Brings word there's fighting going on over there."

Fighting! Damn if Philo Clark doesn't have his hands full now! But we might all be in for it too.

As soon as he had extracted what skimpy information the youngster had to tell, Lee told Bordeaux to get over to Camp Sheridan and bring Captain Burke back with him. They had to put their heads together, perhaps call in Spotted Tail and Touch-the-Clouds, along with their leaders, to somehow forestall for the worst. If fighting had broken out between Red Cloud's friendlies and Crazy Horse's Northern People, then the flames of violence just might spread like a prairie fire whipped by a terrible wind. After all, the Spotted Tail folks had been loyal to the white man and his soldiers a long time, while until this past spring, Touch-the-Clouds had been a Northern hostile, a close friend and fighting companion of Crazy Horse.

It didn't take long for Burke to show up; and the two of them had begun to discuss their strategy in talking with the chiefs they were about to call together, instructing them to assemble outside Lee's office, when a second rider came racing up to the agency buildings with more news.

Black Crow, one of Spotted Tail's most trusted shadows, was carrying the electrifying news that Crazy Horse had reached their camp with his wife and two friends.

"This isn't good news, Lieutenant," Burke murmured all but under his breath as he stood and shifted his gunbelt. "It's a sure thing that the fighting at Red Cloud is going to follow Crazy Horse here. Only a matter of time now."

Bewildered that one of Spotted Tail's most trusted lieutenants would be the one to carry so important a report, rather than one of Touch-the-Cloud's Minniconjou, Lee turned to Bordeaux. "Ask Black Crow if he has any idea what Crazy Horse wants here."

In a moment the interpreter translated, "He asks to stay with his friends at his uncle's agency. Wants to move away from Red Cloud's people."

Burke and Lee looked at each other for a moment before the captain exclaimed, "By the stars, if it doesn't appear Crazy Horse is requesting sanctuary from you!"

Lee agreed. "That's exactly what he's looking for—sanctuary."

"Agent Lee! Agent Lee!"

Turning into the open doorway, the lieutenant squinted into the sunlight, finding an excited interpreter, Joe Merrival, pointing up the road to the Red Cloud Agency. A soldier atop a lathered horse burst through the open stockade gate and reined up in a cloud that threw dust on the half-Mexican translator.

With a salute, the young soldier gulped and eyed both officers, asking, "One of you officers Lieutenant Lee . . . ah, sirs?"

"I am Jesse Lee."

The private pulled a twice-folded piece of parchment from inside the folds of his damp blue fatigue blouse, urged his weary pony forward three more steps, and handed the parchment down to Lee there on the porch of his office.

Tearing open the thin dollop of wax sealing the flap, the lieutenant looked at Burke, and said, "It's from Clark, sir."

"To you?"

"Yes, Captain."

Burke nodded gravely. "Tell me what it says."

Aloud, Lee began to read.

Dear Lee:

There has been no fight; Crazy Horse's band is just go-ing into camp, and will give up their guns without trouble in all probability. Crazy Horse has skipped out for your place. Have sent after him. Should he reach your agency, have "Spot" arrest him, and I will give any Indian who does this, $200.

                                                    Clark

"We've got to get on top of this before it blows up in our faces, Lieutenant," Burke warned. "We damn well know they'll be coming for him, and real soon. Troops and friend-lies both. If we don't convince him to come to the post—or, better yet, to the safety of your agency stockade—we're go-ing to have a major bloodletting on our hands right over there in the Touch-the-Clouds' camp!"

"I suggest we go immediately to see what we can do to convince Crazy Horse that his very life—and the lives of many of his people—might depend on him getting behind the walls of this agency."

"A capital idea." Burke slapped his hat back on his head. "As soon as we get Crazy Horse to return here with us, I'll go straightaway to Camp Sheridan and mount up my two small companies. We'll return and prepare to receive Crazy Horse . . . or prepare for the worst."

Lee waved Bordeaux over so he could give instructions to both interpreters. "Joe, I want you and Louis to go hitch up the ambulance for Captain Burke and me. You two can ride your horses if you prefer. While you're doing that, I'm going to alert Lucy to keep her eyes open—that some rumor or news might come in from any quarter while we're gone."

"Where you want us to go with you?" Bordeaux asked.

"Louis, I want you and Joe to come with me to the northerners' camp."

It gave Jesse Lee no small measure of reassurance that both of his translators chose that moment to quickly glance at each other, something less than bold confidence in their eyes.

CHAPTER TWENTY-SIX

Canapegi Wi
MOON WHEN LEAVES TURN BROWN, 1877

CRAZY HORSE CARRIED NONE OF HIS GUNS, NOT A BOW, lance, nor tomahawk. All he had folded across one arm was that red blanket.

"Stay with me, *Sicun*," he whispered to his spirit guardian as he watched the buildings appear through the trees far ahead of him.

I am with you, Ta'sunke Witko. I will be with you to the end—till you draw your last breath ... and I am freed for the rest of time.

At his right hand rode White Thunder, one of Spotted Tail's headmen. An agency Indian. A good man, Crazy Horse thought, but nonetheless a loafer. At Crazy Horse's left, in that honored position, rode his uncle Touch-the-Clouds. And right behind the Hunkpatila leader was Black Crow, Spotted Tail's trusted comrade. This Sicangu headman carried a soldier carbine across his thighs. Another coffee-cooler. Neither White Thunder nor Black Crow had fought a battle, made war against the *wasicus,* in many a summer, many a summer ... but here they were, escorting him and Touch-the-Clouds as if they were important enough to ride in the shadow of so honored a pair of Northern fighting men.

Black Crow's narrowed eyes clearly showed he was attempting to disguise his fear with haughty indifference. Neither those darting, furtive eyes nor his trembling finger poised over the trigger of that soldier carbine he carried mattered to Crazy Horse. Behind those two Spotted Tail men rode a double-handful of trusted warriors—friends of Touch-the-Clouds—men who had fought beside Crazy Horse in the heat of summer battles, and in the bitter cold of winter skirmishes too. While they did not carry any soldier carbines, these warriors were nonetheless armed with traditional Lakota weapons...and imbued with the same warrior spirit that continued to whisper inside the head of Crazy Horse with every step he took on this road to meet the *wasicu* agent.

Out of a gap in the trees ahead came two riders. Behind them came a soldier wagon, with two men inside. He recognized one of the horsemen—the half-blood interpreter called Bordeaux, who had been present at the council when the Grabber made his lie about going north to fight with Three Stars until there wasn't a white man alive. And the other was the agent for his uncle's reservation.

This is a strange thing!

"Meeting the agent on this road?" he asked his spirit guardian.

Yes. Ever since the day when you surrendered and came in from the north country, the agents and soldier chiefs have called you to come to council. But now it seems this one is eager enough to talk that he comes to you.

"A good sign," Crazy Horse whispered. "Perhaps—as Touch-the-Clouds promised—I can trust this one to straighten out the lies said about me."

After Crazy Horse raised his arm and called out to the approaching white men, the agent turned to speak to the half-blood interpreter.

Translating the agent's words, the half-blood said in Lakota, "I was coming to the camp of Touch-the-Clouds, where I heard you had come. I received the messenger you sent, with word that Crazy Horse had arrived. This must mean there is serious trouble at Red Cloud's agency. It is a dangerous thing to run away when so many are wanting to take you prisoner."

"So you knew about the soldiers' plan to take Crazy Horse prisoner?" asked Touch-the-Clouds.

The white agent nodded.

Then the interpreter said, "Come back to the agency with us. We will make you safe from harm while we work hard to make all the lies straight again."

"We were already on our way to see you," Touch-the-Clouds explained. "Crazy Horse wants to talk. I told him that you could be trusted to do what is right to make the lies and trouble go away so he can come live in peace with me. Here at his uncle's agency."

For a moment the agent listened as the translator made the white man words; then he said, "The agent cannot say if Crazy Horse can stay here at his uncle's agency. That will be decided by the soldier chief at Camp Robinson. But the agent wants you to know that he will do everything in his power to make sure you are treated fairly and have a chance to tell your story—so you can correct those poisonous lies the Grabber and Red Cloud have told about you."

The eyes of both Touch-the-Clouds and Crazy Horse went to stare at the half-blood's face in surprise.

Crazy Horse spoke for the first time, asking, "Do you believe in my truth?"

·Nodding, the man called Bordeaux said, "Yes. With my own ears I have heard the bad words that can come from the Grabber's mouth. As for myself, I don't think you would be fool enough to murder Three Stars in such cowardly treachery. Crazy Horse may not be all things good . . . but I do not think he is a coward who would murder an unarmed man during a peace talk."

"Because of your honor, I want you to stay close to me when I talk to the agent this afternoon," Crazy Horse requested. "I want someone who I can trust when they put my words into the white man's talk."

The agent and the soldier turned their wagon around, and together with the white men and their interpreters, all continued toward the agency buildings, the log stockade coming in sight through the shimmering afternoon heat waves. Along the road were gathering those women and old ones who had overheard the first news that Crazy Horse had reached their reservation. Of a sudden, a great pounding of hooves and shouts from many voices struck his ears. From their left appeared a large party of horsemen, all of them armed, beginning to yell the instant they spotted Crazy Horse. Leading this force was his uncle, Spotted Tail.

Behind him the Northern men began to holler. Crazy Horse turned as one of Touch-the-Clouds' warriors whirled his pony around and galloped off, heading back to the Mnicowaju camp to report the threatening arrival of these friendlies. Spotted Tail halted his men with a wave of his arm, and the horsemen quickly spread out in a broad crescent, the horns of which nearly surrounded the Northern men. Both sides hollered and boasted, shouting challenges to one another, shaking their weapons—either firearms or bows—making curses against the other band until Touch-the-Clouds told his warriors to be silent.

Not to be outdone, Spotted Tail quieted his men, who outnumbered the Northern warriors by more than ten-to-one. More Mnicowaju warriors arrived from the camp of Touch-the-Clouds, narrowing the odds down to no more than two-to-one, but now the scene could not have been more tense.

Swinging out of his saddle, the agent waved his arms and shouted for quiet. Then he turned back to face Crazy Horse, speaking loudly in his white man tongue. Bordeaux talked loud too, assuring his translation could be heard over the noisy clamor of hundreds upon hundreds of voices.

"Crazy Horse. You must go back to the Soldier Town at Red Cloud's agency. That is the only way you can tell your story to the big soldier chief there, the soldier chief who will decide about the lies said of you."

"Go back to Red Cloud's agency?" shrieked many of the Northern men.

Other Northern warriors bellowed, "They are cowards and back-shooters there!"

"We will never let Crazy Horse go back to be murdered by Red Cloud's cowards!"

From behind Spotted Tail came boasting challenges, arguing that Crazy Horse was an Oglala and as such did not belong here.

*You do not belong here? Where do you belong if not
with these people? If Red Cloud's Bad Faces have turned
their hearts from you...don't you deserve a home with
your uncle's people? To camp with Touch-the-Clouds'
northerners? To live out the rest of your days camped beside your father?*

The Sicangu of Spotted Tail became restless behind their
chief, daring to press closer to Touch-the-Clouds' warriors.
At the same time, these Mnicowaju veterans were not about
to be intimidated as they urged their ponies forward, growling their own threats.

Of a sudden, his spirit guardian spoke again.

*You are the only one who can stop the fight from break-
ing out right here, Ta'sunke Witko! You are the only one
who can prevent Lakota from spilling another Lakota's
blood!*

"Stop!" he roared aloud, flinging his red blanket across
his lap and raising both arms in the air—his hands empty to
show that he was unarmed. "We are all the same people! Do
not hurt your relations!"

Mitayake oyasin! Yes—we are all related!

Like he had passed his empty hands over both angry
sides, the voices were suddenly stilled and this patch of open
ground between the agency buildings fell deathly silent.
Only the restive, nervous ponies snorted and pawed at the
trampled earth.

The white agent spoke to his interpreter; then the half-
blood said, "Crazy Horse, the *wasicu* says you are a good
man with your people. You just proved it to him—stopping
the trouble so no blood will be shed here on your account. I
am sure none of your people would see you hurt. And neither will I. I promise you—if you will put your trust in me—
I will see that you get to Red Cloud's agency unharmed, so
you can talk with the soldier chief there."

Instead of responding, Crazy Horse stared at the sky, the
late-afternoon sun slanting through the dust raised by all
those hooves like shafts of gold the color of cottonwood
leaves in autumn. *Autumn, when Three Stars promised us*

our hunt. Autumn, when the Hunkpatila always went in search of the buffalo, to make meat and take the hides that would keep the People fed and warm through another winter. Autumn was a crucial time for the People.... With no hunt, they would have to live on the white man's skimpy handouts of moldy flour and stringy meat from the spotted buffalo.

"If Crazy Horse has no words to speak," Spotted Tail announced in his dramatic and stentorian voice as he slid from the back of his pony, "I have some words to say to him."

Crazy Horse watched his uncle step across what little open ground remained between the two opposing forces, the tall chief stopping right before his nephew.

"For many winters you have roamed around like a fire in the north. You are of the Oglala. The Oglala are your people. Something good should happen to you with them. Instead, you have run away like a wolf with its tail between its legs."

Grumbling arose on both sides, but Spotted Tail raised his arm and quieted the angry crowd. "Look around you, Crazy Horse," he commanded. "At my agency the skies are clear, and the air is still and free from any dust stirred up by trouble. This is my tribe. *I* am the chief here. Spotted Tail ... is the chief. Every Indian must obey me. Sicangu, Mnicowaju, and Hunkpatila too. You say you want to come here to live in peace. If you stay, you must listen to me in all things. We never have trouble here because I am chief. That is what I have to say to you!"

Your uncle—he did not even acknowledge that you are his nephew! Look how he stands, haughty like Red Cloud! He wants to separate you from his family, don't you see? The great Spotted Tail has no nephew named Ta'sunke Witko!

"These are my words, Crazy Horse," Spotted Tail continued, his face passive, not showing the bond of family between them. "If you stay here, you must obey me!"

In the background, Crazy Horse heard the muffled clicking of more gun hammers than he could ever count.

Suddenly, the face of an old friend appeared through the

crowd pressing in on all sides. Chips! The shaman who made for him the bullet-proof medicine of the eagle's heart!

Apparently alarmed by the noisy emphasis given to Spotted Tail's demands by the clicking of all those gun hammers, this Bad Face Oglala had leaped into the open, grabbing the soldier chief's arm.

"Crazy Horse is a brave man," Chips pleaded. "But today he is tired and his medicine is too weak for him to die. If these Sicangu cowards have to kill anyone... tell them to kill me! Kill me instead!"

"No," injected the interpreter as he eased the excited shaman back toward the Mnicowaju line. "No one is going to be killed today."

With deep appreciation in his eyes for what Chips had offered, Crazy Horse turned to stare at his hard-talking uncle.

I still have a few good friends... but who are you, Spotted Tail? The warrior of old? Or another wasicu dog loafing around the white man's forts?

"You are not Sicangu," Spotted Tail continued haughtily when Crazy Horse did not give him the honor or courtesy of a reply. "You are Oglala. That is why I want you to go back to your people before something bad happens to you here. If you come live on this reservation, you must do what I tell you."

Just like the white man, he scolds you! Spotted Tail— the one who was arrested and put in a prison, coming back a changed man. A chief who heeds the scolding words of the white man... and now he scolds you as if you were a naughty child! "You must do this! You must do that!" Or what will happen? Or what, Ta'sunke Witko?

Spotted Tail warmed to his harangue. "The best thing for you to do is go back to your people. Some of my chiefs will accompany you back to your people as soon as possible. I have spoken!"

This great Sicangu chief who once spilled the blood of many wasicu soldiers—he is saying you are no longer his relation? Scolding you to go back to the friends of Red Cloud who lie about you, plot against your life? This is all Spotted Tail has to say to his nephew?

"'It is time that Crazy Horse comes into the agent's house,'" announced the half-blood after Spotted Tail finished, translating the white agent's words. "'You will be safe there.'"

He turned to look at his other uncle. Touch-the-Clouds nodded. "Yes," was all Crazy Horse said to the agent and his interpreter.

Inside the log building with the two *wasicus,* along with Touch-the-Clouds and Spotted Tail too, Crazy Horse felt like a wild animal that had been trapped. He continually gazed outside where he saw the two lines of angry warriors snarling like starving dogs growling over a bone.* The Northern men would protect him from the Sicangu, who wanted Crazy Horse so they could turn him over to Red Cloud's scouts, to get him off their reservation, to put an end to this trouble.

But then the interpreter was talking, asking why he had left his camp.

"I fled only when a great war party of soldiers and scouts came to take me prisoner. They brought two wagon guns with them too, marching toward my camp of women and children. All this might to take one man into their custody? I dared not let the very young and the old, the innocents, be hurt when it came to fighting. And . . . be assured it would come to fighting when they took me prisoner."

"Does Crazy Horse intend to fight instead of going back to speak to the soldier chief so he can get the lies laid to rest and put behind him?" asked the interpreter.

"When I came in I gave my word to the White Hat, and later to Three Stars," Crazy Horse said. "I gave my promise that I wanted peace, that I would not make war again. Then

---

*Lieutenant Jesse M. Lee, military agent at Spotted Tail Agency, estimated that by the time they moved their discussions inside his office, there were more than 500 armed and infuriated warriors ready to fight at the drop of a hat, right there on the agency grounds, while Captain Daniel Burke had just under 100 men to muster at nearby Camp Sheridan.

the soldier chiefs came to me, asking me to go back on that war road for them. I said no. They became very angry with me—wanting me to break the honor of my word! Finally I said I would go north with them, camp my people right next to the soldiers, and we would fight until every Nez Perce was killed."

"So those were the words twisted by the Grabber?"

Crazy Horse nodded. "Yes. He made Three Stars believe I was not to be trusted. I never plotted to go on the warpath against the white man, or to kill Three Stars."

"But today you ran away to the camp of Touch-the-Clouds?"

"Yes," and Crazy Horse looked into the face of the *wasicu* agent. "I brought my wife here, so she could be with my relations, with the people who could help her. Please, understand that I only want what was guaranteed my people when I came in to surrender."

The half-blood asked, "What were you promised?"

Tell him what you were promised, Ta'sunke Witko. Tell this white man you trust exactly what you want from him before you give yourself over to the soldier chief at Red Cloud's agency.

"White Hat and Three Stars told me I would have my own agency in my old country," Crazy Horse said quietly in that hushed room, sensing that his feet were already walking an uncertain road. "I want to know—now—if someone will promise me that my people will have their own agency... before I am taken away from them."

Those last words the interpreter made for them caused the two white men to rock back in their chairs and look at each other strangely. Frantic, Crazy Horse hoped this interpreter he was trusting had not made a mistake like the one the Grabber had committed.

"You know you must leave your people?"

"Yes. I want you to go tell the soldier chief the truth I speak... before I am made to leave this land."

"Your words are good, Crazy Horse," the interpreter said. "But you yourself must go to talk about these things with my chief at Red Cloud's agency. I will promise no harm will come to you. And I promise that I will help get your people moved to this agency."

Crazy Horse considered that, then turned to Spotted Tail to ask, "Uncle, after I go explain all these things to the soldier chief, can I come live beside my father, among the Northern People, here on your reservation?"

"If you obey my orders, and the orders of the agent," Spotted Tail said. "When you go back to your people at Red Cloud's agency, I will give you a good horse to ride as a gift, and send some of my chiefs to ride along with you."

This man who had once been a close relation, had been his uncle, brother to his father's second and third wives—this Spotted Tail had become a different animal for the time he had suffered in the white man's prison. Made over in the white man's image. So now the only relations he still had on this reservation were his father and his mother's uncle, Touch-the-Clouds. With deeply sickening regret, he realized he had nothing left among the Sicangu.

First his old friend, Red Cloud—chief of the Bad Faces—had turned away from him. And now his uncle had thrown him away too.

"I trust you," he said sadly when he had turned back to the agent. "And I trust your promises."

But ... you are a warrior, Ta'sunke Witko! Always have been a warrior. And as a protector of the Lakota People, you have always been prepared to throw your life away if need be.

" 'It is nearly sundown, and I am sure you haven't eaten all day while you were riding here,' " the interpreter spoke the agent's words in Lakota. " 'For tonight, I will give you over to the care of Touch-the-Clouds. You will sleep in his lodge. Come the morning, you and Touch-the-Clouds will return here ... so that we can start on our journey to see the soldier chief at Red Cloud's agency.' "

CHAPTER TWENTY-SEVEN

5 September 1877

Camp Robinson, Neb., Sept. 5, 1877.

General Crook,
Cheyenne.

Major Burke sends word that he, with Touch the Clouds,
Swift Bear, High Bear and Crazy Horse are coming in
ambulance to-day. [Crazy Horse] will be put in guard-
house on arrival. I think he should be started for Fort
Laramie to-night and kept going as far as Omaha, two or
three Sioux going with him so that they can assure people
on return that he has not been killed. I hope you will tele-
graph Gen. Bradley. Everything quiet and working first-
rate.

Clark
1Lt.2d. Cavalry.

LIEUTENANT JESSE M. LEE HEARD THE CLATTER OF HOOVES
out front and went immediately to the window to have himself a look at those riders reining up in the early light.

"Who is it, sir?" called his cook, from the small apartment attached to the back of his office.

"It's . . . Crazy Horse," he answered in wonder, pulling the
big watch out of his vest pocket, looking at the time—just
past seven A.M.—then bringing it to his ear. Nothing wrong
with its reassuring tick, and he clearly remembered winding
it this morning upon rising, as was his habit of many years.

The gray-haired cook was at the doorway leading to their
apartment that next moment, tying the long muslin apron

around her dress. "I thought you told him to be here at nine?"

"I did," he said with a bewildered shrug. "I can't put my finger on an earthly reason why he'd show up so early."

"You're going to make time for breakfast before you start for Robinson, aren't you, sir?"

"Count on it," he said. "I-I'll be back in a moment."

Lee opened the door and stepped onto the plank porch, struck with the cool fragrance of the early morning. One day soon autumn would make its arrival known, crisp and cold. But for now, these mornings on the high plains were like a sweet prelude to the coming closure of winter.

"Crazy Horse," he said in English, stepping off the porch and into the talclike dust. He stared a moment at the man dressed in a dark blue shirt to match the dark blue trade-wool leggings. His moccasins were brightly beaded and the Oglala leader had that ever-present bloodred blanket draped over his lap. "Wait here. Let me get an interpreter."

As Lee started across the compound, he vividly remembered the conversation he and Captain Burke had shared in the ambulance while on their way back into the agency yesterday afternoon, just before the tense showdown between the two Sioux warrior bands had threatened to erupt in violence.

"I agree with you, Captain," Lee had said as they rumbled along. "I too think Crazy Horse could become a great leader among his people. If . . . if he's only allowed to."

"For what reasons do you agree with me, Lieutenant?"

"Because he's never been trained—not like those old chiefs, Red Cloud and Spotted Tail—never trained to use diplomacy and persuasion to gain advantage over another. My experience has been that when he speaks, it is straightforward and honest. That said, I think he can be depended upon to keep his promises."

"My hunch tells me that what promise Crazy Horse makes you," Burke continued, "he will take pains to keep."

"But, sir, the bitter truth is," Lee had replied, "so many of those around him, both Sioux and whites too, aren't any-where as committed to keeping faith with the truth as he is."

Once he found Bordeaux having breakfast with some other employees in the agency canteen, they both hurried back to the office, coffee cups in hand. Lee motioned Crazy Horse, Touch-the-Clouds, and a third warrior to follow them into the office, where they settled on the floor in front of his desk. For a moment Lee remembered the note he had received from William Clark yesterday afternoon, mentioning the reward for the capture of Crazy Horse...and he wondered which of these two Minniconjou would now claim the 200 dollars.

He leaned back against his desk, set his coffee aside, and asked Bordeaux, "I know Touch-the-Clouds well...but who is this man? I don't know him."

"Name is High Bear. A close relation to Touch-the-Clouds. So he is old friend to Crazy Horse."

Lee nodded to the man, then turned on Crazy Horse, saying, "You are early. That means you must be eager to go back to Red Cloud and get your words said to the soldier chief there?"

Crazy Horse didn't appear sullen or withdrawn this morning, his face a mask to his innermost feelings. Instead, Lee could plainly see that the Oglala leader was tense, fidgety, perhaps even trembling at times while Bordeaux translated the words into Sioux.

"No, he comes early because he did not sleep any last night," the interpreter declared. "Crazy Horse comes to the little agent—you—asking that you give him back his promise."

"What promise?"

"That he goes to Red Cloud with you," Bordeaux said. "He wants you to go to the soldier chief for him instead. Tell the big soldier chief of Crazy Horse's words, and get permission so he can live here at Spotted Tail's agency."

That took Lee aback a moment. Stalling for time, he picked up his clay coffee cup and moved around the desk, settling in his narrow chair. It seemed unusually hard beneath his buttocks this morning. "I'm afraid I can't do that, Crazy Horse."

"Why?"

"The soldier chief is expecting you at Red Cloud."

He thought about the letter from Clark, how it had given the impression that everyone seemed to know that Crazy Horse would be placed under arrest once he reached Camp Robinson...everyone except Crazy Horse. Perhaps the Oglala chief did know how things would be played out with his being put in custody, whisked away to the east, even to a sentence in prison.

"You can tell him Crazy Horse stays here," Bordeaux continued for the Oglala. "He will cause no trouble for Spotted Tail or Touch-the-Clouds. He'll live here now."

Clutching his cup between his two palms, Lee said, "We have given our word to one another, you and I. Now we must both see this thing through."

"There is no other way?" Bordeaux asked.

"No. Our feet are on the path to getting these matters made straight, Crazy Horse."

Bordeaux's eyes darkened with worry as Crazy Horse told him something in a near whisper, then the interpreter translated, "It has been told to him that something bad will happen there at Camp Robinson...when he returns."

"Bad?" Lee asked, his belly tightening in a knot, realizing what Clark and Bradley had planned for this man. Crazy Horse knew his return could not be good. "What bad thing could happen to you when you are under my protection, and the protection of the army? None of Red Cloud's scouts will get near you, I promise."

"He is sure something bad will happen, so he wants to stay here."

Eventually he convinced Crazy Horse that he must hold to his promise, that he could not remain behind in the camp of Touch-the-Clouds with his ailing wife. Once again the Oglala leader committed himself to accompany Lee to Red Cloud's agency, but only on certain conditions. First of all, neither of them, Lee nor Crazy Horse, would wear pistols that day. In addition, Crazy Horse asked Lee to promise that he would tell the soldier chief all that had gone on here in the last two days, especially that Spotted Tail had agreed to let the northerners live on his reservation if the soldier chief allowed it. As well, Lee promised Crazy Horse that he would get the chance to tell the soldier chief at Camp Robinson how his words had been twisted, and how he had never threatened to kill any white men.

"Beyond that, tell Crazy Horse that I can't promise him that General Bradley will allow him and his people to live here with Spotted Tail," Lee admitted sadly. "Explain to him that such a decision is made by a higher authority than I : the district commander."

He waited a moment as Bordeaux translated and Crazy Horse stared unflinchingly at the lieutenant's face. Then Lee continued. "But ... you will have your chance to talk to him," he vowed as the rumble of a wagon and the squeak of a brake were heard outside the office. "And I feel certain that when you have made your case, your people will be allowed to move and live here."

Crazy Horse turned to gaze out the open doorway at the ambulance a soldier had just brought to a halt. He stared for a long moment, and when he turned back, his face was even sadder, stonier still. Quietly, he whispered something to Bordeaux.

The interpreter said, "Crazy Horse wants to ride horseback. Says he does not want to go back to Red Cloud's place in the white man's wagon. He is a warrior of his people ... and he's always lived on horseback."

To ride in that wagon would mean he's admitting he has become a prisoner, Lee thought as he stood and moved around the small desk, presenting his left hand to the Oglala leader. Standing, Crazy Horse did not hesitate to take the hand, and they shook.

That was all right about the horse, he told himself. But Jesse Lee could not bring himself to promise a thing about Crazy Horse's hope of coming back to his uncle's reservation. After all, that might well turn out to be an outright lie.

For now, the army had plans to clamp the man in irons and scuttle him off to prison. And Lee could not bring himself to shade or color the truth simply so he could wash his hands of this prisoner.

Maybe I can convince Bradley that Crazy Horse ought to be given a reprieve, the lieutenant brooded as he gazed at the Oglala leader's scarred lip and cheek. *He never said he was going north to kill white people—only Grouard claimed that. And Crazy Horse never plotted to kill Crook. How absurd to think that a warrior of such renown would stoop to such a dastardly act! If only I can convince Bradley to wire Crook, asking for the general to commute the man's sentence.*

Sentence? That's a good one on me! Lee thought. *Crazy Horse has been tried and sentenced, about to be shipped off to prison—all without the benefit of a damn trial!*

"Louis," he said as he held the war chief's hand. "Tell Crazy Horse I know him as a man of honor. Yes, he can ride back to Red Cloud on a horse."

Cheyenne, Wyo., Sept. 5, 1877.

Colonel Bradley
Comdg. Camp Robinson

Accept my thanks for the successful termination of your enterprise and convey the same to Lieut. Clark and others concerned. Send Crazy Horse with a couple of his own people with him, under a strong escort, via Laramie to Omaha. Make sure that he does not escape. Keep up your efforts until you get every Indian in, even if you have to follow them up to Powder River.

George Crook,
Brig. General.

The morning sun felt like a prayer against the side of his face as the small party wound its way along the wide, worn trail taking them southwest to Red Cloud's reservation. There were moments when Crazy Horse thought he could almost drift off to sleep on the back of this pony Spotted Tail had given him...but every time he would remember what he was about to face—and he was jolted awake again.

Just ahead of him the soldier wagon rattled and squeaked. Inside on benches sat the little agent from Spotted Tail, the half-breed translator, and two of his uncle's most trusted associates: Black Crow and Swift Bear. With the leather shades rolled up and tied, one or the other of those Sicangu headmen had his eyes on him all the time, soldier carbines resting on their laps, ready.

A threat to him, Crazy Horse, warrior of the North Country! Who were these little men who had chosen to be coffee-coolers, loafers in the shade of the soldier forts...while the Northern People were defending Lakota hunting ground and their ancient way of life?

On either side of Crazy Horse rode two trusted Mnicowaju friends, fellow warriors: Touch-the-Clouds, and High Bear. Men who had sat through the long, dark night with him rather than closing their weary eyes to sleep. At times he wondered if his uncle doubted his promise not to flee the camp. But he had a sick wife, after all. And where could the two of them go that the friendlies could not find them quickly? Not to mention the soldiers who would follow. Gone like winter breathsmoke were his dreams that just a few of the Hunkpatila and Touch-the-Clouds could slip off alone, taking different trails, later to meet in the shadow of the White Mountains before the first snows flew. He sat rigid with self-doubts in the light of the small fire that turned their faces red, listening to Black Shawl's deep and troubled breathing when she eventually fell asleep. A tense and foreboding quiet had descended upon the night.

As soon as it grew dark, disembodied voices came to whisper to him through the lodgecover, too-quiet footsteps coming and going. Later, a new voice came to offer its advice.

"Crazy Horse!" the whisper would come through the taut canvas near his ear. "You must run!"

"Go now to the Land of the Grandmother!" said another. "Escape to Sitting Bull's people!"

Touch-the-Clouds listened too, as had High Bear, while the three of them sat through that long night without sleep. But there could be no escape for him now. A sick wife, and what with everyone watching him. Even more important: he had given his word—he had allowed Touch-the-Clouds to give the agent his personal guarantee. There was no running now. His only chance lay in getting the agent to give him his promise back come morning.

He had prayed that he could have slept, and therefore dreamed—allowing himself to drift into the Real World of dream, fleeing the bleak hopelessness of this Shadow World. Without sleep, without a chance to dream, he could only sit and listen to the disembodied warnings from the darkness.

Strange how the Mnicowaju were worried enough about Crazy Horse to warn him of the danger he already knew waited for him back among Red Cloud's Bad Faces. Strange...because his own Oglala people had spread lies about him behind his back, had followed him around wherever he went, Red Cloud's spies sniffing in his tracks like predators with the scent of blood in their nostrils.

They were cowards, afraid to confront him in the open. Instead they huddled in groups that made them feel more powerful, like these ten agency Indians who followed a little distance behind him, making sure that his seven faithful friends from Touch-the-Clouds' camp would not somehow permit him to flee. Sicangu men like Good Voice and Horned Antelope, whom the agent called "reliables," good agency policemen who had surely been ordered to prevent his escape at all costs.

More than a third of the way back to Red Cloud's agency, where the trail entered a narrowing of the White River valley, a double-handful of horsemen suddenly appeared on one of the surrounding hills.* The riders waited on the crest

---

*Where the agency trail crossed present-day Bordeaux Creek.

for the ambulance to pass, and Crazy Horse too, then angled down the slope and joined the tail end of the procession with the other Sicangu men. A few of them even dared to ease up on either side of him—not real close but near enough that he could see them without turning his head—where they rode near High Bear and Touch-the-Clouds. But these were not his *Mnicowaju* friends. These were Spotted Tail's agency men, all of them wearing their blue coats with the shiny buttons. Soldier coats like the one Little Big Man loved to parade about in all the time now.

"Do not let this trouble your heart, brother," Touch-the-Clouds said quietly as the sun warmed the back of his neck. "These are petty men, far beneath a man of your stature. Know that there are so many of them . . . because they are so afraid of you."

Crazy Horse said nothing, not for the longest time as they rode on, the dust spinning up from the four iron wheels on the white man's wagon where the two Sicangu with their soldier guns watched him with dark, feral eyes. Farther on,* even more of Spotted Tail's scouts rode out of the trees and joined their march. Now these horsemen were arrayed in long columns spread on either side of the wagon, stretching back to the rear of the formation. Crazy Horse was wondering what they would do if he suddenly bolted and reined away. But he held himself in, fighting down the impulse, and did not bolt away.

Not until early in the afternoon, that is—when another party of scouts joined them. Now there were enough of Spotted Tail's agency men that they dared to inch their horses closer and closer to him. Crazy Horse turned to look this way, and that, slowly making a count of these Lakota who made themselves prison bars around him. He stopped counting when he reached more than six-times-ten around him, while only that handful of Touch-the-Clouds's faithful Mnicowaju rode right behind Crazy Horse.

---

*As the procession neared present-day Chadron Creek.

"Steady, my brother," his uncle cheered soothingly. "They won't dare do a thing as long as you keep your promise."

Promise? What good was his word to the soldiers, good at all to these agency Indians who had filled their bellies with too much flour and pig meat, every one of them forgetting that they were Lakota?

Ha! They aren't Lakota anymore, he decided as his pony carried him on, step by step, toward the Soldier Town. These cowards had been living beside the *wasicus* too long, eating *wasicu* food, and obeying *wasicu* laws to truly be Lakota anymore.

Surprising himself, Crazy Horse suddenly slammed his heels into the flanks of the spirited pony Spotted Tail had sent to Touch-the-Clouds' lodge after the stars had winked into view last evening. "Keee-yiiii!" he cried to the animal as it shot into a gallop beneath him.

"Aiii-eee! Crazy Horse!" Touch-the-Clouds roared in surprise. "Come back, nephew! They will shoot you!"

But even as he heard their snorts of shock and anger, heard them yell to one another and their horses, Crazy Horse knew they would not shoot him. Only two men would ever have that much fury in them—and neither man was in this party that had him surrounded. Not Pretty Woman, who had nursed that humiliation to his boyhood pride for all these many winters. Neither was No Water, a man who suckled himself on a private rage so intense that few men would ever experience such passion. Only men like No Water and Crazy Horse, these two who felt things far, far deeper than most men—be it love for a woman, or hate for the man who had taken her away from him—only they truly understood each other. Both men had tasted the seduction of that very same passion. But . . . No Water was not here to shoot him in the back. Only Spotted Tail's agency police. And Crazy Horse knew none of them would have the nerve to shoot a man of his stature in the back.

Besides, his vision and Chips's powerful medicine had prescribed that he would never fall to a bullet. Death would only come from a knife, and only when the hands of his own people reached out for him, grabbed him, held him prisoner. *These agency scouts have little chance of doing that!*

All of them behind him, yelling in horror—and he could still hear the mighty voice of Touch-the-Clouds yelling for him to stop. The strident voices of the *wasicu* agent and his interpreter—two languages tumbling against each other as everyone tried to yell at once...but those voices were fading, falling from his ears as he burst through the trees and onto the long, open slope that led to the top of the bluff.

Taste the air, Ta'sunke Witko!

Yes! It tasted sweet. Not the same air he had been tasting moments ago. Different now because he was no longer surrounded, hemmed in, made a prisoner by all their bodies moving closer, closer—like those rigid iron bars his friends had told him were what kept a man from escaping the iron lodge at the Soldiers Town. He drank deep of the air that shot into his lungs with a valiant song while the horse beneath him found its gait and stretched out for this run across the flat, making the gradual climb up the long slope, on toward the skyline where late-summer clouds were gathering that afternoon.

Such a fine, strong animal, he thought, his thighs tight around its ribs, riding forward, close to its withers, hearing its eager, heavy breathing coming rhythmically. It could go and go; he was sure of it...go as far as he needed it to—if not all the way to the North Country. He looked over his shoulder and saw that his pursuers were back down the slope and so far behind, spread out and struggling just to keep up with the strong horse his uncle had given him.

Aren't you cursing Spotted Tail now!

His uncle's agency scouts and that white agent would be cursing too—angry that Spotted Tail had given his nephew such a powerful animal. They would never catch him now.

But as he shot over the top of the hill, Crazy Horse saw the next long slope rising to the top of the next hill. And beyond it another. Farther still, one more. On and on it would go. How could he keep on?

She will cry more because you have abandoned her, more than if you ... you had fallen in battle.

And he knew his *sicun* was right.

Yes. You can run, but you have never run from a fight, Ta'sunke Witko. Always you have turned your horse into the battle, unafraid of what lesser men could ever do to try stopping you. Unafraid of throwing your body away.

"I have never turned away from a fight," he answered the spirit guardian, whose words reverberated not just in his head, but hummed within his breast now, echoed down through his belly, and shuddered out through every limb with the same anticipation he always experienced as he rode into battle. Ready to throw his body away rather than turning from the fight.

At the bottom of the hill, in a narrow wrinkle within those rising and falling folds of land, ran the course of a tiny stream* marked by its emerald border of grass and brush. This powerful horse could vault that stream without making so much as a stretch, he knew. And then he would be on the other side, with only the White Earth River between him and all that country beckoning him to come north once more. Tonight he could finally lie again beneath the sky again, looking up at the black so dark it reminded him of the trader's silk handkerchiefs some of the agency scouts wore around their necks, a black so encompassing it swallowed everything but the tiny points of light dusting the star road above where all the warriors of ages past galloped across the sky for all time to come. To lie there in that North Country again and look up, knowing there were no boundaries to those heavens, that those stars could ride forever ... the same way he too could forever ride the country of his birth.

But when the moment came for the man to kick ever more speed out of the animal below him ... Crazy Horse

---

*It seems likely that this incident occurred on or near Dead Horse Creek.

slowly drew himself back from the horse's withers, pulled back on the buffalo-hair reins, and brought Spotted Tail's pony to a halt beside the creek gurgling over its stony bed.

He leaped down, patting the horse on its neck, and watched it step into the stream before he turned around to look at those coming after him. Yelling, shaking their firearms, shouting such anger from frustration and embarrassment that he had broken away, that he could have gotten away so easily. The pride of these agency men was so easy to bruise because they had so little to feel pride for ... no longer warriors. Instead, they played at being fighting men now, full of bluster and bravado as they circled around him, yelling at the top of their voices with fear as all the more thundered down the long slope toward the first who had him surrounded once more—around and around him, threatening with their carbines, shaking their fists and shouting the bad words at him, even yelling some of the *wasicu* words that he did not know, but understood their meaning just the same because they came from so many angry tongues who had learned such talk from the soldiers and miners.

"Do not touch me!" he cried back at them suddenly, catching those closest to him by surprise.

In shock, it jolted most of them. They snapped their mouths closed, eyes wide now that he pointed to one after another of his pursuers—turning slowly, pointing at another, then turning again in a tight circle as they paced their panting ponies in a loop around this Hunkpatila who would be free but for knowing there was only one path left a warrior to complete freedom.

"Yes—you heard me, you little men!" he growled, holding up his empty hands, fingers spread, palms outward to them. Daring them, daring them all. "Do not touch me!"

More of the chasers raced up, their horses skidding in the grass and throwing up dust over those whom they bumped and jarred, horses whinnying with fright. Still not a one of them had the courage to speak, to challenge him ... wide-eyed were they all like their frightened, snorting horses.

"Don't you know who I am?" he bellowed at them, now

that there were more than five-times-ten come to make him prisoner again. "Hey-ya! I am Crazy Horse...and I have come here to water my horse!"

Through the pack slowly came one rider. He was a little older than the rest of these agency police. Older than Crazy Horse. Perhaps not as old as his uncle, but a warrior who would have known the old days of glory when the Sicangu of Spotted Tail had struck back after soldier chief Harney murdered the innocents on the Blue Water. This one would have counted many coups...but eventually turned his heart away from fighting to become a loafer like Spotted Tail. How sorry Crazy Horse felt for the man as the old warrior came up and stopped his pony between the lone Hunkpatila and the agency scouts.

"You came here to water your horse, say you?" he demanded. "Not to run?"

"This horse my uncle gave me, it is full of vigor," Crazy Horse replied with the faintest hint of a smile.

Eventually a small grin came across the man's wrinkled face. He gazed across the creek for a moment, then back at the Hunkpatila standing on foot. Then the old Sicangu said, "This horse would need a lot of water to carry you for such a long, long ride, Ta'sunke Witko."

He smiled back at the old warrior, then nodded once before he turned, picked up the long rein dragging in the shallow creek, and leaped atop the animal's back.

"Ride with me back to the trail and the soldier wagon," the old Sicangu requested gently.

Crazy Horse looked at him, then turned his head to gaze at all these petty agency men, saying boldly, "My uncle's horse...yes—it will carry me now where I must go."

CHAPTER TWENTY-EIGHT

September 5, 1877

Cheyenne, W. T.
September 5

General P. H. Sheridan.
Your dispatch of today received. Crazy Horse was at the
bottom of the whole trouble at both agencies & yesterday
his band was dismembered by the soldiers & our Indians,
mostly by the latter. The members of his band are being dis-
tributed among other bands. Crazy Horse is now a pris-
oner & I have ordered Bradley to send him here. I wish you
would send him off where he will be out of harm's way. You
can rest assured that everything at the agencies is perfectly
quiet & will remain so.... This is the end of all trouble as
far as the Sioux are concerned, outside of Sitting Bull.

Crook.

"YOU EVER DO ANYTHING 'CEPT STAND GUARD DUTY?" SEA-
mus Donegan asked the forty-eight-year-old sentry as he
walked up to the corner of the guardhouse.

William Gentles smiled wryly as he kept on pacing down
the length of the log building, where a shingled awning covered the entire width of the guardhouse. "Nothing else but
sleep, eat, drink up what pay they give me ... and walk this
goddamned Sentry Post Number One."

"When your relief comes?"

"Not till tattoo, Seamus," Gentles groaned. "My dogs
gonna be yapping by then!"

He looked down at the man's bootees. "Them broghams
look to be falling apart on you."

"Quartermaster says he's got more coming up from the

rail in Sidney next week or so," Gentles explained. "Till then, I stuff in some bits of newsprint so the screws workin' up through the soles don't chew up the bottoms of my ol' feet. Still a damn sight better'n the boots we had in the war."

"Blessed Mother of Christ!" Donegan exclaimed with the vivid memory. "A wrap of old canvas was better'n those new boots they give us to wear."

Gentles laughed easy and hearty as he stepped along, keeping time. "Like the blankets they give us always come apart in the rains that fell and fell, and never stopped!"

"Boots did too," Donegan agreed with a laugh of his own. "I was afraid of climbing down from me horse, because it meant I'd have to slog around in the puddles and the mud—sucking the soles off my cavalry boots!"

"I 'member scrounging over the battlefields for to find a Johnny what had feet big enough to fit my dogs," Gentles said with a loud blast of laughter. Then his face suddenly went sad. "But most Johnnies didn't have 'em no good boots anyway. Lots of 'em I saw had no shoes at all."

"I remember that as well," Seamus said, reflecting on those terrible days some fifteen years gone. "We Federals was lucky with what we had."

Gentles straightened, ramrod rigid, and shifted his rifle into both hands as he came to a sudden stop. "Aye, so I keep on marchin' my watch, don't you know."

The old soldier dropped the butt of his Long-Tom Springfield rifle to the ground beside his left boot, clicked his heels together, and saluted the Irishman, snapping his right arm across his breast—fingertips barely touching the muzzle of the rifle where the long regulation bayonet was locked, protruding like a bold exclamation mark at the end of the sentry's rifle.

Donegan snapped his heels together too, returning the salute, fingers touching the wide brim of his well-worn hat. "Carry on, sojur!"

"Aye, Sergeant Donegan, sir!"

That made the Irishman stop and turn back. "I told you I was a sergeant, did I?"

"You did," Gentles said. "And if I'd been the sort could

scrub my arse against a saddle for days at a time, I could think of no better man I'd want as non-com over me than your plucky soul, Seamus dear!"

"That's about the highest praise I feel a man could give, save for looking in the face of my wee boy and knowin' I'm his da. You ever was married, Willy?"

He wagged his head with melancholy. "Soldierin'... that was me mate. Come to it later'n most men does... so we stuck it out together, it appears. Only wish the general'd get around to shippin' me back to my own unit before I'm bound to muster out here at Camp Robinson."

"Not a one of your outfit still here? Just you?"

Gentles said, "Like I told you in the saloon, ever' last bloody one of 'em gone 'cept me—shipped back to Camp Douglas in Utah Territory, while my arse was chained up in this here guardhouse," and he jabbed a thumb back at the low-roofed log building behind him.

"What does the adjutant say about you getting back to your company?"

"When it suits 'em, I s'pose," Gentles replied. "No one seems in the hurry... so as long as there's whiskey to drink up at Paddock's store, I'll walk as many miles as they tell me to walk: back and forth... back and forth."

"Ever you have serious trouble with them what get thrown in here?"

"Them? Naw—they're just soldiers like me." Then he looked at Donegan quizzically. "Here and I took you for a man who'd seen the inside of a place just like this. Didn't you ever spend some time in no guardhouse?"

"Been over ten year, it has," he said, awash with the memories of that cold December in Dakota Territory when a brave but reckless officer marched off with eighty men to punch his way right on through the whole Sioux nation. "Fort Phil Kearny. Fetterman got hisself and a lot of good men hacked to pieces one cold day."

"Aye, another officer leading his lambs to the slaughter."

"I was in on the rescue detail," Seamus declared as footsteps scraped on the boards of the covered porch behind them. "We got there too late."

"If you hadn't, you'd not be standing here, keeping this old soldier from his work," Gentles growled with a smile, raising his Springfield to his shoulder once more.

Seamus turned his head slowly and looked over the small army post. "Things get quieted down some, now that I hear Crazy Horse run off for the other agency?"

The sentry nodded, then shrugged. "Seems to be settled some. Let them others keep him so all the buggers who don't like him will have to find something else to worry us with. Naw, there ain't no bloody excitement to help keep a sleepy man awake when he's ordered to stand a twelve-hour watch on guard duty!"

"Buy you a drink tomorrow?"

"Swear on my grandmother's grave that'll be as soon as I drag my bones outta my bunk," the private replied with a knowing roll of his eyes. "Gonna be a long night of walking sentry here. Thank you for offering, Seamus dear."

"More'n happy to have a cup with an old soldier. Tomorrow, Willy?"

As he set off in a rhythmic pace again, Gentles dragged the back of his hand across his mouth and said, "Aye, tomorrow it is."

Chicago, Illinois
Sept. 5, 1877.

Captain Gillies, U.S.A.,
Cheyenne Depot, Wyo.

Sending the following to General Crook.
Your dispatch of this date received. I will send to you at Green River Station, the latest news of the Nez-Perces. I wish you to send Crazy Horse under proper guard to these Hd. Qrs.

P. H. Sheridan,
Lieut.-General.

Once Crazy Horse came back in sight, Jesse M. Lee felt like he could breathe again, that huge set of iron pincers that had clamped themselves around his chest suddenly freed. As the Oglala leader rode up among that posse of Spotted Tail's scouts, Lee stood at the back of the ambulance and wiped his brow with a damp red kerchief. He felt immense relief that he would not be the one to trust, then suffer betrayal at the hands of the one he had trusted.

"Bordeaux, I want you to tell him he must ride right here," Lee ordered, pointing emphatically at the rear of the ambulance. "Tell him he must not stray from the tailgate of this wagon or I will have him removed from his horse and placed in here with the rest of us."

Crazy Horse listened, turning to glance at the warriors massed on either side of him. Those Brulé were men, Lee realized, who Crazy Horse had just made to look inept, if not like fools. While he was a warrior, a horseman. These agency police would have to struggle to even begin to hold a candle to Crazy Horse.

Lee wiped his face once more, then ordered his driver to resume their march, pressing on up the White River Road. Taking a seat in the jostling ambulance, the lieutenant now kept a constant eye on the prisoner's face.

That's what he is, Lee thought. A *prisoner.* Never before in all these months since the Northern bands had surrendered had the lieutenant ever known anyone to think, much less speak, in those terms. *He's a prisoner, for God's sake! Surely Crazy Horse knows that, if only by looking around to see the way the scouts have him surrounded, the way he was pursued so doggedly. A man of his stature and history must surely be chafing from this prison he finds himself inside already* . . . because these reliables had already moved within a couple of arm lengths of the Oglala. *All around him now, like the bars on a prison cell.*

Lee got his first sight of the magnificent Crow Butte a little less than fifteen miles from Camp Robinson. It was here that he ordered a brief halt while he took out a small tablet and his pencil, writing a short note for Luther Bradley at the post ahead.

> *DEAR GENERAL: I have Crazy Horse with me, about 15 mi out. Please send word by return courier. Take him to the post or agency? I respectfully suggest that we use all tact and discretion in securing Crazy Horse so that we do not precipitate serious trouble. Additionally, sir— since I have promised him that he might state his case to you, I request that arrangements be made accordingly for him to see you.*

> LEE, agent

"Bordeaux, call for Horned Antelope," the lieutenant instructed. "He's on a good horse, you said?"

"It's a strong, leggy one," the interpreter responded, then hollered for the Brulé to come forward.

Having positioned himself right behind Crazy Horse's left heel, the agency scout now had reined aside and around the prisoner, no more than a few steps, to halt at the rear of the army ambulance.

"White Hat," Lee said in English. "Bordeaux, tell him to take this note to the White Hat—just as fast as he can ride. And tell him he's to wait for word from White Hat, wait to bring back a letter from him for me."

He watched Horned Antelope turn his horse away, parting the crowd of more than sixty faithful friendlies, then kick the animal into a lope that quickly rolled into a gallop. Lee brought his eyes to Crazy Horse as he sat back down on the wide seat at the side of the ambulance. Once more the Oglala looked as he had when he showed up at the office early that morning. Like a small, trapped, feral animal that finds itself in the company of snarling predators. Not that the man could ever be considered timid in the way a jackrabbit was a timid creature ... but the way even the bravest, most courageous and noble of animals would become when it realizes that there is no escape from its enemies, no flight possible from the predators on its heels.

His heart ached for the man. And he began to feel the first twinges of guilt, looking now at Crazy Horse as the ambulance lurched into motion once more.

Predators, Lee thought, *that's what these others are. Predators who will never be anywhere as magnificent and noble as their prey.*

It suddenly struck him that there were more and more of the Sioux showing up now at the heart of this post, easing in from all directions. Lounging in the late-afternoon shade offered by the log buildings, the older men, women, and children were doing nothing that made Donegan suspicious as to their motives. Just that . . . there was one hell of a lot of them.

For the most part there were more women and children, along with bent, ancient ones too, than there were any men of fighting age among the growing crowds—but over the moments he stood watching, Seamus began to see that the men were showing up. Whereas the women and children arrived on foot, their men showed up on horseback. And many of them were wearing some item of war regalia tied onto or strapped over their soldier tunics. As Seamus stopped there close to the adjutant's office, not all that far from the guardhouse where Private William Gentles continued plodding through sentry duty at Post Number One, it struck him that many of those horsemen showing up among the crowd were also proudly displaying their army carbines.

It didn't take that wide saber scar down the middle of the great muscles of his back for Donegan to sense that something was afoot. Although he did not feel any ominous dread or threat, Seamus nonetheless sensed a tremor of misgiving at the pit of his belly and turned, intending to strike out for their little camp—just to assure himself that Samantha was still playing with little Colin by the tent, that they hadn't become frightened by the appearance of so many hundreds of Sioux—

"Seamus!"

He wheeled around at the cry of that familiar voice, finding Valentine McGillycuddy waving at him from the covered porch on the front of the adjutant's office.

"Over here!" the doctor yelled to him when it was apparent Donegan was troubled about making the decision between turning off to camp and detouring for a talk with his friend.

McGillycuddy stood at the edge of a loose knot of more than half-a-dozen officers, young and old, all of them watching the gathering of the Sioux from the narrow porch at the front of the adjutant's office, lowering their heads from time to time to make a whispered comment to their fellows. Many of them puffed on pipes, or sucked on black-fingered cheroots, as if this were the best entertainment they'd had all week.

"Just the man I want to see," Seamus called out cheerily.

"Come over to find out what's going on?" McGillycuddy answered as the Irishman approached.

"Naw. Was looking for you," Donegan explained. "Wanted to know if you'd look after Sam and wee Colin for a few weeks."

"What have you got on your mind?"

He took a step up on the low porch and took a place beside McGillycuddy beneath the overhanging awning. "I've heard what the wire has to tell. The Nez Perces are coming to Crow country—they'll be on the Yellowstone soon."

McGillycuddy studied him a moment. "What does that war have to do with you, Seamus?"

"Miles is up there. A fighting man if ever there was one," Donegan declared. "If them Nez Perces are coming to Yellowstone country, it's for damned sure that Nelson A. Miles will have a mix-up with 'em before it's over."

"You'll offer yourself to scout for the man again?"

"Aye, that's it," he answered. "So say you and Fanny will watch over my bride and son. I've got money to leave you for food."

"Sam doesn't eat that much," McGillycuddy said with a grin.

"That mean you'll do it?"

The physician nodded. "When you plan on leaving?"

"Come morning. Soon as I see Sam and Colin are took care of."

"We'll see to them while you're away, Seamus Donegan," McGillycuddy said. "Just make sure you ride back here when Miles is done with the Nez Perce."

"I'll be back before you have a chance to miss my cheery company!" Seamus responded.

Rubbing his one left eyelid that drooped, McGillycuddy looked up at the taller, gray-eyed man, the smile disappearing from his own face. "Too bad you couldn't just take them two with you when you leave Camp Robinson."

"Take 'em with me?"

"Yes. Not a good time here...right now," the doctor replied, turning his head so that he could stare once more at the crowds.

Finally Seamus asked, "You mean all the Sioux popping into the post?"

"You've hit the nail, Irishman."

He nodded once, a bit grimly. "Damn right. Don't all of them showing up make something itch inside you?"

McGillycuddy glanced at him with a small measure of appraisal. "The old warrior seeping out of your pores again, is it?"

With a shrug he said, "What kept me alive this long, I suppose. By the by, why the devil are you here yourself, Doc?"

"'Stead of being over at the hospital?"

"You ain't got no sick to tend to? No stewards to order around, have you?"

"I came this way looking up someone who might know just what it is brings all these folks out of Red Cloud's camp."

"Any of 'em Crazy Horse people what made their stampede yesterday?"

"I'll bet a good number of 'em are."

"Makes sense," said Captain James Kennington, officer of the day that Wednesday. He stuffed the pipe stem back between his teeth and returned to studying the Sioux filling the parade ground and all the spaces between the buildings.

"What makes so much sense?" Seamus whispered to McGillycuddy after he tore his eyes from the ceremonial sword slung from Kennington's belt.

"Reasonable there's gonna be a lot of Red Cloud's people and Crazy Horse's here both," the doctor explained. "The Red Cloud folks have been very suspicious of Crazy Horse, for the longest time. And, the Crazy Horse people are here to watch their chief being brought in."

"T-they're bringing him in?" Seamus asked in disbelief. "I thought word was he'd run away to the north while his folks scattered and made it hard to follow him."

Shrugging, McGillycuddy said, "Guess not. Not long ago one of Spotted Tail's couriers brought a note in for Lieutenant Clark. Came from the agent over at Spotted Tail. It was news that he was bringing Crazy Horse in to see Bradley."

As the open ground before them began to fill with soldiers formed up for the daily parade, it took a moment for that to start to sink in. "If that don't beat all. What'd Crazy Horse do to get hisself arrested? Did he give up peaceable? Or did they run him down last night and they're dragging him back in chains—"

"Nothing so dramatic as that, from what Billy Garnett got out of that Sioux courier while Clark wrote a letter back to Agent Lee," McGillycuddy declared. "He showed up at a friend's camp and asked to stay there with his mother's people. But Lee and post commander Burke somehow convinced him that he can't move there till he gets his problems put to bed back here."

"Problems?"

"The Grouard thing," McGillycuddy growled as Kennington and the other officers stepped off the porch and onto the parade to take up their positions.

Down the middle of the open ground came a procession of flags. It all seemed a little unreal to Donegan, watching this afternoon ritual performed this day for the first time in front of thousands of too-quiet Sioux.

"Don't remind me about that double-talking bastird," Seamus hissed angrily. "The man can't be guilty of anything to do with Grouard!?"

Whispering as Kennington shouted orders that echoed over the parade, Dr. McGillycuddy said, "Story has it one of Red Cloud's men slipped up by Crazy Horse's lodge a few nights back and heard the chief plotting with his best friends to murder Crook and Clark when they showed up at a peace council away from the post."

A sudden gust of laughter escaped his lips. "Sorry!" he whispered when some of the officers turned and glared at him over their shoulders. "I couldn't help but laugh about that! Crazy Horse? Him? Stupid enough to think he could kill them two officers and get away with it?" He sniggered with laughter again. "Tell me, Doc—who's the bleeming idiot believed in that scheme to kill Crook and Clark?"

Lieutenant Henry Lemley turned and leaned back to say, "Crook and Clark themselves."

The smile drained from his ruddy face. "Crook thinks Crazy Horse would actually murder 'em.... and then try to run off to that country up north what ain't theirs no more?"

"General Crook believed it enough," Lemley explained quietly, "that he gathered all the chiefs who don't want Crazy Horse around and put them up to arresting the man."

He shook his head, dumbfounded. "This all been going on here?"

"Last couple of days, Seamus," McGillycuddy replied.

"Good friend you are," Donegan growled. "A juicy piece of news like this and you didn't tell me."

"Well, here's a news bulletin for you," McGillycuddy said. "The agent bringing Crazy Horse in says he wants to have an audience with Bradley, so he can get all his problems ironed out before he moves his people over to Spotted Tail, where his father and the rest of the Northern People are camped."

For a moment Donegan looked off to the southwest, thinking of her and the boy back at camp. Growing more than concerned that with all these Sioux crowding in, all hell could break loose when they brought Crazy Horse onto the post and attempted to put him under arrest. "How soon's this gonna happen—him coming back to talk with Bradley?"

Dr. McGillycuddy reached out with both hands and turned the taller man back around so Seamus faced northeast now. The soldiers on the parade were breaking up, heading back to their barracks as a hush fell over the post. Donegan stared, transfixed, as everything came to a halt while the sun began its final descent. The only object moving was an army ambulance that had begun to part the immense throng of Sioux, thousands of whom started to shout and yell. Close on the tailgate of the ambulance followed a tight knot of horsemen, at the center of which rode Crazy Horse.

Damn, Seamus thought, *if he don't have the look of a man being dragged off to the gallows.*

CHAPTER TWENTY-NINE

5 September 1877

HOLY MOTHER OF GOD!" THE INTERPRETER WHISPERED sharply beside him.

Bordeaux had yanked the words right out of Jesse Lee's mouth as they stared in utter awe at the masses of Sioux who had packed themselves tightly together on the grassy parade, and in among the log buildings, when their ambulance rumbled up from the White River crossing and onto the grounds of Camp Robinson. On the hard plank seat across from Lee and Bordeaux, Swift Bear and Black Crow were yammering loudly between themselves, gesturing and looking about at this unbelievable scene.

Lee turned with sudden recognition that Crazy Horse had to be watching the same scene. He found the Oglala, along with Touch-the-Clouds and High Bear, all three staring ahead, transfixed, as if in complete disbelief. Never before had any of them—white, red, or half-breed—ever seen the Sioux gather at this post in such numbers. Perhaps such an occurrence could happen over at the agency, but only on ration day.*

He suddenly looked for his Lucy, squinting in the late-afternoon light at the porches along officers' row, noticing all those white officers, their wives, and enlisted men on the

---

*The total number of Sioux comprising this throng was estimated at the high end by Dr. Valentine McGillycuddy at more than 10,000 Indians, while other—and more conservative—estimates put the number somewhere between 3,000 and 6,000 Sioux. You have only to visit old Camp Robinson (not the more modern Fort Robinson across the road) to see firsthand how even the lowest estimate would have made for a dramatic and potentially explosive situation.

periphery of the fort, come to witness this momentous historical event. What a sight to remember: all of Red Cloud's Oglala come to watch their once-esteemed war chief brought back a prisoner, under guard by his uncle's agency scouts. Lee realized his wife had to be watching, somewhere among those white women, because Lucy would have heard he was on his way with this famous prisoner.

As soon as the first of those at the edge of the crowd heard the noisy approach of the ambulance and the hoof-beats of more than seventy horses clattering up from the river crossing, the throng fell silent. On the parade that silence swept across the waiting crowd like a wave as more and more of the Sioux learned of their approach. Then the ambulance was forced to slow, and began to inch its way into the mass of Indians reluctantly parting to let them through. As soon as Spotted Tail's scouts passed by, the by-standers were closing their ranks once more, sealing up that narrow tunnel they had opened for this procession.

First one woman began to keen. Then more women took up that sad lament. Old men raised their reedy voices in war song. Some men simply shouted curses or praise. The eerie effect started out low and indistinct, but eventually grew in discordant volume as the ambulance made its way past the cavalry stables. Skirting around the saddler's shop, swinging west, the prisoner's procession moved closer and closer to the adjutant's office—where Lee hoped he would find Bradley.

Three years before the lieutenant had taken a personal hand in construction of Camp Robinson...so Jesse Lee knew that less than seventy yards of open ground lay between that office and the post guardhouse. Why hadn't he thought of that before? *They mean to throw Crazy Horse behind bars without the slightest charade of justice!* Yet he hoped—no, Lee prayed—that the prisoner would be allowed to speak a few words to Bradley. After all, he himself had given Crazy Horse his personal promise.

Sensing the first tremors of misgiving he would not allow

to become fear, Lee kept his eyes moving across the crowd, all the way over the extent of the parade to this building and that along officers' row, searching not for Lucy now, but for the face of Lieutenant William P. Clark. He was the one who had sent a message that Lee was to bring Crazy Horse to Bradley's place. So where the hell was he?

Then it struck him how dangerous a spot he was in, as the lone soldier who was bringing in Crazy Horse...and here were all his fellow Oglala. Lee turned and quickly looked over Spotted Tail's Brulé horsemen. They appeared as nervous as he felt—fear, apprehension, and an impulse to fight on their faces as they cocked their rifles and held them close, ready.

But in that next moment, Lee read the mood of the crowd—and realized that the great majority of the crowd were not singing out the praises of Crazy Horse, nor calling for the prisoner's release. Instead, these Sioux were crying out in anger at this man he was bringing back to them...a captive.

Lee turned and glanced at his prisoner, worried.

Still, on Crazy Horse's face registered no sign of fear, nary an emotion. Instead, the stoic mask of a true warrior confronting the inevitable...but the man's eyes danced constantly. He had to be looking over the crowd that clamored around him, sang his praises or cursed him for the trouble they believed he had brought down on their heads—perhaps he was looking for a friendly face, someone who might pluck him from this noisy madness.

More soldiers appeared in view ahead, a solid phalanx of blue in front of the office as the ambulance slowed.

"Lieutenant Lee!" cried James Kennington.

"Captain!" he called out, standing unsteadily, gripping the sidewall as the ambulance shuddered to a halt. "I was expecting to see Lieutenant Clark. He sent me a message—"

"General Bradley directs that you turn over your prisoner to me, the officer of the day," Kennington interrupted curtly.

When Kennington took a step down from the porch, Lee saluted him, struggling to gather his wits about him.

"B-but..." Lee stammered. "No, not yet, Captain. I'm hoping Crazy Horse can say a few words to the commanding officer before he is...before...this is done. I've promised...you see, I told him—"

"You'll have to take that up with the commanding officer himself," Kennington said as he approached the side of the ambulance in the manner of a man in full recognition of his authority at that moment as thousands looked on. "No one can answer for the general but the general himself, Agent Lee."

"Of course, sir." And Lee turned, threading his way between the knees of three other men, and leaped from the back of the ambulance.

Immediately going to Crazy Horse's side, the lieutenant looked over his shoulder at the interpreter. "Bordeaux, get over here!" As the translator stopped at the rear gate of the ambulance, Lee looked up at the Oglala and said, "Crazy Horse, the general wants me to turn you over to another officer."

Behind him, Bordeaux was beginning his halting translation.

"I know I promised you could talk with the general when you got here," Lee plunged ahead. "So I'm going to talk to the general now, let him know you're here. His office is right over there."

He watched Crazy Horse's eyes follow the direction of that arm he held out, pointing all the way across the parade, through all those gathered thousands of Sioux. Then the man's intense eyes came back to the young officer who stood at his knee. But his lips did not say a word.

"I want you to go inside with Bordeaux," Lee continued. "Sit down with Touch-the-Clouds and High Bear. Black Crow and Swift Bear must go with you too," and he pointed at the door to the adjutant's office. "You wait in there and I'll come right back when I've told the general that you want to talk to him."

As his English faded off and Bordeaux's Sioux translation continued, Crazy Horse's eyes moved from the lieutenant to the open doorway. When the interpreter finished, the prisoner looked again at Lee. He nodded, dropped from his horse, and stood waiting for the four Sioux to gather around him as the crowd began to murmur in whispers now. While Bordeaux started them toward the office Lee whirled about on his heel and plunged through that narrow gap the Indians in the crowd made for him as he scampered across the parade.

All 200 yards of it, holding himself to a half-trot because he wanted so to run, constantly reminding himself to keep it to a fast walk instead. The porch was crowded with officers and two white women as he bolted up the steps. They cleared a path for him to the door. Almost before he had finished knocking, a uniformed striker* was there to open the door for him. This long-faced young private showed Lee into the parlor, then left. In a moment Bradley came in, finishing with the buttons of his tunic.

Lee saluted. "General, I respectfully come to ask that you have a few words with Crazy Horse." He went on to explain in the most earnest and solicitous language why he felt Bradley should listen to the prisoner, then concluded, "I know you to be a most fair and generous commander, sir. That's why I took it upon myself to give the man my word that you would listen to what he had to say in way of explanation—"

"You gave your word, Lieutenant?" Bradley cut him off.

"Y-yes, General."

Then Bradley turned to the side and gazed out the window at the crowded parade. "It's too late," he sighed as if with a great weight pressed upon his shoulders. "Talking to him won't be of any use, Mr. Lee."

"But sir, if you would only hear him tell you himself that he never said anything about killing white men," Lee de-

---

*Usually a private who served as a personal attendant to an officer of high rank.

clared desperately. "That he never conceived any plan to murder General Crook."

"The general's order is peremptory," Bradley said gravely, still staring out the window rather than meeting Lee's eyes. "There's nothing I can do to change it here and now."

"Or-order, sir?"

"In fact, I doubt that General Crook could change the orders he gave me." The man finally turned to gaze at Lee. "This directive comes from Chicago, Mr. Lee. Orders from that quarter don't get changed by men like me."

"But, sir, isn't there some room left for you hearing the man out—"

"Mr. Lee," Bradley interrupted sternly, eyes narrowing. "There is nothing further to be said. Now, go about your duty as a soldier...and see that Crazy Horse is handed over to the officer of the day. The sooner you do that, the better."

Pleading, he said, "I gave him my word that if he returned here peaceably, you would see him."

Bradley shook his head. "It's just too late to have any such talk. Everything has been decided by those higher in command."

His mind burning with a thousand different scenarios of how he would return to the adjutant's office, Lee asked, "C-can he be heard by you in the morning, General?"

Slowly, deliberately, the commanding officer turned away, back to the window. "Turn your prisoner over to the officer of the day. Instruct Crazy Horse that he is to go with Captain Kennington and not a hair on his head shall be harmed."

For a long moment he stared at the back of the colonel's shoulders. Every fiber in Bradley's constitution had the make-up of a soldier. To him an order was unequivocal. The orders he had received from above were law and gospel. They were to be met with instant and unswerving obedience. And—as Lee had come to learn about the man in the past few months since Bradley had arrived to take

over command of Camp Robinson from Ranald Mackenzie—woe be to the subordinate who dared to question his
orders.

Of a sudden he was struck with the stark realization that
he best end this interview. Better that these orders from far,
far away be obeyed, and obeyed quickly.

Out the door without ever hearing it closed behind him
by the striker, off the porch and onto the parade, plunging
into the crowd, once more parting the masses that continued
to whisper and murmur, some of the women keening, others
sobbing quietly as he struggled to get back to the adjutant's
office. He suddenly remembered Lucy, wondered if she had
been watching him from one of the porches.

"It's too late," he recalled Bradley saying. While the
colonel certainly must have meant that it was too late for
anything but the arrest and incarceration to proceed un-
changed...Lee decided that he could explain it away to
Crazy Horse by telling him it was too late in the day.

Just as he reached the end of the crowd, the sun leaked
out of the sky, the last of the sharpest shadows gone in that
heartbeat. His own began to hammer with the fear of insur-
mountable failure.

"Tell Crazy Horse this," he huffed as he bolted through
the office doorway and snagged Bordeaux's arm. "Night is
coming on and the general said it's too late for a talk now.
Bradley said for you to go with the officer of the day...to go
with this man," and Lee indicated Kennington. "If you go
with him, you will be taken care of, Crazy Horse. And the
general wants you to know: not a hair of your head shall be
harmed."

For a breathless moment after Bordeaux finished his
translation, there was complete silence in the spartan office,
save for what high-pitched, eerie sounds of keening reached
them through the open doorway. Suddenly the four Sioux
who had accompanied Crazy Horse into the office shouted
collectively.

"Hau!"

It was a good sign. They were all smiling. Crazy Horse got to his feet and went to the door where Captain Kennington stood and held out his left hand. They shook. The two of them filed onto the porch, two armed soldiers stepping up as escort. Touch-the-Clouds started to join his nephew, closely followed by the other three Sioux.

But Lee reached out and managed to grab the tall man's arm. "Bordeaux, tell them I want them to wait here and listen to me."

Instead of translating, Bordeaux whispered, "We better get out of here! If they go to put him in the guardhouse, there's gonna be hell to pay and the two of us gonna get killed because we're the ones brought him over here!"

"You're going to stay right here with me and do what I tell you," Lee snapped.

His face carved with worry, Touch-the-Clouds watched after his nephew a moment longer. When Crazy Horse did not turn in farewell, but instead wore the look of complete trust in the soldier who was escorting him off the porch, the Minniconjou chief shifted his full attention on the young agent. Lee quickly explained to the three that he had done his best to secure an audience with Bradley, but that orders had been given from the highest command for the arrest of Crazy Horse.

"I hoped to again make my case in the morning before he was moved from the post."

"The army is taking him away?" Touch-the-Clouds asked when Bordeaux had explained.

"Yes, like Spotted Tail was taken away for a time," Lee explained lamely.

"You told him the soldier chief would listen to his words," Touch-the-Clouds said sternly.

"There isn't anything more I can do as a soldier," the lieutenant said. "I am subject to a higher authority now."

"Who is this?"

Lee wagged his head, hopelessness sinking in. "Someone . . . a soldier chief far, far away."

The chief fell silent, and all Lee heard was the breathing of the four other men as the voices of the crowd floated into them.

Touch-the-Clouds turned back to the lieutenant and asked, "So he will be safe tonight?"

Lee swallowed, daring to answer, "No one can hurt him now."

CHAPTER THIRTY

Canapegi Wi
Moon When Leaves Turn Brown, 1877

Ta'sunke Witko! I will come with you!"

He spotted his old friend emerging from the edge of the crowd that had begun to part for the soldiers who were walking in front of him.

"Little Big Man," Crazy Horse called as the stocky warrior moved up on his right side. The soldier chief walked on his left, and now a friend at his right. "Did you come chasing me yesterday?"

"Yes," he admitted without the slightest shame, allowed by the soldiers to step right up and walk beside Crazy Horse.

"Did you come after me for the reward White Hat was offering to the man who caught me?"

"No," Little Big Man asserted firmly, his face stony and serious. "Man Afraid and I came along with Red Cloud's men to be certain that no harm came to you."

"No harm?"

The muscular *akicita* nodded. "Yes. We were afraid that *you* might do something that would cause the others to hurt you—even . . . kill you."

"Lakota injure Lakota? Why, this is unthinkable . . ." Then his voice drifted away as they started across the patches of dirt and of trampled grass.

Because he remembered No Water, and reached up to touch the scar at his left cheek, felt the way it had drawn up his lip as the skin healed. Every heartbeat of every day, it had served as a reminder.

"I will stay with you now," Little Big Man vowed. "Wherever you go, I will go with you and stand by you."

"It is good," he heard himself saying. "Even though your feet are now walking a different road, and you have become a metalbreast for the agent . . . I am glad you are here to help me understand."

In front of them two soldiers slowly cleared the way through the noisy crowd. These white men did not carry the long rifles of the walking soldiers, nor the carbines of the horse soldiers. Only pistols on cartridge belts strapped around their waists. He glanced to the left at Kennington's belt. A pistol there too. And that long, shiny knife slung from his left hip so it swung with every step. Little Big Man did not carry any of his soldier guns on him, only the knife on his belt.

Between the place where he had made his talk with his uncle's agent and that log building where they were leading him now lay a patch of open ground. Here at sundown it was packed with many of his faithful, people who had endured terrible winters, suffered through the summer chases, lived on in the old way even though the soldiers burned and destroyed everything they had been forced to leave behind. Some of his supporters cried out his name, while others wept or quietly keened. After so many of his Northern People had attempted to escape to the four winds, it was reassuring to know they had come to see him at this difficult time.

Among all those Lakota faces at the edge of the crowd, Crazy Horse suddenly saw a white face he recognized. It was the *wasicu* healer, pushing himself through the narrow gap between two of Red Cloud's agency police. The white man reached out an arm.

Smiling at the healer, Crazy Horse said, "Hau, Kola!"

As the escort passed the white man, he called back, "Kola!"

It was as if the healer wanted to say more, but could not—Little Big Man was moving him on so quickly.

Crazy Horse shifted the red blanket from his right arm to his left, feeling the reassuring hardness of that new knife soldier chief Bradley had given him as a welcome gift after his arrival. Still hidden there in the folds of that red blanket, it had remained a secret from the moment he had awakened before dawn in his uncle's lodge. That seemed so long ago now, so far away too . . . this very morning back where he belonged near his beloved Beaver Creek, camped beside his father and his two stepmothers. Where he and Black Shawl could live out the rest of their days in peace because no one would talk against him there. No one would spread lies about him on that reservation. No man could convince the soldier chiefs there that Crazy Horse meant to do any white man harm . . . the way they had managed to convince the soldier chiefs here.

But tomorrow morning he would speak to these white doubters, if need be saying more words than he had ever uttered in public. And he would make them understand that he had laid down his rifle, untied his pony's tail, and vowed to stay peaceful—

Ta'sunke Witko!

He paused a moment, believing someone in the crowd had called out his name. But Little Big Man took a firm hold of his right arm, nudging him into motion again. Crazy Horse realized it was the voice of the true one inside his head. His spirit guardian talking to him not through the mouth, but within his own heart.

Breathe deep now. Taste this air. Is this the air of freedom and peace that you hoped for back when you gave your body over to these soldiers and Red Cloud too? Did you really mean to throw your body away to these fools? Or will you remain faithful to the oath you made so many winters ago: that you will only give your life away as a warrior?

"I was a warrior," he said in a whisper. Yet neither of the men on either side of him heard, not for the noise of the crowd as they neared another low-roofed log building.* "Now I am just a man. No longer a leader. Just a man."

---

*In September of 1877, the one-story Camp Robinson guardhouse was composed of two rooms. You entered the building through a lone doorway at the east side, on the north wall. An awning extended along the full length of that north, or front, side.

Only the rocks and sky live forever, Ta'sunke Witko! A warrior does not die an old man.

Looking ahead between the two soldiers just in front of him, Crazy Horse noticed the lone guard with the long rifle turn on his heel at the near end of the covered porch and slowly pace away with his back turned. And for the first time he realized how many wagon guns were lined up in front of this place where he supposed the soldier chief wanted him to sleep until morning, when they could finally talk and all would be made better for it. And at the edge of the crowd sat Red Cloud and his pompous son-in-law, American Horse, both of them glaring down at him from the bare backs of their big horses.

"You are a coward!"

The throng went quiet at that shrill cry from a man's throat. He stopped, looking for him. There!

"I thought you were a brave man," shouted the warrior who wore one of the soldiers' blue coats. "But we can all see you are nothing but a coward now!"

In a sudden, blind fury, Crazy Horse lunged for the Red Cloud man, arms outstretched to seize him by the throat, but Little Big Man held fast to his right arm, and pulled him back.

"Do not worry about what he says," Little Big Man said quietly as he returned Crazy Horse to his place.

"Yes!" the shouter cried with a loud snort, and other men around him laughed. "Go along with the soldiers now, you man of no fight!"

His attention was snagged in the opposite direction as a door was drawn open by a soldier who stood right inside, beneath the awning, partly wrapped in shadows. Little Big Man tightened his grip on his left elbow as they turned left and stepped under the shady awning, onto the porch. For the first time, the soldier chief reached out to grip his right arm, tightly there above the elbow as they approached the door.

"Crazy Horse."

He turned at the familiar voice. From the faceless crowd stepped another old friend. "He Dog," he said with relief.

Now there would be two trusted companions at his side in this difficult time. But when Little Big Man threw up his arm to halt He Dog from approaching any closer, Crazy Horse grew uneasy.

So He Dog took a step back and warned, "This is a hard place you are going into, Ta'sunke Witko."

When Little Big Man tugged on his arm in a rough manner, pulling him away from He Dog, Crazy Horse moved on, following the two soldiers in front of them as they stepped onto a wooden porch and filed through a narrow opening that forced his old friend and the soldier chief to fall behind him momentarily.

Stepping through the doorway, Crazy Horse did not turn to Little Big Man when he asked his old friend, "Is this where we will sleep together tonight?"

With both feet inside he opened his eyes widely, glancing left and right, letting the eyes grow accustomed to the dim light in this place, now that the sun had fallen and night would soon draw itself like a blanket over the land.

"Yes," Little Big Man answered quietly at his right ear, stopping right behind Crazy Horse. "This is where you will sleep tonight, my fr—"

—at that very instant Crazy Horse realized where they had him!

This was the terrible place others had described to him! Tall shafts of iron extending from floor to roof . . . and behind them he spotted the dirty, bearded faces of soldiers who wore heavy iron shackles clamped around their wrists and ankles too. And what a foul stench assaulted his nose! The air so close, suffocating . . . his eyes darted—realizing the prisoners had no windows to look at the sky. Only tiny air holes chopped up high in the log walls.

"Where have you brought me!" he cried in horror.

Out of the reeking gloom appeared six soldiers: the two who had escorted him into this dank, repulsive, confining place . . . and four others, who held shackles and chains in their hands. Ready to make him a prisoner like these pitiful *wasicus,* who appeared to have been wallowing in their own filth. To throw away his freedom like this would be worse than death!

"No-o-o-o-o!" he shouted, whirling around on his heel, knocking away the soldier chief who had been gripping his left arm.

"Ta'sunke Witko!" cried Little Big Man. "No! No! They will hurt you!"

Growling with the fierceness of a grizzly, in one lunge Crazy Horse was at the doorway, his fingers frantically stabbing through the folds of his red blanket. In a second lunge he found himself barely through the open door, where the crowd immediately gasped and most started to scream. Inside that foul, stinking place behind him, the soldiers were yelling too. Clatter of metal against metal, clanking iron and jangling chain, scuffling feet, all landed upon his ears.

Onto the porch ahead of him bounded the two Sicangu, who were his uncle's closest shadows, men who had come with him on this journey only to make sure he was locked away in this terrible place. Swift Bear and Black Crow wore hard faces as they pounced toward him, but Crazy Horse lowered his head and threw his shoulders into the two agency police. With a grunt, they both fell aside, arms reaching, hands grabbing at his legs as Little Big Man charged up behind him. Their momentum carried them off the porch.

Behind you! Ta'sunke Witko, watch behind you!

To his left, out of the corner of his eye—he saw the old soldier still some distance away at the corner of the log building. The soldier suddenly looked over his shoulder, beginning to whirl around at the same time, his long weapon slowly coming down from where he had been carrying it at his shoulder. A last shaft of sunlight glinted off the long knife affixed to the muzzle of the weapon.

"Don't do this, my friend!" Little Big Man shouted behind his right ear. "No! Don't do this! You can only hurt yourself!"

He felt his friend's mighty arms thread around him: the left ensnaring him around the waist, the right looping across

Crazy Horse's chest, that hand immediately ensnaring Crazy Horse's left wrist as the red blanket spilled from his forearm.

But he had managed to pull the knife into sight.

"A knife!"

Angry voices thundered around him while the shrieks and cries and wails became deafening.

"That son of a bitch has a knife!"

As he staggered beneath the great weight of Little Big Man on his back, in a blur Crazy Horse saw how American Horse threw down his soldier carbine on him with a sneer—but in the next moment some of the Northern People leaped in front of American Horse and prevented him from shooting. Snarling in frustration, American Horse shouted his shrill order.

More than ten agency men charged in from the edge of the crowd, their soldier pistols drawn, forced to swing their weapons side to side, trying to take careful aim at the two wrestlers.

Atop his pony, Red Cloud shook a fist and hissed at his scouts, "Shoot low! Shoot to kill!"

As Little Big Man struggled to get a powerful hand around his right wrist, Crazy Horse felt his old friend's hot words behind his ear: "Stop fighting, my friend! They will harm you if you fight!"

From the crowd a woman shrieked in horror, "His arms! His arms!"

Another woman screamed, "See? They are holding his arms!"

Off to the side he saw the soldier chief appear, rushing into view as he wrenched his long knife out of its shiny scabbard, waving the long blade at Red Cloud's and American Horse's agency men—clattering its deadly weight down against the barrels of their army pistols.

A coward runs!

"I am not a coward!" he roared in anger at his *sicun*.

Stand and fight them as a man!

"Don't you see? I am the last warrior!"

"No war to fight! No war to fight!" Little Big Man shouted in his ear, beginning to squeeze and twist Crazy Horse's right wrist painfully. "Stop fighting and you will not be hurt, my friend!"

He would never be able to throw off the strong one who held him in such a painful vise, two powerful arms squeezing around his middle to make breathing impossible.

"Drop your knife!" Little Big Man ordered, catching Crazy Horse's right wrist, immediately wrenching downward on that hand gripping the sharp weapon. "Drop it before they hurt you!"

"Let me go, my friend!" he snarled back at his old comrade of the war trail. "Let go of me!"

They grunted against each other, wrestling as they had when they were mere boys. But this was different now—both men knowing who was the stronger...both friends knowing who would remain the warrior unto death.

Inch by inch his right arm was pushed down, then suddenly drawn back by Little Big Man. It was an old fighting tactic to catch your opponent off-guard by using his power against him. So for an instant Crazy Horse let that right arm go limp, which caused his friend to relax but a heartbeat.

This was his only chance at escape, his only road to freedom now.

Show them how a warrior looks death in the eye!

His legs bent slightly, Crazy Horse raked downward through the air with the knife, felt it strike something more than air, but slashed onward.

"Arrggg!" Little Big Man shrieked, his hands suddenly flying free.

Heaving upward, Crazy Horse threw his right shoulder into his old friend, flinging the bigger man backward. He raised his face to the red-tinged sky, shouting his most stirring battle cry: "Strong hearts to the front! Cowards and weak hearts to the rear!"

"Private, stab the bastard!"

He sucked air into his lungs, still in a crouch as he cried at the crowd, "It is a good day to die!"

"Stab him, goddammit!"

Little Big Man spun away, blood flinging from his opened wrist, clutching the wound tightly in his right hand as he stumbled backward, staring at Crazy Horse with wonder and pity in his eyes.

No! Crazy Horse's mind burned. *I only meant to free myself—not to cut you!*

"Stab the son of a b—"

His ears rang with the angry *wasicu* words he could not understand, interrupted by a loud clunk of metal against wood.

"You stupid Mick bastard!"

The women's screams began to ring even louder in his ears.

"Dammit—you heard my order: Stab the son of a bitch!"

Behind you! Remember that death will come from behind you, Ta'sunke Witko!

With a mix of sorrow turning to horror, Little Big Man called out, "Look out, my friend—"

From his left he felt the movement rushing toward him, more than seeing the approaching danger. Remembering his youthful vision received on the great rock in the middle of the prairie: danger approached from behind.

Out of the corner of his eye as he began to whirl, Crazy Horse caught the blur of blue, the glint of oiled wood and dulled steel lit with the crimson of sunset.

Then sensing the long blade pierce the small of his back, just above the left hip, sliding on below the bottommost rib—a sudden, painless shock coming from the realization that he was staring into the eyes of the old white man who had him impaled on the end of his long gun. The soldier's weary, red eyes did not show anger, nor sadness either. In that instant he found their souls touching, the *wasicu*'s eyes said nothing.

From the circle of red and white faces around him issued a gasp of utter shock.

For another heartbeat his eyes gazed over his shoulder at the old soldier—saw the blank eyes just then widening with recognition. Then Crazy Horse felt the long blade slowly pulled from his back as his knees weakened, unable to hold him up any longer. The hands of all those reaching out to grab him, to hold him back, suddenly flew from him.

In his chest as he slowly collapsed, Crazy Horse felt his heart labor, pumping blood through his unresponsive limbs. Felt the desperate flutter of wings as his spirit guardian struggled beneath his breast.

The moment his knees struck the ground, an icy white heat exploded from the long river of pain low in his back. Slowly, Crazy Horse rocked forward onto his hands, barely able to keep his eyes open, the pain was so great. The sort of agony that could easily make a man lose himself and wet his leggings. He fought to stay awake. Gritting his teeth, angry and despairing of ever rising again—feeling his strength ebb from him.

Stand and fight them to the end, Ta'sunke Witko!

But he knew he could not. It was the sort of wound that took all of a man's fighting strength from him with one breath. He might not die for some time...but he had been dealt a death blow.

"I-I can...not," he whispered, flecks of spittle collecting at the corners of his lips. "He...he has killed me now."

As he gazed upward at all the hundreds of blurry faces dancing back from him, mouths open, aghast at what they had just witnessed, he drew in one mighty breath, hoping it would be enough to allow him to stumble back to his feet... but his legs were leaving him, like water seeping through the crack in a worn, old kettle.

"My friend," the familiar voice said quietly in his ear.

He looked down at the hand on his shoulder, saw the bright blood dripping off the fingers. Then raised his eyes to gaze into the face of Little Big Man.

Through teeth he had clamped together in an angry, crimson agony, Crazy Horse grunted, "Let me go!," then drew a second breath that sent a wave of renewed pain through his belly. "Let me go....Can't you see you have got me hurt enough?"

He blinked, his eyes unable to see so well now. It reminded him of the black silk handkerchiefs the traders sold. Gloom seeping through him, only some tiny pinpricks of light shooting across the inky void. Surely they must be the earliest stars of an evening—but for the moment there were more than any one man could ever count...all of them turning, turning, turning upside down high above him.

Yet...that star road of fallen warriors was no longer where it had always been, where it should be, to guide him on his final journey. Instead...the star road had turned upside down and was now sweeping its great arch lower and lower. Closer and closer it sank toward earth, descending for him. All the better to gather him up in their mighty arms.

Here at last he would join the immortals.

CHAPTER THIRTY-ONE

September 5, 1877

SEAMUS COULD NOT BELIEVE HIS EYES!

Witness to that obedient old soldier bounding up while the officer shouted for him to stab Crazy Horse, seeing how Gentles missed with his first wild lunge—striking the door-jamb instead because of the way Crazy Horse was wrestling with another, much more muscular Indian in a blue scout's tunic. With a grunt the old private yanked his bayonet free of the wood and immediately sent it home with his second lunge. The moment he did, the crowd of yelling, shrieking Sioux jumped backward with a collective gasp.

"The wolf's let out to howl now!" he roared above the noise to the physician standing at his elbow, near the corner of the porch attached to the adjutant's office.

McGillycuddy turned to stare at Donegan with a mix of horror and dread. "I gotta do what I can."

He gazed over the doctor's shoulder at the muscular Indian who knelt over Crazy Horse the moment the injured man crumpled to his knees. Donegan turned at the sound of angry voices, watching the giant of an Indian hunch out of the low office doorway and quickly survey the scene outside the adjutant's office. He knew the tall one had come with Crazy Horse, perhaps a captor. But from the wounded look that came to the Indian's eyes, Donegan could instantly tell they were more than friends.

"I'm going to help!"

He wheeled around at the cry from McGillycuddy, finding that the surgeon was bounding off the porch, into the crowd, tearing his way through them with his hands, shoving Indians this way and that without giving a thought to his own safety. An instant later the towering Indian shoved his way through the stunned officers on that same porch, bumping past Donegan as he leaped onto the ground, shouting in

Sioux at the thousands of onlookers. A hundred or more fell away from him like wheat parted by the wind until he caught up with the shorter white man. Both McGillycuddy and the tall warrior reached what small open ground remained in front of the guardhouse door where Crazy Horse raised one arm and pushed away the offered hands of the muscular Indian.

All Donegan could think about was how those howling Indians were going to tear up the doctor friend right before his eyes if he did not help. Without an instant's hesitation, Seamus leaped into the crowd, shoving his way through the screaming, wailing hundreds—every step of the way praying none of them would jab a knife between his ribs as he carved a path toward the horrendous scene. The officer of the day was waving his sword in the air and shouting orders. From somewhere soldiers gathering, officers with pistols drawn, sentries with their Springfields lowered, those terrifying bayonets ready to impale the first of any attackers who came bolting out of the surging crowd. Behind their protective crescent stood old Private Gentles.

Donegan's eyes found the Irish soldier's for a heartbeat. In them rested a weary fear—not so much a fear for his own life because he had just stabbed this famous Sioux chief right in front of his people . . . but more so a fear that was beginning to sink in for what he had done. Slowly, Gentles's eyes fell to stare again at the blood that glistened the full length of the bayonet, a crimson stark and shiny against the dull steel. Then Gentles was nudged back even farther by his fellow soldiers, guided toward that open guardhouse door as the protective knot of frightened soldiers retreated inch by inch. All the while that captain waved his sword menacingly at the crowd, bellowing orders across the parade, where more men in blue were swarming out of barracks and offices, forming up, shouting among themselves in confusion.

Between them and this tiny patch of empty ground where Crazy Horse had collapsed milled several thousand Sioux about to erupt.

Muscling his way through the innermost ring of Indian

onlookers, Seamus recognized the clicks of at least a hundred hammers when he found himself standing over McGillycuddy and the tall Indian—both of them crouched over the bleeding man. The ground beneath Crazy Horse was already blackening with blood as he writhed in the dust and the grass, gritting his teeth, eyes clenched in torment. Moaning the wordless agony of the dying.

As he quickly looked around him, it became clear that the Sioux weren't really pointing their weapons at that double-guard of twenty soldiers who continued to inch back onto the porch and start through the doorway. Instead, the Indians had divided themselves into two forces, one large and armed with the finest of army carbines and pistols, the other side pitifully small, those wild Northern warriors who gripped more clubs and tomahawks than firearms. What illegal guns they had pulled from under blankets and shirts were now cocked and aimed at Red Cloud's men. With unrequited fury both sides shouted their challenges back and forth, willing to turn this into a bloodbath.

"Doc," he cried as he leaned over McGillycuddy, reaching out to grip the physician's shoulder.

McGillycuddy desperately pressed both of his bloody hands against the large patch of crimson that was spreading across the back of Crazy Horse's blue-cloth shirt. He glanced up at the Irishman, saying only, "He has a death wound, Seamus."

"Then we gotta get 'im outta here," Seamus whispered urgently. "Get you outta here."

As a trumpeter blew the first notes of Boots and Saddles, McGillycuddy leaped to his feet immediately, glanced down at both of his hands wet with blood. Without a word he darted toward Kennington.

"Captain!" he raged as he jolted to a stop before the wide-eyed officer shaking his ceremonial sword at the scouts who were brandishing pistols as they screamed. "The man is going to die! I've got to get him to the hospital to put him at ease—"

"You forget yourself, Doctor!" Kennington interrupted.

"You are a soldier. My orders were to put that prisoner in the guardhouse, so into a cell he will go."

"You're a mule-headed son of a bitch!" Donegan growled as he came up behind McGillycuddy protectively.

Kennington glanced at him, then back at the physician's face. "We have our orders, Doctor. You take a leg, I'll take the other, and we'll have a guard take his head—"

"Not to the guardhouse, for God's sake!" McGillycuddy protested.

"We're not going to stand out here till someone else gets killed for what's already been done!" Kennington growled, jamming his sword back into its scabbard. "Help me, Surgeon! That's an order!"

They quickly knelt and started to raise the wounded man off the ground, but the tall Indian suddenly clamped his big hand on McGillycuddy's shoulder and shook his head ominously. Except for the wailing of the women, the crowd grew quiet.

Through the knot of soldiers arrayed against the guardhouse stepped a white-faced Baptiste Pourier. "For God's sake, Captain!" he yelled in fear. "Stop! Or we're all dead men!"

Both white men gently laid Crazy Horse back in the dirt and trampled grass, and that giant Sioux took his hand from the surgeon's shoulder.

In panic the doctor turned to glance back over his shoulder as American Horse, still perched imperially on his pony, pushed his way through the crowd, inching toward them. But it wasn't the chief, McGillycuddy pointed out now. "Look, Seamus! It's Grouard."

McGillycuddy raised his arm as American Horse came to the edge of the menacing, noisy mass of Sioux. Seamus spotted the dark-skinned scout peeking around the corner of the nearby commissary. Rising to step away from Kennington, the doctor impatiently waved for Grouard to come. But the interpreter shook his head and disappeared from sight.

"God-blamed coward!" Donegan snarled, while the trumpeter blew Boots and Saddles a second time on the warm air of that late-summer's eve.

"There!" McGillycuddy said, pointing in another direction. "Johnny! Johnny Provost! Come help us!"

For the briefest moment Seamus stared over the heads of the crowd at the commanding officer's quarters. Bradley stood in the midst of a few of his officers, watching from that safe distance, arms folded across his chest as a man might watch a cockfight. "Seems your post commander ain't gonna do a thing to help you, Doc."

McGillycuddy glanced up as interpreter Johnny Provost reached his side, long enough to recognize that Colonel Bradley was refusing to become embroiled in the near riot threatening to erupt. "Johnny, stay here. I'm gonna need you to translate." Then he darted away.

"Where you going, Doc?" Donegan cried.

He looked over his shoulder to shout back at the Irishman, "To make the man act like a leader."

Damn little chance of that! Seamus thought to himself as he stepped behind the tall Indian who was still crouched over the writhing, groaning Crazy Horse. Bradley was a coward who would always stay behind the safety of fort walls when civilians were attacked, or out of harm's way when it seemed certain a general Indian war was about to flare up.

Sprinting back in minutes, McGillycuddy huffed, "The general repeated his orders to put the prisoner in the guardhouse."

"Then it's our duty to obey those orders, Doctor," Kennington declared.

"You realize what'll happen?" McGillycuddy shouted. "This chief is related to Crazy Horse. He doesn't want us to move him. So what do you think will happen if we attempt to move him into the guardhouse?"

"I say you go ask the friendly scouts," Seamus suggested.

"Yes," McGillycuddy said, hope back in his voice as one of the Indians at the edge of the crowd began shouting, pointing at the sky as he seemingly trembled with fear.

Around him more and more of the Sioux turned their

faces at the evening sky, some of them putting their hands over their mouths as that Indian continued to shriek.

"Who is that, Johnny?" McGillycuddy asked of the interpreter.

"Name's Black Crow. One of Spotted Tail's friends."

Donegan grew irritated with how the man was working on the crowd. "What's he saying to 'em?"

Provost listened for a moment more, staring at the sky too. "He says that cloud up there, the big one—'Look! Look!' he says, telling the others it looks like a man riding a white horse. Most of these people remember Crazy Horse always rode a white horse."

"So now they're getting spooked?" Seamus asked, grimly preparing for the worst.

Grabbing Johnny Provost's arm, McGillycuddy sprang away toward American Horse, who sat stoically atop his pony at the edge of the innermost ring of agency police, his army carbine cocked, positioned across his left arm.

Seamus watched how the surgeon implored the agency leader through the interpreter, how American Horse shook his head in refusal. That hit Donegan as a contradiction: that this agency leader would not give his permission to have Crazy Horse moved into the guardhouse—even though he was no friend to the dying man.

"Crazy Horse is a chief," Provost explained to McGillycuddy in English, loud enough that Donegan could hear. "A chief must not go into prison."

McGillycuddy whirled on his heel, his face blanched with frustration. "I'm going to ask Bradley for help once more."

Across those 200 yards of parade crowded with shouting, wailing Indians, Seamus watched the way McGillycuddy held his arms up to the colonel on that porch, imploring. Over their heads blared the brassy notes of the army bugler's call to arms that would not end. Finally the doctor wheeled about and darted back through the crowd a second time.

Reaching the open ground where Crazy Horse lay gasping, drawing his legs up in agony but twitching less and less, McGillycuddy breathlessly announced, "The general's agreed to a compromise, if I can get the chiefs to go along."

"What compromise?" demanded Kennington abruptly.

"I told Bradley the man won't last the night. He's going to die anyway. There's no purpose served by forcing a show-down and carrying him into the guardhouse," McGillycuddy gasped. "But the general did agree we could remove him to the adjutant's office."

Slapping McGillycuddy on the back once, Donegan said, "A damn fine plan."

The doctor turned away with Provost, stopping at the knee of American Horse, where the interpreter explained the plan. This time the chief nodded and legged down from his pony.

Freeing the blanket from around his own waist, American Horse unfurled it on the ground right beside the bleeding man. Rising again, the chief called out, motioning a half-dozen of his young men forward from the crowd. Provost bent over the back of the tall Indian, explaining what was to be done in a whisper.

Nodding in reluctant agreement, the giant gently eased Crazy Horse onto American Horse's blanket, then rose and took a step backward.

Gesturing toward the wounded man, American Horse be-gan shouting to the crowd.

"What's he saying, Provost?" McGillycuddy demanded.

" 'Maybe this man is badly hurt,' he's telling them," the interpreter translated. " 'And maybe he is not. We will take him into the same place where they had the talk, and see how much he is hurt. Probably the Indian healers can save him. It will not do to let him lie here while he dies.' "

That announcement made to the masses, American Horse spoke his instructions more quietly. The six warriors went to their knees, secured their hands around the edge of the blan-ket, then slowly stood together as the clamoring crowd fell silent.

To Provost, McGillycuddy said, "To the adjutant's of-fice." And he pointed at the building some sixty yards away.

American Horse started away beside the tall Indian, followed by the six carrying the dying Crazy Horse. They so
reminded Seamus of pallbearers carrying the body of their
wounded comrade . . .

But even though these six were Sioux, they certainly
were not supporters of the wild chief of the north. They
owed their allegiance to Red Cloud, a man clearly jealous of
all the adulation paid to Crazy Horse.

"Seamus," McGillycuddy said, having stopped and
turned suddenly. "You're coming with me?"

He thought only a moment, then shook his head. "No,
Doc. This is something you and Crazy Horse don't need me
for. I already seen men die slow deaths . . . enough to last me
a hundred lifetimes."

Without another word, the army surgeon blinked and
turned away. Following his patient through the hushed
crowd, on their way toward the adjutant's office.

Looking over his shoulder, Seamus hoped to find William
Gentles among those soldiers arrayed in a protective crescent around the guardhouse door. But the private was not to
be found. The soldiers already had him tucked safely away.

Over the heads of that silenced throng came the shrill
keee-awww of a hawk. Like so many others, Donegan turned
to look into the sky. But nowhere did he find a bird on the
wing.

Of a sudden, Seamus realized where he was needed most.
Back with Samantha and Colin.

Ta'sunke Witko!

For the first time, the voice of his *sicun* whispered when
it called out his name.

Hands had moved him. And now they moved him again,
each time causing such agony to jolt through him. Then he
felt himself lifted, believing it was the star road and those
warriors gone before him in battle who had bent to earth to
scoop him up.

But as he peered through the slits of his eyelids, there
were no stars. Only the copper faces of the young men who

grunted on either side of him, struggling. They were carrying his body—where he did not care. He had thrown it away and so wanted to leave the pain behind. With this faithless undoing of his life by old friends, how he wanted to leave the betrayal behind and feel his spirit take wing.

Around him he heard voices, some speaking the *wasicu* tongue he could not understand, others speaking Lakota, but words he could not make out. They jostled his body; then Crazy Horse felt the hard firmness beneath his tormented body as the six grunted under his weight. Feet shuffled away as he strained to open his eyes into slits once more. And immediately found the face of the *wasicu* healer hovering right over his.

Whispering Lakota, he husked in a series of gasps, "It was...one of the long knives...on the soldier's gun... stabbed through my body. I will die before another sunrise."

And listened as a *wasicu*-talker translated his words for the healer.

This healer was the one who brought the trader's daughter to your camp, into your lodge, Ta'sunke Witko.

Yes, he answered his spirit guardian, but spoke inside himself now. *Still, I won't blame the man for what she did to me...did against me, to help Red Cloud's friends and the White Hat too.*

You made it one more battle to fight, one more contest you had to win.

Those days are past now. I will soon release my body, throw it away. It won't be long now...not long at all until you too are free.

But you are coming with me, old friend. We will mount on these wings of mine and never truly be apart again.

Crazy Horse felt himself smile at that. *Yes. As soon as I finish this one last battle...I will go with you.*

In many ways, this will be your hardest fight.

Why does it have to be so?

Because you cannot stand on your own feet. Mostly because you have no hope of winning this final battle.

*I have been up against it many times before. Why can't I
fight back now?*

**Because... your day has passed, Ta'sunke Witko. Don't
you see that your people no longer need a warrior, no
longer do they need you. Your strength comes from the
past. Now other men will have to lead your people into the
future. Your day is over, and the sun is setting on all you
held so dear.**

My father?

He is on his way to you. Soon, he will be at your side.

Black Shawl?

She will know before this night is through.

Before a new sun rises... I will see my daughter too?

**Yes, along with your young brother, and your kola
Hump as well.**

Then... I truly am going to join the stars.

**Where all great warriors ride through eternity, Ta'-
sunke Witko.**

H-how?

**When you finally believe you can fight no more... you
must let go. Open your fists and... just... let... go.**

CHAPTER THIRTY-TWO

5 September 1877

Camp Robinson, Neb.
Sept. 5, 1877.

General Crook,
Green River, Wyo.

Crazy Horse reached here at 6 o'clock, his pistol and knife had not been taken from him and in getting these, he made a break, stabbing Little Big Man in arm and trying to do other damage, but we have him all right and I think there will be no further trouble. I had selected several Indians here and cannot speak too highly of their conduct, particularly of Little Big Man. Crazy Horse's father and Touch the Clouds are now with him; the latter in the melee was cut in the abdomen, but not seriously. The Indians I selected simply did better than I can express and deserve great credit, and I hope may get it.

Clark,
1LT.2d. Cavalry

IT TORE AT MCGILLYCUDDY'S HEART TO WATCH HOW THE old man ran his fingers over his son's pale face as the light seeped from the sky outside this lonely log building.

At times Crazy Horse fought death more valiantly than any other man the doctor had watched slip slowly away. Each time it appeared the pain had returned, Valentine gave the war chief another injection of morphine, so that he could go quietly, without any of the struggle that had marked those first agony-ridden minutes after the soldier lunged forward with his bayonet. From the site of the wound, and the bruising of skin entirely across the small of Crazy Horse's back, McGillycuddy believed the weapon had pierced not just one, but both kidneys. A death blow to any man, no matter how strong.

As the hours dragged on, the doctor continued to reflect on how things could have turned out much worse than they had. Had one mistake been made, one gun fired, how many would be dead or dying right now?

Valentine remembered his sprint through the crowd to reach Colonel Bradley's house, begging the post commander to rescind his order that Kennington put the wounded Crazy Horse in the guardhouse.

He had begged the stone-faced officer, "General! This will be the death of a good many men and Indians before you succeed in getting the body moved, for the Indians are ugly."

"Crazy Horse is dying?"

"He has his death wound, General."

After flexing his jaw for some moments, Bradley finally relented, "Move the body to the adjutant's office. I'll decide on the disposition of the corpse after you pronounce his death."

How quickly the last dim trail of twilight had begun to abandon the western sky now as he rose to strike a match, lighting the lone kerosene lamp to be found in this tiny adjutant's office. Foul-smelling that it was, the lamp strained to hold back the gloom as night settled down upon them all.

The door had opened again, and once more it was James Kennington. With evident relief, the captain said, "The last of the Sioux have left the post. But I think General Bradley still fears some reprisal."

Valentine had nodded, realizing it was well past retreat, thinking how so many of Crazy Horse's followers had hurled themselves onto the backs of their ponies, galloping away from the post, firing their carbines and pistols in the air, screaming their bitter curses and insults on Red Cloud's and American Horse's betrayal of their beloved leader. Within minutes of their arrival at this office with the dying man, the faint throb of drums and wild singing began to float toward the garrison from the surrounding camps. Bradley, indeed all the officers, feared a night attack, and put every available man on alert.

Looking down at his patient on the floor, laid out upon American Horse's blanket, McGillycuddy said, "Thank you for bringing that news, Captain."

"I also came with the man's father."

Looking over his shoulder at the officer, Valentine had noticed the old man inching up behind the captain's shoulder, easing around Kennington's side to stop at Crazy Horse's feet. A soft, pitiful groan escaped the old one's lips. Then his tired, rheumy eyes slowly climbed—this time landing on the face of the tall chief who had maintained a faithful watch over the wounded man from the moment American Horse's men had laid Crazy Horse upon a pallet of blankets nestled in a corner of this nearly empty office. Touch-the-Clouds stood, stepped back, and motioned the old man over.

When the Minniconjou chief had asked Kennington to remove his nephew to die in a lodge in one of the nearby camps, the captain categorically denied that request. So Touch-the-Clouds asked if McGillycuddy would allow him to spend the death watch over his nephew; Kennington agreed only if the chief turned over all his weapons to the soldiers outside the door.

"You may not trust me," the chief said to the officer, speaking through the half-breed interpreter who had asked to join the death watch. "But I will trust you. You may take my gun."

When Kennington backed out of the office and quietly closed the door, Valentine whispered to his interpreter, "What's the old man's name?"

"Worm," said Billy Garnett. "He used to be called Crazy Horse, until he gave his name to his son many years ago."

"How do you say that in Sioux?"

After Garnett had told him, McGillycuddy said, "Waglu'la,

I am glad you have come to spend these last hours with your son. Tell him that."

After the translator had spoken, the old man trained his eyes on the white man. "You are the healer who helped my son's wife when our shamans could not. Your power must be great...but this night your medicine isn't strong enough to hold back the hands of death."

"No, my healing is nowhere near that strong."

Worm gazed down at his son, stroking Crazy Horse's brow and cheeks with his gnarled and callused fingers. "We were not agency Indians. We belonged in the north, on the buffalo ranges. We did not want the white man's beef. We asked only to live by hunting for ourselves."

While Garnett translated, Valentine sensed that the old man had a story he wanted to tell. Quietly, the doctor settled on the floor, across Crazy Horse's body from the grieving father.

"During this past winter," Worm continued, "Three Stars sent runners to us—time and again—saying, 'Come in; come in.' So we came in, and hard times fell upon us."

McGillycuddy could see how painful it was for Worm to talk about the bitterest of memories, yet he had shed no tears.

"My son was a brave man. Only thirty-six winters have passed over him," Worm explained; then his lined face went dark, and hard as chert. "Red Cloud was jealous of my son. He was afraid Three Stars would raise my son to be head chief over him. We were getting tired of that man's jealousy and would not have remained here at the agency much longer. Red Cloud and our enemies here, they were trying to force us away, maybe drive us back to our hunting grounds in the north." He paused a long time; then with a sob he finished, "Now see what Red Cloud has done to him."

Worm bent low and laid his cheek against Crazy Horse's cheek for a long moment. When he stood, the old man stepped back into the dimmest shadows, crossing his arms with a whimpering sigh as his son stirred, barely opening his eyes. The dying man's eyes no longer appeared glazed with the effects of the morphine, and a low groan escaped his throat as he slowly shifted his gaze to the side. Crazy Horse mouthed something to the old man and Worm immediately sat again, bending low to hold his ear to his son's mouth.

Rocking back, the old man nodded, then looked up at the doctor. Crazy Horse's eyes slowly danced again until they found McGillycuddy.

"H-hau . . . Kola," he whispered from his dry lips.

Garnett explained, "He calls you his friend."

"I know those words," Valentine declared. He bent close to Crazy Horse, looking into the war chief's eyes. "Hau . . . mita kola."

It was an easy thing to watch the rising of the pain as it came over the dying man, how it drew up his face in a tortured mask, made Crazy Horse clench his eyes shut, twisting his mouth in a pitiable groan as he fought against the unseen enemy of death. Both his blood-crusted hands wadded up the blanket he lay upon, shuddering in agony.

In an instant, McGillycuddy hunched over his bag, removing the glass stopper from the bottle of morphine, drawing another injection of the drug into the hypodermic needle. When he turned around and pushed up Crazy Horse's sleeve to expose his upper arm, he laid the needle against the skin atop the vein—but stopped right there.

Worm had clamped his hand around the doctor's wrist.

"Touch-the-Cloud, tell him why I'm doing this for his son. It's only to ease his pain. He will die soon."

Garnett translated; then the Minniconjou chief spoke softly to convince the old man. After another moment of hesitation, Worm released the doctor. McGillycuddy slid the needle into the vein and slowly injected the pain-numbing morphine. The four of them watched in silence as the transformation took place once more. Crazy Horse's eyes were no longer clenched, the agony slowly draining from his face. Crazy Horse rolled his head a little so he could look again at the doctor.

" 'Healer,' " Garnett translated the dying man's words.

" 'You told my father I am going on this long journey to meet death. I have known this for a long time.' "

"I only want to make the journey easier for you, my friend."

His dark eyes began to sink back in his head, clouding over with the glaze brought on by the drug, and the soft turn of his lips made it seem that Crazy Horse understood as he turned his head away.

Silence came over the tiny office once more. McGilly-cuddy could hear the measured cadence of the sentries right outside the door as darkness deepened and the lamplight softened. The moon fell from the sky.

Now only the stars remained.

It felt as if the drums were throbbing in his marrow, their agonized rhythm stabbed him so deep.

With his wife and many of the other officers, Lieutenant Jesse M. Lee waited on the porch in front of Colonel Luther Bradley's residence for what would become of this uncertain and starless night. Moments after the stabbing, the commander had put the entire post on the highest alert. Every enlisted man now stood at an assigned post around their perimeter, issued extra ammunition and instructed to demand recognition from any Indian that might venture onto the Camp Robinson grounds, on penalty of death.

Along with those incessant drums, the faint wails and shrieks floating in from the surrounding camp were beginning to tell on his dear, sweet Lucy. For the first time in the last thirty-six hours Lee doubted his having left her here at this post when he and Spotted Tail took off downriver in the dark early-morning hours of 4 September—the day Bradley's troops and Red Cloud's police were to have arrested Crazy Horse. Back then, who would have known they both would be witness to this awful event, this day of tragic death and bitter reckoning?

Those drumbeats and that wailing only served to heighten their tensions as they waited out the hours, knowing how very real was the possibility of attack by the dying man's supporters. Realizing that Crazy Horse's people fully blamed Agent Lee for bringing their leader here as a prisoner, to be stabbed by that nameless sentry . . . to die an agonized death. As an immeasurable guilt weighed down his shoulders, Lee felt it was only natural the Northern Indians blamed him for this tragedy.

Just moments after American Horse's six Oglala scouts had carried Crazy Horse into the adjutant's office, that surly chief came back outside to address the thousands of onlookers and hundreds of mourners. Red Cloud's son-in-law had stepped to the edge of the porch and shouted, "We have the body now and you can't have it!"

An uproar began anew. The Crazy Horse supporters shouted their curses on the agency Indians, while Red Cloud's Oglala cheered, clearly ecstatic that their leaders were holding the wounded man hostage.

"We've been arguing over this!" American Horse yelled above the noisy clamor of the thousands. "But we've got him in this lodge now, and you can't have him!"

Lee had just begun to explain to Lucy and some of the other officers how that arrogance on the part of the agency forces was certain to inflame the passions of Crazy Horse's people when a half-dozen warriors spurred their horses across the empty parade, heading straight for the commanding officer's home.

"How'd they get on the post grounds?" one of the officers was demanding.

Another officer shouted for enlisted men to come on the double.

Yanking back on their reins right at the edge of the porch, the Oglala horsemen immediately began screaming in Sioux at the soldiers.

"What are they saying?" Lee and others demanded of their interpreters.

Baptiste Pourier explained, "That one, he's Crazy Horse's uncle. Named Little Hawk."

Indeed, the angriest of the antagonists appeared to be the wounded man's uncle, who suddenly dragged a pistol from under his shirt and waved the muzzle directly at Lieutenant Lee, that gun hand shaking in fury.

On the far side of the parade, Lee could see that more than three dozen of Red Cloud's policemen were already rushing toward this tense scene, but in those moments before they arrived, Little Hawk spewed out his vilest hatred for Lee, as well as the interpreter at Lee's side, Louis Bordeaux—both of whom had accompanied his nephew to this place where he had been killed by a soldier's bayonet.

Had a single bullet been fired in those tense seconds, a massacre of small proportions would have taken place on Colonel Bradley's porch. White women, officers, and enlisted too, along with Crazy Horse's people and Red Cloud's police—all would have died there and then. But the reservation scouts made a mighty show and convinced Little Hawk and his warriors they stood little chance of getting away with murder.

Their fury still unquenched, the Northern men wheeled about, shoving through the agency police who outnumbered them more than six-to-one. Little Hawk and his warriors raced away, shouting their oaths and firing their pistols into the air.

Jesse put his arms around Lucy's trembling shoulders, realizing just how frightened she had become at this brush with sudden death.

"They blame me," Lee confessed with a deepening sadness. "Even though I did everything I could to get him that audience I promised he would have with you, General Bradley . . . Crazy Horse's people blame me for his murder."

"You did everything expected of an officer and a gentleman," Bradley advised. "There's nothing for you to be ashamed of."

"Then why is there such a big hole inside me right now?" Lee asked. "A hole big enough that all the explaining away in the world isn't going to make it better."

"You're Agent Lee?"

Jesse turned at the question from an unfamiliar voice, discovering a dark-skinned civilian standing at the bottom of the steps. "Yes, I'm Lee."

"My name's Provost. John Provost."

Bradley stepped up to explain, "Provost is one of our post interpreters. Had a Sioux mother."

"What do you want with me, Provost?"

Staring up at the lieutenant, the half-breed said, "Doctor said you're wanted over at the office."

He momentarily gazed across the parade. "McGilly-cuddy?"

Provost nodded. "Sent me to tell you Crazy Horse wants to see you."

"C-crazy Horse?" he said in disbelief.

"Doctor sent me to get you," Provost said, turning to point back at the adjutant's office. "Said to come in a hurry."

Quickly bending to plant a kiss on Lucy's cheek, Jesse bounded off the porch, the interpreter falling into a trot right beside him.

That evening word had it that many of Crazy Horse's people had bolted out of the surrounding camps of agency Indians, some to scatter upon the winds, while others headed directly downriver for Touch-the-Clouds's camp at Spotted Tail Agency. Yet most had chosen to stay and mourn right there, across the river from Camp Robinson—because, Lee thought, they must have realized that if they ran, the soldiers would come hunt them down...the way the soldiers had always hunted them down. So instead of running this time, they wallowed in their grief: wailing, keening, singing, drumming the darkness down. Lee knew the men would be giving voice to coup counting and their most fervent brave-heart songs, for these were the warriors who had faithfully followed Crazy Horse against the soldiers at the Platte Bridge fight, or the Fetterman massacre, or the other victorious skirmishes and battles to defend their northern hunting grounds, like the Rosebud and the Little Bighorn. Men who had vowed to follow Crazy Horse...tonight they had no leader.

Not just the men—but the women, children, and old ones too. While the men had charged into the battles, still it had been these innocents who had suffered most, enduring beyond all human endurance when, time and again and again, they were forced to abandon all their possessions, or were forced to watch the soldiers burn everything they owned along with their stockpile of winter's meat too. So these un-sung women had placed the weak and the old with the little babes on the pony-drags and plunged into the icy snows, fol-lowing their men...warriors who had vowed to follow Crazy Horse to the end.

What to do now? Now that these poorest of the Oglala, the Crazy Horse people who had endured unimaginable loss, privation, and death...now that they had no leader?

"Agent Lee, come in; come in," Valentine McGillycuddy said, gesturing with a hand, bringing him over from the doorway where Captain James Kennington stood guard. "He's heavily medicated—to kill the pain."

"Provost said he wanted to see me?"

The surgeon scooted back some. "Come closer. Kneel here, where he can see your face. Yes, Lieutenant—he wanted to talk with you before...Crazy Horse knows he's going to die soon."

Inching sideways on his knees, Jesse came even with the wounded man's shoulders and leaned down slightly. Crazy Horse's half-lidded eyes seemed to spot him, and his scarred face turned toward the lieutenant. His dry, cracked lips be-gan to move, a bare whisper of words.

Provost translated, phrase by phrase, " 'My friend, I do not blame you for what happened today. Had I listened to you, this trouble would not have happened to me.' "

It made hot, unexpected tears come to Jesse's eyes to hear those words. He laid a hand on Crazy Horse's shoulder. Lee said, "At Red Cloud Agency, you may have been a little chief, and your word may not have been trusted much...but I would have seen that your good words were spoken to the soldier chief tomorrow if..."

And his voice drifted off into silence.

" 'Thank you,' " Provost translated. " 'I do not blame you for what others did. You were a good man to me. I am use-less now to help my people. Do what you can for them when I am gone.' "

When Crazy Horse turned his head slightly and closed his eyes, Jesse waited in expectation with the others for the wounded man to breathe again, worried that those last words might indeed be the death rattle. But after agonizing seconds, they heard Crazy Horse's labored breathing resume, watched his chest rise and fall with a slight shudder.

"He's growing weaker and weaker as we watch, Lieutenant," McGillycuddy said.

Patting the dying man's shoulder, Jesse nodded and rose to his feet.

"Ever since I arrived here with this man and Bradley refused to see him," Lee said quietly to the surgeon, "I worried that I would be made the goat of this affair. But now ... now it just doesn't seem to matter anymore."

He swiped at the tears that spilled down his cheeks and gazed across the tiny office at Touch-the-Clouds. Lee gestured toward the tall Indian and said, "This chief ... you can rely on him for anything you need during your death watch, Doctor. I regard him as honest as the sun."

McGillycuddy nodded before he laid two fingers into the groove of thick muscle on Crazy Horse's neck, feeling for the weakness of the pulse.

Sensing the immense burden of guilt bearing down his shoulders, Lee put his hat back on his head, stood rigid, and saluted the dying man on the floor. "Tell him ... try to explain to him why I don't think I can stay here anymore ... waiting, watching while he dies."

CHAPTER THIRTY-THREE

Canapegi Wi
MOON WHEN LEAVES TURN BROWN, 1877

SOMEWHERE OUTSIDE HIMSELF, CRAZY HORSE HEARD THE soldier trumpet blow. Muffled, beyond the log walls of this place where they had brought him.

For a moment he wondered if it were this death road that made him hear such a thing.... Then he remembered why the soldiers blew their trumpets. He had heard their brassy call raised so many, many times in battle.

Crazy Horse thought on all those people gathered to watch the little soldier chief and Spotted Tail's *akicita* bring him back to the Soldier Town. It seemed as if all of Red Cloud's people had turned out.

Now a soldier was blowing his war trumpet so he feared that fighting had broken out between the army and his people. But... he heard no gunfire. No screams of women, no strong-heart songs from the men. Why was the trumpet blowing?

He stirred fitfully, blinking, hoping to see more than the wispy edges of pale light—waiting, anxious for the first gunshots, the cries of men rushing into battle, the shrieks of the women and little children fleeing...

But there were none. Only the melancholy notes of that soldier trumpet, fading into the darkness that was closing in around him.

Sad that the soldiers had put down their roots and raised their log houses in this land that lay in the shadow of the majestic Crow Butte—where as a boy he and his best friend had hunted the tiny creatures among their burrows. Sometimes they had used their small bows and arrows. And other times they had hunted with rocks. That was before the soldiers came to take this land from them all and then give it over to Red Cloud...as long as Red Cloud obeyed the White Hat and Three Stars too.

Looking back now, it seems to be a whole lifetime away, Ta'sunke Witko.

Then he heard the whisper of his father, and looked up to find the old man bent low over him. Even felt Worm's fingertips gently caress his face. It was good his father was here for this coming of death. And his uncle too. Instinctively, he knew Touch-the-Clouds had never left his side.

Fitfully, pain rising again, he remembered how the soldier wagon had led them down toward the leafy trees at the crossing of the White Earth River, all of Red Cloud's people gathered to watch him in this time of trouble. With so many unfamiliar and hard faces pressing in around him, it had surprised Crazy Horse when his old friend had stepped out of the crowd, dressed as a warrior once more—wearing those powerful clothes he had always worn into battle...all those battles the two of them had fought together.

You see He Dog in your dream. But fail to remember how he abandoned you, his old comrade, and went over to Red Cloud's camp.

Maybe he went to stay in his uncle's camp so he could save his women and children, Crazy Horse answered the soft voice that reverberated in his marrow with a galvanic electricity. *He Dog will always be a warrior.*

Remembering now the recent memory of his old fighting *kola.* No matter that they had disagreed and He Dog had moved across the river. He had been there at that terrible moment they brought him to the hard place, and the two of them were together again. But Little Big Man became just as hard as that terrible, reeking place...and kept He Dog away.

Oh, had He Dog only been beside Crazy Horse when his arms had been held from behind! Had He Dog been close to protect his back, then Black Crow and Swift Bear could not have trapped him as he rushed from the doorway; then Red Cloud and American Horse could not have penned him in, to prevent him from breaking free.... None of them could have made him stop and struggle until the soldier's long gun knife tore apart his insides.

None of the evil-talkers were there at his final struggle. Not Woman's Dress, No Water, not Lone Bear nor Little Wolf—the two who had spewed out the lies about him plotting to kill Three Stars. None of them were to be seen in the noisy crowd. Only Red Cloud, sitting majestically and triumphant beside American Horse, both chief and son-in-law enthroned imperially on their ponies—watching this final undoing of the man they believed to be so much a danger to them and their exalted positions of influence. Come now to see Crazy Horse humiliated before his people, stripped of dignity, and scourged by the soldiers for nothing he had done by his own tongue, much less his own hand.

Those Oglala, his own people...how ugly they had turned against him.

From afar he heard footsteps on the tiny rocks outside, measured steps—like those of a man's dance. Crazy Horse wondered if he should have been a dancer like the others. But his medicine had told him no. Slow, rhythmic steps came into this place where he lay. Measured beats like the drum he felt reverberating within his breast. Each beat oozing a little more blood from the awful tear in his body.

After riding on the crest of some rising pain, he felt like sleeping again.

And when he awoke, Crazy Horse still heard those drumbeat footsteps, felt the rhythm inside him as it grew in volume and pain. So deep in his bones that it had to be the very heartbeat of the earth itself—the mother, the womb of his people.

He stirred a little, his breathing become ragged as he fought the swell of fiery agony through his belly. Sensed his father's face hovering over him, his uncle's hand on his shoulder, comforting. Against his arm, he felt the healer press.... Ah, the sleeping water slowly warmed his veins again.

"F-father..." he muttered as his eyelids grew too heavy and he felt himself succumb to sleep once more.

"I am here, my son."

Too late, for he was already dreaming.

Crazy Horse had only wanted to tell his father to let him go.

Camp Robinson, Neb.
Sept. 5, 1877.

General Crook,
Green River, Wyo.

In the melee, Crazy Horse got a prod in the abdomen, possibly from a bayonet, but probably from a knife when he attempted to stab Little Big Man: the latter I am trying to persuade all the Indians. The Doctor reports that [Crazy Horse] has no pulse in either arm, and it will be impossible to move him to-night. His father will be allowed to move his lodge near the guard-house and take charge of him should he be alive in the morning.

Clark,
1Lieut. Commanding.

He pulled the watch out of his vest pocket and tilted its face slightly, toward the greasy yellow light of the smelly lamp. Wasn't too long and it would be midnight.

Dr. Valentine McGillycuddy returned the watch to his pocket and listened to the sound of gravel underfoot outside, whispers rising from those faceless soldiers who came and went beyond these walls, and the muffled sobs of the old woman who had come to sit in the shadows, crumpled against a wall, her blanket pulled over her head in mourning. Beside her sat the old man, holding fast to their vigil with Touch-the-Clouds. The giant never moved from the dying man's side.

From time to time Valentine laid his two fingertips along the groove of the great muscle in the neck, searching—then finding—the faint and thready pulse. Measuring how it weakened hour by hour. Yet his patient was suffering little from all the morphine—only a little at a time, just enough to help him sleep himself into death.

God, but what a way to go.

He suddenly thought of the small, leather-covered flask he had along, and dug it from the bottom of his bag. Chances were that some of the brandy would magnify the narcotic effects of the morphine, make these last long minutes all the easier on Crazy Horse. Valentine unscrewed the pewter cap, poured it full, then slowly lifted the wounded man's head on one arm. But as he brought the cap to Crazy Horse's lips, Worm rocked forward to clamp his hand around the doctor's wrist. The old Indian shook his head emphatically, whispering.

"What's he say?" McGillycuddy asked Garnett.

"Doesn't want you to...to whirl his mind," Billy explained.

With a reluctant nod, the doctor gently returned Crazy Horse's head to the folded blanket beneath it. Gazing down at the brandy in the cap, he quickly tossed it back, enjoying how the liquid burned all the way down his throat, briefly robbing him of breath.

The old man certainly had some understanding of the white man's whiskey. So Valentine decided it was better that Worm did not fathom how this morphine was affecting his son. No earthly reason why the living should be allowed to subject the dying to this agony of a slow death, all in the name of courage and stone-faced warriorhood...when McGilllycuddy had it in his power to help his friend, Crazy Horse, in his final moments.

He had been thinking for some time, deep in his own thoughts, when the dying man stirred, moaned softly in his sleep. That sound of fitful dreaming made McGillycuddy's heart lurch in sympathy; he turned away with a sigh, forcing his hands into busy-ness again with the morphine bottle and the hypodermic. He had it filled once more and slowly turned to Crazy Horse, finding both Touch-the-Clouds and the old man at the wounded one's side. They were touching him, whispering so quietly it seemed as if their lips were only moving...but then his ears heard their faint singing.

Sioux words, mournful as a death march, a plaintive melody sung in time to the marching footsteps of those sentries posted outside the door.

Crazy Horse's head turned slightly as his eyes opened halfway, gazing at the face of his father. The moment he moved, Worm and Touch-the-Clouds silenced their song. Crazy Horse spoke something in a whisper as a single, waist-long braid slipped to the pallet of blankets. The tall chief of the Minniconjou gently placed the braid back on the dying man's red blanket.

Worm scooted close, leaning over his son's face, as if to listen. Then he whispered something to Crazy Horse. The dying man mouthed more words to his father. Then his lips moved no more.

Surprising McGillycuddy, a brief rush of air escaped Crazy Horse's lungs and his sunken eyes fluttered fully open—wide for a long moment. So long that the doctor thought he might be struggling to revive himself. But as quickly those eyelids relaxed and fell, while his head slumped to the side.

In the darkened corner where the lone kerosene lamp barely penetrated, the old woman began to sob and keen. Much louder now.

Worm looked up at the doctor and spoke sad words in a voice that cracked with grief.

Billy Garnett tried to translate . . . but the half-breed could not utter a single sound.

Placing the hypodermic back inside his bag, Dr. Valentine McGillycuddy scooted closer still, his knees touching Crazy Horse. Held his ear over the nose and mouth, not breathing himself as he listened. And eventually rocked back so he could place his fingers along the carotid artery again. Nothing.

Nothing but the mournful sobbing from that woman in the shadows.

"Son, I, am here."

And Crazy Horse felt the sure hand of his uncle as he

struggled to speak to them. Somewhere close, he heard a woman's keening, and prayed it was not for him. Yet Crazy Horse realized it was, knew that these tears were shed for him...so he wanted to cry out that his final battle was almost over.

Do not weep or mourn! You should rejoice for me!

Even though he had been betrayed by his own people, not once had he forgotten what he was. A warrior of the People.

But as soon as they no longer needed him, the Oglala threw him away.

The pain had become like a warm, shallow pool where he lay unable to move now. No longer flushing cold or hot through him. As the pain had warmed its way into his limbs, Crazy Horse got used to the idea of this throwing away of his body. He knew he wouldn't need his arms and legs anymore.

Slowly turning his head, he mouthed a few words toward the blurry faces swimming somewhere just above his eyes.

Worm bent low, placing his ear against Crazy Horse's lips, and said, "Tell me again, my son. I am here."

"Oh, f-father. I am sorely hurt," he whispered on faint puffs of shallow breath, all that his lungs could hold now that his body was being torn away from him. "T-tell my people it is no use to depend upon me anymore now...."

With a slow seeping blackness the one great eye that was his Lakota heart closed and everything inside him turned to night. It took a moment, but he suddenly felt freed. Light as goose down that wafts on a breeze, he was lifted, lifted... the sobbing and those mournful Lakota songs gradually fading from his hearing.

The approaching brightness surprised him, sparkling shafts of intense light somewhere above him. He turned slightly, with great curiosity, aware for the first time of the wind lifting him, as would the wind beneath an eagle's wings, carrying him ever higher toward the light so intense it made him shudder with joy.

Higher and higher he climbed, as if on a rising current of warm air, making for the heavens...leaving his beloved earth, family, and friends behind. Climbing toward the magnificent Star Road that arched across the night sky.

Such utter joy it brought him to feel the power and magnificence of the light that began to radiate from him now, a brilliance that burst forth from the heart of what he always had been.

What he now would always be.

CHAPTER THIRTY-FOUR

September 6, 1877

Red Cloud Agency, Neb.
Sept. 6, 1877.

Commr. Indian Affairs
Washington

Crazy Horse resisted last evening when about to be im-
prisoned. Had concealed weapon. Fought furiously and
was killed. Considerable excitement prevailed through
the night, and most of his band got away, but probably
went to Spotted Tail to join other Northern Indians. I
think everything is quieting down this morning. Little Big
Man was wounded by Crazy Horse.

Irwin, Agent.

WHEN HIS HAIR WAS PULLED BILLY JERKED AWAKE.

In the darkness beyond he heard the faint, steady throb of
Indian drums drifting in from the nearby camps, listened to
the high, pained keening of the women.

Trembling with sudden recognition, Garnett whirled in
the bed that was shoved right against an open window, discovering the old man peering in at him through the narrow
opening. When he recognized Worm's wrinkled face, another shudder of fear shot through his veins as he stuffed his
hands under the pillow and found his two revolvers. He
loosed a snort of relief that the old Oglala hadn't attempted
to snatch his pistols and done the three of them in while they
were sleeping—

"Nephew, get up," Worm said sadly, softly. "My son is
dead. I want the bow and my arrows now."

"Ta'sunke Witko is dead?" Billy asked in Lakota, shifting

his weight on the straw tick where he and the two other interpreters had laid down to attempt a little sleep sometime
before midnight.

On his right, Baptiste Pourier stirred and rolled over—a
heavy sleeper. Curled up at Billy's left elbow lay Louis Bordeaux. The interpreter from Spotted Tail's agency grumbled
unintelligibly as he rubbed the heels of his hands into his eyes.

"Touch-the-Clouds is with him now," Worm continued. "I
want to go back and tell our people that my son is gone."

Bordeaux snapped awake with that, rolling onto his hip
and reaching under the pillow to pull his own two guns into
sight. "What will become of Ta'sunke Witko now?"

"The healer said I will go back for his body after sunrise,"
Worm declared. "Give me my bow and knife now before I
go back to the camp."

Warning squirted through his veins with a red heat. Garnett realized that when a Lakota mourned for a loved one
who had fallen at the hands of a white man, their culture approved them killing any white man in retaliation. Billy dared
not return any weapon to the grief-stricken father.

"Bat! Wake up!" Bordeaux growled, reaching over Garnett to jostle Pourier's shoulder.

All three of them had scrunched together on Lieutenant
William Clark's narrow bed in the officer's tiny quarters.
Clark himself slept in his office, which lay on the other side
of a thin wall. On a canvas cot less than five feet away lay
Frank Grouard, propping himself up on an elbow at that very
moment and beginning to laugh at the three interpreters below the window where the old Oglala's gray head was
framed in muted starlight.

"What are you laughing at, Grabber?" Worm demanded
angrily. "You should have been killed a long time ago! What
you did to my son got his death walk all started!"

"Your mouth is full of horse dung!" Grouard snapped at
the old man.

"You and Red Cloud are a pair worse than women!"
Worm snarled at Grouard. "Him and all his kind were jeal-

ous of my son, and it was you who let the lies go on and on—"

"Shut up, old man!" Grouard shouted, his smile gone.

"Shut up yourself, Grabber!" Bordeaux hollered. "I was there. I heard with my own ears what you did. Twisting Crazy Horse's words around—"

"To hell with all of you!" Grouard roared as he rolled on the bed and his boots hit the floor. "Ta'sunke Witko was looking for death and he got what he deserved!"

"You sad son of a bitch!" Pourier growled angrily in his heavy-tongued English. "Every time we are up against anything dangerous, you always are in the way. You're a god-damned coward, Grouard!"

Grouard slapped a hand to his waist. "I'll cut out your tongue!"

Pourier immediately pulled one of his two guns from his lap, dragging back on the hammer as he said, "That old man could have reached in the window and snatched up one of our pistols! Could've killed Billy or Bordeaux before we could've shot him—just so he could kill the bastard he blames for getting his son killed."

"Nawww! He's just a harmless old man," Grouard scoffed with a mirthless smile, waving his hand as he got up to stand next to the door that would take him into Clark's office. "You're the coward, Bat. Got to be an old woman in your old age, ain't you?"

As Grouard turned the knob and disappeared through the narrow opening, banging the door behind him, Billy turned back to Worm.

"I can't give you your bow and knife yet," Garnett explained gently.

"Why can't you give them to me? They are mine. I handed them over to you so I could go sit with my son while he died. So he would have his father at his side when he took his last breaths—"

"I can't do anything about it right now," Billy responded with a little irritation. "It's the night. All the soldiers are a little nervous now. Come morning, I'll see the big soldier chief about your weapons."

"Go to him now."

Shaking his head, Billy said, "I won't go to him now. It's night—"

"No one is sleeping," Worm argued. "The soldiers are everywhere, awake—waiting for an attack. Don't they realize no fighting is going to come? Let me have my weapons and I'll go away till sunrise."

"I'm sorry. You'll just have to cry it out for now and I'll get your weapons for you when you come back to get your son's body."

Instantly feeling regret for having snapped such cruel words at the grieving father, Billy reached out to touch Worm. But the old man tore his arm away from the windowsill.

"I trusted you," Worm said quietly. "Because *my son* trusted you. Now you have forgotten your mother's people."

Garnett watched him turn away and trudge off into the night. Eventually Billy turned around, overhearing Grouard telling Clark that Crazy Horse was dead.

The lieutenant sounded groggy, really very angry for this interruption. He growled, "Go back to bed, dammit! All of you! Leave me be till morning!"

"Don't you care that your prisoner finally died?" Garnett hollered from the back room.

"You boys are all played out," Clark snapped. "We all are. Now just go back to bed and let me get some sleep—"

"Sleep?" Grouard asked. "How can we sleep now?"

Clark responded, "You are afraid of him, aren't you? Well, Crazy Horse can't hurt you now, Grouard!"

Leaping to the floor so he could stand in the doorway between the two small rooms, Garnett hissed at the lieutenant, "All you brave soldiers were afraid of Crazy Horse! That's who's afraid of him—alive or dead!"

"Go to hell, Garnett," Clark grumbled, rolling away from them and drawing the blanket back over his legs.

As he returned to the bed and stretched out, with Bordeaux and Pourier taking their places on either side of him, Billy kept both pistols in his hands, arms crossed on his chest.

Any man who wasn't afraid of someone so mighty, someone as *mysterious* as Crazy Horse was surely a fool, Garnett ruminated as he stared at the beams of the low ceiling overhead, his mind buzzing with what all could happen now that the greatest war chief of the Lakota nation had been murdered by a white man.

Any man was a fool not to be afraid of a living, breathing Crazy Horse...

And he'd be a goddamned suicidal idiot not to be afraid of a stone-dead Crazy Horse.

Camp Robinson, Neb.
Sept. 6, 1877.

General George Crook,
En route to Camp Stambaugh, Wyo.

Crazy Horse died at 11:40 P.M., last night. Some lodges have left and gone to Spotted Tail, the excitement last night being intense; but the Indians here claim that they will get them and will be responsible that none go north. Everything seems to be working well, though we have not heard from Spotted Tail. The death of this man [Crazy Horse] will save trouble.

Clark,
1Lt.2d. Cavalry

Valentine McGillycuddy hadn't been able to sleep, not with the far-off pounding of the drums, nor the mournful wailing of the squaws either. Maybe because his mind just couldn't let go of that image of Crazy Horse's last breath.

For some time, Touch-the-Clouds and Worm sat motionless, watching the body as if waiting for breath to return. Eventually the tall Indian dragged the wounded man's red blanket over Crazy Horse's face.

"It is well. He has looked for death and it has come," Touch-the-Clouds spoke with grief as he got to his feet and pointed at the body. "That is the lodge of Crazy Horse. Now the chief has gone above!"

As Touch-the-Clouds held out his right hand to McGilly-cuddy, they shook. The chief gazed at the doctor and said, "I touch your hands to show you I have no bad heart for any-one."

Worm stepped up and asked to take his son's body with him.

After briefly glancing at Captain James Kennington, Valentine said to Garnett, "Billy, tell Worm that I cannot turn the body over to him yet. Not until morning. Ask him to come back after sunrise. Then I can give him an ambulance to take his son back to the village."

When he had listened to Garnett's explanation, Worm said, "No. I do not want your army wagon. I want a flat wagon. No army wagon."

The doctor escorted Worm and Touch-the-Clouds from the adjutant's office, watching them move off in the dark-ness, their shoulders sagging with grief. For those few cool moments that remained before midnight, they stood in si-lence on the porch, beneath the immensity of the late-sum-mer sky.

"I'll post a double-guard until morning, Doctor," the offi-cer of the day eventually spoke, still staring after the two In-dians disappearing in the inky light.

"They'll want his body come morning," Valentine ex-plained.

"As soon as Bradley says we can hand it over, the old man can have his son," Kennington promised.

When McGillycuddy started away from Kennington and his four sentries, Touch-the-Clouds reappeared from the night and stopped in front of the doctor, speaking the words that Billy Garnett translated.

"He wants to go with you."

"Why?" McGillycuddy asked suspiciously.

"He says to protect you," the interpreter said.

"Why do I need his protection?"

With a shrug, Garnett explained, "Maybe because the Lakota will know soon enough that you were the one with Crazy Horse when he died. Maybe because the old man will tell them you gave Crazy Horse the sleeping water."

He stared up at the tall Indian. "Ask Touch-the-Clouds if he thinks I did anything to kill his nephew."

"No, he does not think you hurt his nephew," Billy replied. "That's why he is coming to stay the night with you. And keep watch so others do not harm you."

Without a word of reply, Valentine nodded at the chief, and in silence they started across the parade together, when McGillycuddy suddenly thought of a friend and his family. At the commissary the two of them turned west, walking toward the cottonwoods along Soldier Creek, moving quietly through the dark. But not quietly enough.

"Who goes there?"

The two of them froze for a moment. "It's me, Seamus."

"Doc?"

As McGillycuddy and the chief resumed walking toward the pale outline of the wall tent, he looked into the darkness but could not see the Irishman. "Where are you, Seamus?"

Off to his left from the cover of the trees stepped the tall Irishman, both hands filled with the long-barreled Colt's revolvers. McGillycuddy stared down at the army pistols, then glanced at the tent. "Samantha and the boy all right?"

"Yeah," Seamus said in a whisper, then wiggled his guns at the Indian. "What's he doing with you?"

"This is Crazy Horse's uncle."

"Yeah—I recognize him. But that don't explain why the dead man's uncle's standing here in my camp. Any more of 'em come along with you?"

Valentine said, "You're 'bout as nervous as a scalded cat."

"Ain't you?" Donegan said. "Just listen to that."

They both put their ears to the night, hearing the drums and the singing, the wails and the grief easily enough. "I don't think any of them will come, Seamus."

"That noise is enough to put any man's nerves on edge. Them Sioux is mourning something terrible right now. So how come you're so sure them Injins won't attack?"

"Why don't you come to our place, all three of you?" McGillycuddy offered. "Sam and the boy can sleep in with Fanny."

Donegan wagged a pistol muzzle at Touch-the-Clouds. "Where's he going?"

"With me," Valentine declared. "Said he wanted to come along to protect me."

For a long moment Donegan stared at the Indian; then he slowly shoved both pistols back into their holsters tilted at the front of his hips. "You don't mind having company tonight, Doc?"

"No. I'd be insulted if you turned me down."

Seamus disappeared behind the tentflaps, then reappeared within minutes with the sleeping babe cradled across his arms, Samantha at his elbow, a wool mackinaw pulled over her dress. Without any more said, the three of them followed the physician and Touch-the-Clouds toward the surgeon's tiny residence, where he found his Fanny still awake, sitting in a chair.

"I was worried sick you were in the middle of things," she admitted, glaring over her husband's shoulder at the tall Indian.

"I was," he confessed. "Crazy Horse is dead."

Fanny put her fingers to her lips as she watched the Donegans stepping up behind the Sioux. "Oh, my . . . is there trouble for it?"

"No, I think things will be quiet, dear," Valentine said. "But I brought our friends over to stay with us until the post quiets down again."

"As soon as I heard of the stabbing," Fanny sobbed as she wrapped her arms around her husband, "I grew so frightened. But it helped when you sent someone with word that you were all right, and going to stay with the death watch until Crazy Horse died. Come in, Samantha. Oh, please come in."

With the Donegans bedded down on pallets in the small bedroom McGillycuddy used as a sometime office, and he and Fanny stretched out on their bed, still fully dressed, Valentine pulled his watch out of his vest pocket and stared closely at its face in the dimmest of lamplight. The hands stood just shy of one A.M. He set it on the upturned hardtack crate that served as a bedside table and interlaced his fingers across his chest as Fanny nestled her head against the groove of his shoulder.

At the door, he listened to the low, whispered cadence of Touch-the-Clouds singing a mournful death song. In sign, the Minniconjou chief had pantomimed that he was going to post himself at the McGillycuddys' bedroom door. There he would sit through what dark hours were left until morning, when fears of the night and the unknown could be dispelled, and Crazy Horse laid to rest.

CHAPTER THIRTY-FIVE

6 September 1877

LIEUTENANT JESSE M. LEE SAT AT THE SMALL WRITING desk in Colonel Luther Bradley's office, his hands trembling as he reached into his coat pocket and pulled out the small diary covered with a soft kid leather. Quickly he flipped through it from the back, until he located the first blank page. He gazed at his wife, Lucy, for the longest time as he collected his thoughts, grateful that she had finally fallen asleep on the pallet he had arranged for her beneath the small window.

With a sigh he slid the diary beneath the lamp he turned low. Staring at the flickering flame as he rolled the wick down to dim its light, Lee felt anger and frustration bubbling within his belly. There was nothing left for Lee to do but lay the blame where the blame belonged. Clearly, the U.S. Army, and Lieutenant William Philo Clark in particular, had overestimated Crazy Horse's political ambitions. While Sherman, Sheridan, Crook, Bradley, and Clark too could maneuver, flatter, and cajole both Red Cloud and Spotted Tail to accomplish what the white man wanted to see done by those Sioux leaders... they simply could not fathom that Crazy Horse held no ambitions to become an important chief, no desire to be vaulted above others.

He had wanted only to be left alone.

Eventually, he gazed down at the blank page. On the topmost of those faint blue lines, he wrote in the date, then began to form into words the tragedy that had overtaken them.

Thursday, Sept. 6, 1877.

No one can imagine my feelings this morning. I often ask myself, "Was it treachery or not?" To the Indian mind how will it appear? My part in this transaction is to me a source of torture. Started Touch-the-Clouds and Swift Bear to Spotted Tail agency in the ambulance, and told them to look out for the driver. Explained matters to Touch-the-Clouds and he seemed fully satisfied that I was not to blame. He thought "his people would censure him for coming down with Crazy Horse."

I had a long talk with Gen. Bradley. He did most of the talking. I felt so miserable that I could scarcely say anything; but told the general how our course was to get Crazy Horse, and that I felt that MY power had departed; my influence over the Northern Indians had gone; I was short of my strength; that this whole trouble was the result of mismanagement on the part of Philo Clark, and mis-interpretation on the part of Grouard.

Finally he set the pencil aside and rested his throbbing head upon his arm. Closing his eyes to the tears, Lee shuddered with grief. Not for Crazy Horse, because there was no longer any purpose to grieve the dead.

Rather, Jesse Lee mourned for the living, for Crazy Horse's people. Where were they to turn? What would become of them now?

Headquarters Dist. Black Hills,
Camp Robinson, Sept. 7th, 1877

Adjutant General
Department Platte, Omaha.

Sir:
When Gen. Crook arrived here on the 2nd inst. he ordered me to surround and disarm Crazy Horse's band the next morning...

Crazy Horse and his friends were assured that no harm was intended him; and the chiefs who were with him are satisfied that none was intended; his death resulted from his own violence. There was a good deal of excitement among his people following his death, but it is quieting down. The leading men of his band—Big Road, Jumping Shield, and Little Big Man—are satisfied that his death is the result of his own folly, and they are on friendly terms with us. Crazy Horse's band is being reorganized under Big Road, a moderate, prudent man, and I think most, if not all, the band can be kept quiet.

Very respectfully, your obed't. serv't.
L. P. Bradley, Lieut. Col. 9th Inf.

BY TELEGRAPH
———

News from the Northwest—
Death of Crazy Horse.
———

Indians Driven Out of the
Black Hills.
———

All Scotland Uniting to Honor
General Grant.
———

Annual Reunion of the Army of the Tennessee.
———

THE INDIANS.
———

Claiming the Black Hills—
Crazy Horse Reported Dead.
———

CAMP SHERIDAN, September 4.—Shedding Bear, with fifteen lodges of Lame Deer's band, numbering about eighty persons, surrendered this morning to Major Burke, of the Fourteenth Infantry, commanding this camp . . . These are the Indians that have been committing depredations in the vicinity of the Black Hills, and their coming in leaves that country and the Big Horn country entirely free of Indians . . .

CHICAGO, September 6.—Orders have been issued for
the apprehension of some of the principal agitators among
the Indians in the disturbed regions of the west, with a
view of placing them in confinement in Florida, a practice
which has proven effective in quelling disorders among the
Indians in the Indian territory and elsewhere. Army officers
here do not anticipate any serious commotion on account
of the death of Crazy Horse.

It surprised McGillycuddy to find the two of them on the
front porch, tall shadows in the gray pre-dawn light. Touch-
the-Clouds sat on one side of the door in complete silence,
his back against the wall, and Donegan was reclining in a
ladder-back chair. Both of them appeared to be listening to
the distant keening from the Sioux camps. Both men lost in
their own faraway thoughts.

*Likely the two of them are thinking about the same north
country, but for different reasons,* McGillycuddy reflected.

Touch-the-Clouds would be brooding on what had been
until only months ago—the freedom and their ancient way
of life come to an abrupt end. And the Irishman would be
yearning for the freedom those free and open plains always
gave him, no matter that in recent days he had talked more
and more of returning to Montana to fight another Indian
war.

One man whose heart had been broken when freedom
was torn from him. The other a man whose very heart hungered after what had been ripped from the Sioux they both
had harried, chased, and fought through long months of heat
and dust and endless rains. But the Sioux and Cheyenne had
been defeated, herded onto these reservations.

As the inevitable result of his inability to live confined
and useless, one solitary man had been killed, a man whose
very way of life had ended when he decided he would bring
his people in to the agency—knowing that he was throwing
away everything that he had ever lived for. Knowing that the
reservation would eventually mean the death of him.

With some crude sign, he made Touch-the-Clouds understand they would now return to the adjutant's office where the body of Crazy Horse rested. Behind them Donegan's chair clattered on the planks of the porch.

"You going over to where you left him after he died?" Seamus asked.

"Want to come?"

Donegan glanced a moment at the tall Indian, then said, "Yes. Do what I can . . . to help. He was a . . . a . . ."

"I think I know what you're trying to say, Irishman. A noble enemy. A man you fought, but came to respect?"

"That's close enough, Doc."

As they neared the office the sun was just beginning to splash the eastern horizon with a brilliant bloodred, a crimson so vivid that it reminded Valentine of the strips of meat Crook's soldiers had ripped from the flanks of barely dead horses during that starvation march after fighting Crazy Horse's warriors at Slim Buttes.

"Sky's bleeding this mornin', Doc," Seamus whispered as the eight sentries at the front of the building watched the two of them approach with the tall Indian.

"It's got good reason to cry too," McGillycuddy added. But there wasn't a cloud to be found marring the morning blue.

After asking one of the soldiers to fetch the officer of the day, McGillycuddy entered the office with the Irishman and Touch-the-Clouds, finding the body outstretched in a corner, resting on the blankets on the floor, completely covered with his own red wool blanket . . . just as Valentine had left things.

"May I look at him one last time?" Donegan asked.

For a moment, McGillycuddy looked at the Minniconjou chief. Touch-the-Clouds seemed to understand the desire of the white man and nodded, stepping over to kneel beside the body. Seamus knelt opposite the doctor as Valentine pulled back the red blanket.

How pale he looked already. Never had been near as dark as his Sioux brethren. But his pallor was all the more striking now. McGillycuddy had just repositioned the blanket and they were standing when the door opened.

"The old man is coming," Lieutenant William Clark announced as he came in with two more officers on his heels.

"Bradley?"

"No. I think it's Crazy Horse's father," Clark explained. "They were coming this way."

"They? How many men does he have with him?" Valentine asked.

"Just a woman. Old like him."

"Probably one of Crazy Horse's stepmothers." The doctor went to the window, looked out, and saw the pair approaching the soldiers who were about to stop the Indians. "She was here with Worm last night, keeping watch."

Clark went to the open door and shouted to the sentries, "They can come in. This is the dead man's parents."

Stepping aside, the guards let the old couple climb onto the low porch, then quietly enter the office.

As they knelt beside the blanketed form on the floor, Clark stepped to McGillycuddy's elbow and whispered, "I've sent for the wagon, and that coffin I asked for last night."

"We can turn him over to his parents?"

"Sooner we do, the better the general will feel," Clark said. "Bradley's going to be nervous as hell till Crazy Horse is off this post."

Valentine watched how the pair of old Sioux stroked the arms they had pulled free of the blanket they left over Crazy Horse's face. "Alive or dead, that man still brings fear to a white man's heart."

Clark swallowed. "Damn shame things had to turn out like this. But he brought about his own undoing."

"Did he, Lieutenant Clark?" McGillycuddy asked, feeling the fury rise in him, turning to gaze steadily at the young lieutenant. "Or do you say that only because he was the one Indian you discovered you would never control?"

Clark opened his mouth to speak as the snort of horses and the rattle of bit chains announced the arrival of the springless wagon* right outside the door.

Adroitly stepping between the physician and the red-faced lieutenant, Donegan offered, "I'll help bring in the box."

Inside the cramped office, Valentine, Donegan, and Touch-the-Clouds dragged off the top of the coffin, set it against a wall; then the three of them gently lifted Crazy Horse and laid him into the crude pine box before replacing the warped and ill-fitting lid. Clark called in two more soldiers. After they turned their Springfield rifles over to the lieutenant, the two young men knelt with McGillycuddy and Donegan, raising the coffin off the floor, carefully positioning it on their shoulders.

After squeezing through the narrow doorway, the four of them slid the box into the back of the wagon.

Clark stepped over to the soldier who leaned against the front wheel, his arm wrapped lazily around the brake handle. "Soon as you get the body to the village, I want you to get on back—"

"Beggin' pardon, Lieutenant," the middle-aged soldier interrupted as he straightened, "but you can't make me drive this wagon into that camp."

For a moment the officer stared at the older soldier, work-

---

*This turned out to be the same wagon that had been readied to whisk prisoner Crazy Horse away from Camp Robinson after midnight that 6 September 1877. Orders were given and plans had been laid for Second Lieutenant H. R. Lemley and his E Troop of the Third U.S. Cavalry to escort their famous captive south to Sidney Barracks, located on the tracks of the Union Pacific Railroad, near present-day Sidney, Nebraska, manned that autumn of 1877 by a unit of the Fifth U.S. Cavalry. From there a shackled Crazy Horse was to be hurried east to Omaha, on to Chicago to meet General Sheridan himself, and eventually to the Dry Tortugas, off the coast of Florida.

ing that around in his head. Then Clark turned and looked over each of the sentries standing at the front of the adjutant's office, some watching him with great curiosity, others showing the barest interest.

"Any of the rest of you?" he asked. "All I need is a couple of volunteers to take this wagon into the camp across the river."

"Ain't what I'd call safe duty, Lieutenant," observed a different soldier.

A third said, "Not something for a sane man to do."

While Clark was looking from man to man to man, Valentine figured he had to agree with the reluctance of these enlisted men. Wasn't a savvy soldier who would willingly step forward and volunteer to take the body of this particular chief into a village where the angry occupants had been nursing all night long on their hatred for the white men who had killed one of their leaders.

"Might be best to find some of Red Cloud's men to drive the wagon," McGillycuddy suggested.

A hard expression on his face, Clark stomped away across the parade. In a few minutes he was back with two of his U.S. Indian Scouts, both of them proudly dressed in their blue soldier coats. Without waiting for further instructions from the lieutenant, the pair clambered up the front wheel and settled on the plank seat, where they turned to peer over their shoulders at the tall chief who stood between the old man and woman.

"Maybe they'd like to make the ride in the back of the wagon, Lieutenant," McGillycuddy suggested. "Sit with the coffin."

Clark made sign to Touch-the-Cloud, offering to let the three of them ride in the wagon with the dead relative's body, but the chief only shook his head.

"No, they want to walk," explained Clark before he signaled the pair of scouts at the front of the wagon.

The two-horse hitch lurched into motion, followed by those three mourners who clung near the rear gate, as this sad little cortege started toward the shallow crossing of the sluggish river.

For a moment McGillycuddy watched as the wagon inched its way through the trees. Then he gazed up at the cloudless blue sky, wondering why it wasn't raining.

EPILOGUE

SEAMUS HAD BEEN UNABLE TO SLEEP, WHAT WITH FUSSING over all the affairs he must see to before setting out in the morning.

Two new, strong horses purchased from Long Joe Laravie, one of the traders set up for business near the Red Cloud camps, along with a pair of new blankets, and another brace of Colt's revolvers. Before all the Sioux drifted onto the post grounds yesterday afternoon, Donegan had given a going-over to three new Smith & Wesson pistols trader Johnny Dear had behind the counter in his store at nearby Red Cloud Agency.

"Company calls 'em the Scofield model," Dear had explained. "G'won—put 'em in your hand and see how they feel to you. Break it down there, right: with the catch on the frame that breaks the barrel and cylinder forward. Looks to me like they'd be quicker to reload than these Colt's you're wanting to buy."

Sure enough, with a flick of the thumb the Irishman could break open the cylinder for reloading—six cartridges at a time—instead of loading one cartridge at a time before he had to turn the cylinder to the next chamber in the Colt's pistol.

"What'd I tell you?" Dear proposed. "You want to try two of those Scofields instead of these Colt's you picked out?"

"No," Seamus answered, wagging his head as he laid the pistol down on the scrap of blanket Dear brought out when showing off his pistols. "What's a man on horseback going to do? Neither gun makes it easy for me to reload in a fight, what with me having to hang onto my horse's reins. Only choice I got in a scrap is to stuff the reins between my teeth."

Dear scratched at his two-day growth. "Hadn't give a thought to how a man'd get that done in the saddle."

"Aye, there's the rub," Seamus replied. "So tell me what you want for them two Colt's I picked out here. If a man can't reload up in the saddle and on the run...then he sure as hell needs to have more'n two belt guns on him, Johnny."

Eighty pounds of salt pork and another fifty of hardbread he would load onto the packhorse. That and all the ammunition he was taking along for that big Sharps buffalo rifle a packer had put in his hands after the Rosebud fight in June of '76.* Not to mention the cartridges he was packing for the Winchester, a model '73, and all the ammunition Seamus figured he might need for those four single-action Colt's. No frills this trip. The horses would be burdened with enough weight as it was. Speed was what he was counting on: crossing north-northwest to Pumpkin Buttes, striking almost due north from there for the mouth of the Tongue, praying he would reach the cantonment of the Fifth Infantry before Nelson Miles put his regiment of fighters into the field against those Nez Perce who were coming his way.

While he wasn't taking along the new straight razor with the ivory handle that Sam had bought him because, as he had explained to his wife, he was going to grow a beard against the coming of winter winds to the northern plains, he had purchased a new toothbrush with stiff, brown bristles...in addition to a pair of photographs he would carry in the breast pocket of his wool shirt, right over his heart.

Back in late June, when the post and agency was being overrun with one photographer after another, all of them eager to be the first to capture on a glass plate an image of the wild Northern chief Crazy Horse, Donegan had ended up wrangling a deal out of one of the best of the shadow catchers. Two days later the three of them had dressed in their finest, and scrubbed their faces raw, rid now of the dirt and grime and smudge from campfire smoke. After Samantha had used her fingertips to brush what little hair Colin had atop his head, she had taken up her brush and turned her attention to her gray-eyed husband. When she finally had his

---

*Reap the Whirlwind, vol. 9, the Plainsmen Series.

shoulder-length hair neatly parted in the middle, she finished up by giving a quick going-over to his mustache and Vandyke goatee.

They posed as a family: Seamus perched on a stool in front of a painted canvas backdrop hung from the side of the photographer's wagon, little Colin supported on his lap, and Samantha standing beside her husband, one hand on his shoulder, the fingers of the other barely touching her infant son. It took two tries before Donegan managed to hold the boy still enough for the photographer.

Then Seamus had stood, backed away, and asked Sam to plant herself on the stool, taking Colin into her lap, propped there for a much more informal sitting.

"You're sure this is what you want?" asked the photographer.

He saw how the boy gazed up at his mother with such love, his little fingers knotted around one of the many buttons running down the front of her bright blue dress. Diffused sunlight poured through a canvas awning, giving a blush to her cheeks.

Seamus replied, "Oh . . . yes. This is just the way I want to remember them, sir."

Those two photographs he would carry, having left a copy of the family portrait with Sam to remember him by . . . along with his taking along that big turnip watch she had purchased for him back at John Collins's store, Fort Laramie. Whenever he would hold the watch against his ear—she had instructed him—the tick would be the beat of her heart, drumming out her love for him while he was so many, many miles and so many, many days away.

"How about Sam and our boy bunking in with the two of you till I'm back come November?" he asked Valentine McGillycuddy as they sipped at coffee in the dark that Thursday morning, September 7.

"I thought I'd already made a decision on that," the doctor replied, blowing across the surface of his coffee.

"You talked it over with Fanny?"

"She's the one came up with the idea," McGillycuddy admitted with a grin. "I think it's a fine idea. Women belong together, Seamus. It's men like you and me can do without company for long stretches of time."

His eyes misted a little as he peered at the doctor. "Especially a fella like me. I'm in your debt, friend."

"Oh, you will be by the time you get back!" McGillycuddy snorted. "I'm keeping account of how much Sam is going to eat!"

Reaching way down into the deep front pocket of his canvas britches, Seamus pulled out a thick roll of army scrip. Seizing hold of McGillycuddy's empty hand, he filled it with the roll of paper money, then closed the physician's fingers around it. "You keep this for me, and take what you need to feed the three of you while I'm gone north to fight with Miles."

In stunned disbelief, McGillycuddy stared down at the wad of neatly rolled bills tied up with a soiled piece of string. "My god! How much money is this, Seamus?" he exclaimed in an astonished whisper.

With a shrug, he answered, "Don't rightly recollect how much I've got left now, after trading off for new horses, guns, cawtridges, and all. But...if I don't come back... want you to see that Samantha gets all that's left."

Valentine quickly stuffed the money down an inside pocket of his morning coat. "I'll make sure Sam gets every last dollar of it, Seamus."

For a moment, he could not speak, staring as he was into the eyes of this friend. "Th-thanks, Doc. You'll watch over 'em for me?"

"Like they was my own, Seamus. Like the two of them was my very own."

All too soon it was time for him to step away from that officers' barracks and fetch up his horses, lead them over to the tent where most everything he was taking was buried under their blankets. With the animals saddled and ready to go, he put his new pair of binoculars into the off-hand saddlebag and buckled the three straps. Sighed, and led the horses back to the porch where McGillycuddy waited with Touch-the-Clouds, the two women, and his little boy.

She stepped down from the low porch as he dropped the reins and moved toward her.

"Sh-sh," he whispered in her ear as he took both of his loved ones into his arms. "There's nothing else we can say. Got it all said last night."

And when Samantha pulled back a few inches and looked up into his face, she set Colin in her husband's arms and then went to wiping the damp tears from Donegan's ruddy, bristly cheeks, already furry with a three-day growth of new beard.

"We'll be waiting here, Seamus," she said softly.

"By Thanksgiving," he vowed. Then thought better. "No later than Christmas."

"Then we'll be staying for the winter?"

He stroked her hair for a moment. "Unless we get a stretch of fair weather and can strike out for Deadwood. Here, or up there, we're not going to make it to Last Chance Gulch before late spring now."

"These are good people," she said, trying hard to smile.

"No finer people to look after those I love."

Then she pressed herself against him, flinging her arms around both of her men, quietly sobbing. "I knew this was what you were when I married you, Seamus. A soldier. A fighting man...a warrior. But just knowing doesn't make the parting any easier."

"Long as there's Injins running over the land, killing white folks 'cause so many white folks has killed them and stole their hunting grounds...I can't take you two north with me."

He felt her nod her head against his thick wool shirt. Leaning down, he kissed her forehead before she stepped back. Then he raised Colin up to the full length of his arms and gently rocked the boy side to side.

"Take good care of your mama now, son. You pa's going away for a few weeks to do what he can to put things right again. Till then, I don't want you learning to say a single word or take a single step, neither one...not till I get back to bounce you in the air meself."

Gradually bringing the boy back down to his own damp and upturned face, Donegan smothered Colin's face with a dozen tiny kisses. Then turned him back over to his mother.

At her ear, he whispered, "You both are all I've ever had to care about."

Then briefly pressed his open mouth against hers, quickly turned, and stuffed a big boot in the leather-wrapped stirrup. Dragging a coat sleeve beneath his nose, he touched his heart with his fingertips, blew her a kiss, and reined both horses around in a tight half-circle, jabbing the saddle animal with the blunt ends of his brass spurs.

Don't look back, he told himself over and over as the horse carried him away. *Just don't look back.*

There were friends he owed his allegiance to up there at the mouth of the Tongue River. Fighting men and comrades-in-arms.

And there was a wide swath of Montana Territory he had to see was put back to rest. Only then could he come back to Samantha and Colin with a heart not burdened by duty to his adopted country, not fettered by loyalty to old friends.

Only when the flames of this Nez Perce War were snuffed out could he come back to family, and once more take up their search for a home.

AFTERWORD

We did not ask you white men to come here. The Great
Spirit gave us this country as a home. You had yours. We did
not interfere with you. The Great Spirit gave us plenty of
land to live on and buffalo, deer, antelope, and other game;
but you have come here; you are taking my land from me;
you are killing off our game, so it is hard for us to live. Now
you tell us to work for a living, but the Great Spirit did not
make us to work, but to live by hunting. You white men can
work if you want to. We do not interfere with you, and again
you say, why do you not become civilized? We do not want
your civilization! We would live as our fathers did, and their
fathers before them.

AS EARLY AS THE SUMMER OF 1877, DR. VALENTINE T.
McGillycuddy first credited this speech to Crazy Horse. But
many historians have lined up to express their skepticism
that Crazy Horse ever said these things to the army's con-
tract surgeon at Camp Robinson. The truth is, these historians claim, Crazy Horse never did say anywhere near this
much at any one time.

However—I, for one, believe Crazy Horse did utter these
heartfelt sentiments to McGillycuddy during the final
months of his life, sometime after the *wasicu* healer had
earned the Oglala leader's trust by managing to ease Black
Shawl's suffering. Far from being the words of a defeated
man, they were instead the unerring defiance of a man who
would never be corralled, tamed, or "civilized."

You will remember how Crazy Horse dared to go against
the ways of his own people, finally turning his back on the
ineffectual shamans by inviting McGillycuddy to help his
wife, Black Shawl. In fact, Helen Laravie was the first interpreter the physician brought along to the Oglala camp. If not
through his subsequent translator, William "Billy" Garnett,
then perhaps through the young half-breed woman who

eventually became Crazy Horse's "third" wife, this famous war chief expressed his renunciation of all that the white culture offered.

He might have brought his suffering people in to Red Cloud's agency, but Crazy Horse never once acted as if he had surrendered to his enemy. Never acted as if he had been subjugated by the *wasicu*. The army had yet to defeat him in battle.

Why, I ask those skeptical historians, wouldn't Crazy Horse speak to the white healer he reluctantly had come to trust? Never before was there any occasion, much less a need, to speak to a white soldier, or a civil official, in such an informal manner. Beginning with the time his youthful friend, Lieutenant Caspar Collins, was killed in the Platte Bridge Fight of 1865, until a dozen years later, when his relationship with McGillycuddy was kindled, Crazy Horse always spoke to the white man through others: men like his uncle, Little Hawk, or fellow Shirt Wearer He Dog, or even good friend Little Big Man, back in those days when white commissioners were first attempting to "buy back" the sacred *Pa Sapa*.

If Crazy Horse trusted the physician enough to medicate his wife, and saw with his own eyes the improvement in her health, why wouldn't Crazy Horse feel enough at ease to believe he could express his unmitigated bitterness with his new "condition" to this white healer? Is it impossible to believe that Crazy Horse thought: if McGillycuddy had proved himself powerful enough to heal Black Shawl, perhaps his medicine would be strong enough to improve conditions for the Hunkpatila?

He was exactly what Red Cloud and Lieutenant William P. Clark feared he was. Crazy Horse was, and always would be, an "unreconstructed" warrior.

Another matter that has become abundantly clear to me over the years is how most historians, along with the great majority of Crazy Horse's white admirers, have failed to plumb the depths of his spirituality, a mysticism that guided him throughout the years he was known to the white man . . .

but most especially a spirituality that guided his every step during these last days of his short life.

In *To Kill An Eagle*, authors Edward and Mabel Kadlecek succinctly explain the bedrock of a Lakota warrior's belief: "When an Indian dies, he is believed to travel to the Milky Way."*

The Lakota believe that the Great Mystery—or *Wakan Tanka*— gives to each baby a ghost, or *niva*, which originates or comes from the stars. Therefore, each person is possessed of a spirit, or *nagi*, what author Raymond J. DeMallie calls an "immaterial reflection of the body." After death, DeMallie goes on to explain, this *sicun*, or spirit guardian, was believed to escort the spirit of the departed human back to the spirit world just beyond the Milky Way. Then the person's body, now empty of all spirit, rots and becomes nothing.

Through dream, a man was able to leave this day-to-day secular world and briefly return to the sacred world that knew no earthly bonds. Every Lakota grew up learning how dangerous it was to attempt to stay in that sacred world for very long. So it was that I imagined a Crazy Horse, chafing more every day with the weight of his unseen shackles and chains, making more and more attempts to leave behind this temporal world of strife and worry—this cramped existence on Red Cloud's agency, where the chief's jealous and conspiratorial *wagluke*** mocked him—daring to take more and more of those perilous journeys into the sacred land of dream where Crazy Horse saw his life as it ought to have been.

Leaping more and more into the realm of sacred dream, could it be that Crazy Horse had come to believe he could experience an exalted resurrection?

In those last seasons of bloody warfare that preceded his death, Crazy Horse had oft instructed his friends and relations

---

**Wanagi Tacunku, or "Spirit's Trail," otherwise known as the Star Road, or our Milky Way.
**The "loafers," or "coffee-coolers," who hung around the white man's army posts.

on what he himself had been told in dream by the sacred ones, instructions regarding how the others must care for his body should he be killed. His fellow warriors were to paint his body red, then plunge it into fresh water, at which moment Crazy Horse would be revived and returned to life. But if his friends forgot this sacred ritual, Crazy Horse prophesied his bones would turn into rock and his joints into flint.

While his spirit undoubtedly rides across the night sky far above us, the body of Crazy Horse has returned to dust, somewhere. Trouble is, there's more controversy and speculation as to his final resting place than there ever was over how he was killed, or who dealt him the fatal deathwound.

What we do know is that Worm took his son's body into one of the nearby camps, where he and others transferred it from the army wagon to a travois. Then the grieving father and at least one of his two wives started east with it, because the old man did not consider Red Cloud Agency to be hallowed ground. At Spotted Tail's agency, a temporary sepulcher was constructed for the body, which the women bathed and sewed inside a ceremonial blanket. Ironic that the white man's cattle wandering the agency grounds were drawn to that sepulcher, beside which Worm and the two women remained, fasting and mourning for more than three days and nights. Near the end of the fourth day Worm begged the agent, Lieutenant Jesse M. Lee, to protect his son's body from the cattle that apparently enjoyed rubbing their itchy hides against the rough timbers of that crude sepulcher. By himself, Lee rounded up the wood and constructed a fence around the three-foot-tall bier where the body would remain, at least until the Lakota were forced to migrate east to new homes on the Missouri River.

Eighteen days after Crazy Horse's death, on September 23, 1877, in an article more suited to the white man's stereotype than having anything to do with Lakota practice, the *New York Sun* reported that

> [Crazy Horse's] favorite war pony was led to his grave and there slaughtered. In his coffin were placed costly robes and

blankets to protect him from the colds, a pipe and some tobacco, a bow and quiver of arrows, a carbine and a pistol,
with an ample supply of ammunition, sugar, coffee, and hard
bread, and an assortment of beads and trinkets to captivate
the nut-brown maids of paradise.

The following year, when the Oglala were finally allowed to
escape that desolate patch of ground beside the Missouri and
return west to a new reservation that would one day be
known as the Pine Ridge, Worm brought the body of his son
with him. This is where things get really murky and
shrouded not only in legend, but in controversy too. In later
years some Oglala testified that the body of Crazy Horse
was secreted away to the north when many of the Northern
bands were able to slip away from that forced march to the
Missouri River, unnoticed by the army escort as the column
strung itself out more and more across the rolling prairie.
One school of thought believes his bones made it all the way
across the Medicine Line when a few of the Northern People
reached the camp of Sitting Bull. Others believe Crazy
Horse was eventually buried somewhere along the Powder
by those who escaped the migration. And, in reading the
Kadleceks' book, as well as that of Robert A. Clark (see selected bibliography, which follows), you will learn of the
case made for Crazy Horse's bones being buried in the valley of his beloved Beaver Creek, on the old Spotted Tail
Agency.

As for me, it simply doesn't matter where the bones of
this mystical and enigmatic leader were finally laid to rest.
Crazy Horse does not lie here, or there, or even over there.
He is a thousand winds that will forever blow across these
Northern Plains.

For those of you who do want to learn even more about
the controversy of those final days and the killing of Crazy
Horse, or you want to read more on the conflicting theories
about just where the remains of Crazy Horse were laid to
rest, you can ask your local bookstore or librarian to locate
the following titles:

Autobiography of Red Cloud, War Leader of the Oglalas, edited by R. Eli Paul

"*Big Bat*" *Pourier: Guide and Interpreter, Fort Laramie, 1870–1880*, by Hila Gilbert

Blood on the Moon—Valentine McGillycuddy and the Sioux, by Julia B. McGillycuddy

"The Bordeaux Story," by Virginia Cole Trenholm, *Annals of Wyoming* (July 1954)

Buffalo Soldiers, Braves, and Brass, by Frank N. Schubert

"Campaigning Against Crazy Horse," by David T. Mears, *Proceedings and Collections of the Nebraska State Historical Society*, 15 (1907)

"The Capture and Death of an Indian Chieftain," by Jesse M. Lee, *Journal of the Military Service Institute of the United States* (May–June, 1914)

Caspar Collins: The Life and Exploits of an Indian Fighter of the Sixties, by Agnes Wright Spring

"Chief Crazy Horse, His Career and Death," by E. A. Brininstool, *Nebraska History Magazine* (1929)

"Crazy Horse," by Guy V. Henry, *Army and Navy Journal* (15 September 1877)

Crazy Horse and Custer—The Parallel Lives of Two American Warriors, by Stephen E. Ambrose

Crazy Horse: The Invincible Oglala Sioux Chief: The "Inside Stories," by Actual Observers, Of a Most Treacherous Deed Against a Great Indian Chief, by E. A. Brininstool

Crazy Horse: The Strange Man of the Lakota, by Mari Sandoz

The Crazy Horse Surrender Ledger, edited by Thomas R. Buecker and R. Eli Paul

Custer's Conqueror, by William J. Bordeaux

"The Death of Crazy Horse—A Contemporary Examination of the

Homicidal Events of 5 September 1877," by James N. Gilbert, *Journal of the West* (January, 1993)

The Eleanor H. Hinman Interviews on the Life and Death of Crazy Horse, edited by John M. Carroll

Fifty Years on the Old Frontier, by James H. Cook

Firewater and Forked Tongues, by M. I. McCreight

Fort Robinson, Illustrated (published by *NEBRASKAland Magazine*)

General George Crook: His Autobiography, by Martin F. Schmitt

A Good Year to Die—The Story of the Great Sioux War, by Charles M. Robinson, III

Great Plains, by Ian Frazier

Indian Heroes and Great Chieftains, by Charles A. Eastman

The Indian Sign Language, by W. P. Clark

The Killing of Chief Crazy Horse, by Robert A. Clark

Lakota Belief and Ritual, by James R. Walker

Lakota Society, by James R. Walker

The Last Days of the Sioux Nation, by Robert M. Utley

Life and Adventures of Frank Grouard, by Joe DeBarthe

The Life and Death of Crazy Horse, by Russell Freedman, drawings by Amos Bad Heart Bull

Man of the West: Reminiscences of George Washington Oaks, 1840–1917, by Ben Jaastad

"The Man Who Captured Crazy Horse," by Bailey Millard, *Human Life* (September, 1910)

My People the Sioux, by Luther Standing Bear

The Oglala Lakota Crazy Horse: A Preliminary Genealogical Study and An Annotated Listing of Primary Sources, by Richard G. Hardorff

"Oglala Sources on the Life of Crazy Horse," by Eleanor H. Hinman, *Nebraska History* (Spring 1976)

On the Border With Crook, by John G. Bourke

Paper Medicine Man—John Gregory Bourke and His American West, by Joseph C. Porter

"The Passing of Crazy Horse," by H. R. Lemley, *Journal of the Military Service Institute of the United States* (May–June, 1914)

Phil Sheridan and His Army, by Paul Andrew Hutton

A Pictographic History of the Oglala Sioux, by Helen H. Blish (drawings by Amos Bad Heart Bull)

Red Cloud and the Sioux Problem, by James C. Olson

Red Cloud—Warrior-Statesman of the Lakota Sioux, by Robert W. Larson

Red Cloud's Folk: A History of the Oglala Sioux Indians, by George E. Hyde

Rekindling Camp Fires: The Exploits of Ben Arnold, by Lewis F. Crawford

Sacred Language: The Nature of Supernatural Discourse in Lakota, by William K. Powers

The Sioux: Life and Customs of a Warrior Society, by Royal B. Hassrick

The Sixth Grandfather: Black Elk's Teachings Given to John G. Neihardt, by Raymond J. DeMallie

Spotted Tail's Folk: A History of the Brulé Sioux, by George E. Hyde

The Surrender and Death of Crazy Horse: A Source Book About a Tragic Episode in Lakota History, by Richard G. Hardorff

To Kill An Eagle: Indian Views on the Last Days of Crazy Horse, by Edward and Mabel Kadlecek

Unpublished personal journal by Lieutenant John G. Bourke, photocopy contained in "Crazy Horse File," at Fort Robinson, Nebraska (1878)

"War or Peace: The Anxious Wait for Crazy Horse," by Oliver Knight, *Nebraska History*, 54 (1973)

Warpath and Council Fire: The Plains Indians' Struggle for Survival in War and in Diplomacy, 1851–1891, by Stanley Vestal

West From Fort Pierre: The Wild World of James (Scotty) Philip, by James M. Robinson

He is a thousand winds that still blow.

Like Mari Sandoz, I see Crazy Horse—who she called the "Strange Man of the Oglala"—as a mystic. But even more, I see him as the central, lead figure in a tragic passion play.

A Shakespearean tragedy is this, a tale fraught with New Testament overtones. Consider, if you will, the striking similarities when you compare this story you have just read with that final week in the life of Jesus, the poor carpenter from Nazareth. Neither Christ nor Crazy Horse ever set out to become wealthy or powerful in the secular world of mankind. Both were exalted by others, summoned to their fate by others: while Jesus was called to his ministry by God, Crazy Horse was anointed by the Big Bellies, the old ones who selected the Oglala band's Shirt Wearers.

Consider, too, Christ's triumphant entry into Jerusalem, the joyous cries of the crowds, the happy wailing of the women, along with the gall-tinged jealousy Jewish officials must have felt for this rebellious and ragged upstart who had been performing miracles among the poor out in the countryside. How dare this carpenter's son call himself a rabbi! Why, the high priests must have exclaimed, was this Jesus of Nazareth proclaiming himself to be the Son of God? How dare he anoint himself as our long-awaited Messiah!

Then remember the scene of Crazy Horse's grand entry into Red Cloud's agency—how the men, women, and children lined the road for the last two miles, just as they had for Jesus, waving scarves and feathers and medicine bundles instead of palm fronds, crying out in unrestrained joy to their hero: this fighting chief who for ten winters had given his all to be their savior. Think now how that spontaneous and heartfelt celebration at his arrival had to raise the gorge in Red Cloud's throat, angering the chief's jealous minions— even Crazy Horse's own uncle, Spotted Tail—as these reservation Lakota were forced to watch the adulation heaped upon this ragged upstart who had refused for so long to come in and give himself up to the white man.

Why, Crazy Horse did not even carry a title of his own! He wasn't even a chief!

It took less than a week for the sinister whispers spoken behind the back of Jesus to grow into an angry cry. Whispers of the most powerful religious officials eventually growing in volume to become the cry of the crowds. Even though it was the priests themselves who convinced Judas that it was for the best to betray his leader, look back and see how it all was played out under the majesty and the might and the fluttering banners of the Roman Empire. It was on behalf of those high priests, who were frightened, and jealous, and ultimately very envious of the upstart who had begun to shake the temple to its very foundation, that Roman soldiers arrested the rebel leader. In front of thousands of the prisoner's own people, soldiers hauled their captive off for his final sentencing. On behalf of the wary priests, the Empire's soldiers carried out the death warrant: pounding nails through the rebel's flesh and hanging him from the timbers of a thief's cross.

More than eighteen centuries later, out on those plains of northwestern Nebraska Territory, it took much longer than a week for the jealous and suspicious chiefs to undo Crazy Horse. They needed a few months not only to convince the white officials and army officers that this last of the holdouts could not be trusted . . . they needed ample time to work the other side of the equation too: After laboring so hard throughout that spring to convince Crazy Horse he had no choice but to trust the army and agent to whom he would give himself and his people, they now set about convincing Crazy Horse that he never would be able to trust the dishonest *wasicus*.

With agonizing slowness, this tragedy of great passion was played out under the majesty and might of the stars and stripes, the banner of the United States of America. Day by day, week by week, the chiefs who had so much to lose to Crazy Horse hammered away at the rebel's own people, finally convincing them that their leader could no longer be trusted to do what was good for them. Just as the high priests had whispered doubts and charges of blasphemy into the ear of Judas, so too did Red Cloud and his grasping allies concoct their betrayal of those Hunkpatila closest to Crazy Horse, luring them away from their leader. Eventually, most of the Crazy Horse people came to believe that Crazy Horse was about to ruin everything for them if he were not stopped.

(It is here I pause to be sure you understand that I do not in any way, shape, or form agree with Red Cloud's biographers when they howl in protest to this dark, evil view of Red Cloud, claiming that the Oglala chief was, at the very best, an innocent who was used by Lieutenant Clark and General Crook, an otherwise noble figure who was much maligned by Mari Sandoz, or, at the very worst, Red Cloud was not the insecure and evil chieftain who manipulated people and events to bring about the fall, if not the death, of Crazy Horse. Make no mistake, dear reader: I firmly believe that Red Cloud's hand—not to mention those of Woman's Dress, American Horse, and many others—are forever stained crimson with Ta'sunke Witko's blood.)

After months of delicate, and some not-so-delicate, machinations comes September 5, 1877. On behalf of this conniving chief Red Cloud and his faithful courtiers—who were frightened, jealous, and extremely envious of this upstart who was getting so much more attention from the white man than a ragged non-chief ever should enjoy—the U.S. Army cajoled Crazy Horse, convincing him of his personal safety even while they were in the process of arresting him. In front of thousands of his own people who packed the grounds surrounding the adjutant's office, Camp Robinson soldiers took their prisoner into custody and marched him off to the guardhouse, prepared to lock him away until the middle of the night, when plans were for Lieutenant H.R. Lemley's troop of cavalry to whisk the trouble-maker far away from those few Oglala he might still influence.

Yes, things had been quite comfortable at Red Cloud's agency ever since Colonel Ranald Mackenzie and the Fourth U.S. Cavalry disarmed and unhorsed the Oglala in the autumn of 1876. The obstinate chief was made malleable: he could be brought around to the agent's, and Lieutenant Clark's, way of thinking. Red Cloud's Oglala had adjusted to their new way of life. No one wanted Crazy Horse to shake this peaceful existence to its very foundation. Not the army. Least of all the Oglala leaders, who had the most to lose.

In a Shakespearean climax of catastrophic proportions—even though chief American Horse and other angry headmen were fully prepared and willing to kill Crazy Horse by their own hands—it was a lone soldier who carried out Red Cloud's and American Horse's most fervent wish.

The most potent rebel voice was silenced. Trouble snuffed out by a fateful conjunction of the fears of a trouble-maker's own people with the fears of their powerful captors.

Colonel Luther Bradley ordered every man on the alert that night of September 5, the soldiers fearing reprisal by the Lakota. But despite what wailing and mourning took place in the surrounding camps, everything remained surprisingly calm. Crazy Horse's supporters were fleeing toward Spotted Tail's agency. Very few of the Northern People remained nearby.

Do you remember how Red Cloud and his headmen met with General George Crook and offered to kill Crazy Horse a few days before the arrest? That night, as Crazy Horse lay dying, and in the days to follow, those chiefs came to Lieutenant Clark to assure him that, indeed, they were glad that the trouble-maker was no more. They believed they had done their part to see that the source of all discord at the two agencies had been removed. The chiefs promised the White Hat there would be no outbreak of violence... and there wasn't. These coffee-coolers did all that was necessary to stamp out the first flames of the white man's fear of a whole-sale uprising.

That suicidal uprising would not come for another thir-teen winters.

So with Crazy Horse out of the way, the immediate item on the chiefs' agenda was their crucial journey to Washing-ton City. Twenty-two scant days after Crazy Horse passed on to the ages, Red Cloud, Spotted Tail, and the rest of the delegation were in the nation's capital, having their first au-dience with President Rutherford B. Hayes. Within the walls of the White House that twenty-seventh day of September, Hayes promised the chiefs he would do everything in his power to fight the opposition in Congress, a powerful lobby that had lined up enough votes to overrule the president and banish the Lakota south into Indian Territory, the present-day state of Oklahoma. But Carl Schurz, Hayes's brilliant and courageous Secretary of the Interior, would eventually succeed . . . and the Lakota would be allowed to come back to new homes in Dakota Territory.

But that autumn of 1877, even before the chiefs and headmen had returned from Washington City, the army and agents went about packing up the Red Cloud and Spotted Tail people for their march east to the Missouri River, where they could be more easily supplied by steamboat than by long-haul freight-wagon outfits. As the weather turned cold with the foreboding of an early winter, those long, sad pro-cessions started east for a new home promised on the banks of the Missouri. As the days wore on, the columns strung out and some stragglers found it hard to keep up. With nowhere near enough soldiers to keep an eye on everyone on that gen-tly rolling landscape, the Northern People began to slip away, a few lodges at a time. Some disappeared into the bad-lands, on their way back to their beloved hunting grounds in the Powder River country. Others pointed their noses farther north for the Land of the Grandmother and kept right on go-ing until they crossed the Medicine Line, rejoining the Sit-ting Bull people.

But as I've already mentioned, the bones of Crazy Horse stayed with his father that terribly cold winter of 1877–1878 when starvation howled wolfishly at every lodge door. In the spring, the tribes were informed that they could return to new agencies near the reservations they had been forced to abandon in the autumn of 1877. Tradition holds that Worm brought the remains of his son back to Beaver Creek. It was somewhere high along the borders of this valley—where Crazy Horse fasted, prayed, and meditated many times in his brief life—that tradition holds Worm buried the bones in a secret place. A place few Lakota would ever know. A place no white man would ever see.

Back to the here and now, I have concluded my years of research and feel ready to make a final pilgrimage to Fort Robinson, once more seeking out Tom Buecker, the savvy historian and museum curator who doesn't mind kicking around the "what ifs" with me. But even more, I have returned here so that I could walk this ground once more—to stand right here outside this reconstructed guardhouse and wonder how things might have been different had Crazy Horse not attempted to bolt from that narrow doorway. How long would the government have kept him at the Dry Tortugas? Would they have held him until he died, unable to break his spirit, unable to tame so wild a rebel? And if he had ever been allowed to return to the Oglala—like his uncle, Spotted Tail, returned to his Brulé—would the man who came back ever have been the same Crazy Horse, the Ta'sunke Witko who loved and lived, fought and died on the high plains of the far west?

Or, in my wildest imaginings, how would things have played themselves out if he had escaped the reservation in time—putting into motion his hopes of slipping away a lodge or two at a time, eventually to reunite with his few faithful friends and followers before the first snows fell somewhere in their beloved hunting grounds, there in the shadow of the Bighorns? It is easy to believe that Sherman, Sheridan, and Crook would not have rested until the escapee was hunted down, until Crazy Horse was captured or killed.

Brought in dead or alive. Just as easy as it is for me to real-ize that once Crazy Horse had been forced to taste the bitter gall of reservation life as accepted by Red Cloud, American Horse, and Spotted Tail...Crazy Horse would never again let himself be taken alive.

How different things would have turned out for history had Ta'sunke Witko gone down fighting in his beloved homeland.

Instead of crumpling to his knees, all fighting strength seeping from him, collapsing on this dusty patch of summer sun-baked ground where I now stand. Tears in my eyes, I clearly see a dripping red bayonet yanked out of his back, his fellow Oglala suddenly leaping away in dismay and shock. In utter fear that this unkillable warrior was about to die.

It was here, on this patch of grassy dirt at old Camp Robinson—where I find myself sitting in the shade because I feel my own knees buckling with overwhelming emo-tion—that the great hoop of the Lakota Nation was irretriev-ably broken.

Not when Sitting Bull managed to escape north to Canada. Not when the other fighting chiefs decided to give up and come in to the reservations.

On this hallowed ground the greatest Lakota warrior fell...never to rise. His people never were as mighty again.

No one would ever mend the hoop, no matter the efforts of Sitting Bull and Gall when they returned south of the Medicine Line and gave themselves over to the *wasicus* some four years later. It would take thirteen more years after Crazy Horse's death for that broken hoop to be shattered be-yond all repair—when the white man ordered the arrest of Sitting Bull, and the old chief was killed at the hand of his own people. Such a terrible thing could happen only because the power and might of the fighting bands had been broken for all time in that spring of 1877...only because the spirit that had once made them mighty was now crushed.

With Crazy Horse out of the way, no Oglala ever took up the mantle and carried on the struggle.

But in the midst of the emotions that threaten to engulf me, I suddenly remember that Crazy Horse is not here, nor does his spirit infuse this ground with tragic sadness.

A thousand winds that will forever blow across this stark and beautiful country.

While a mighty life has been snuffed out, all one need do is to walk out onto the prairie, away from the contaminating wattage of modern man . . . and gaze up into the greatness of the heavens. Let your eyes and your heart guide you to that Star Road, a thick dusting of countless points of light. Resting there among the best of the Lakota . . . shines the spirit of Crazy Horse.

He who would have considered his image being carved out of a mountain in the sacred *Pa Sapa* as the ultimate profanity, because Crazy Horse had spent his whole life steadfastly refusing to have his image taken from him! It is this Crazy Horse you must remember. The sacred and mystical war leader of the Oglala. Not some artificial and obscene rock face that's been blasted out of the side of a mountain.

I sit here in the shade of this log building, taking great solace in the words of Black Elk, who wrote many years afterward of "The Killing of Crazy Horse":

> It does not matter where his body lies, for it is grass; but where his spirit is, it will be good to be.

So tonight when it grows quiet and your find yourself needing to close your eyes in sleep—I want you to walk outside and look up at the dark canopy overhead. There . . . you'll find it in the untamed fires of the night sky: the true fighting spirit of Ta'sunke Witko rides across the heavens forever.

Terry C. Johnston
Camp Robinson, Nebraska
September 5, 1999